THE COLOR OF TRAUMA

For information about this title, contact the author:
Hollie Smurthwaite
hollie@holliesmurthwaite.com
https://holliesmurthwaite.com

ISBN: 978-1-7371189-3-0

Cover Design by Sarah Hansen, Okay Creations
Interior Design by Olivier Darbonville
Edited by Steph Morgan

First Edition

THE COLOR

of

TRAUMA

HOLLIE SMURTHWAITE

For Randy—

Thanks for having and holding and all that stuff.
I don't always make it easy, do I?

CHAPTER ONE

Kiera

THE MEMORY TRANSFER WENT WELL ENOUGH. Kiera didn't even vomit.

She'd warned Emma and Emma's mother, Alicia, of the possibility. Alicia had sniffed as if the hefty price of removing Emma's trauma meant that puking would have been unprofessional. At least, Kiera had sidestepped that issue.

Kiera rose from her chair, more stable than not, despite her brain bloating like a frightened puffer fish. She squeezed her eyes shut, desperate to reconnect with reality.

She imagined the parts of her River North Chicago office that felt like home: a fuchsia vase on her lacquered credenza; a yellow-framed picture of Kiera and her brother on her glass desk; a turquoise pillow on the black leather couch.

When she opened her eyes, the normally calming frosted windows disoriented her as if she were seeing everything from underwater. Emma's mother sat on an armchair, awaiting the announcement that Kiera had achieved the impossible. Clients really wanted the past to disappear with the memories, a return to who they had been before the event.

Alicia jumped to her feet. "Well?"

Kiera ignored her and focused on her rib cage—easy breath in, easy breath out. She had to calm the storm inside her.

"Emmy?" Her mother's voice quavered.

Kiera regarded Emma, and they studied each other in a *Freaky Friday*-esque moment. Like a lot of clients, Emma looked shell-shocked, but she managed a smile. "It's so bonkers," she mumbled, shaking her head as if trying to find whatever memories Kiera had extracted. The movement swished the shield of death-metal purple hair away from the scarred side of Emma's face, exposing patches of tight, waxy skin. When Emma didn't immediately adjust the tilt of her chin to compensate, Kiera smiled.

Maybe this won't be so—

Emma's memories scalded Kiera's awareness like globs of lava from an erupting volcano. *This is my face: burn scars forever. My hair doesn't hide the wreck of my face well enough. Shave the hair on the good side, draw attention there. Need to stop looking. Can't stop looking.*

No.

Kiera stared at her ragged cuticles, the sight of something so familiar grounding her enough to sink Emma's memories into the background.

Soon. Kiera could go home soon. But first she had to tend to Emma. "We'll talk in a few days and check if the level of memory is good, okay?"

Kiera sculpted memory, taking only the shock, the raw, the hot and throbbing, just enough so the person hopefully could move forward. Memory transfers were a form of art and, therefore, inherently imperfect. She'd done her part; now Emma needed to fill those gaps with something positive.

Emma glanced at her mom before bobbing her head. "Okay."

Kiera walked Emma to the door. Had it really been only eleven years since she'd been Emma's age? Seventeen was a lifetime ago. She barely had enough room for her own past, and now she was a lockbox for dozens of the most painful memories imaginable.

As always, with the misery so fresh and unmanageable, she asked herself why she continued the transfers. Materially, Kiera had all she wanted. She didn't do memory surgeries for the money, she did them for . . . Why the hell did she do them? Added security? Out of habit? Self-hatred? Because she could? Fuck if she knew.

It did give her clients a chance for a little peace. This might enable Emma to reclaim some of her childhood. Her use of the word *bonkers* was a promising sign. Not that anyone could go back to who they used to be, not really, no matter what you remembered or what you forgot.

"Do you call us, or do we call you?" Emma's mother asked, reedy and restless like a bird with no feathers. An imperious, demanding bird.

Kiera had barely opened the door. "I'll call Emma this weekend."

"What time?" Emma's mom asked.

Kiera sighed. No questions afterward—she'd been clear. She might have stabbed the mother in the eye if she'd had a pen or some other kind of pointy tool. And the energy.

"I don't know yet but sometime on Sunday."

Alicia pursed her lips like she wanted to argue.

Emma, clearly the brighter of the two, grabbed her mother's arm and tugged her away. "Let's go, Mom."

* * *

HER DRIVER, TONY, KNEW TO STAY SILENT AND DROPPED HER OFF AT home without a word. Manny at the security desk nodded but didn't try to talk to her—he followed the routine too. Even with the privacy of the empty elevator, Kiera had a strict policy of not losing her shit until she was safe within her condo. Her hands shook as she hit the code to unlock her door.

Once in her relaxation room, she collapsed onto the velvet chaise, pulling an angora blanket over her as she curled in on herself and let go of everything. Her desire, her control, every thread holding her fragile being together.

The memories, once Emma's and now her own, rolled through her like the storm clouds of a hurricane—churning and whipping, making the tiniest debris suddenly deadly.

Tears fell with the remembrance of searing heat and Emma's reflexive lurch away from the splattering oil. The popping, spitting sound of the pan. No pain at first, only the convulsive jerks. But the pain caught up, overwhelming and agonizing. Her screams echoed in her ears.

Skin too tight, too smooth, too ropy.

Frank, horrified gazes tracked her every move afterward. Behind her back. Right to her face. Real, imagined, incessant.

I'm a monster. I'm a monster. I'm a monster.

Not Kiera's thoughts, but that didn't matter.

The memories were true or exaggerated by Emma's perceptions, but they hurt like tiny needles in her eyeballs. Kiera felt like a freak inside. Emma felt like a freak on the outside. Now Kiera bore the weight of both, the pressure bearing down on her in a way she couldn't avoid no matter how she shifted her body on the couch.

It's too much.

No, she could handle it.

Too much.

No, she'd gone through far worse and survived.

But it hurts. It hurts. It hurts. It hurts.

She took a deep breath. This was temporary; it would fade. It always did. She just had to wait it out. Kiera closed her eyes and crammed the wisps of Emma's memory into their own mental prison.

No end in sight. Whether it was Emma's memories or the universe preparing to push her past the breaking point, she couldn't shake the feeling that someday soon she'd find no more room at the inn and the trauma would all break loose, swarm and spin her, and she wouldn't recognize what was real, and she'd never be herself again.

CHAPTER TWO

Dean

DEAN STARED DOWN AT THE INERT BODY OF Brittany Kolchek. Her medical chart logged three stab wounds to the abdomen, multiple contusions and abrasions, and ligature marks about the wrists. Bandages obscured the part of her scalp the offender had taken. Pink-and-purple skin swelled, making her face appear inhuman.

She almost looked stable, but despite all the advances of modern medicine, Brittany would die, likely within the week. Already her seizures had increased, and the doctors had insisted she wouldn't wake from her coma.

He closed his hands into white-knuckled fists. In Dean's six years in homicide, he'd had many cases where the victim hadn't died at the scene, but he rarely had a quiet moment alone with an unconscious one.

Dean wanted just five minutes to talk to her because, right then, they had nothing to point them to who might have done this.

This case was different. Attacks like Brittany's, that level of brutality, were uncommon. Two other cases in Chicago had enough similarities that they would soon be officially linked. Sexual assault, ligature marks, stabbing, mutilation. Chicago had a serial killer, the kind filmmakers made miniseries about, and Brittany Kolchek was his third victim.

History would judge Dean on how he handled the case. History, the department, his parents. More importantly, his gut insisted the offender would kill again, extending the line of photographs of beautiful, pitiable victims. Finding the offender was his responsibility, his burden.

What about an M&M—memory muncher—memory surgeon? What might one uncover?

He shook his head, a sure sign that arguing with himself had hit a new low. This case could safeguard or break his reputation. Or it could break his mind. Better to rely on traditional tactics.

Whoever fights monsters should see to it that in the process he does not become a monster.

Never a good sign when Nietzsche quotes rattled his thoughts.

And if you gaze long enough into the abyss, the abyss will gaze back into you.

The abyss had been gazing into him for years, so how close was he to becoming that monster? Not that he had a choice now. He had to perform at an Olympic level, pushing everything inside him to find that edge that would solve the case, no matter what it did to his psyche.

Or his reputation?

Shit. His old University of Illinois Chicago adviser, Dr. Cranston, studied the phenomenon of memory surgery, and he'd assured Dean over drinks one night that though most were fakes, true memory surgeons existed. Dean respected Cranston enough to take his word that some people could read another's thoughts. But the Chicago Police Department was not as open-minded. He'd be the joke of the department if word got out, even if memory surgeons gained some sort of national validation—which they wouldn't. And everyone would scrutinize each choice he made on the case. No chance the bosses would approve of him trying something so woo-woo.

He looked at Brittany. At the depth of the injuries that made her death inevitable. Whoever had done this to her had enjoyed the act, but a passing vehicle had interrupted the ritual. That interruption would've cut into the bastard's satisfaction. No evidence of frenzy, so he'd been calm or at least

14

controlled. The Memorial Day holiday and abandoned location of the crime spoke of premeditation. He'd chosen that filthy spot, perhaps as a fitting end to a person he didn't view as a person.

"Oh my God!" came a voice from the doorway.

Dean turned slowly to look at the new arrival, the vestiges of the imagined offender clinging to his mind.

A middle-aged woman in a floral, sleeveless blouse and white skirt stood just inside the room with a hand over her mouth. She wore a pearl necklace, an adornment from another age. The jewelry reminded Dean of his mother, who never left the house without a strand.

"That . . . that can't be Brittany. My little girl."

He reached her elbow as her knees buckled. Dean held her upright until she steadied herself, then helped her to a chair at the side of Brittany's bed. She clasped her daughter's hand and brought it to her forehead.

Focus, Matthson.

The victim needed him, and so did her mom.

"Mrs. Kolchek, I'm Detective Dean Matthson with the Chicago Police Department." He left out that he worked homicide, not wanting to remind the woman that her daughter would likely die soon. "I'm so sorry this has happened to your daughter and your family. I'll give you a few minutes with her. When you're ready, I'll be outside. I've got some questions for you."

"You'll catch him." Not a question. Though her back was to him, her posture screamed resolve.

"Ma'am, I will do my very best."

He couldn't promise, though the impulse crawled up his throat to choke him. As a cop, he'd learned fast that life provides no guarantees, no slam dunks, no sure things.

The idea floated back to the surface of his consciousness: memory surgeon. Risky. Crazy.

This wasn't a simple heater case; it was napalm hot with too many eyes for him to risk snagging one of the charlatans.

If he chose that route, the whole thing had to be beyond reproach.

15

Memory readings weren't even admissible in court, and that wouldn't change any time soon. But Cranston could probably find him someone real. He could potentially unleash a trove of information. Inadmissible data could lead to admissible evidence and vital clues.

From outside Brittany Kolchek's hospital room, he heard the distinctive keening of her mother's sobs. He couldn't save Brittany; all he could hope to give her family was closure and an attempt at justice—because nothing could balance what had been done to their daughter.

Dean wanted more time before attempting something radical this early in the investigation. His professional distinction along with his clearance and confession rates placed him in high esteem of the department. People respected him; he had several commendations and recognition, but cops were a fickle bunch. And a reputation could be easily tarnished. Did he have the balls to put the case ahead of his good name?

CHAPTER THREE

Kiera

KIERA STOPPED SCRATCHING HER ARM, THEN ceased tugging on her earlobe. Her tapping foot was the last body part to still. Perfect. Now she'd appear normal as she waited for Dr. Patty to start the memory-surgeon therapy group. Except Nadira shifted her attention from her sketchbook, and her eyes marched over Kiera's skin like fire ants.

It wasn't Nadira, really, but the aftereffects of Emma's memory surgery wouldn't quiet down no matter how tightly Kiera bound them. Pain was one thing, but this was something else. A longing had awakened inside Kiera at the positive moments she'd glimpsed in Emma's memories. The recollections of healing touches, of being held, of safety—they all blazed.

Kiera didn't know what to do with something so sweet that her head buzzed. She thought her dreams of love had died years ago. Turned out, those romantic yearnings wouldn't stay dead, no matter how unrealistic.

"What?" Kiera snapped as Nadira continued to stare.
"What's wrong?" Nadira whispered. Her long black hair had fallen forward over her sketch pad, but she tucked the cascade behind her ear, revealing the perfect oval of her face.

"Nothing." That was the truth. She just wanted to discuss relationships. Certainly, that futile subject didn't warrant twitchiness.

Kiera focused on her surroundings to avoid Nadira's stare, though there wasn't much to note: the same old square room with linoleum floors, wood paneling, acoustic-tiled ceiling, and zero decoration—unless she counted the row of five flags that were presumably brought out for parades and whatnot. But shouldn't a Veterans of Foreign Wars hall also have purple fez hats, or bloodied bayonets, or scythe-like swords—some deep-cut, foreign-war shit? What was the point of going to war if you weren't going to bring back some cool spoils?

Kiera peered at Nadira's drawing. She had penciled in Dr. Patty's perfect posture, her knees and ankles together, her hands folded in her lap. Dr. Patty appeared ready to run a Pampered Chef party or an etiquette class, not a group therapy session for the Chicago area's memory surgeons.

"Shall we begin?" Dr. Patty asked in a high-pitched voice that coordinated perfectly with her blond hair, pastel sweater set, and televangelist smile. She held court at the apex of a semicircle, three chairs on either side of her, seven chairs total, though only six of them were ever filled. She needed to be in the center of everything. Or maybe she was saving a spot for Elijah or some patron saint of the mind fucked.

"Anyone want to start?" Dr. Patty prompted. She sounded extra perky, or maybe Kiera's maelstrom of conflicting impulses only made it seem that way.

Kiera resolved to nut up. Her hand shook as she lifted it, keeping her elbow tight to her body.

"I've had a horrible week," Amy began.

Fucking Amy.

"What sort of issues came up for you, Amy?" Dr. Patty asked, her lips stretched into an inviting smile, one that showed how sincerely she cared.

That kind of open-ended question might take up the entire hour. Kiera shifted in her chair again and jiggled her knee. What Kiera hated most about group was Amy. Stupid, Jesus-loving, self-involved, narcissist Amy—soft-spoken with huge brown eyes like a cow and tears like a crocodile. Since she had joined group three weeks ago, each session had been primarily devoted to her. Dr. Patty loved her because Amy drank in all her advice, swimming in it, gargling with it, probably douching with it.

Amy pursed her lips. "I've had the worst nightmares. I don't think I've gotten more than six hours of sleep any night this week."

"You sleep six hours a night?" Beth said in her scratchy voice, though cross talk was forbidden. "I'd kill to sleep that much."

"Now, Beth, we're not here to pass judgment, and this isn't a competition to see who suffers the most," Dr. Patty admonished.

If it was, Amy would lose. Amy had come to group after her first and only memory surgery. One trauma, a car accident. The memories had been of a girl trapped for three hours, in agony, thinking she was going to die alone. That certainly qualified as traumatic. But that experience paled compared to gang rape, beatings, and abandonment for dead by your boyfriend, or Daddy sneaking in your room every night for four years. And those were only a few of the client memories Kiera had experienced, transferred, and stored in her own mind. Yeah, hard to pity Amy.

Still, if Amy had said on the first day that she'd only done one transfer, and it wasn't that big of a deal, and she didn't even know why she was there, they all would have rallied around her. Kiera would have argued that nobody could quantify anyone else's pain and blah, blah, blah. But Amy assumed that everyone would automatically give a shit about her because they all shared the same "gift." And she never . . . shut . . . up.

Kiera lived in terror that Dr. Patty might reinstitute the talking stick. When group had first formed, Dr. Patty had brought a long, hollow chunk of wood that she presented to them so they would have an orderly way of determining who was to speak. However, in the early days, only Kiera, Nadira, and Beth attended, none of whom had wanted to talk, and they sure as shit didn't want to hold a tree branch when they did.

Amy rocked forward in her chair, as if she were sharing a juicy secret. "I wake up in the night sweating, and I'm not sure where I am, and I'm so scared, but I don't want to wake anyone else, so I sit there crying. I try to be quiet, but my mom's a light sleeper, and she always hears me, and then I feel guilty that she's not getting enough sleep too."

Bullshit. Kiera didn't believe for a second that (a) Amy didn't want to wake anyone, (b) that she tried to be quiet, or (c) that her mom was a light sleeper. Amy bawled her head off until someone came to her room, like an infant.

"Did you use any of the tools we talked about last week?" Dr. Patty asked, reaching out to pat Amy's arm.

"Jesus Christ," Kiera muttered loud enough that everyone heard her. If she had to listen to a single-nostril-breathing symposium again, she might explode.

Beth crossed her arms across her prodigious chest and tilted her head to the ceiling, taking huge, audible breaths. Her brown helmet of hair didn't move at all with the motion.

"I used all the techniques!" Amy cried, as if Kiera's mumbling and Beth's breathing had been over their belief that Amy wasn't trying hard enough.

"You need better affirmations," Kiera suggested, though she usually restrained from such comments until the coffee shop afterward with just Nadira and Beth. "How about 'I will not be a narcissistic drama diva'— oops, that's a negative."

Nadira put a hand over her mouth to hold in a laugh, and Beth sputtered.

"That's uncalled for," Dr. Patty said. "I think you owe Amy an apology."

An unnatural silence settled over the group for a moment. The air conditioning ticked and whooshed; the odor of stale Pine-Sol hung like low fog. Okay, she'd been a bitch, but someone had to refocus the group on the group, not just the most self-involved member. Her skin wouldn't stop squeezing her. It burned. It itched. It had to stop.

"Apologize? To that pampered princess? I'd rather have my left tit cut off. And I know how painful that would be, by the way." That wasn't exactly true. The transferred memory she was referring to had included the removal of a nipple. Kiera hated the word *nipple* and refused to say it out loud. *Tit* was close enough.

Amy put a protective arm over her left breast, as if Kiera had threatened to cut Amy's breast off and not her own. Kiera wanted to smack Amy until that stupid deer-in-headlights look fell off. Maybe with the talking stick.

Nadira, the one person Kiera allowed to touch her when she was so agitated, placed a hand on Kiera's arm. She gave Kiera a hold-my-beer look that disrupted her psycho spiral.

"I think if anyone should apologize, it should be Amy for wasting so much of our time." Nadira straightened her already perfect posture. "We spend most of group on her bullshit."

Bullshit? Nadira rarely swore.

"Yeah," Beth agreed. "Can't we have a session where Amy shuts her trap for the whole thing?"

A delicious tension pulsed, akin to an arsonist's high when the fire catches. Yes, sisters. *Burn, motherfucker, burn.*

Emma.

Kiera closed her eyes. Andre, Emma's boyfriend, peered down at her—at Emma—studying her, tracing the scars across her neck and chest. Her mottled skin didn't matter to him. He saw the girl underneath. And for once, she'd felt beautiful to someone. For once, another person's touch—

No.

That wasn't meant for her. She had left that memory for Emma, of course, but though she hadn't taken it, the experience still haunted her. Nobody had ever looked at Kiera like that. She'd never been seen, and no one had lovingly touched her scars. Her invisible scars.

She wrenched herself back into the moment.

Ramon, the only male in the room, spoke in his usual quiet voice. "No Amy? I can't imagine what that would be like."

He had joined the group a few months back, and his input was always thoughtful and direct. *He* had earned their respect.

"They're ganging up on me," Amy whined, cowering next to Dr. Patty.

Kiera rode on fury and frustration. "Find a new group and tell them about how mean we all were." No other group existed for memory surgeons, but Amy could join Narcissists Anonymous and save Kiera anger-management tutorials.

Dr. Patty lifted her hands. "Let's all take a moment to calm."

"When's that ever helped?" Beth said. "We been doing this six months. I ain't no better. Still can't go out at night, can't ride a bus, can't be with too many people, can't go on a damn date."

Kiera's skin flared like a rash. Yes! At last. How did they date or love? How did they roll in the sheets without throwing up on their sexual partners? There had to be an answer between Kiera's hey-I-pay-a-professional-for-sex, Nadira's revolving-door policy, and Amy's proud declaration that she was saving herself for marriage.

What did Beth do? What did Ramon do? Dr. Patty probably exorcised her Miss Ray of Sunshine persona as Ass Handler Patricia. She provided "therapy" with a cat-o'-nine-tails and a tubful of Crisco but was unlikely to share those details. God forbid group got interesting.

Beth gestured wildly and her scratchy voice began to lose its pitch. "I practice all them stupid exercises: meditating, the I'm-in-control stuff, the visualizations, everything. I ain't got nothing else to do, so it ain't like I forget a day. When does it get better?"

Kiera's throat clamped like she was choking on a pill. She wanted to touch Beth's arm or pat her shoulder, but she never managed it. Kiera didn't have Nadira's ease with physical contact. It was a skill Kiera envied. She wished she were more affectionate or friendly or whatever but had no idea how.

The flash of Emma's memory came again. She wanted to find a way to have that.

"Recovery has no timetable, Beth. Nobody can tell you how long it will take, but you've been making progress," Dr. Patty encouraged in her unflappable manner before glancing at her watch. "Let's shift focus for a moment." She craned her neck toward the door, as if expecting someone, smoothing her perfect hair. "There's something important I need to ask everyone." Her eyes locked on Kiera. "Please don't get angry."

CHAPTER FOUR

Dean

DEAN HATED USING PEOPLE, BUT THE STAKES WERE too high. When he'd met Patty Morten, the grad student who ran the therapy group as a thesis project, she'd looked him up and down and blinked a few too many times. If her crush on him made her more persistent with the group, he'd take it.

Through the window of the closed door, he watched the memory surgeons inside, including the one Dr. Cranston had warned him about. Kiera Brayleigh. Her parents in interviews had called her a wounded animal, but from his internet search, she resembled more of a feral one, snarling refusals for interviews.

She could either be his biggest asset or an explosive waiting to go off.

Didn't matter. He couldn't take the chance of that unstable bomb taking off his face and half of Chicago. One of the others would say yes.

The door opened. Dean held his body still.

Patty smiled, but it didn't reach her eyes. Damn.

"Well, they aren't happy," she said. "But I persuaded them to give you five minutes."

Five minutes. Not a lot of time, but he would make it enough. Would they refuse him? Maybe. He patted Brittany Kolchek's photograph through his jacket pocket. They would find refusing her far more difficult.

* * *

DEAN APPROACHED THE SEMICIRCLE WITH AUTHORITY AND CONFIDENCE. He recognized all but one from his research. Patty gestured to the open seat beside Ramon Aguirrez. He appeared exactly like his DMV photo: twenty-three, Latino, with dark eyes and hair. Handsome and haunted. According to Dr. Cranston, he'd grown up Catholic and worked almost exclusively with the church.

"I'm Detective Dean Matthson." He looked at everyone in turn, while he remained standing.

Next to Ramon was a young silver-blond woman, the only one he didn't recognize. Cranston missed one. She blinked up at him like someone nearsighted. Patty sat beside her and nodded at Dean in encouragement.

Next to Patty was Nadira Shula, who looked like a fashion model with her red high-heeled shoes and tailored clothes. She wore a forced, polite expression. Her area was physical abuse of children, making her less than ideal.

Then sat Kiera Brayleigh, Queen M&M. She supposedly worked the heaviest cases: rapes, tortures, and incest. She didn't appear nearly as nuts as the online photos portrayed. However, the ever-present hostility of her glare was in abundance. The brilliant shade of blue of her eyes with her black hair made her intense. No way he wanted her on the case.

On the end was Beth Hamilton, the small-town girl who had the most wide-ranging experience in trauma transfer, from cheating husbands to home invasions. His top choice. But she chewed her lip and refused to hold Dean's gaze.

"I'm not sure how much Ms. Morten has shared with you, but—"

Kiera lifted a finger; thankfully, her index. "*Dr. Patty* told us you had questions about memory reading as it might apply to one of your cases. Read memories aren't admissible in court. You're wasting your time."

"I don't need evidence like that," he said, deciding not to point out that Patty hadn't graduated yet and wasn't, technically, a doctor.

"Whew," the blond he didn't recognize said. "It's one of the frustrating things about what we do." The memory surgeons all winced when she spoke, though the blond didn't appear to notice.

"What's your name?" he asked.

She beamed. "Amy Carter."

"Do you mind telling me what's your specialty?"

"Bitching and complaining," Kiera replied in a tight voice.

Amy's lips compressed, but she didn't say anything. Was Kiera the group's bully? Was that how she controlled the narrative? Everyone looked to her, even Patty.

Kiera sighed. "Dr. Schwartz is the expert in the field. Look into his research. Gilfoile and Roberts are hacks, and the rest don't know shit but still want to capitalize on the memory-surgeon thing."

He wrote down "Schwartz" in his notebook, surprised at her generosity. "Thank you."

She stared at him with those blue eyes that didn't blink enough. "That all?"

"Not quite."

"Yeah, I figured." She shook her head. "They don't fully understand how memory works, so it's going to be a while before they figure out how we're able to access people's memories and how they can be removed and kept in someone else's mind. We can't help you with the science stuff."

"I'm more interested in how it works from a practical standpoint." He directed his questions at everyone else, but the only one looking directly at him was Kiera. Fine. If he won her over, the others would follow. "I'm trying to ascertain what you can and can't do."

"Why?"

No time to finesse. With his attention still on Kiera, he handed Brittany Kolchek's picture to Ramon and asked him to look and pass it on.

"I've never seen her before," Ramon said. "Is she missing?"

Dean waited until everyone had viewed the photo, because he didn't want to give them the opportunity to refuse.

Beth looked last, and she studied Brittany for several seconds. "She seems nice." Then she walked the photo back to him.

"Her name is Brittany Kolchek," he said. "She's in a coma." As a group, they cringed, even Kiera. Good—they cared. "The doctors say she won't wake."

"You don't want information. You want one of us to jump into her memories," Kiera said, her face as hard as her voice.

"We believe she's the third victim of a serial killer targeting young women. All three scenes have little physical evidence. This might be our only chance to catch a break." When nobody spoke or moved, he added, "He'll kill again."

"Would it work?" Nadira asked Kiera. "Going into a comatose woman's memories?"

Kiera shrugged. "Doesn't matter. It isn't ethical. She can't give consent."

"I talked to Brittany's parents, Sarah and Sam," Dean said, giving their names to personalize them. "They gave approval already. They're desperate to have her killer caught."

Kiera sighed. "A memory isn't like a medical record. Someone else can't give permission to intrude like that."

"It ain't like she can get embarrassed," Beth said.

Kiera rubbed her thumb between her eyebrows, as if to stave off a headache. "She's still got to give up the memory."

"What do you mean?" Dean asked.

"We can't just read minds. The person has to let us in. Consent. If she's in a coma, I don't know if she can do that."

He kept his voice even. "Would one of you be willing to try?"

Their eyes flicked to one another again, the hive mind at work. He hadn't anticipated that. Everyone watched Kiera. She shook her head without hesitation.

Another dead end.

He could search for an out-of-town M&M, but it had taken too much time just to find this small group. Brittany Kolchek was going to die and take the knowledge of her killer with her.

But what about the new girl, Amy? None of them liked her, but that made her an isolated antelope—a people pleaser and susceptible to authority. When she noticed him staring at her, she blinked in surprise and smiled in a reflexive way.

"Amy," he said softly. "Are you the one to help me?" He paused. "To help Brittany?"

The room went quiet, as if he'd announced an active shooter in the building.

"What?" Amy turtled her neck into her shoulders.

"I understand that what I'm asking is very hard," he said. "But I'm an expert at reading people, and I think you're the kind of person who can't sit by and let a killer run free." He let the weight of his words settle in silence.

"You're an expert at reading people?" Kiera asked, her lips tight. "I've got something for you to read."

"Kiera," Dr. Patty admonished. "Detective Matthson is only asking for help. Everyone has to be allowed to make up their own minds."

"It'll take a lot of bravery." He should stop, but Amy was waffling. Corny would work. "Brittany needs you."

Kiera snorted.

"I'll do it," Amy said. Then she straightened in her chair and addressed the rest of the room. "We were given this gift for a reason, and I want to make a difference."

"You can't," Kiera said with enough snap to make Amy deflate. "You don't comprehend what you're getting into."

"I'm a memory surgeon, same as you," Amy retorted, though she lacked Kiera's bite.

"You're comparing your experience with mine?"

Dr. Patty wielded her Zen calm like a weapon. "Kiera, each person owns their individual truths. All we can do is support one another."

Kiera threw up her hands. "I'm trying to warn her about what she'll be feeling later. She's never done a reading on a victim of violence." She grabbed the bottom of the metal chair and stared at Amy. "You won't ever be able to go back."

"You should consider Kiera's advice, Amy. Take time to make a decision if you need it," Patty said. "You aren't obligated."

Damn.

"I can do it," Amy said to the fists clenched on her lap, her resolve solidifying. "I'm going to do my part, like everyone else."

Yes.

Finally, a break. Armed with a memory surgeon, he could do this. But then Kiera stood, arms crossed, looking ready to rip his head off and kick it back to him.

CHAPTER FIVE

Kiera

AMY DIDN'T HAVE THE STRENGTH NECESSARY TO transfer traumas. That first surgery should have been enough to convince her. But Amy was a fucktard of epic proportions. She couldn't handle a hangnail, but somehow thought she'd be fine to read a rape-murder victim. A fucking *murder* victim. Nothing anyone attempted would make the victim's life better, not if she didn't wake from her coma.

Nadira stood and put a hand on Kiera's arm. "If she wants to do it, let her." When Kiera gaped at her, Nadira shrugged. "Some people only learn the hard way."

Amy stood too, glancing at the group. Her legs visibly shook. "I'm ready to go."

If she left, the rest of the time was guaranteed to be Amy-free. That should have pleased Kiera.

Detective Matthson put an arm out to Amy, as if to touch her. Amy was about to hop in a car with him, a stranger. Had anyone verified he was a police officer? Sure, he had the vibe, but he also had dimples. Cops shouldn't have dimples or that gentle, therapist-like manner. Or look that rugged-handsome hot, with his short blond hair and lean, tall body. Manipulative bastard.

Amy rose from her chair, her hands gripping both straps of her knockoff Birkin bag as if she wanted to hug it to her chest like a teddy bear. Naive, impressionable, and so fucking vulnerable with her wide eyes and panting breaths. Fear wafted off Amy more potent than her overly floral perfume, marking her like the word *victim* tattooed on her face.

He couldn't do that to her. Goddamn sonofabitch fucktwisted . . .

"Stop," Kiera said. That should have been enough. Her experience, her advice, should have been enough. But Amy just blinked at her.

"Don't," Nadira said, her voice rising. Nadira didn't lose her cool like that. "If she wants to play hero, let her."

"I can't." Kiera couldn't explain it to Nadira because she didn't understand it herself.

Nadira reached out and took Kiera's hand. "I recognize that look in your eye. You're not ready."

Was Kiera seriously considering volunteering as tribute? If Emma's surgery had been a rape, Kiera couldn't have done another. But this one hadn't drowned her—just discombobulated her. She remembered drowning in someone else's memory, and she couldn't picture Amy surviving the anguish.

"Nadira's right," Beth said, getting to her feet too, bringing them into a memory surgeon's version of a huddle. She gave Kiera an elbow nudge, keeping the contact brief. Beth always perceived Kiera's discomfort with touch. "Who knows what he didn't say. The po-po never tell everything."

Beth and Nadira were both right. If anyone had told Kiera an hour before that she would intervene to protect Amy from a traumatic reading, she would have laughed her ass off.

"I can do it," Amy argued, crossing her arms over her chest. Only a foot stomp was missing from the spoiled teenager routine. "I'm the one he wants. There's something special about me."

"Yeah, your gullibility," Kiera said, breaking from the huddle. Time for hard truths—even if they hurt, this would save Amy. Kiera marched up to the other woman. "You have yet to deal with that car accident. You think you can't sleep now? What are you going to do when you wake up screaming and puking in the middle of the night, and you have no fucking clue what's real and what isn't? Are you willing to risk psychiatric hospitalization because you want to play hero to some smooth-talking cop who doesn't give a fuck what happens to you?"

Amy slapped her hands over her ears. "Stop yelling at me!" Tears gushed everywhere, completely proving Kiera's point.

Kiera glared at the detective, promising him with her eyes that she would make it her new life mission to ensure his misery if he took Amy. She had plenty of time and money and could use a pet project.

He held her gaze with equanimity but didn't say anything, then reached some internal decision. "Ms. Brayleigh, if you feel that strongly, I'd very much appreciate your assistance."

"I can do it," Amy said with a sniffle and desperate swipes under her eyes.

Kiera didn't break eye contact with the cop. "Not today. Today, I'll do it."

CHAPTER SIX

Dean

T HEY STOOD ALONE IN THE FOYER OF THE VFW
hall studying each other. Kiera Brayleigh tapped
her foot as if wanting to either attack him or sprint away. Dean agreed with
Cranston's warning of Kiera's volatility and his belief in her genuine gift.

If Dean had to endure Kiera's ball busting to not squander his one
shot, he would. He'd developed quite a thick skin over his time as an
officer. Dean could take the abuse. Amy's complete breakdown at nothing
more than a verbal confrontation made her an unfit choice, and he was
relieved not to find out the harder way.

Kiera hefted a gigantic pink leather purse that could hold a Shetland
pony. The corded muscles of her shoulders rose as she slung it over her
shoulder. She had the kind of physique that only came from weightlifting.
She stared at him from behind a lock of hair, savage despite her elfin
features.

"Let's see your badge," she growled.

Dean pulled out his wallet and flipped his police ID out to her. She
studied everything.

"Patty and I shared the same adviser at UIC." He wanted to shift gears
and start collaborating, but he'd dug his own hole there with his heavy-

handed tactics. Now he had to ensure it didn't turn into a grave.

"Who?" she asked, as if she'd caught him in a lie.

"Dr. Robert Cranston."

Her eyebrows rose. "Is he still working on a paper about the effects of trauma on memory encoding and retrieval?"

The question sounded like a test, and it confirmed he'd chosen correctly. Her eyes glared, but the rest of her said nothing of her internal thoughts.

"Not that he mentioned to me."

She nodded. "He wanted to talk to me too, but he didn't have the audacity to crash group. Or he had too much respect."

Dean endured the pull of Sarah and Brittany Kolchek and the ticking down of time. "Shall we go?"

"Which hospital?"

"Northwestern. I can take you and drop you back here when you're finished." He gestured to the exit.

She snorted. "My driver will take me. I'll meet you there."

His eyebrows rose. She had a driver? "It's no trouble."

"Says you," she muttered, then dug in her bag up to her elbow and rummaged around. Finally, she pulled out a phone and hit a few buttons. "Hey, Tony. Can you come fetch me now? I need to go to Northwestern Hospital." She frowned and jiggled her head. "An hour or two . . . Thanks." Kiera breathed deep, held it, and exhaled. She slid her eyes to Dean. "I'll meet you there. Which building and where do I go once I get there?"

"The emergency services on Huron, fourth floor, room 4112. The victim's name is—"

"Brittany Kolchek," Kiera finished, as if affronted by the thought that she might have forgotten.

Dean hoped she didn't let that venom loose on Sarah and Sam. "Her parents are both there. You'll want a word with them first?"

"Certainly." Her voice had no inflection.

If she waited for him to leave and then ditched him, he wouldn't find another memory surgeon. Dean noted the quick rise and fall of her chest, the way her gaze wouldn't settle. He retrieved a business card from his breast pocket, where he always kept two. "I'm going to warn the Kolcheks you're coming." Dean handed the card to her. "They would be devastated if you didn't show after I gave them hope."

She snatched it. "I said I'd do it."

He thought about telling her she was a hero or a good Samaritan or Brittany's last chance, but he kept his mouth closed. Flattery would likely piss her off. Another self-dug hole he'd probably never climb out of, so he'd settle for sincerity. "Thank you." He lightly touched her elbow. "Truly."

One side of her lips quirked into a smile and then was gone. "Right behind you."

CHAPTER SEVEN

Kiera

A s Kiera waited for Tony's distinctive honk (long blip, short blip, long blip), she thought about Detective Matthson's tie. From a distance, it was like any old tie, blue and boring, but up close, the pattern wasn't a curved scroll, but handcuffs. She had barely stifled a laugh.

His body was lean and long, making him appear taller than he was. He wasn't basketball player tall, but she'd had to tilt her head to glare at him. He'd been wholly unaffected by the glower, as if her ire slicked right off his skin. Probably an essential quality in a detective.

He cared. Not about her, that was for sure, but about Brittany. Kiera smirked, pleased she'd thought to ask Beth the victim's name again before she'd left. Beth remembered everything.

The expression on the detective's face when she'd smacked down Brittany's name had satisfied her more than crème brûlée with a thick, crisp crust. She should stop breaking his balls, but come on, anyone who slipped into that level of charm offensive, even to help someone, was as much con artist as detective.

At least, he was using his powers for good or whatever. Antagonizing the detective wouldn't serve Brittany—not that anything would—but it alleviated some of Kiera's tension.

She thought about how her own parents would react if she were in a coma and snorted. They'd hold a press conference to display their grief. If it were her brother, Ash, though? They'd seize the top three brain specialists from anywhere in the world. Her mother might even streak her mascara. For Ash.

Tony beeped, and Kiera brushed the frigid air from her arms and pushed out of the VFW hall. Maybe her question—the idea that her ability included a limit, a bottom, a breaking point to the trauma—might be answered today. Or her mother had been right all along. Kiera's "gift" possibly did insulate her, make her abler to weather the storms of terror and hurt and despair. Because despite the icy coating in her gut, part of her couldn't stop wondering if she could join with a person in a coma, how the memory would differ, and if she might help catch a murderer.

CHAPTER EIGHT

Dean

“I GOT ONE,” DEAN SAID, UNLEASHING HIS GRIN, though Curt couldn't see it through the phone.

Curt, of course, had to piss all over his clover. “More wasted time.”

“Come on. Aren't you the least bit curious?” Dean wanted his partner there with him. If Curt left Area Central now, he could reach the hospital in time.

“The very least.”

“You're not coming?”

“I would, but I'm running a séance in the conference room in about ten. We'll compare notes afterward.”

“Fuck you.” He'd anticipated Curt's refusal.

“Dean,” Curt said, suddenly serious. “I realize you want to believe in this, but keep your head, okay? We need evidence-based theories, not psychic bullshit.”

“I'll channel my inner Curt and be the most skeptical motherfucker on the planet.”

“Good. Call me when you're done.”

Despite Curt's refusal to back him up in person, Dean felt better. Facing Kiera Brayleigh's wrath had put a chink in his armor. If memory reading turned out to be total bullshit, Curt would make sure he at least got a laugh out of the spectacle. And he could tell himself that he'd flipped over every rock. He would meet Brittany's parents with a clear conscience.

* * *

Dean relaxed when he arrived at the hospital in time to prep Sam and Sarah Kolchek. He had gotten tentative approval from them before tracking down M&Ms, but victims' parents were always unpredictable.

Brittany's folks were stock-photo attractive: Sarah, a dyed blond, Sam with thick, salt-and-pepper hair. Both middle-aged, holding hands as they sat side by side at Brittany's bed, their affection clear, their bond strong. They stood when he entered, tense and wide-eyed. Their hope hurt. "Let's step outside to talk for a moment. I found a memory surgeon who's agreed to try and reach Brittany."

Sam and Sarah followed Dean to the waiting room just as Kiera arrived. She greeted the parents first. Dean was amazed at the difference in her disposition; she was almost another person. The snarky cactus had been replaced by someone calm and kind, like an aloe vera plant.

"I'm sorry for the reason we're meeting like this. I'm Kiera Brayleigh." She surveyed the area and the smattering of people in the gray fabric chairs that surrounded the space. She extended her hand. The Kolcheks hesitantly shook it. "You're familiar with what I do?"

"You were in that documentary we watched," Sarah blurted.

Kiera's shoulders quivered, but the smile didn't leave her face. "Everything presented about me was unauthorized and undoubtedly inaccurate."

"But your parents—"

"I'm told your daughter is in a coma."

Although not a snap, the words struck Brittany's parents. Sarah bent her face and cried with as much dignity as she could muster. Sam wrapped a protective arm around her. "Maybe this isn't a good idea. I don't know if we're ready to see what happened to our girl."

Kiera and Dean exchanged a glance, and Dean gave her a nod of encouragement.

"It's not like I'm a projector," she said with surprising gentleness, unperturbed by the intense emotions from Brittany's parents. "It's mind-to-mind contact and may not be possible with her in a coma. All I can offer is to try, but that's up to you."

*　*　*

FIVE MINUTES LATER, DEAN OBTAINED USE OF AN EMPTY ROOM. Negotiating was more comfortable without a bunch of worried families and patients gawking at them if this turned fractious.

The Kolcheks sat on a hospital bed, Dean occupied a guest chair with his notebook resting on his leg, and Kiera paced in a three-foot path. "I'll need an hour. You can use that time to grab something to eat or—"

"You want us to leave her?" Sarah's tiny voice, so different from when he'd first met her, made his heart thump like a fist pounding a heavy door.

"It might not even work," Sam said to his wife as if she hadn't been present earlier.

Sarah sighed and rested her head on his shoulder. "If these are her last moments, I don't want her reliving the worst parts of her life. Maybe we should forget this memory thing and just sit with her and share all the good memories instead."

Not a total surprise, nor the first people to hesitate. Dean opened his mouth to soothe them, but Kiera spoke first.

"My clients don't relive the memories when I read them," she said. "It isn't painful or disturbing. I always ask afterward, and everyone says that it feels like daydreaming, their thoughts wandering at random. We may not connect, but I wouldn't do it if I thought she might be harmed in any way."

The Kolcheks watched Kiera, suddenly in rapt attention. Dean found himself leaning toward her, also curious about the experience.

"Here are some other myths," Kiera said. "I can't make your daughter

39

do anything. I can't change her memories or manipulate them. She won't wake up, and I won't talk out loud or reenact anything. I won't be removing anything. It takes a lot of work and energy and"—she hesitated, then finished—"can't help her." She paused and tucked her hair behind her ear. "Any questions so far?"

They shook their heads. Kiera had snagged their interest.

Keep going, sweetheart.

"Okay. Here's what I do: I sync my brainwaves to your daughter's, and when we're aligned, I'll go into her memory. The trauma, when acute, is always right on top, and I'm going to see what led up to the attack, getting a description and a breakdown of events so the police have an MO or whatever helpful information I can find. Detective Matthson will be in the room with me the whole time."

He tried not to appear pleased, because he suspected she was trying to needle him. He'd never leave her in the room alone with Brittany.

Kiera clasped her hands together. "Once we're done, Detective Matthson will pass on whatever I have, and that's it."

"Can you give her our love?" Sarah asked.

Kiera's face softened. "It doesn't work that way. We won't be having a conversation in her mind. I wish we were. All I can do is access her memories." She reached out as if to rest a hand on Sarah's but stopped and balled her hand into a fist. The stilted motion caught Sarah's attention.

Sarah put a hand on Kiera's arm. "I know you would if you could."

Dean added his own argument. "If anything changes, I'll call you immediately."

"The doctors did say she was stable for now," Sam said, rubbing his wife's shoulder. "And I do want us to do everything we can to catch that devil."

"I hate the idea of any more mothers having to go through this."

And just like that, the tide turned. When Dean looked at Kiera one corner of her mouth twitched, and he suspected she'd surprised herself by helping to convince the parents. He inclined his head to one side in thanks. She rolled her eyes, but the gesture seemed more for herself than him.

Prickly as she was, she had a sense of humor. He let out a long breath he hadn't even realized he'd been holding.

Kiera shifted and Sarah's hand dropped from her arm. Sam shuffled his feet and asked, "Um, how much would we owe you for this? We don't have a lot of money."

Dean hadn't considered that. The city wouldn't pay anything, certainly not without a shitload of paperwork and several meetings, during which he'd be a punch line, then a punching bag. But Brayleigh waved her hand. "Don't worry; I don't need anything."

The Kolcheks stood, still clasping hands. "I don't want to go far. Maybe just to Au Bon Pain?" Sarah asked Sam.

"Okay, honey." Sam studied Dean. "You'll call?"

Dean nodded. "I will, and I won't leave until you get back. She won't be alone."

They shuffled out of the room together, Sam opening the door for Sarah. Kiera watched them go. She rubbed her temples. "Keep in mind that memory reading isn't like finding video footage. Memory can be hazy, distorted, and disjointed. And the memory isn't mine, so oftentimes it's hard for me to sort through what's real and what's some kind of weird perception."

"Okay."

"My initial recollections are always the most accurate, so I'll give you all the pertinent details right away. Like with any memory, the further away in time, the more vulnerability to outside influences."

He tamped down his surprise. Google wasn't the best source of information, but he expected better than he got. "Good info."

She half smiled at him, more nervous than friendly. "I told the Kolcheks the read would take an hour, but it won't." She ignored Dean's frown. "If she's in a coma from the trauma I'm going to search for, all she has is the root memory."

"Root memory?"

"The initial experience. When something traumatic happens, you experience it, right? And then you start to replay the events—that's an echo of a sort. She won't have much of that."

He nodded.

"The memory won't take long to find. But sometimes I need time to recover, and those people don't need to see me freaked out. I'll be long gone before they get back." She shook her head and rubbed her hands across each other. "I hate this shit."

CHAPTER NINE

Kiera

K IERA ENTERED THE HOSPITAL ROOM, HER HEART beating in her throat. She hated hospital rooms. Too many sharp memories—both others and her own.

The beeping was expected, but the hushed quiet surrounding it was creepy. The florescent lights didn't help, giving the room a ghastly, flickering glow, and the closed curtains around Brittany appeared sinister. Kiera set her purse on a chair next to the bed, then braced herself as Detective Matthson pulled back the curtain.

The form on the bed was barely recognizable as human. Her face was doughy and bruised; gauze wrapped around her head where not enough blond hair peeked out. Kiera's heartbeat expanded from her throat to her eyes and temples. Was Brittany missing part of her scalp?

Kiera's pulse pounded everywhere as if taking over her body. She would have to relive that suffering. And it would be bad. Shockingly, horrifyingly bad.

Her mouth trembled as she looked over Brittany's body. He should have told her. She understood why he hadn't, but . . . he'd maneuvered and trapped her and had the nerve to look so fucking *innocent*. Brittany had not just been assaulted. She'd been butchered.

Kiera rammed the heel of her hand hard into Dean's chest, and even she didn't know if she wanted to hit or push. He stumbled back into the wall with a thud.

"You motherfucker!" she hissed.

He held up his hands. "Ms. Brayleigh, please calm yourself."

"Calm myself?" She gripped her head and squeezed. "Are you fucking kidding me? Left out some pertinent details, didn't you, Detective?"

"No, I just didn't think—"

"Bullshit. You were thinking plenty." Kiera kicked the garbage can, which tumbled a few times before bouncing off the wall. "Fuck. Fuck. Fuck." She pressed the heels of her hands into her eyes. "Fuck."

He watched her as if she were a caged animal.

Her voice broke. "Why would you do this to me?" Not quite what she'd intended.

Dean spoke in a gentle voice. "Look at her face." Despite herself, she glanced at Brittany, her inert form and too-swollen face. He continued in that low tone. "I can't make that right, no matter what I do."

Tears sprang to her eyes because she'd had the same thought so many times over so many women.

He remained calm. "Sometimes I do things I don't want to do to find some justice. For victims like Brittany."

"'Victims like Brittany.' Fuck you," she muttered to herself, running her numb hands through her hair. She wanted to quit, to storm out, but his determination to help Brittany by any means had somehow snagged her admiration.

She threw a box of tissues from the sideboard to the other side of the room. In the brief moment his eyes followed it instead of her, she attempted to retrieve her composure.

"I'm going to need a few minutes to calm myself down after all this bullshit," she said, gesturing to Brittany. "Bring me that garbage can. I'll probably need it."

She wished she'd thrown the box at him. She wished she'd slammed him in his handsome face.

Dr. Patty would say that a controlled breath could slow the heart, but she'd never faced an impending rape and assault—if only in her mind.

Kiera pulled her thoughts from Dr. Patty and closed her eyes, envisioning her relaxation room with the fountain, the massaging chair, the fainting couch with the plump cushions, the hint of lavender in the air, and the temperature a little too cool. Endure the next hour, and then she could go home and put herself back together again. She would prevail.

Kiera opened her eyes. "You ready?"

He nodded.

For a few seconds, she tried to steady herself, but her body wouldn't stop shaking, so she simply took Brittany's hand, the one not attached to some sort of IV drip. Her palm was warm and dry, and Kiera wanted to apologize for her sweaty one.

It was selfish to think, but Kiera hoped the read wouldn't work, that the woman's brain would clamp shut. Then she could congratulate herself that she'd done the right thing without having to face the consequences. She closed her eyes and reached out to the woman whose hand she was holding, reached down and out, searching for that spool of color, the coil of memories that told Kiera they were synced. And she found it.

If Kiera ever wrote a memoir, which she would never do, she would title it *The Color of Trauma Is Pink*. Memories shone as filaments, thin and tight, spooled around each other, like a ball of yarn. The worst memories were always a shade of pink. Kiera had long ago ceased to care why.

Brittany had a fuchsia memory at the top. The metallic sheen was a grim sign. The thickness of the strand, wider than any echoes, told her it was a root memory. Kiera saw few echoes of that memory, which had the same color. That was promising. She wouldn't have to dig through other terrible memories, and it might indicate a shorter memory, though the filament lengths rarely corresponded to a commensurate length of time.

She could always say she couldn't find anything. Nobody would argue. She could walk away, go home to her relaxation room, smoke a joint, and count herself lucky. But she'd have to live with the guilt if he killed someone else.

Kiera didn't know Brittany. She didn't owe her anything. But when she recalled Brittany's slack, battered face, she wanted to burn down the world.

Fuck. *Just decide.* Before she wimped out, she grabbed hold of the filament.

And everything changed.

The difference between a conscious person and someone in a coma was apparent right away. No barrier blocked Kiera from Brittany's memories. No walls had to be deconstructed; Brittany's mind opened with no resistance or pause.

The memory started with a knife to the neck. From the tenuousness of the filament and that first peek at the event, Kiera knew the trauma etched deep. But she'd touched the thread, so the recall would run no matter what she did. If she pulled out now, the experiences would slam into her in a jumbled mass, which was always worse. She had to ride out the encounter.

With a tight hold to the thread, she backed up to the block of memories just before the knife.

* * *

"Hey, I think you go to my church."

Brittany looked up from her book. The guy was hot, with electric-blue eyes and a sweet undercut paired with curly, floppy hair that was gelled within an inch of its life. She studied the man for a moment. His low-slung jeans and faded T-shirt were mackadocious. Two black hoops circled his bottom lip. No way he went to her church. "I don't think so."

"Holy Trinity on North?"

Holy shit, that was her church. How had she missed Mr. Hottiness? "Yeah, I do go there. Sorry, I don't recognize you."

He smiled. Brittany forgot to not look stupid for a few seconds. He took a step closer. "No worries. I take the piercings out for church. I'm Dillon, by the way."

She laughed. "Brittany."

Dillon took her hand and kissed the back like a movie hero. She had thought him in his midtwenties, but now she thought early thirties—

* * *

Kiera wasn't taking the memory, and nothing had happened yet, but dread threatened to taint the recollection. Her gut gurgled, and she couldn't feel her hands. No matter how much she wished to stop, it was too late. She couldn't even slow the fall.

* * *

They took the bus back to her place. She ducked into her bedroom to change, a nonstop grin on her face. But when she returned to Dillon, he was gone. Someone grabbed her and yanked her backward into a hard body. The guy was too tall to be Dillon. She froze from a sharp sting at her neck. Weren't there, like, a million blood vessels in the neck?

A knife.

"Don't fucking move, bitch. Don't make a sound. Do exactly as I say, and you won't get hurt." The voice was lower than Dillon's. Where was Dillon?

But, of course, he was Dillon.

He kept her on the bed, face down, hands bound behind her back, her panties ripped from her body. The savage yank and tear stung and left her open, exposed, and vulnerable. That was when Brittany realized she was in real trouble. Before then, she told herself that he kidded, a not-so-funny practical joke.

Dillon held her head down flat against the mattress, on top of her grandma's quilt, as if she had been struggling. Had she? He widened her legs farther and farther, past when her muscles screamed. He bent her feet back and tied them to her hands, leaving her at his mercy. His breathing turned snorty and rough like a beast. He probably grew tusks or horns. He raped her from behind, and she was glad that she couldn't see his face, but the sick heat of him on her skin made her eyelids flutter like a spasm.

Her grandma's quilt would have to be stuffed into the deepest part of her closet. She was going to need a new bedspread. She would need new clothes too, black with a few browns or grays, all in muted tones. What was a tone? Colors had tones and sounds had tones...touch had tones too. Dillon's tone was deep, like a foghorn, like the sound a submarine makes before it dives into the black of the ocean. Brittany wanted to dive down.

Pain was a funny thing. Her body flinched and jerked and flailed, all without her input. It tried to inch away from the agony, searching for an angle that ached less. Dillon pulled out, and she thought him finished. Then he spread her cheeks.

Her lucky dress was riding up to pool under her breasts. The seams ripped, like her insides ripped, like her life ripped. Dillon talked to her the whole time, calling her a slut, telling her how much she liked it, telling her that this was what she deserved, telling her that she was his, and he could do anything he wanted, he was in control. "Whore! You fucking whore," he hissed into her ear, his hands gripping her hair so tight her scalp screeched.

She tried to scream, but he shoved her face into the mattress so she couldn't breathe. Every molecule in her body woke up and struggled, as if she'd been tossed into an ice bath. "Do that again, and I'll slit your throat just enough so it takes hours for you to bleed to death," he said when he'd lifted his hold. Brittany could only breathe.

* * *

KIERA'S LUNGS ACHED WITH THE LACK OF OXYGEN—OR TOO MUCH oxygen. Her body didn't realize that the experiences weren't real—not for her. Her mind disconnected, then reconnected like a reboot.

Focus, Kiera. Focus on the details.

But all she could grab were slivers of color and movement and pain.

* * *

He duct-taped a balled-up athletic sock in her mouth that he'd found in her dirty clothes' basket, and she worried she would catch some sort of athlete's foot. She pictured a thick, white paste coating her tongue, and her breath would be atrocious. Plants would wilt if she breathed on them. Her mouth would itch too. Maybe she would teach herself to eat spicy food. She was going to learn to love curry, she decided. Curry reeked like feet to her, so it made sense that curry would be the cure.

Dillon continued, talking and talking and violating her for forever. Shouldn't he be done by now? He was impotent. No, that was when a man couldn't get it up. And then he did climax, or she assumed he did. He grunted and tensed, then collapsed onto her back. He was heavy. Then he was gone, as if he had turned to mist. She hadn't heard him leave. Had she fallen asleep?

Someone was going to miss her. Church tomorrow. Her parents would miss her. They'd call, and when she didn't answer, they'd worry. They'd come by. They would find her. Oh, God, would they discover her like this? Trussed up like a pig, naked and bleeding, clearly violated? What would they think of her? She'd let a strange man in her apartment. Why had she done that? She wanted to go back in time, back to the bus stop and say, "Another time," and then Dillon would disappear and find somebody else. He knew what church she went to. Had he been following her? She searched her mind, but she didn't find him. But someone from church would recognize him. Father Thomas! Oh, God. He could be identified. Did that mean he was going to kill her?

Her thoughts circled and circled around what had happened, what was going to happen, and how the entire ordeal might never have happened. She heard the television, the flush of a toilet. The ropes wouldn't budge, wouldn't loosen. She slept fitfully, her legs and arms cramping, her neck stiff and aching from being wrenched so far to the side.

He woke her in the night, gripping her. Her chest rattled, but then her bonds broke. Her body screamed, a flood of achy pain overtaking her. Dillon grabbed her hands and slid the blade between her and the twine. He stuffed the cut rope into his pocket. She tugged down her ripped dress, arranging herself as well as possible.

He was leaving. Thank God. The room swayed. But, no, he was taking her with him. No. No. No. But he did. He held the knife to her rib cage, threatening to stab her if she moved or yelled. He stole her grandmother's quilt, stuffing the covering into his backpack. He must have guessed how much it meant to her.

"Grab your purse. You'll need money and your keys."

She wouldn't need her purse if he was going to kill her. Right?

* * *

Kiera's heart jumped and scrabbled like a startled cat. A trapped animal, scrambling for escape though the cage had already shut. The imperative to run blocked by the inability to do so made a kind of insanity.

* * *

Dillon shoved her into the back of the van and closed the door behind them. The vehicle stank of dust and rust. "Sit down," he barked, and she all but collapsed. "Do I have to tell you everything? Put your wrists in the manacles."

Manacles. Manacles. What a funny word.

She set down her purse and complied. He snapped her in place, and Brittany was relieved the fit wasn't tight, though she couldn't slip her hands through. Dillon retrieved his bike, shoved it next to her in the back, and walked to the front. He tossed his backpack on the passenger seat and started the van. Mexican music filled the space with the sounds of trumpets, guitars, and accordions.

He took her someplace industrial and deserted with a loading dock that reminded Brittany of when she had been in a production of Rent *in high school, only real. A dark, spooky stage littered with papers and leaves, stinking of motor oil and something—oh God, pee.*

Dillon showed her his knife, spinning the blade in his hands and singing a song she didn't recognize. She cried. He slapped her, openhanded. Then backhanded. She stumbled and screamed, tasting blood in her mouth. He gripped her shoulder with his knife hand and then punched her in the abdomen hard enough she stopped breathing for several seconds. Just as she recovered her breath, he pulled her upright and stabbed her deep, low in her stomach. "That's right. I'm the one that kills you," he whispered.

At first, she felt more pressure than pain. He stared into her face. His eyes were so blue. So blue, blue, blue . . .

* * *

STOP! KIERA LET GO OF THE MEMORY, WHICH MEANT IT RAN FASTER AND deeper, gripping into her with claws that cut. She hadn't made a mistake like that in years. Oh, fuck. Nothing stopped the onslaught of terror and confusion, and it hit her all at once.

* * *

A jerk. A hot, sharp pain seared her forehead. Feet slid. Red. Warm liquid dribbled into her eyes. Blood. Her hair. Scalp. Going to die. Didn't want to die. Want to go home—her parents' home—her bed that still had a canopy.

"Daddy." Daddy always made her troubles better. He always scared away the monsters. Headlights swam over her. Scream!

CHAPTER TEN

Dean

K IERA SAT IN A CHAIR CLASPING BRITTANY'S HAND, her posture and countenance rigid. Her eyes were closed. Dean studied her in detail as he bounced a notebook against his thigh. She had a pronounced jaw and a sharp chin, but in repose, she appeared sweet. Pretty.

He expected twitching or eyeballs moving behind her eyelids, little spasms, and gasps. She wasn't relaxed, but she didn't move. At all. Her breathing was fast, but no more so than when she had begun. If she were faking, though, she would be doing something.

He should have mentioned the brutality of the attack to Kiera, but she would have refused if she comprehended the extent of the assault, even to protect one of her own. Guilt served nothing, so he pushed it away.

Then she made a tiny sound, like a scared kitten, and Dean's heart bounded into his throat and stuck there. The urge to comfort her almost overcame his common sense. He barely stopped himself from touching her. Like she would have appreciated that.

Her breath turned rapid and shaky as color drained from her face. Was she going into shock? Dean needed to stop this, though he didn't know how to retrieve her.

With a lurch, Kiera bent over and threw up in the wastebasket next to her chair with a groan. "Fuck, fuck, fuck, fuck, fuck," she chanted after she'd thrown up twice more.

She wiped her mouth with a tissue she dug out of her jeans pocket. Her eyes were red-rimmed, and tears streamed down her cheeks, but the color was back in her face. She tried to sit up straight but couldn't hold the posture. "He said his name was Dillon. Brown hair, longish and kind of floppy on top, cut close to the sides." Kiera crumpled, both hands on the floor, her head hanging down. "Bright-blue eyes. He's tall. He's got two hoops through his lower lip, near the center about a centimeter apart. Black. The hoops, not him. He's white, pretty pale."

Dean knelt next to her, his notebook cast aside, careful not to touch without permission. "It's okay. You're okay. I can wait for—"

She shook her head, as if trying to shake off something, then continued, words crashing over one another. "Write it down now. He was strong or seemed strong to Brittany. He knew where she went to church. Holy Trinity on North. He said he's been going there for a month, but she didn't recognize him. Talk to a Father Thomas."

Dean took notes on autopilot.

Kiera slid upright, her back against the bed, and wrapped her hands around her legs before resting her forehead on her knees and rocking herself, making a high-pitched keening noise. Dean pressed the pen so hard into the paper it should have ripped. She hadn't just observed but suffered an immersive experience. He had done this to her.

She cried for several minutes before picking up her head, keeping turned away from him. "She was at a bus stop after shopping at Mariano's. Afternoon. He was there and asked her out. He had a bike, Trek, old, blue or gray, I think." She blew her nose. "They rode the bus together, his bike on the rack. He . . . helped with the groceries and asked her to change. No. He said she *could* change, and she did. When she came out of the bedroom . . ."

Her voice choked, and she gasped twice. "He was waiting behind the door with a knife and grabbed her from behind. He tied her up, hog-tied her, and raped her both vaginally and anally. Much later, he took her to another location. He brought a white van—"

Dean's heart stumbled. "Did you catch a plate number?"

"No. Don't interrupt. This shit fades fast," she snapped. "In the van . . ." She closed her eyes, and Dean winced at breaking her concentration. A license ID would have been gold. "Old, service-like, metal on the floor, some sort of bar running along the sides. He had restraints there, manacles, and she was attached at her wrists. He took her to a warehouse of some kind. On the loading dock, he stabbed her in the stomach or uterus. He said, 'I'm the one that kills you.' He was scalping her when headlights flashed by. Before she screamed, he must have hit her in the head. How the fuck is she still alive?" Kiera's voice rose at the end. She resumed crying, covering her face with her hands. "Oh, God," she said over and over again.

Nobody could invent something like that, hitting so many confirmed details. She had seen the killer. He had a witness.

She curled over herself and shook. Dean squatted down next to her, moving the wastebasket out of the way. He wanted to comfort her, but people in crisis didn't always want that, and he had been the one to put her in this situation. Her mood might snap, and then she might slap him. He certainly had it coming.

But it wasn't anger radiating from her. It was raw pain. She made mewling sounds like a wounded animal, and he couldn't stop himself from putting a tentative hand on the back of her head. She leaned into him, almost knocking him off balance, burrowing into his chest.

Words tumbled out her mouth into his shirt, gaining speed and strength. "She kept calling for her father. That fucker was killing her, and she was crying for him. You can't ever tell him that. He can't ever know how much she suffered. Promise. Promise me you won't tell him how she needed him. Please."

"I'll do all I can." No parent should have to hear the particulars of what their murdered child had endured. Dean believed in the truth, but truth wasn't the answer to everything. However, if the killer was caught alive and the case went to court—they'd know the details, whether they wanted or not.

"I hate you," she said into his shirt, crying, face pressed to his chest, her hands clinging to his arms. "You're a bastard."

"I know." She was a wreck because of him. He stroked her hair once, then a more confident second time. "But I'm the bastard who's going to catch the motherfucker who did this."

She pulled away to look at him. Her face was red and splotchy and haunted. He let his determination show in his eyes. She gripped his shirt tight, undoubtedly wrinkling it—not that he cared. "You fucking better, Matthson."

CHAPTER ELEVEN

Kiera

K IERA WOKE IN THE RELAXATION ROOM, HER HEAD foggy from her dose of Valium. Memory surgeons had high instances of suicide and drug addiction. Kiera had no intention of becoming a statistic, so she had strict rules regarding self-medication. One Valium a month. Period. No exceptions. One sleeping pill per month. No exceptions. Weed twice a month and no more than four hits at a go. Nothing harder than that. Pain was sometimes better than the cost of relief.

No alcohol.

She thought of her mentor, Doreen, whose struggles had inspired the rules. Doreen hadn't met a line she wouldn't push. Kiera, for all her faults, always held firm. After all, a line that moved was no line at all. She ached at the memory of Doreen.

The rule was simple: no alcohol as *medication*. That wasn't a slippery slope but a precarious precipice that Doreen had tumbled over. Kiera sometimes drank a glass of wine with her brother, Ash, or Nadira and Beth, but never if she thought she needed it.

Her shrink wanted to put her on antidepressants, but Kiera had refused. Of course she was unbalanced. She experienced a fresh trauma every month or two piled on top of old ones. Medication was more for people who should have been over it by now. Okay, that was unfair, but it didn't change her belief that antidepressants were not for her.

She kept her eyes closed, absorbing the sound of cascading water. That fountain was the best money she had ever spent. Spending five minutes listening as water splashed and trickled was enough to calm her.

It didn't last.

The memory of the sharp sting of the knife zipped through her thoughts. Kiera had several stab memories, and she ran a comparison, though she shouldn't let her mind run over the trauma again so soon after waking. She should give herself time to heal a little, carve some distance, perspective. But something about that particular pain was odd, hotter than the others, thinner. Why? Because of the location on the scalp?

Stop thinking about it.

She was okay. One day she wouldn't be, but today she was okay.

Kiera's stomach had settled, but she wasn't in the mood for food. Instead, she changed and went to the workout room. She hopped onto the VersaClimber and climbed. She started off with slow speed and high resistance. Sweat dripped into her eyes, her heart pumped, and her lungs heaved. She increased the resistance. Her thighs and butt burned. Her arms felt hot and rubbery. When she thought she couldn't continue, she set her stopwatch. After five minutes, she took off all the resistance and cooled down for another ten minutes. Her legs shook as she kicked off her exercise clothes. Leaving them on the floor, she padded to the bathroom to shower.

She wore a healing blue tank sundress, though for a moment she recalled Brittany putting on her dress, the red one with the shelf bra. Her lucky dress. God, what a joke. Tears brimmed, and Kiera slammed shut the memory. With her hair in a towel turban, she called Nadira.

"Come over," Kiera barked into the phone.

* * *

"Don't you dare say, 'I told you so,'" Kiera said as she opened her door.

"Wouldn't dream of it," Nadira was such a liar. "So, what happened?"

Kiera reset her security alarm and followed Nadira to the living room, where they plopped down at opposite ends of the shaggy couch she'd named Goliath. Kiera tucked her feet beneath her and plucked at the soft fur upholstery. Nadira sat like a lady.

"That victim was raped, beaten, and cut—and not a little and not in a five-minute window. Hours." Kiera said, her voice misty.

"Oh, no."

"I figured the memory would be horrible when I saw her, but I'd told the cop and the parents I'd do it."

Nadira reached out and put a hand on Kiera's knee. "You still should have said no."

They sat in silence for a handful of seconds before Kiera dropped her head into her hands. "You're right."

"What's your coping strategy?" Nadira asked.

"Well, I used up my Valium for the month."

Nadira sniffed. She often expressed the opinion that Kiera's rules for self-medicating were stupid. Nadira was a walking pharmacy. Then again, she'd never met Doreen. "So, what else?"

At least, Nadira didn't pull anything out of her bag to tempt Kiera. In her state, she might take anything. That scared her. All she had to keep her tethered to sanity were her rules. She had to hold on to them.

"My plan?" Kiera raised the pitch and slowed her voice like Dr. Patty. "I'm going to breathe into my third-eye chakra as I place my hands into a calming mudra." Kiera extended both middle fingers, swirling them around her own face as she took a deep breath.

Nadira laughed.

Kiera sighed. "I'm going to have to talk to Detective Dickhead sometime tomorrow. I didn't let him grill me beyond what I spouted off from memory."

"Screw him."

Despite her mood, Kiera giggled. "Not remotely tempted."

Nadira laughed too. "You sure?"

She didn't tell Nadira that she'd leaned on him, that he'd cupped his hand on the back of her head, stroked her hair. Kiera didn't want Nadira knowing how she'd gripped his forearms, face to his chest, vulnerable, taking comfort from the person who had forced her through such misery. How grateful she'd felt. Kiera was too embarrassed by her reaction to him, and she had an irrational fear of losing Nadira's respect, though they'd always supported each other.

"I have to talk to him, though, so he can catch that psycho fuck-prick. He was the worst kind, Dir, the kind you can't see until he's right on top of you. You know?"

"Yeah." And, of course, she did. Everyone in group would understand. Except Amy.

"I want to ask you a favor, but you can say no." The idea had come to her on the ride home, and she had mixed feelings about asking.

"I'd do anything for you, Kiera."

Tears sprouted hard enough to slip down her cheek before she blinked them back. "Thanks." She swallowed, and the movement hurt. "I'm hoping you can sketch him for me."

Nadira froze, and Kiera hated herself for panicking her friend. "I think I can cut a segment of the memory. I'll use my root memory of the read, so it won't be perfect." She reached out and touched Nadira's shoulder when Nadira curled inward. "Not the assault, only the initial meeting. I won't give you any of the bad shit, I swear to God. I would *never* do that to you."

Nadira sat up straighter. "You can do that?"

"I want to try. I'll make a clean copy, so there's no danger. I wouldn't ask, Dir, but I'm scared they'll make me search through mug shots, and I can't bear the thought of seeing all those faces. What if I recognize someone else?"

Nadira nodded and licked her lips. "And you don't want to spend the hours with a forensic artist."

"I'll screw that up. I'm not great with the descriptions, but you're fantastic. If I show you his face, you'll capture him perfectly." The praise sounded fake though it was true. Kiera was acting as bad as the detective, coercing her friend to look at a rapist murderer, so she wouldn't have to flip through photos of criminals.

"Bring me some water. I'll take a little something, and let's see what happens," Nadira said with forced cheer to match Kiera's forced praise.

Kiera bounced to the kitchen. "For this, you're getting the Fiji Water and some brownies."

"Herbal brownies?" Nadira asked, breaking into a real grin.

* * *

"Matthson." The detective's voice was crisp and short, sounding cop-like.

"It's Kiera." Too informal. "Brayleigh."

"Ms. Brayleigh, thank you for calling. How are you?" He now sounded shrink-like. *And how do you feel about that?*

She smiled, unsure exactly why. "You have questions for me, right? For tomorrow?"

"Yes. You can come down to the station, or we can come to you."

Not a tough decision. "You can come here."

CHAPTER TWELVE

Dean

THE CONDO BUILDING WAS SITUATED RIGHT ON Lake Shore Drive, the highway running along the shore of Lake Michigan. The structure appeared almost quaint next to the high rises on either side. The lake stretched out unobstructed before it, the water dotted with boats and personal watercraft.

Dean and Curt had known she lived on the ninth floor but not that it was the penthouse. The doorman needed to slide a card into a slot for the ninth-floor button to work. She owned the entire floor.

The entryway highlighted the condo's luxury with white marble inlaid with seams of black and gold, the midday sun making it glow. A scrolled metal side table with an oddly shaped silver bowl was positioned beside the door. Inside the bowl sat a wallet but no keys. Her door had a keypad, so perhaps she didn't need any.

Kiera Brayleigh stood barefoot and barefaced, wearing a casual red halter dress of a T-shirt-like material. "Detective Matthson," she said in a dead tone.

"Ms. Brayleigh," he replied, holding out his hand. She let his hand hang for a few seconds, shook it once, and focused over his shoulder. Guess she still harbored a grudge.

Dean gestured to Curt. "This is my partner, Curtis Haze."

Curt held out his hand. "Call me Curt."

"Call me Kiera." She shook his hand and looked him in the eye. Many times, people had a hard time believing he and Curt were partners, since they were so opposite to each other: Dean thin, white, and six foot; Curt broad and fit, black, and five feet eight. Kiera, however, didn't act surprised.

She stepped aside for them to enter. "Come on in." Once they entered, she armed her alarm system.

"Expecting trouble?" Dean asked.

"Always."

Dean and Curt synced up with a few glances as they followed Kiera into her condo. This woman had money, and she was a few centimeters off-center.

And then there was the place itself. As he watched her walk, the vastness of the space hit him. Ten-foot ceilings, huge photographs on the walls, all nature scenes: oceans, rivers, mountains, meadows, and cliffs.

The flooring stunned him. Gorgeous hickory cut in a herringbone pattern—real craftsmanship. She must have paid a pretty penny for it.

Curt muttered, "I wish Mark could see this." Curt's husband sold real estate and had a passion for interior design.

"It is beautiful," Dean said under his breath.

The living room had a decent fireplace and impressive mantel, and she had the strangest sofa—large, black, and furry—but he held a neutral expression. Until he saw the high-end kitchen.

As he gawked at the frosted glass cabinets and high-end appliances in the kitchen—thinking of his own half-demolished, never-ending remodel—Kiera wandered to the embedded glass countertop along the back wall and picked up a piece of white copy paper. She flipped it over, considered it, then handed the page to Dean. "This is your guy."

Curt and Dean peered down at the drawing. Someone had rendered a pencil sketch of a youngish man with high cheekbones, a sharp chin, and a lip pierced with double rings. As she had described in the hospital, the man had hair styled into a messy pompadour on top with close-cropped sides.

"You drew this?" Dean asked.

"God, no. I have an artist friend. This is what he looks like, though."

The likeness was a positive development. "Can I keep this?"

"I certainly don't want it." She crossed one arm over her body, scratched the other arm, shifted between her feet, and looked around until her eyes landed on the island counter. Next to the cooktop was a food processer's bowl filled with a yellow paste. "I prepped enough for all of us, if you're hungry," Kiera said, fidgeting with the side of her dress, as if the fabric had become twisted.

Dean usually partook when victims or victim's families offered, because it gave the people something to do, some way to feel as if they were helping. Curt, though always hungry, was leery about eating or drinking unvetted food. So, Dean was surprised when Curt said, "Yes, ma'am. This seems a lot nicer than Taco Bell."

Kiera snorted. "I should hope so."

"What're you making?" Dean asked, though his iron stomach would have been just fine with Taco Bell.

"Grilled cheese." Her face remained stiff. The paste in the bowl must be some combination of cheeses.

"How can we help?" Curt asked.

"Do you guys want salad too?"

"Absolutely," Dean replied as he noticed a subtle tremor in Kiera's hands. If he and Curt sat back and watched her cook, the shaking might worsen. He took the drawing back to the little side table near the door.

When he returned to the kitchen, she was pulling food out of the refrigerator. Something buzzed.

"Goddamn it," she muttered and slammed the fridge door. She tossed a tube of goat cheese onto the counter.

"What's wrong?" Dean asked.

Kiera shook her head and wiped a hand over her face. "My washer was stopping in the middle of the cycle once in a while, and now it's freezing all the time."

"Do you know why?"

She crossed her arms. "No, I don't speak washer."

This could be advantageous for him—he had a knack for all things mechanical. He loved the tangible, definite accomplishment of making something broken function again. Police work was rarely that cut and dry.

"Can I take a look?"

Kiera studied him for a moment, then threw one arm in the air. "Knock yourself out."

He followed her down a hall to a small laundry room, all in white: appliances, walls, tile. The only color was a small border of neon-green leaves around the walls near the ceiling, probably made from vinyl. The high-end washer had an "LE" message displayed. Dean pulled out his phone and did an internet search on the code.

"Can I finish making lunch?" Kiera asked from the doorway, her body tilted away, as if she wanted to bolt.

"Of course."

She disappeared.

According to the web, the error meant the motor was overheating. The room didn't smell acrid, but that didn't necessarily mean anything. The problem could also be the sensor. Luckily, the drawer stand under the washer was on feet that made it easy to slide the machine forward. He unplugged the unit and found the back panel. He needed a screwdriver.

When Dean reached the kitchen, Kiera and Curt were arguing about salad ingredients.

"I don't care for walnuts," Curt said. Understatement. Curt *hated* walnuts, from some traumatic walnut-fudge experience when he was a kid.

"You mentioned that," Kiera said, hands on her hips. "I'm not saying the salad needs walnuts. My point was that if we're going to go pecan, goat cheese is not the right choice."

"What are you thinking?"

Kiera opened the fridge and brandished a blue-veined chunk. "Blue cheese."

Curt looked ready to snatch the cheese but tilted his chin instead instead. "That'll overpower the radicchio."

She squared off in front of him, only a foot away. "Not if we add some arugula."

They were acting so much like gunslingers that Dean couldn't keep a smile off his face. He stayed out of the room, not wanting to disturb the standoff.

Curt grinned, his eyes cutting to Dean, knowing he was there. "I like this girl."

"Girl?" she said before flipping the sandwiches.

"Woman," Curt amended. "I like this woman."

"That will make lunch less awkward," Dean said. Then he asked Kiera, "Have you got a screwdriver?"

"Phillips head or regular?" she asked as if proud of her terminology.

The proper term was flat-head and not regular, but he didn't correct her. "Phillips head."

"Sure, just a second." She called over her shoulder to Curt, "You're in charge of the sandwiches. Don't you dare burn them."

"Yes, ma'am," Curt said.

Kiera disappeared down another hallway.

"Radicchio?" Dean whispered.

"Greens ain't no joke."

"Isn't radicchio red?"

Curt made a shooing motion. "Stick to repair and vacate yourself from my kitchen."

CHAPTER THIRTEEN

Kiera

KIERA RETRIEVED HER TOOLBOX, A SAD RED-METAL contraption, and found what Dean needed. "Here you go."

Did Dean Matthson play at home repair often while he interrogated? Maybe they taught it at police school. The strategy worked because she couldn't stay mad.

Dean had his head bent over something in the back of the washer. "Sometimes it's a sensor."

"Tell me about it," Kiera replied with an air of authority, propped against the doorjamb.

"I think the problem is in the wiring." He ducked his head around to peer at her. "Couple of wires are burnt out."

Kiera stared at him blankly. Was he serious?

"If you have wire cutters, strippers, and electrical tape, I think I can fix it," he said.

"You can fix it?" Kiera tried to comprehend a regular person repairing a washing machine. She had been sure he was going to invent some bullshit diagnosis and tell her she needed to call a proper repairman. He kept surprising her.

"We serve and protect," he said with a grin.

* * *

Kiera stifled a smile as the cops exchanged yet another glance at each other between bites of food. "How long have you guys been partners?"

"Forever," Curt said.

"Forever in human years or dog years?"

"Both," Dean said. "We've been partners off and on for ten years." He looked at Curt and grinned. "Mostly on."

"How old are you?" she asked. It was a rude question, but he fascinated her, and he appeared too young to have been a cop that long.

"Thirty-three. I joined the force when I was twenty-one." He took a bite of pear from the salad. "Curt was my second partner after I was off probation."

Kiera almost bit her tongue. "What did you do to put yourself on probation?"

Both men laughed, which made Kiera wonder if she'd said something dumb.

Dean smiled. "Sorry. Everyone begins on probation. You have your field training, a few more months on the street, and then you're off probation."

"Oh." She had more questions, but the conversation sounded more like her interrogating them. She wasn't used to talking to strangers.

Luckily, Joel, the concierge, interrupted her conversational floundering with the electrical tape. He handed it over with a guileless smile. "You can keep that, Ms. Brayleigh."

Joel was in his early twenties and always blushed in her presence. Kiera found his shyness adorable, which was a nice break from the sick dread she usually experienced when men showed attraction.

"Thanks, Joel."

When she returned, the detectives were done eating. Their heads were close together, and they were clearly arguing, though Kiera couldn't catch whether it was fun or getting serious. "Everything okay?"

"We should jump right into the case details from your, uh . . . reading," Curt said, as if he wanted to put *reading* in air quotes.

If he was pissed at his partner, he didn't need to take that vitriol out on her. She'd forgotten that they were there on business. "What do you want to know?"

"Everything," His eyes were as hard as his voice, as if he had flipped a cop switch.

Detective Curt Haze vibed like a skeptic. Offended disbelievers abounded, but they didn't come to her home to ask for help. Maybe he was playing bad cop. Something sharp, like jagged metal, dropped into her stomach. "You'll have to be more specific, Detective."

Dean stood and shot a warning glare at Curt. Was he attempting to protect her—or Curt? "Let's move this into the laundry room. I'll work on the washer as we talk."

They all walked to the laundry room, Kiera and Curt carrying bar stools from the kitchen. Dean ducked into the space between the back of the washer and the wall to examine something. Curt sat outside the door and pulled out a notebook. Kiera arranged her stool so she could see both men.

"Start at the beginning," Dean said in an easy voice.

Kiera rubbed between her eyebrows with the knuckle of her thumb. *Calm down. Just get it over with.* She'd gotten only a few sentences into the story before the first interruption.

"How tall was he?" Dean asked.

"Your height."

Curt scribbled in his notebook. "Six feet tall. Right-handed or left-handed?"

She cocked her head to the side and ran down the memories. "Right-handed."

"You're sure?" Curt asked.

Maybe they had discovered some evidence he was left-handed. She shrugged. "He held the knife in his right hand."

Tension frizzled in the small room. The two detectives each stared as if they wanted to pummel the other.

"You two want a moment alone to plan your next move?" she asked. No way did she want in the middle of some sort of police pissing match.

"No, we're fine," Curt said, his voice suddenly thick and rich as caramel sauce.

Dean went back to pulling out wires. He used the handles of one of the tools to pull off the coating on some of them. She hoped he knew what he was doing.

"Shouldn't I turn off the electricity?" she asked, images of Dean frying running through her mind.

"I unplugged the machine," he said, as if trying not to laugh.

Kiera stared at Curt, who appeared bored. She sighed. "Shall I go on?"

"Please," Dean said, now wrapping some wires with black tape.

She continued. "He hooked his bike on the front rack, and they rode the bus together to her stop."

"How did she pay?"

Kiera tapped a hand over her mouth. "He paid. He used his Ventra card. Can you find him that way?" she asked. The concept that they might find him so easily made her dizzy.

"Depends," Dean said. "We can obtain access to CTA records, but not all Ventra cards are registered. Any idea of the time?"

She closed her eyes. People rarely thought about the time, but she examined her recollection of the memory more deeply. Dillon had suggested tea, not lunch. "Two o'clock?"

"That will help us narrow down records."

"They got off at Sedgwick and walked to her apartment. He left his bike leaning next to the steps and helped her with the groceries."

"Did he lock the bike?" Dean didn't look up from his work.

What difference did that make? "No, but there was a wrought-iron fence, so the bike wasn't on the sidewalk."

Curt took copious notes, as if the bike leaning against the stairs would be the key to the case. "Once upstairs, she put all the refrigerated stuff away but kept the rest on the counter."

"You're sure?" Curt tapped his pen on his notepad.

"Yeah. That's not something that would be muddied by trauma. Why?"

"Nothing was left on the counter when we checked out her place." His voice was neutral, but Kiera got the impression he was trying to catch her in a lie.

She resisted the urge to shrug. Still, where *had* the food gone? "He put the groceries away? Strange."

"You're sure Brittany didn't?"

"Positive. She changed her clothes after putting the cold items away, and he bound her as soon as she came out. Can you get fingerprints off the boxes and stuff?"

Dean jumped back into the conversation, no longer fiddling with the wires, his eyes gleaming. "Possibly. He wasn't wearing gloves or anything?"

"No, not that I saw. I mean, she saw." She put her hand to her mouth. "Oh."

"What?"

Kiera's memory read wasn't a camera in the room. She only knew Brittany's perspective. "He had her tied up in the bedroom for a long time, hours. Who knows what the hell he did during that time. He could have had gloves in his pocket, or wiped down everything, or made himself a fucking sandwich and left his DNA everywhere. Don't your guys check all that?"

"We found no evidence to suggest she'd been assaulted there," Curt said in a dry tone.

Kiera had never cared if people believed her. Fuck them. This time, however, she needed to be believed. Real evidence might be all over Brittany's place. She needed Dean to believe her. "She was raped on her bed. Vaginally and anally." Her voice was rising, a tinge of hysteria making her shrill. They'd doubt her now—dismiss her as overly emotional—but she couldn't pull back. She rose and gestured wildly with her arms. "On her bed. Her own bed!" A detail fell into her mind that would help prove her case, but her words came out spastic. "Call the Kolcheks!"

She paced in the small space. "She was on top of a quilt. But he took it with him." *What else? What else!* "Her grandmother made that quilt, mostly blues and whites, flowers, polka dots."

Dean reached for her, and it was only the frantic pace of her mind that kept her from swatting his hand away. It was too much.

Then he rested a hand on her forearm from around the washer. People had tried this before—something about physical touch shaking you out of a triggered state—but it never worked with her. Any touch and she tended to explode.

Not this time. His skin was warm and dry, the contact solid. He quieted the chaos with his long brown lashes and his blue-green eyes—steady, calm.

"Listen," he said, his voice a near-whisper that stilled her body. "Chicago has the Crime Lab, whose evidence technicians are specially trained. We'll look into it. I promise you."

Kiera's face roasted with the humiliation of her hysterics. "Thanks."

"Was that all he took?" Curt asked, ignoring her discomposure, which she appreciated.

"Yes, he—wait. He had her bring her purse." She flinched. "Brittany thought for sure that meant he wasn't going to kill her."

The detectives exchanged another look.

"What?" she snapped, tired of the juvenile bullshit.

"Her purse at the scene and the fact that her apartment appeared untouched made us believe she'd been attacked somewhere else," Dean said.

She hoped they believed her now.

The interview continued with one relentless question after another. Her pores wept sweat with every unearthed detail. She'd turn to a quaking mess later as she had to wait until next month for the blessed relief of Valium. Rules were rules.

"What else did you see? Be specific," Curt said.

A wave hit her all at once—not of what she'd seen, but what she'd felt—helpless and isolated. She'd essentially died alone with that maniac. The last thing she'd seen was grime and garbage and blazing headlights that seared—

"Can you hold onto this?" Dean's voice brought her back into the room.

He could have set the tools atop the dryer. Somehow, he'd perceived she'd hit the rumble bumps and was about to career down a steep embankment. He held out the wire-stripper things like a peace offering.

Kiera opened her fist and stretched her hand out to him. When he placed the tool in her palm, his warm fingers brushed her skin.

For that second, she'd never felt more present. "Thanks," she murmured.

"Anytime."

Curt seemed oblivious to the moment. "Anything else that might have relevance?"

"Can't think of anything," she said, glad her voice sounded normal.

Dean tilted his head. "Fair enough." He rapped his knuckles on top of the washer. "Okay, let's test this bad boy." He plugged in the cord and stepped around as if to admire his handiwork.

The timing wasn't suspicious. Not at all.

She smiled and restarted the cycle, only remembering as the clothes tumbled—

Oh. My. God.

A blush filled her face as bright bits of bras and panties rotated as if they were giving her the finger.

She refused to avert her gaze. No weakness, none, never. Not even when Dean Matthson had gotten an eyeful of her underwear.

CHAPTER FOURTEEN

Dean

I F THE KOLCHEKS HADN'T RENTED BRITTANY'S apartment for her, Dean couldn't have returned. No judge would sign off on a search warrant based on a memory surgeon's testimony, and they'd finished processing the scene days ago. But Sam had given Dean the key and his permission to enter the space and do whatever he deemed necessary.

Belinda, one of his favorite evidence techs, scowled at him without much heat. He appreciated her processing the apartment with him. Only a few inches shorter than him and just as broad, Belinda managed to exude a lightness, a leave-nothing-behind essence that served her well as an ET. She collected the bedding, then started to pull prints from the nonporous surfaces in the apartment.

Belinda dusted the cabinets first, and Dean left her to it with a list of individual grocery items to process from Kiera's statement. He walked the rest of the apartment with his new understanding, imagining the assault unfolding according to Kiera's description. The violence. The brutality. The disconnected urge to take what the killer wanted when he wanted, how he wanted.

"You were right," Belinda said, breaking his reverie.

"Huh?"

She knocked her ball cap back an inch and gave him a toothy grin. "We couldn't lift any usable prints off the bread, but we have quite a few viable partials off the Triscuits, Vlasic pickles, and stevia, and they could be a match to the cabinet handle and the counter. Two sets."

* * *

Spurred by the new evidence, Dean met Curt at Mariano's. There would be some video there, at least of Brittany. If the offender had followed her from the store, there might be some footage of him too. Grocery store chains like Mariano's usually had decent video.

They found footage of Brittany entering and exiting the store. Nobody appeared to follow her. There were several more cameras in the area, but none of the camera angles helped.

* * *

The next day, they checked the CTA video footage of the North Avenue buses from 1:50 to 2:30. There were four. All the buses had video except one, which only had a dummy camera. Unfortunately, Brittany and the offender weren't on any of the three buses with footage.

Dean and Curt canvassed the bus stop at North and Clybourn. There was a convenience store across the street where they would have boarded. The clerk was slow to call the manager, but eventually, they were given permission to review the video footage. It was a lucky break the footage was stored on-site. Usually, video took days or weeks to gain access.

CTA had sent them the exact time the fourth bus had been at the stop, so they were able to fast-forward to the right time, 2:06 p.m. And there he was, the offender attaching his Trek bike to the front of the bus.

"Oh shit," Curt murmured, his shock making Dean roll his eyes. Kiera had proven herself to Dean that first day.

The video quality was poor, and there was traffic and a bus between the camera and suspect, but they saw his brown hair, short on the sides and a loose pompadour on top, exactly like Kiera's drawing. Brittany sat at the window closest to the convenience store, the side view of her face visible. The man with the bike sat next to her, and she turned her head to speak to him.

*　*　*

THEY HAD EVEN BETTER LUCK AT THE SEDGWICK STOP. THERE WAS A camera in the alley. Once they tracked down the appropriate person from the building's management company, they found footage of the offender wheeling his bike and talking to Brittany.

The offender rested his bike against the concrete stairs and reached his hand out to take two of Brittany's grocery bags. There was another side view, this one clearer than the previous footage but still blurry. The time stamp had them entering Brittany's building at 14:13.

Dean's stomach quivered with a pleasant sort of nervous energy, the way it did when clues and evidence came together. They fast-forwarded through the day.

"Stop!" Curt said.

Dean backed up several frames. Brittany and the offender were leaving. The offender had a hand on her upper arm. They couldn't see his other hand, but from the twist of his shoulder and Kiera's statement, the offender had a knife at Brittany's side. They walked together down the steps and out of the camera's view. Time stamp 23:44.

Nine and a half hours. He had assaulted her for nine and a half hours. *Bastard.*

Did his sexual pleasure grow with every moment he had her under his control? The high of invincibility likely dumped serotonin into his system.

Dean ghosted that sensation through his body—reaching, inhabiting. So good. So powerful. He never wanted it to end.

Dean rubbed his chin. "I want to see the warehouse again in person."

Curt grabbed his keys. "Good idea. We can verify how long it takes to get there."

* * *

THEY BOTH WALKED AND STUDIED THE AREA, DEAN PLAYING THE SERIES of events in his head. The tape and evidence tags were gone, and the rain had washed away most of the blood, but he could still picture the scene as it had looked the night of her attack. He and Curt finally ended up at the same spot, in front of the faded bloodstain, the ghost of Brittany's life.

"Must have gone down pretty fast, I'm thinking," Dean said.

Curt nodded. "Never completed the scalping. Probably left right after the car turned around."

"And didn't take the time to make sure she was dead."

The fat droplets of blood on the floor didn't have any tail trails, indicating Brittany had not been moving when the blood hit the cement. The long tails on a few splatters on the back wall were consistent with a forceful blow at an angle. Two different wounds; two different patterns.

I'm the one that kills you.

Dean draped the killer onto his psyche.

I'm the one that kills you.

This was right. So right. He was the only God Brittany would ever know, and he found her wanting.

"What are you going to tell the LT?" Curt asked.

Dean closed his eyes for a moment, coming back to himself with the uncomfortable reminder of their lieutenant. "Let's see what Sergeant Mike thinks. At this point, I don't think we can keep Kiera Brayleigh out of this." He glanced up and down the street. There was no traffic going past. "Dennison is going to be pissed, but he'll find out anyway once the profiler gets here. I think he'll be more pissed if he finds out later rather than sooner."

"Can I sit out of that conversation?" Curt asked with a smile.

"No, you can't. You have to back me up," Dean retorted, glaring.

Curt groaned. "This is going to suck."

* * *

"You used a memory surgeon without getting permission from Sergeant Plynt first?" Lieutenant Dennison barked.

Sergeant Mike Plynt stood to the side, posture erect, barrel chest prominent, square jaw tight. His mouth opened as if he was going to jump in to back up Dean, but Dean shook his head. Dennison had a point.

"I thought it best to keep it quiet unless it worked."

"Worked?" Dennison moved into Dean's personal space. "Kolchek died this morning. We're going to the press tonight, and you drop this bomb on me? What am I supposed to say if word gets out that a fucking memory muncher had a hand in this investigation?"

The news of Kolchek's death made him want to kick something, but Dean kept his voice calm. Dennison always whipped into a frenzy if challenged. "She also provided us with information that led to the biggest breaks in the case we've had so far."

"So, I should tell the press that they can relax because M&Ms are solving our cases for us?"

Breathe in. Breathe out.

"No reason to tell the press anything about Ms. Brayleigh's contribution."

"You think?" Dennison held his position long enough to make his point, then took a step back.

Curt stood behind Dean. The lieutenant focused on him for a moment. "And what do you have to say?"

"The evidence speaks for itself, LT," Curt said in a voice that sounded as if were attempting to avoid a Cubs-versus-Sox debate.

Dennison glared at the pair of them. "If this blows up, you two assholes are taking the heat." He stalked out of the detective area leaving Dean and Curt with their sergeant.

"Could have gone worse," Mike said with a wolfish grin at Dean. "We catch this guy, and it won't matter how we did it."

* * *

DEAN WALKED OUTSIDE THE STATION. AREA CENTRAL WAS LOCATED IN the second district station on the south side of Chicago on Wentworth. The building was uninspired both inside and out. No storm clouds shadowed the sky, but the air hung pregnant and muggy. Oppressive. The weather matched his mood and the neighborhood.

Dean had worked the last eighteen days in a row. Foolish. But he had Dennison on his ass, never-ending reports, too many court appearances, and his contact lenses wouldn't stop scouring his eyeballs.

He still had an hour before the press release. Kiera merited hearing about Brittany from him first.

There was no place to stroll in the neighborhood, so Dean confined himself to the parking lot. The afternoon late shift was on the street, so there wouldn't be much movement in and out. The lot was relatively private, despite the outdoors. The 90/94 traffic was audible but not loud. Dean pulled out his phone and took a deep breath. He pictured Kiera in her condo, barefoot, lying back on a chaise lounge on her deck, drinking a glass of red wine.

"Did you catch him?" she asked the moment he gave his name.

Shit. He'd never make it to Wednesday, his next day off. "Not yet."

"Oh."

Dean nudged a few cigarette butts to the edge of the cement. "I wanted to thank you again for your assistance. We're going to find him sooner because of your help."

"I hope so."

Get to the point.

"There's going to be a press conference in a few minutes that will air on the ten o'clock news and run consistently after that. We're going public with the case to warn people that a serial killer is in Chicago. They're going to show your sketch, and we've been able to locate some video footage of the offender. We're hoping this leads to a quick identification."

"Should I watch?"

He swallowed. "No, that's not why I called." Time to man up. "Brittany Kolchek died this morning."

Kiera gasped. "Fuck."

He hated the thought of her hearing this alone. "I wanted you to know before they announced it."

"Thanks." She took an audible breath. "I knew it was coming. You told me that the first day. So, I don't understand why I feel bitch punched."

He let her talk.

"If she'd lived, her life would have been hard," she finally said. "Maybe she's better off."

He paced the parking lot, walking in loping circles, the phone held to his ear.

"Oh, bullshit," Kiera said. "She should have the chance to pick herself up and piece together some kind of life. It's just . . ." She took in a ragged breath and pushed on. "I don't want to think that those memories were her last." She made a growling, gurgling noise. "Goddamn it."

The energy had shifted. He could feel she wanted him to talk now.

"At least, she sort of got to tell her parents she loved them one last time," he said. "I passed that message along. Remember?"

"How did they take her death?"

"Sarah called me. We didn't talk long, but she was calm and composed when we spoke. She said that Brittany was in a better place now." Dean never disagreed with that sentiment, though he rarely shared it. He, too, wanted Brittany to have the chance at a life.

"Better place. What's a 'better place?'" Kiera asked. She answered her own question. "Hawaii."

He chuckled. It was a good thought. "No argument there."

His teammates, Tam and Liu, pulled into the parking lot from a food run. Dean waved at them, then quickly turned his back, so they would know not to disturb him. "Do you have someone who can come over and stay with you while you process this?"

"Are you offering?"

"What? No. Just my bereavement training kicking in. I'm working."

I'm working? What the hell was wrong with him? But he couldn't—

She laughed. "I'm just fucking with you."

He exhaled, and when he took in his next breath, it came easier. "I see your sense of humor is still intact."

"Always." After a moment, she said, "Do you have anyone there to help *you* process?"

Nobody had ever asked him that before, and her concern made his belly flip. "Are you offering?"

Kiera snorted. "When I'm offering, you'll know."

Maybe he'd make it to Wednesday after all.

CHAPTER FIFTEEN

Kiera

KIERA WOKE TO BLACKNESS. THAT DIDN'T FRIGHTEN her. Her bedroom was always dark when she slept. Other memory surgeons liked to sleep with a light on. Easier to check whether the bedroom was empty. Kiera preferred the advantage of finding her way through the blackout of her own space. Anyone trying to attack her while she slept would be at a disadvantage—if they decided to sneak in and not turn on any lights and didn't have night-vision goggles.

It was stupid. She knew it was stupid. But she still kept her room pitch-black.

She went to the kitchen and pulled out a glass and orange juice. The sweet, tart flavor of the juice woke up her mouth but not her brain. Her mind was somewhere else, working, searching, finding. In the deepest part of night, three or four in the morning, dark thoughts flowed freely.

While sleeping, she had recognized the killer. Something about his smirk or his posture or the cadence of his voice. If she could remember what it was, she might find the memory of when she had met him.

She went out on the deck and stood at the railing, admiring her clear view of Lake Michigan, the calm water before her, the city behind. Despite the warm air, she shivered.

Come on, come on, think.

Wind whipped her hair across her face, but Kiera felt oddly at peace. She should have been shaking and crying and keening. Shadows moved behind her eyes. They were always there, the memories, like sharks swimming deep in the ocean of her mind, never sleeping, always hunting, always hungry. But this time, she wanted to find a specific shark.

She ran the killer's face through her thoughts. His face had changed throughout the ordeal. Stress causes strange things to happen in perception. Vision tunnels or darkens or brightens, sounds distort or muffle, and smells—the worst.

His scent. Something potent and familiar.

Bounce fabric softener or Irish Spring soap. Kiera's mom had used Bounce—so it had to be Irish Spring, or she would have known immediately.

She fetched her phone, then thought better of it. Should she wake up the detective for a huge break in the case of . . . Irish Spring soap?

Kiera squinted against the brightness of the phone and froze. Her backlit fingers tripped the trigger. The killer had the odd quirk of fidgeting with the fingers of his right—? Yes, right hand. He rubbed his index finger back and forth across his thumb, fast, like he was drizzling salt over something.

Her stomach rolled. She did recognize the killer. Not his identity, but his presence. Or rather—one of her clients had.

* * *

AFTER BUSINESS HOURS HIT, KIERA TOOK A SINGLE DEEP PULL ON THE joint she'd allow herself for this call. A stronger person wouldn't need a little green to pass go, but she wasn't a stronger person.

She called her assistant at the office for Vanessa's phone number. She hadn't talked to her former client, her first client, Vanessa, in over five years, but people tended to keep their cell numbers.

It felt wrong to call her. Vanessa had paid to abolish her traumatic memories, and calling would only remind her, refresh the pain. Of course, not calling wasn't an option. A serial killer. A sicko.

I'm the one that kills you.

Briefly, she considered telling the cops the pertinent details and not involving Vanessa at all, but Vanessa deserved to make the decision about participating. She'd had too many choices taken from her already.

Kiera watched the cars, imagining the passengers, their destinations, their lives. The ache to be one of them, cruising down Lake Shore Drive with the window down, her hand catching the air stream, was overwhelming.

She took a stuttered breath, as if her lungs realized a regular inhale wouldn't be enough and sucked in a bit more. Kiera hit the send button and endured the rush of I-hate-my-life that filled her to bursting.

"Hello?"

They hadn't spoken in years, but she recognized Vanessa's voice instantly. "It's Kiera."

The pause that followed made Kiera want to sit, but she locked her knees. "There's no easy way to say this, but the man who attacked you has been hurting others."

"Is he coming for me?" The desperation in Vanessa's voice matched the pitch of Kiera's churning thoughts.

"No, Vanessa. No." He'd no reason to come back after ten years. "But the police will want to talk to you."

"I don't remember anything!" Too loud. Too desperate. Maybe calling had been the wrong decision, but it was too late now.

"I know," she said in a soothing voice, resisting the urge to crawl inside herself. "You can't tell the police about the attack, since I hold all those memories, but they'll want to ask questions about what you were doing at the time, people you knew, that sort of thing, trying to find a link between what happened to you and what happened to the others."

After an agonizing pause, Vanessa said, "Others?"

"Others." No point in sharing how many. It was just a guess anyway. "If the police can contact—"

"No. We have a confidentiality agreement. You're not allowed to talk about this."

Should have toked twice.

"If you don't want me to share your name, then I won't."

"You can't share *anything*!"

"If you say no, then I won't." She pressed a hand over her forehead, willing the conversation in another direction. "But, Vanessa, he's *killing* women now. Knowing where he started and what he did might help catch him."

Heavy breathing and choking sobs. It took Kiera a second to realize some of them were her own.

"If I participate, he'll come after me," Vanessa said with hushed urgency.

Kiera wanted to assure her he wouldn't, but of course, she knew better than to make promises she couldn't keep. "If you could just talk to them for—"

"No. Tell them what *you* know, but you keep me out of it."

"Okay."

"Where is he?"

"Chicago. At least, that's where his latest victim was assaulted."

"And you're sure it's him?"

"He's unforgettable." Kiera hoped for an ironic chuckle but got nothing. She turned her back to the sun. "How are you? I mean, before I called."

"Good days and bad days, you know?"

"Talking to anyone?"

"Already done my time on the couch."

"Just a friend then?" When Vanessa didn't respond, Kiera dropped the subject. Vanessa had to want to get better. Kiera pushed aside the little voice asking if that applied to her too. "Level of memory we left still working for you?"

"Yes. Whenever I find myself tempted to remember what occurred, I remember that I paid six figures to forget." Vanessa did chuckle then but without humor. "Think I'll take a sabbatical to Europe for a few months. You contact me when he's caught."

Vanessa talked so differently from when she'd been assaulted: stiffer, formal, controlled. The reaches of trauma were deep and winding and invaded the strangest places.

CHAPTER SIXTEEN

Dean

DEAN'S PHONE RANG WITH A GENERIC TONE. Probably a sales call, but at least, it wasn't work.

"Matthson."

"Detective? This is Kiera Brayleigh."

"Oh." He was surprised but pleased. "Hi."

"I've got something for you."

She didn't sound remotely flirtatious. "Okay. Hold on a sec." He grabbed his notebook, his heart rate perking like a dog ready to go on a walk. "What do you have?"

"Your guy uses Irish Spring soap. Well, before he took Brittany, anyway."

Oddly specific and wouldn't help, but he didn't want to appear ungrateful. "Great."

"The other thing is complicated, and it's going to sound weird. I know, big surprise. I'll give you everything I can, but it isn't everything I could, and I'm sorry, but—"

"Kiera, I'm confused. What's up?"

"I recognized the attacker from another client."

"What?" He'd followed so many bum leads in the last few days, a real lead electroshocked his system. "You know who he is?"

"Not exactly. He raped one of my other clients, ten years ago. She never went to the police, and he was a stranger to her, so I don't have an ID. And she won't let me release her name to you. She's pretty pissed I'm talking to you at all."

"This guy's now killing women, Kiera. I need that victim's name."

"You think I don't know that? Fuck." She whispered the last word but sunk real feeling behind it. "I can give you the details of the rape. In fact, I'm the only one who can give you those. I'm not chapping your ass for sport."

He didn't push. He needed what information she had, and he'd worry later, if he needed more. "Thanks."

"My driver isn't available until after two, but I can come down to the station this afternoon, if that works for you."

And just like that, he discarded his first day off in weeks. Fatigue dragged at him, but the adrenaline of another strong lead would have to keep him awake. This information was too critical to wait. It was easier and faster if he went there.

"Can I stop by your place for a few minutes instead?"

CHAPTER SEVENTEEN

Kiera

DEAN STOOD IN HER ENTRYWAY, DRESSED IN NAVY dress slacks, a white shirt with no tie, badge necklace, gun on his hip, and Clark Kent glasses. The glasses startled her, making her disoriented as if she hadn't really known him, which was stupid, because she *didn't* really know him. Kiera liked the glasses.

"Follow me," she said, determined to keep this all business.

She led him to the library, the best place to do the reading. Kiera's favorite reading chair was a tufted, overstuffed quarter-circle nest.

Dean sat in a more traditional armchair. "You need to take a minute?"

She grimaced. "No clue."

Her mouth was cotton dry, but she didn't want to drink anything. He waited for her to sit before seating himself. She tugged the cashmere blanket over herself as if the softness might cushion the memory.

"You all right?" he asked.

She shrugged. Her hands shook, but that was normal. "I did the trauma transfer ten years ago, and I've done so many others since then. I have to go back into her memory."

He got up and walked to her, squatting in front of the chair where she had cocooned herself. "You don't have to go through it again. Just tell me what you remember." He put his hand on hers resting in her lap. The gesture was sweet and intimate and confusing. She wanted him to stay like that.

He squeezed her hand. "Jesus, you're freezing."

How had he skated right through her defenses? Kiera never trusted her mistrust, because she mistrusted everything and everyone, but she always trusted her trust, because it didn't come around very often.

He appeared concerned, with his frown and drawn eyebrows. There were shadows under his eyes and fine lines at the corners. He wasn't sleeping enough.

Kiera swallowed. "I can do it."

"Without vomiting?" he asked, his eyes flicking to the empty garbage can next to her chair.

She huffed a laugh. "I make no guarantees. Did you bring a splatter guard?"

"No, but I've got a rain poncho in my car. Should I go get it?"

"Maybe." Her hand clenched his like a reflex. They were still holding hands, and it felt natural. She'd freak out about that later. "All right, back off. I'm ready." Her voice had more punch than earlier, but still a weak version of itself.

Dean returned to his seat and opened his notebook.

Kiera closed her eyes. "Ask questions as they come up. I'll try to go slow."

"She's better now, the victim?" he asked in a quiet voice.

"Yes, but she's still damaged. The trauma transfer can only capture the episodic memory." His eyebrows rose. Delaying the dive into the memory, she continued. "The removing of the memory takes place, as far as they can tell, in the frontal lobe of the brain and parts of the parietal lobe. That's where they believe recollections of events are stored. But my talent can't stretch deep enough to reach the limbic system, where our emotions come into play. So, I can take the recollection of the event, but the anger, the fear, and the pain are all still in there."

Dean cracked his knuckles. "What does that mean?"

"The trigger and the emotional response, the PTSD type of reactions—

sweating, racing heart, dry mouth, all the fun stuff—are still there, but now there's no context. Imagine how disconcerting it would be for you if tomorrow you were walking down the sidewalk and smelled roses, then burst into tears. You had to bend over you were crying so hard, but you had no idea why."

"I'd think I was losing it." His voice was quiet. "So why bother?"

"I can't remove the trigger, but I can eliminate the narrative, and the narrative is the driver. If a person is ready and willing to do the work, I can take out the pattern of thinking that keeps them spiraling down. They'll still need coping mechanisms, and they need to reprogram their thoughts." She gave him a wry smile. "I leave enough memory that they remember something happened, but not the specifics. The brain hates a vacuum, so they have to have something ready to jump into the space the traumatic memory leaves."

He nodded. "That's impressive. You let them keep just enough memory that they can let go of the rest?"

"Hopefully. And they retain who hurt them, to protect them from being hurt by the same person again."

"Right," he said, but his raised eyebrows showed that even he knew she was stalling.

Fuck it. "Okay, I'm ready."

Kiera could find any memory by sight and feel. The memories were stored in little boxes in her mind, like old-school card catalogs. Each box had a faint pink glow, the color of the trauma. Vanessa's was pale, like pink champagne. She opened the box and took hold of the fattest, shiniest filament. The root of the initial trauma. She didn't hesitate.

* * *

Huh?

There was someone in Vanessa's room. Gabby was always sneaking into her house at night when her dad got drunk.

"Gab?" Vanessa mumbled, trying not to wake all the way up.

The figure in the room pounced on her, snatching a pillow and pressing it over her face.

She couldn't breathe.

Vanessa struggled, her body like a puppet whose master had a seizure, every limb flailed, striking out, tugging at the pillow. Air! Air! Air! *The pillow moved. She took hulking gulps of air.*

"Make a noise, and I'll kill you," a graveled voice hissed.

* * *

"He used a fake deep voice, like he was trying to sound like Batman." To her own ears, Kiera sounded like she was in a tunnel.

"Same voice?" Matthson asked, his voice far away.

"Can't tell because he's disguising it. Is he afraid she'll recognize him?" That gave her body a jolt, either of excitement at the possibility or dread.

"Got an idea of height and weight?"

"She was lying down, so it's hard to tell height, but he's bigger, bulkier than he is today. Not football big, but he's got some muscle on him."

"Hair or eye color?" Dean prompted.

She concentrated. "Ponytail? Longer hair anyway."

"Anything identifying, like scars or tattoos?"

* * *

Vanessa froze. She wanted to live. She'd do anything to live.

How had he gotten into the house? The doors were always locked.

Gabby's route.

Had he climbed up the trellis and broken into the guest room? Not that he had to break in since she left the window unlocked for Gabby. Vanessa hated Gabby for making her vulnerable. He dug his knee into her back, and Vanessa whimpered, causing the hand on her neck to grip harder.

He tugged her sleep shorts down.

Oh, God. No. *No!*

She struggled, her body overriding her mind for a moment. He punched the back of her head, and she stilled, dazed. She was jittery and lethargic at the same time, like mad bees trapped in a jar.

The pain was sharp and continued on and on and on.

* * *

"He raped her vaginally only." As if that were somehow better, more merciful. *Thank God, I was only vaginally raped . . . said nobody ever.*

"Any similarities beyond the position?" Dean asked.

Kiera swallowed. "He grunts like an animal." The sound echoed in her head in stereo. "It isn't a noise of pleasure, but violence, if that makes sense."

"It's the same?"

"Yes. I'm sure."

Through the tinny barrier, Dean sighed.

* * *

Suddenly, the weight was gone. There was nothing tethering her to the bed, but Vanessa didn't move. Her mind contemplated the pattern of her pillowcase and didn't want to return to her body.

"Nessa, look at me," the demon said.

She didn't want to, but her eyes snapped to his. How did he know her nickname? What else did he know about her?

* * *

"Brown eyes," Kiera reported. "Hair light brown or dirty blond."

* * *

He fastened his jeans. "Got a present for you." He threw down a small stack of photos like a john tossing cash at a prostitute.

Vanessa couldn't stop herself from staring. The photos were all of her. Horrible photographs. She recognized the outfit from Molly's party last weekend. The night she had gotten blasted and passed out.

She had thought that was funny.

He'd been there. No other possibility. He'd put her in lewd poses, the worst with a Michelob Light bottle sticking inside her, her head lolled to the side, but her hand wrapped around the label, as if she were screwing herself. Had he raped her then too? She couldn't remember.

"Would be a shame to see that on Facebook." His fingers twitched, his thumb rubbing over a finger in some sort of evil gesture.

She had told her parents she was spending the night at Kitty's house. Nobody would believe she'd been drugged against her will. People would laugh at her. The pictures would be seen by everyone. She'd have to leave school, the state.

He loomed over her then, bending enough for the light to glint in his shark eyes. "Relax. This is just between you and me. As long as it stays that way, nobody else needs to see these."

* * *

"HE DIDN'T USE A CONDOM," KIERA SAID.

"Did she go to the hospital?"

"No. She went to Planned Parenthood the next day and got a morning-after pill, though. So, no pregnancy, no rape kit."

Vanessa had been the perfect candidate for a memory surgery because she wasn't one to pick at the edges of memory, attempting to recall what had happened, despite knowing it was bad enough that she'd paid six figures to have the recollection removed.

"He had to have been stalking her beforehand," Kiera said. "He knew how to sneak inside her house."

"Any details about the party?"

"Happened the weekend before the attack. She thought she'd gotten blackout drunk, but he had to have drugged her somehow." One thing had been bothering Kiera in particular. "He didn't hide his face. Is that common?"

"No. Maybe he was disguised at the party. Did he leave the pictures? Does she have them?"

Kiera shook her head. "He took them with him."

"Can you give me the dates of the party and the assault? The age of the victim?"

Finally, something she could actually give him. "Westchester, Illinois, for the attack and the party. She was seventeen at the time, a senior in high school. Ten years ago." That wouldn't lead to Vanessa's identity. It probably wouldn't lead to much at all.

Kiera hoped what she told the detective would help, that she hadn't reopened that wound for nothing. There had to be something. Please. One little thing. "He does this weird gesture." She mimed the action, her thumb rubbing across her index finger. "What the fuck does that mean?"

Dean had moved, silent and unseen, and was now sitting on the coffee table, his knees inches from her. He was close but not on top of her. He was frowning but not at her. "No idea."

Kiera clamped down her emotions. "If you get the chance, please shoot him in the face."

He chuckled and closed his notebook. "I can't just shoot a suspect in the face."

Kiera was disappointed. She wanted a detailed description of the wrath the detective was going to bring down on that prick.

Dean half smiled. "Prison is a worse fate than a quick death."

She snorted. "That won't change what he did or make any of his victim's lives different. I don't want him to suffer. I want him to end."

"I can't just shoot him," he repeated, rubbing his stubbled jaw. "Not that the idea isn't tempting, but it isn't worth risking my career and my freedom. And *I* want him to suffer."

"Do you want something to drink?" she asked as she stood, needing a break.

"No, thanks, but you go ahead." He didn't push to continue.

Kiera opened the fridge and pulled the cranberry juice. How could taking on so much make her emptier? How did the physics work?

The tears wouldn't stop. Somewhere the man who had hurt Vanessa and Brittany and countless other women was moving through the world unencumbered. Was he happy? Did he ever think about Vanessa? Or did his victims disappear the moment he left them? Vanessa, despite the memory gone, probably glimpsed the void daily. She moved through the world knowing she wasn't right, knowing something had been taken from her.

"You okay?"

Kiera jumped, rubbing her hands over her wet face, blushing, sputtering, trying to gather the scattered pieces of herself together. "I'm fine," she said.

"Clearly."

She burst into sobs. They exploded out of her like blood from a gunshot wound. She tried to yank them back, but the pain was too big a gush to be contained. Dean put his arms around her, loose, as if waiting for her to push away. But she didn't want to break away. His arm, more muscular than she'd imagined, turned out to be a decent flotation device in the flood.

"Let's take a break," he said in a quiet voice. "Want to sit outside?" With his glasses on, he looked so kind and concerned.

* * *

THEY ENDED UP ON THE DECK, STANDING AT THE RAIL, GAZING AT LAKE Michigan. The sight never failed to refresh her.

"I can almost see my buddy's boat from here," Dean said, pointing toward Navy Pier and the Columbia Yacht Club just south of it. The sun made his blond hair shine, and a gust of wind ruffled his short locks.

"Well, don't you run in elevated circles," she replied. There were few dock spaces in Chicago, and the docks near Navy Pier were highly coveted.

"Old money," he said with a sage nod. "He rarely takes the boat out, though, which I will never understand. He and his wife like to party at the dock. But I'm hoping to talk him into taking me out today for at least an hour or so. They've got a couple of Jet Skis too."

"Today? Is it your day off?"

"Ah, I never really get a day off." He nodded his chin in the direction of Navy Pier. "But after this, yeah, I get to relax."

"Oh God. I'm keeping you from having fun."

"Don't worry. You're doing great. I'm not supposed to meet him until noon or later." His posture was relaxed as he stared out at the lake.

When the restful silence between them evened out her mood, she said, "I would have talked to someone else."

Probably *should* have talked to someone else. She liked him too much and suspected her comfort with him might be the sign of an impending stroke.

He shrugged. "I'd rather be the one to talk to you."

Kiera was glad he'd been the one. She needed his strength to dive back into the pain and misery.

CHAPTER EIGHTEEN

Dean

W HEN THEY RESUMED THE INTERVIEW, DEAN sensed her mood dropping. He had no idea how to pull her back, not with what lay ahead of them. Delving into the similarities and differences between the two attacks wasn't going to brighten her day.

Kiera stared at him for a moment, then sighed. "Let's finish this, okay?"

As he'd feared, the follow-up questions dragged her down like a body trapped in cement shoes. He wanted to offer her something hopeful, but he couldn't give her what he couldn't give himself.

She was sure the rapist was the same man, and everything—words, tone, gestures, body language—all confirmed she was telling the truth. Having an association with two of the offender's victims, though, exacted a toll on her. He'd had witnesses fall apart plenty of times, but observing Kiera was worse because the pain shouldn't have been her burden to bear.

He studied Kiera with her head in her hands, her breath fitful. He couldn't imagine ever allowing himself to have a memory erased or taking on someone else's nasty trip. Denial as a coping mechanism wasn't inherently bad, but those holes in memory had to become weaknesses, didn't they? A person couldn't just remove their trauma. They had to integrate it or live in that fight for the rest of their lives.

Or maybe that was his take-it-like-a man upbringing talking. His parents had always been kind, but strict gender expectations were foundational for them.

Men don't cry.

It had taken him until college to realize how messed up that was. He might still unconsciously hold similar beliefs.

* * *

THEY FINISHED AT NOON. "HOW LONG WILL IT TAKE YOU TO GET THERE?" she asked. Dean frowned, confused by the question. "To the dock," she added.

He sighed, so close to being free for the day. "Not more than fifteen minutes."

"Don't you have to go home and change?"

"Got casual clothes in my car."

She laughed. "I can't imagine it. I can only picture you sitting on a boat in your button-down shirt with the sleeves cuffed. What do you do with your gun?"

Dean shrugged. "The gun goes everywhere with me."

"You take it out on the Jet Ski? What happens if it gets wet?"

"If I go out, I'll leave it on the boat in the downstairs cabin."

"What do you mean if you go out? Jet Skis seem like so much fun."

"They are. You've never been on one?"

"No." She wiped a hand over her face. "I don't get out very often."

And what a shame that was. That vibrant woman barricaded herself in a tower, watching the world from a distance because she sacrificed her own peace of mind so others might find their own.

He could invite her to come with him.

That would be weird. And yet, it made perfect sense. Spending the last hours with her garnered him some insight. She wouldn't venture out on her own, and the way she'd melted into him when she cried spoke of trust. Somehow, he'd earned her confidence, and now he had the opportunity to show her that she wouldn't regret it.

"Want to go?" He liked Kiera, and he thought going outside, getting out of that condo, might be what she needed. Leaving her alone to freak out didn't sit well with him.

"You can't just invite me to someone else's boat," she said, not addressing his offer.

"Sure I can. I'm an officer of the law. Take note." He called Jack. A slumbering, self-preserving part of himself awakened. What the hell was he doing? He didn't simply want to do her a kindness; he wasn't that selfless. He wanted to spend more time with her, a happier time, learn more about her. And he didn't have the space in his life for that. His attraction would complicate everything.

Jack answered with "You're late. You better not be canceling. Lorelei and I both took off work for this."

Dean hadn't been expecting Lorelei to be there, and the presence of another woman might help make Kiera more comfortable. Nothing needed to turn romantic. "I'm not canceling. I'm checking if it's okay to bring a friend."

"Lady friend?" Jack's tone suggested he would make trouble for Dean.

"Yes."

"Please, then. I can't wait to tell Lorelei." Jack, an overgrown toddler since the moment they'd met in college.

"Don't get too excited. She hasn't said yes yet." He disconnected and found her vibrant blue eyes and a face still pink from crying. He'd done the right thing, inviting her, but would she accept?

* * *

KIERA REGARDED HIM WITH AN EXPRESSION OF AMUSEMENT MIXED WITH horror. She was shaking her head. "I—you have no idea how complicated it is for me to go out in public."

"It isn't in public. It's a private boat, and you need a code to reach the docks," Dean said. Now that she might agree, he really wanted her to go.

They were standing next to the fur couch in her living room. Her place made sense to him now; each object was beautiful or comfortable, often both. All her furniture had texture—from the furry couch to the cool smooth silk of the chair he'd sat in when in the library, or her chair, with its thick, bumpy weave. Blankets were thrown everywhere, all angora or alpaca or something else warm and comforting. Her hallways were light and ethereal, weightless.

Her condo was her refuge and oasis but also her prison. He understood how hard it would be to leave a place so carefully designed to make her feel safe.

"I'd have to see if my driver's available. How long do you think I'd be?" Kiera sounded unsure. She gazed at the fur couch, as if she were longing to stretch out over it, then back to him, then to the day outside and back to him again.

He liked her eyes on him. "It's Wednesday, so if you're interested, we can stay to watch the fireworks from Navy Pier, but we don't have to. And you don't need a car. I'll take you home whenever you want, even if you want to leave after fifteen minutes. It's the least I could do." No doubt he owed her, and Dean hated owing people. "And I could always go back if I wanted."

She bit her lip but surprised him by looking him in the eye. Oh no, he liked that a little too much. A warmth heated his ribs and then dropped into his gut. Her lips parted, and he wanted to believe she felt it too, the intense connection between them.

"Come on. For a few hours, I'll stop being a dick, and you'll stop being an M&M," he said in his most cajoling tone.

He knew he'd fucked up as soon as he said it.

She narrowed her eyes. "What's an M&M?"

CHAPTER NINETEEN

Kiera

SHE BARELY KEPT A STRAIGHT FACE WHEN DEAN'S face went ashen.

"Nothing," he said.

She held steady, determined to stare and say nothing until he told her. This was power—the heady way he fidgeted in front of her. Kiera could have remained just like that all day.

He grimaced. "Memory muncher." He raised his hands as if to fend off her fury. "But I don't—"

Kiera burst out with a deep belly laugh. "Awesome. I can't wait to tell my group!"

"Kiera, no!" He appeared genuinely panicked despite her obvious amusement. "It's a nickname and something we only use among ourselves at CPD. Please, if word gets out that law enforcement—"

"Oh, please. M&M is adorable." She couldn't stop laughing, though the term wasn't that funny. It was just so unexpected, and his discomfort made him seem so human, and for once she wasn't the one embarrassed. "Better than memory whore or mind fucker."

"Those are harsh."

She cocked her head to the side. "Well, yeah. And you guys call yourselves dicks?"

"Dick as in detective, not as in asshole."

Kiera held up her hands. "Whatever you say."

He smiled, his dimples popping out. "So, you'll come with me?"

CHAPTER TWENTY

Dean

I F DEAN HAD THOUGHT ANYONE ELSE WOULD BE riding in his car, he would have cleaned it or at least gotten rid of the piles of garbage. He slowed as they approached his car. Was there any way to remove the trash without her noticing?

"I just need to straighten up first," he said.

"Yeti balls on a stick," she said with a laugh as she peered through the back passenger-side window.

"I'm really busy," he said as he collected all the fast-food bags into one. Kiera opened the back passenger door and did the same.

"You don't have to do that," he said, wanting to pull the garbage out of her hands.

"You need an intervention."

Dean set his mega bag down and proceeded to make a second. "I need more time in the day."

"Or a maid. If I find a box of doughnuts, I'm going to laugh my ass off."

"If I'd known, I would have gotten some just for that."

She smiled—a real smile—and continued to stuff bags together. Kiera held a Burger King bag out to Dean. "Hey, this one still has some fries! You want some?"

"No." They'd stopped being potentially edible a week ago. "That's scary."

"Not as scary as your car," she said and dropped her own mega bag onto the sidewalk. "Did you know there's a seat back here?"

"Funny," he said as he ran the three mega bags to a corner garbage can, filling the can to overflowing. When he returned, Kiera stood in the open passenger door to let more of the heat escape. She'd changed into a bright-yellow sundress that he assumed was to cheer herself. Though the fit wasn't tight, it flattered her figure, which he should stop noticing.

Then she smiled at him. He'd never courted trouble or stepped out of line, always so aware of his reputation, but she made him want to let go of his tight control and see what would happen. Most likely, disaster, but he found he didn't care.

* * *

THE COLUMBIA YACHT CLUB HAD PARKING, AND JACK HAD ASSURED HIM he could park there without fear of a ticket or towing. He grabbed his bag from the trunk, and they made their way to the boat, circumventing the yacht club, whose speakers were blaring "Pass the Dutchie," until they reached a metal security gate. Dean punched in the code and opened the door for Kiera.

Jack's boat was one of the bigger ones, a yacht amid sailboats and motorboats—at least in his row. Dean liked the boat, even docked. It was like a mini condo on the water.

To the north spun the great Ferris wheel of Navy Pier. To the south was the substantial Columbia Yacht Club. The skyline rose in the west, and the spread of Lake Michigan filled the east. The dock was picturesque, on the edge of a hulking city on a gorgeous day with the breeze keeping everything comfortable. The relaxation in her lips, the openness of her chest, and the slight tilt to her head told Dean that she liked the spot.

When their eyes met, she smiled. The faded gray wood of the dock thunked under their feet, seagulls squawked as they rode the wind currents, and the occasional sailboat clanged as something metal flapped against a mast. The sounds of the city, so close, were muffled. Only the faint murmur of traffic managed to reach them.

The air only reeked a little like fish, which was fortunate, because sometimes the stench was downright nauseating. With the warm sun and slight breeze, it was shaping into a perfect day.

They reached *The Doctor's Couch*. Jack was sitting on the bottom deck of the boat on a folding chair, reading a book. When Jack heard them approach, he jumped to his feet. "Prodigal son!" His gaze shifted to Kiera.

"Hey, Jack," Dean replied with his hand up in a wave.

Jack stared at Kiera, lips moving as if he were talking to himself. Finally, his words went audible, too loud. "You brought Kiera Brayleigh to my boat?"

At first, Dean thought Jack knew her but soon realized that he only knew *of* her. "Yes. Jack, this is Kiera. Kiera, this is Jack." A fissure of dread snaked through his gut. Something was wrong. He gave Jack a glare to prompt him into better manners.

"Hi," Kiera said, standing a few feet away without moving a muscle. Her face was devoid of emotion, which meant she was feeling something. Embarrassment, maybe. Apprehension?

"I'm representing a client against Ramsey Adams," Jack said, like an accusation.

Oh no. No. Not today. Jack was in his "jackass" mode. In college, Dean had loved jackass mode—observing Jack verbally assault some pretentious blowhard or arrogant prick. It had been hilarious to watch Jack lose his cool and rant about some random injustice, like people putting garbage in the recycling bin or not using an Oxford comma. Jack, especially if he'd been drinking, had a way of cornering people and debating them down to the size of dust mites. Dean could see Jack gearing up to do that to Kiera.

Of course, Kiera had faced far greater adversaries than Jack and even Dean hadn't come away from their arguments unscathed. Still, he readied himself to jump in if Jack continued. Dean brought Kiera to improve her day, not ruin it, so he needed to protect her, if the situation devolved.

Kiera frowned. "Who is Ramsey Adams?"

Jack crossed his arms over his chest. "A memory sucker like you."

She stared at him for a moment, then tossed her head back, and laughed, hard and bitter, not her real laugh. "You think we have a fucking guild?"

Dean was about to retreat when Jack's wife, Lorelei, opened the sliding door and poked out her head. When she saw Dean, she smiled. When she saw Kiera, she blinked. "Kiera?"

Dean hadn't expected Kiera was that famous. Or infamous. He wasn't sure what to do, but it was too late.

"Oh, hey, Lorelei. I didn't realize you had a boat." Kiera sounded confused. Then she added, "Or an ass-clown husband."

"How do you know each other?" Jack asked, edging in front of Lorelei.

Lorelei scowled and put her hands on her hips. She was short and wiry, with fire-red hair and a matching personality. Dean waited to see the direction her ire was going to flow. "Quit being Jackass Jack." Jack frowned. Lorelei threw up her arms. "Kiera runs the Center, one of the cosponsors of the Green Tie Ball. Without them, we'd never have found the funds to implement our new, at-risk youth outreach." Lorelei moved to stand directly in front of Jack. "She's a professional."

Jack patted his thinning hair, as if ensuring it was still there. "You never mentioned you knew Kiera Brayleigh," he said as if Kiera weren't there.

"Yeah, there are a lot of people I know that I don't mention to you. Why are you being so rude?"

"What about my case against Ramsey Adams," Jack hissed, as if his case were confidential, as if he hadn't already announced it.

Kiera and Dean exchanged a look. He eased a hand to the back of her arm, not to hold her, but to signal his allegiance to her. If anyone could talk Jack down, it was Lorelei.

Lorelei stared at Kiera and Dean for a second and then rounded on Jack. "She's a memory surgeon. So what? Just because one dentist feels up his patients under anesthesia doesn't mean they all do. Ramsey is a sociopath. Kiera isn't."

Dean thought this was progress, but Kiera's entire body remained stiff, her hands white-knuckled on her tiny purse. "What did Ramsey Adams do?" she asked.

Both Lorelei and Jack turned to her. "He ran a 'hypnotherapy couple's counseling business,'" Jack said, using air quotes.

Kiera held her hands up to stop Jack talking. "I get it." Her jaw clenched. "What a fucktwist."

Dean tried not to smile. *Fucktwist.* Very professional. "What does that mean?" he asked, since he appeared to be the only one clueless about what was happening.

Kiera stepped on a small stone and rolled it under her shoe. "Motherfucker pretends to be a therapist, but what he really does is erase women's memories of their husband's infidelities, and/or physical or emotional abuse, or her inheritance. It's the worst betrayal of trust." She sounded as if she were gearing up to go track him down herself. "I hope he goes to jail for a very long time."

Kiera's anger pushed Jack out of jackass mode. "This is a civil suit."

She shook her head. "He should go to jail." She turned to Dean. "Can't you do something?"

"No." Everyone stared at him as if he were an asshole for not immediately leaving to arrest the guy, as if working a serial-killer case on top of all the cases that continued to filter through his team and testifying in court on those cases they managed to close wasn't enough. "I want the same thing you do, but this isn't Mayberry. I can't just go around arresting people without a warrant or while they aren't actively engaging in an illegal activity because they've done something you think is a crime."

"It is a crime," Kiera said in a low voice.

"That doesn't change the fact that it isn't a homicide, and it isn't a case assigned to me, and there are only twenty-four hours in a day." He brushed a hand through his hair and tried to keep his tone even. "And it's my first damn day off in three weeks, so maybe you can all cut me some slack here."

Kiera squinted at him and bit her bottom lip. "I probably could."

"Yeah, well, I probably can too," Jack said with a smirk. "Want a beer?"

Dean licked his lips and tried to take a full breath. Kiera slipped her hand in his and squeezed once. Something hot flashed between them, incinerating his burnout like a match to paper, leaving him lighter than he'd felt in days. Maybe he should rant more often.

CHAPTER TWENTY ONE

Kiera

KIERA HAD NEVER BEEN ON A BOAT BEFORE, AND she expected more movement. The deck rocked some, but she didn't need sea legs to stay standing or anything like that. Dean had disappeared with his duffel bag into the cabin through a sliding glass door, past a small living room on one side and a smaller kitchen (galley?) on the other, and down a short bit of stairs. His mood had shifted gloomy for a few seconds, and she imagined he needed a break too. The moment he had boarded the boat, his unflappable manner returned.

She pictured him taking his clothes off. He would take off his glasses, unbutton that crisp, white shirt, baring his chest. Was he hairy or smooth? Was he talking to himself to keep his emotions light or was he naturally able to slough off the strain? Maybe she should focus on something other than Dean.

Lorelei smiled. Kiera had always liked Lorelei Dochart and, at one point, had considered asking her to be her therapist. She worked in the same practice as her shrink, Dr. Trent. The only reason Kiera hadn't chosen her was that Lorelei's temperament mirrored Kiera's, and that wasn't what she needed.

"So, you have a boat," Kiera said. Luckily, Lorelei understood her abrupt brand of conversation.

"The boat is Jack's, though it's in my name." Lorelei snickered and drank a swig of beer. "He wanted one for so long, so I said he could have one if it was named after me. If he ever makes me truly angry, I can sink it without the fear of prosecution."

Kiera laughed. Yep. Lorelei was too like her. "That work out well?"

Lorelei leaned forward. "Truthfully, I love this damn boat more than he does." She sighed. "He's not usually so unsociable. I hope you can overlook his behavior."

"Lucky for him, I only tolerate people less rude than myself. That still leaves a lot of room for dickishness." Kiera surveyed the boat, equipped like an efficiency apartment.

"Trust me: he needs a lot of room for his dick."

Kiera grinned at Lorelei. "That explains everything." She could hold a grudge—well within her wheelhouse—but she wouldn't. More than being Lorelei's husband, Jack hadn't been wholly wrong. "I hate those charlatans too. It's like performing nonconsensual surgery. Those people should be put in jail."

"Hey, nothing heavy today," Dean said, his head poking up out of the stairs. He wore a red T-shirt with the Flash's logo and black swim trunks. His feet were bare and just there for her to see. His smile was easy. It tightened Kiera more than loosened her, but in a pleasant way. "What does a guy have to do to acquire a Jet Ski around here?" he asked in a loud voice. "Kiera's never been on one."

"Oh, well, we better gear you up." Jack glanced uneasily at Kiera as if he expected her to do something. Maybe he thought she would raise her hands and call up the winds. She wished she could, just to see the expression on his face.

"My life jacket should fit you," Lorelei said as Dean pulled off his shirt. Mostly smooth.

"We're going out right now?" Kiera stood but didn't move. But not because she'd become absorbed in admiring the light trail of hair between his pecs. And lower.

"Oh yeah," Dean replied.

Yeah? Shit, she was going to ride a Jet Ski.

Kiera went downstairs into the little cabin to take off her sundress. Whipping it over her head wasn't more titillating than Dean taking off his shirt, since she had her suit on underneath, but that didn't matter. She took a moment to compose herself. Shedding clothing didn't equate to intimacy. Dean offered friendship, nothing more, and her infatuation needed to remain hidden.

The bikini wasn't skimpy, but it did have open buckles across her hips instead of solid fabric. She'd never had the chance to wear it. Once the life jacket was on, covering her chest and torso, she relaxed. It was like a bulletproof vest.

When she looked at Dean, he grinned at her, anticipation clear on his face. Suddenly, the idea of Dean viewing her body heated places inside her that had never been warm. She worked out compulsively, needing routine, physical release, the mental break, and tangible strength. Kiera enjoyed the firmness of her muscles with the kind of pride that comes from earning something, and she wanted Dean to notice.

After brief instructions, Kiera and Dean were each on a Jet Ski and ready to go. Kiera followed Dean out of the harbor, crawling through the no-wake zone. Once they cleared the breaker, Dean let loose and skipped out over the water. The lake was choppy but no huge waves or anything. Kiera slid a few inches backward every time she accelerated. The engine had a kick.

People terrified Kiera, but machines intrigued her. Kiera learned the gist of the Jet Ski within ten minutes. The lake grew colder the farther out she ventured, but she didn't care. Kiera found herself pushing the machine and herself hard. She chased boats and wakes, and when she couldn't resist, she chased Dean.

At one point, she hit a wake exactly right and rose high in the air. At first, she'd kept hold of the steering, but her body left the seat and twisted, and she figured more danger lay in holding on than letting go. She flipped over and landed first on her arms, then belly, narrowly missing a face-plant on the water. Lake Michigan shot up her nose, and she surfaced with a snotty face and stinging body. The adrenaline in her system made her giggle like a teenager.

Dean came speeding over to her, killing his engine as he got close. Her own Jet Ski was about fifteen feet from her, bobbing innocently. So much for her dignity. Still, she'd crashed so spectacularly, she was proud.

"You okay?" he yelled.

She couldn't stop laughing, so she nodded, extended a thumb, and swam for her Jet Ski.

"You need help?"

That made her laugh harder. She shook her head. When she reached the Jet Ski, she was afraid she wouldn't be able to haul herself back aboard, but the machine held steady as she heaved herself out of the lake. Her hands trembled with cold as she reattached the lanyard.

Dean was watching her. "Ready to quit?" He sounded so concerned.

"No fucking way. That was awesome."

He leaned forward, one elbow on the steering bar. "That was pretty epic. I give it a nine point seven; the dismount was a thing of beauty."

A bubbling giggle tumbled out of her. "Raw talent."

They laughed. Kiera wiped her eyes and restarted the engine, taking off with a wave to Dean, skipping over the water.

For a while, she was untouchable.

CHAPTER TWENTY TWO

Dean

KIERA WAS TELLING JACK AND LORELEI ABOUT HER spill when Dean docked his Jet Ski. She pulled off her life jacket. "At least I didn't land face first."

He'd kept his eyes firmly on her face when they'd geared up, but he snuck a glance now. She looked like a *Sports Illustrated* model, the sun reflecting off all the droplets on the exposed skin of her chest and stomach. Her breasts weren't *Sports Illustrated* big—not even a handful—but they appeared firm, and he wanted to cup one in his palm. Her body was curved, her torso long and cut, her legs muscled.

"That was so fun." She threw her arms around his neck only for a moment, but long enough for his body to tune to hers.

"Anytime."

Luckily, she pulled away before his shorts tented. He turned and took deep, deep, *deep* breaths until that part of him settled down. If only the rest of his body would do the same.

She all but flounced onto the boat. Lorelei handed her a towel, the blue reminiscent of her eyes. Kiera bent over and raked the towel over her hair. Dean scrutinized her body as she dried off, content to drip on the dock.

Jack tossed him a towel and gave him a knowing look. Dean stopped ogling Kiera.

In a completely obvious move, Lorelei announced she needed to go to the yacht club for ice and asked Dean to accompany her. Curiosity compelled him to follow Lorelei off the boat. Kiera could handle Jack for a few minutes.

The Columbia Yacht Club was impressive, there was no denying it, and Dean liked that it was an actual boat. Or ship. He was sure there was a difference but wasn't sure it mattered.

He'd only been inside the club once before, at Jack and Lorelei's engagement party. They'd entered via the oversized plank that stretched from the dock to the door—cut right out of the ship's side. That had been kind of cool. But what delighted Dean most were the portholes in the bathroom.

Lorelei stopped outside the gate and pulled a single cigarette out of her shorts pocket. So much for quitting.

"She likes you, and she doesn't like many people, especially men," Lorelei said. A yellow lighter appeared from her cleavage.

Unsure how to respond, feeling both flattered and confused, he said, "She's different."

Lorelei lit her cigarette. "She'll understand the hours, the commitment, and the secondary trauma."

Dean rolled his eyes because Lorelei was always talking to him about secondary or vicarious trauma. He handled the stress of the job fine. Better than most. And he didn't need to smoke to do it. "Maybe I need someone who is trauma-free."

"Like Lyndsey Lynn?"

Dean had dated Lyndsey Lynn for over a year, and the relationship had been serious. Sort of. She'd never understood him or even tried. His world was too dark for dating.

"I don't think Kiera likes me as well as you think."

Lorelei exhaled a plume of smoke. "Kiera Brayleigh doesn't casually touch people. I've never seen her hug anyone other than a client, and that was awkward. I'm telling you, Dean, she likes you. No doubt about it." Lorelei flicked her ash and sang under her breath to the song on the loudspeakers attached to the yacht club: "The Warrior."

Ah, the hug. The idea that her hugs were rare pleased him. And Dean wanted to please her. He wanted to do anything that made her comfortable, made her smile.

Lorelei sighed. "But you still need to be careful. I've seen her snap at someone putting a hand on her shoulder. You'll want to pay attention."

"Earlier you mentioned the Center. What is that?"

"It's Kiera's counseling practice where she meets her memory clients. She employs four talented therapists too for regular counseling. You should visit sometime; it's a beautiful space."

"Does she have enough clients to warrant an office? I thought she didn't do that anymore."

Lorelei chuffed. "You don't know her that well, do you?"

He shrugged. "She consulted on a case."

"She charge you?" Lorelei seemed sure she hadn't.

"No."

"Of course not. Kiera takes only one or two paying clients a year. The rest, she does pro bono. We refer about fifteen cases to her a year. She doesn't take them all, but she chooses some. And she does it all for free."

"Then why isn't that common knowledge?"

"So she can be besieged with people wanting free memory erasure? Really? Only a few people know, so keep your trap shut, Dean Matthson. And quit being a dick."

"You forget. I'm a professional dick." And an unprofessional one. He remembered his first meeting with Kiera, when he'd suspected her a shrew, when he'd manipulated her into experiencing such pain and horror. Worse, he wasn't sorry he'd done it. Because he had leads, and he had her spending the day with him. Definitely a dick.

CHAPTER TWENTY THREE

Kiera

"**W**ELL, THAT WAS SUBTLE," KIERA SAID IN her most sarcastic voice as Dean and Lorelei left to "fetch ice."

"What?"

Kiera rolled her eyes. "Lorelei's obviously talking about me, so in the interest of fairness, you need to give me some dirt on the detective." Also, she would never find another opportunity to learn anything that wasn't self-selected about Dean. She wanted to know everything about him, every sinister secret, each detail that made him human and not perfect.

Jack bumped up his ignorance game. "What do you mean?" He was unimpressive. Middle height, middle weight, middle brown eyes, and waning brown hair—not much to note. She stared at him without saying anything else until he scowled. "Why should I tell you anything?"

"Who's your expert witness on the Ambrose case?" she asked. There was a morass of "experts," with few knowing anything of value. If Jack had one of the real ones, she wouldn't have any bargaining power, but statistically, there was a decent chance he had one of the posers.

"You mean the Ramsey Adams case?"

Whoops. She was always getting names wrong. She envied Beth, who had a knack for both names and faces.

Jack continued, tone guarded. "Miller O'Sullivan."

Kiera rubbed her chin. "How would you like a real expert? Like the guy the military calls when they need a consult?"

Jack stared at Kiera, his eyes glittering like a cobra about to strike. He became suddenly interesting, almost attractive. "I've known Dean a long time. In what specific areas do you want damaging information? You want to hear about Lyndsey Lynn?"

She pressed her lips together and tried not to laugh. "What is a Lyndsey Lynn?"

"Worst girlfriend ever."

"Proceed."

His stories of Lyndsey Lynn made Kiera happy. Kiera knew that she was far more trouble than she was worth, but she wasn't vapid. Not that Jack had used that term, but he'd described it perfectly—a woman obsessed with the shells of things: appearance, material goods, status, herself.

Not that Kiera wasn't selfish. Because she was. Her entire life centered on keeping herself centered, but she had a legitimate reason. Kiera was helping catch a killer. It sounded as if Lyndsey Lynn had only been useful for catching sales. Splendid fodder.

Jack related tales of drunken stupidity. There were other wonderful embarrassments Jack shared, such as Dean eating raw fertilized eggs on a dare and making Darth Vader's theme song the ringtone for a girlfriend and having it discovered while at dinner with her parents.

By the time Dean and Lorelei returned, one small bag of ice in tow, Kiera was armed and ready for whatever he might have learned about her.

"Help me with the salad," Lorelei said to Jack. She turned to Dean. "You guys go on up to the top deck."

Lorelei needed to work on her tact.

Dean sat a cushion away from her on the top deck seats. The extra distance wasn't lost on Kiera. She had been right to think that Lorelei had said something about her. But what Kiera had learned had been, no doubt, more embarrassing. "Should we play the exchange information game?" Kiera asked, keeping her voice light.

"What do you mean?"

"I'll tell you what Jack said about you, and you tell me what Lorelei said about me."

He cocked his head to the side. "What makes you think Lorelei said anything?" His smile was smug, his eyes narrow. He was toying with her.

Kiera smirked. "You don't want to play?"

"I'll tell you what," Dean said, his tone stony. "Your game. You go first."

Maybe this was better, each of them learning embarrassing things about the other through a conduit. She opened with the least innocuous tidbit. "Apparently, your ex-girlfriend insisted everyone call her Lyndsey Lynn—not Lyndsey or Lynn or Lynds, but by her full name, and she used to get upset because she'd be giving you the cold shoulder for days, but you never noticed until she finally told you, even though you're a dick." Kiera snickered at that, couldn't help herself.

Dean didn't react.

Her mouth couldn't keep up with her mind, spilling details like an up-tempo rap song. "She's the one who came up with the stupid idea for your facial hair. Seriously, you might want to rethink the stubble thing."

He raised an eyebrow and crossed his arms, his almost smile hinting at both discomfort and amusement.

Kiera picked at the corner of her lip where some lip balm had pilled. Time to drop the most mortifying anecdote. "And you also passed out once with your face in a toilet." He stared at her, lips parted. "And almost drowned."

Dean walked to the ladder to the main cabin, and called down, "What the fuck, Jack?" He didn't sound angry, but he didn't sound amused. His reacting at all was a victory.

Jack laughed. "Your girl bargains like a pro. I'd have told her bed-wetting stories if I'd had any to share."

117

Dean grunted and propped his shoulder against the frame of the canopy over their sitting area. "Lorelei talked about all the charitable work you do for people and how she refers several clients to you a year."

Well, shit. Lorelei had been talking her up, not sharing juicy bits of gossip. She studied the pink polish of her toes. It was a great color, a vibrant neon pink. Kiera loved the shade because it didn't match any of the trauma transfers. Her toes held no memories.

"True," she said to break the silence.

"Apparently, you have a very nice office."

Kiera thought of her beautiful work space. "Also true." Maybe she could salvage this misstep. "Did she mention my impeccable dental hygiene?"

"No, she didn't. Quite the oversight." He squinted and focused on her mouth. "Let's see."

She bared her teeth at him in a feigned snarl. "Twice a day flossing, baby, my secret weapon."

So, that happened; she'd called him baby. Corporal Awkward, at your service.

To her relief, he didn't seem to notice. "That's dedication."

Kiera shrugged. "Which is why Lorelei should have waxed poetic about it."

"She actually said quite a few complimentary things about you," Dean said. Then, almost as an afterthought. "Lorelei also might have mentioned that you're a little weird about touch."

Weight fell on her shoulders, like a too-heavy coat. The distance made sense now. Lorelei had warned Dean to be careful, and now he would treat her differently. Every time they touched or didn't touch, he would be reminded that she was broken.

Dean cleared his throat, but she didn't look at him, just stared out at the water, her eye continually drawn to the breakwater—that small sliver of land that jutted out into the lake making the dock a harbor and not simply open water. That small, tiny mass somehow kept huge waves from capsizing boats in a storm.

Dean tilted toward her, but he didn't move closer. "I'm sorry if I . . . if earlier today, when I put my hand—"

"Don't." It came out sharper than she wanted, and right behind the word came a welling of anger and frustration. And longing. She wanted him to look at her like he had when they'd jet-skied, even if she had no business wanting that. "I'm not one of your victims, Dean."

They stared at each other. She leaned forward, proving he didn't intimidate her. Dean walked over and plopped down next to her. The proximity was unexpected—she assumed he would never sit close to her again. A ravenous lust shot up her body. She licked her lips, the movement catching his attention, his eyes flicking to her lips before back to her eyes.

He moved his mouth to her ear. "I think your game sucks."

She laughed like a popped balloon. He shifted to the side, back against the seat, and she followed, so they were sitting shoulder to shoulder, his body touching hers. The warmth was comfortable and easy, and everything hadn't been ruined.

"What's wrong with the stubble, by the way?" he asked.

She mock-shuddered. "I'll bet it's wicked scratchy."

Dean wiped a hand over his jaw. Then he slanted his eyes to her. "Why do you care?"

"I don't." Her face burned.

He grinned at her. "It's not so bad. Go on, feel it."

"I'm not going to touch your face."

"Because you're weird about touch."

She gaped at him. "I'm weird? You can't ask near strangers to touch your face."

"You brought it up. I think you secretly want to touch my face."

Kiera spluttered. "With my fist."

"Tenderly. With much affection. I think I'm growing on you." He was teasing her, trying to force a reaction, and it worked. Dean Matthson was charm incarnate, and she couldn't stop blushing.

119

CHAPTER TWENTY FOUR

Dean

"THERE'S NO DIFFERENCE BETWEEN BLACK Forest ham and Virginia ham," Dean pronounced.

"Of course, there is, or there wouldn't be two different names," Kiera countered.

"They do that to charge more for one."

"Which one?"

"Like I know. I have a real life, Brayleigh."

Lorelei stepped back from the small table where she'd laid out the food. She pointed to one of the piles. "This one is the Black Forest. It's smoked with fir or pine. The Virginia ham is smoked with hickory or apple wood."

Kiera clasped her hands together. "If we have wine tonight, can you serve one with notes of cherry and chocolate with a hint of oak?"

Lorelei shook her head. "You're getting box wine."

"Does it have hints of cherry and chocolate?" Dean asked. "Because that does sound tasty."

"Grow up," Lorelei grumbled, though she couldn't hide a half smile.

"Yeah, Dean, grow up," Kiera muttered under her breath.

They laughed like kids, and something that had been tied up for so long, he hadn't known it was there, relaxed in Dean. When Lorelei did pour the wine after setting down a platter of grilled shrimp and thick slices of watermelon, he and Kiera became more obnoxious trying to outdo each other with pretentious comments on the legs (Dean), the high notes (Kiera), and the mouth feel (Dean). He was doing well, but then Kiera said she thought she detected a base note of chicory, and Dean couldn't stop laughing. Jack ignored them, but Lorelei stared at the two of them as if they were a pair of talking carp.

Lorelei persuaded Jack to take the boat out onto the lake, probably to avoid the juvenile humor. Kiera grinned like mad when the boat hit open water and moved fast enough for a wake. If she had grown up differently, she would have been one of those adventure people, climbing K2 and participating in ultramarathons. She was too pretty and clever and rich for him to pity, but he did feel a strange sense of loss at what her life could have been.

Of course, he could say the same thing about himself. If he didn't work eighty to a hundred hours a week, what might he have accomplished? He wouldn't be going on four months with half a kitchen and several fire hazards; that much was certain.

Kiera grabbed his forearm to steady herself and kept her hand there, smiling up at him. He forgot about his kitchen, his case, his reservations. He forgot everything.

CHAPTER TWENTY FIVE

Kiera

THOSE GLASSES. WHEN THE HELL HAD DEAN'S glasses suddenly become so sexy? But they were. And then there were the eyes behind them. Now that she'd gotten a closer look, she found an aura of brown around the irises of his bluish-green eyes. And that he looked so vulnerable—no, not vulnerable—accessible, appealed to her.

They sat on the top of a yacht under a canopy of fireworks, their shoulders and hips touching. Epically romantic.

God, she wished he would kiss her.

But, of course, he wouldn't.

Dean Matthson was a professional. Kiera Brayleigh was a freak. She had given up the idea of ever having a normal life before she'd turned twenty. Normality wasn't something just out of reach or an elusive shape in the night. It was like trying to imagine a flying unicorn landing on her deck to take her away. Could she picture it? Sure. But she had to bend her reality like a Celtic knot to do it. Dean didn't make her *feel* normal, but she could *see* normal from there. Her body liked him, accepted his touch in a way it didn't for most others. He made her feel like a person, which sounded corny and stupid, but people usually saw her as a tool or an object.

"You okay?" Dean asked.

Kiera swallowed, reminding herself that caring wasn't always sharing. Instead, she rested her head on his shoulder and closed her eyes until a flash made her eyes flutter open. Green and gold sparkled in the sky.

Dean watched her. His eyes were too alive, too active, though they didn't move. What was he thinking? Lust made her lady bits twist in a pleasure-pain way. She had to master herself before she did something embarrassing, like trying to kiss him. He had extremely kissable lips, full and curved the slightest bit upward. Would they be soft and gentle? She pictured it. Would they be rough and insistent? She pictured that.

He swallowed and didn't pull away, allowing the delicious tension between them to grow. Fireworks flashed different colors across his skin and reflected off his eyes. Kiera tried to hold onto everything crackling through her.

* * *

They returned to the dock sooner than she expected. The goodbyes were quick but not awkward. Kiera and Dean were back at Dean's car by ten fifteen. In another life, she would have walked home. But she understood what could happen to a young woman even while minding her own damn business. Kiera sighed and got into the passenger seat of Dean's car, which still stank of greasy burgers.

As they got close to her home, a sinister wisp of dread circled into her bones. What if someone had broken into her home? The idea was irrational. The front was manned 24-7, a key card was required to reach her floor, and she had a fancy keypad lock and alarm. Nobody knew where she lived. She worked hard to have the title and all the bills in the dummy name of K. Bray. Nothing was tied to her name. She was untraceable. Yet the fear held her tight. Someone was there. Someone was waiting for her.

Dean pulled up to the front of her building.

"Can you check and make sure nobody is in my condo?" she blurted.

123

"What makes you think someone's in your condo?" As if there might be a logical reason.

"Paranoid tendencies is what my shrink calls it."

"And what do you call it?"

"Pathological pessimism."

He tapped his fingers on the steering wheel, more piano than drum. "And me coming up will help?"

"No way am I lucky enough to have an intruder in my home the one night a cop comes to check the place out." She desperately wanted him to laugh, and he did.

"I'll take a look if it'll make you feel better."

If she'd been standing, she might have collapsed in relief. "You can park next door. I have a parking space there."

"Isn't your car there?"

"Are you kidding? I can't drive. All I need is to have a panic attack because 'Shock the Monkey' came on the radio. No, I use a car service. The parking space is for guests."

"'Shock the Monkey' gives you a panic attack?"

"Once." She wished she were kidding.

"Why not listen to NPR or subscribe to satellite radio and listen to the comedy station?" he asked after a few seconds of silence.

Kiera had almost forgotten what they were talking about. "Easier to call my driver when I need to go somewhere."

"Isn't that expensive?" He must be thinking about her money—how much she had, how she had gotten it. Most of her wealth now came from investments, not clients, but she didn't tell him that, because her net worth wasn't any of his damn business.

"What do you care? It's not taxpayer dollars."

"I don't care, but it seems like a waste of money, particularly when you have a parking spot available. But, okay, you're not comfortable driving, so why not take a taxi or an Uber?"

Kiera didn't want to explain, but she needed him now to ensure her safety. She sighed, hating to sound cracked again. "I don't get in a car with someone I don't know. Ever. So, having my own driver available is worth the expense."

He turned off the car but didn't make a move to get out. "Sorry. I keep forgetting what you live with."

She popped open her door. "I wish I could forget."

* * *

THE CONDO WAS DARK WHEN SHE OPENED THE DOOR, ONLY THE GHOSTLY light of the alarm pad flashing. That was what she hated the most. If she had known she would be gone so long, she would have turned on a few lights. The place was stuffy and quiet, like a crypt.

Kiera was afraid to go inside. Her brain dumped freak-out chemicals—cortisol and epinephrine—into her system. A voice in her skull said, "Don't go in there" and "Run." Everything in her said that someone was in there. Waiting for her. Her rational mind insisted that was highly unlikely. But her rational brain had to admit that it wasn't impossible.

"Are you going to go inside?" Dean asked.

She wanted to say, "Hell no, I'm never going in there again," but that was ridiculous. This was her home, and her alarm was beeping, waiting to be disengaged.

Dean studied her, eyebrows raised. So, she disregarded her instincts, which the experts said you should listen to—but then they meant for normal people, and she wasn't normal—and entered her condo. Two steps. She flipped the entry light, shut off the alarm, and moved aside for Dean to enter.

Her purse and the Target bag with her wet swimsuit slapped against her leg. Useless weapons. She dropped them to the floor, freeing her hands. Dean brushed past her and stood to her right, looking up and down the hall. Kiera waited, back pressed to the wall, where nobody could come up behind her. Her mouth was dry, palms wet, heart spazzing, skin crawling.

Dean looked concerned, and although she knew it didn't mean he thought her insane, it was hard not to interpret it that way.

"Should I walk around?" he asked.

She nodded. "Please. Check everywhere." She should have stopped there, but she couldn't help herself. "And please check like you think someone might actually be there and not like you check for monsters in a kid's room, okay?"

He paused for a moment. "Sure."

She stayed by the door, reengaging the alarm, prepared to sprint should the need arise. Part of her felt guilty over exposing Dean to danger to save herself, but he was a police officer. Surely, someone not ready to take on an intruder had no business being a cop.

He took slow and measured footsteps as he turned on all the light switches. Each illumination made her relax a little more. The illumination provided less cover for an assailant. As Dean walked through her condo, she strained to hear any strange thuds or grunts or signs of a struggle. Her hand was on the doorknob, twisting and untwisting, like a nervous tic. When Dean came back, she let go of the knob, trying to act casual.

He brushed a hand on her shoulder. "That side's clear. Let me check the other."

She nodded.

The other side was faster—just the kitchen and living room, open spaces with few places to hide. She stood next to the door but managed not to hold the handle this time.

Dean returned. "Nobody here."

"Do you want dessert? I don't have anything made, but I can make chocolate mousse or cookies in less than half an hour, if you want." She wanted him to say yes. The longer he stayed, the safer she'd feel.

"You can make chocolate mousse in less than a half hour?" He grinned. "I'd like to see that."

Kiera kicked off her shoes. Cooking was better in bare feet. She whipped eggs and cream, melted chocolate, and tempered the eggs, all the tasks melding together in a rhythm like dancing.

To impress Dean, she used a vegetable peeler to shave chocolate off a bar. He peered closely but said nothing. Kiera distributed the mousse between the two glasses and topped them with the chocolate shavings.

"Fancy," Dean said with a whistle.

"No, I have edible gold leaf. If I'd added it, *that* would be fancy." She raised her eyebrows. "You want some gold leaf?"

"No thanks. I'm not a fan of eating metal, even the fancy kind."

She nodded. "It doesn't add to the flavor, but the pretentious factor is through the roof."

"We just spent the day on a yacht. I think we've covered the pretension factor."

Now finished—sans gold leaf—Kiera laughed and led Dean to the deck to eat their dessert in the cool night. There was the barest sliver of moon in the sky and no clouds. A small breeze kept the air moving and fresh. Her skin gave off the faint smell of the lake.

"Damn, this is delicious," Dean said after his first bite.

A plume of pride filled her.

"I'm glad you like it." She took a bite of her own. The consistency was a little too dense—she should have whipped the cream slower—but the taste was exceptional, and the mouthfeel was excellent. She was tempted to tell him she could do better, but kept her mouth shut. Her longings were intensifying again, and there was no telling what else she might say.

CHAPTER TWENTY SIX

Dean

As Kiera relaxed, her movements became more flowing and natural. He liked the way she gestured with her hands and flashed smiles whenever he said anything she thought was funny or clever. He worked hard to charm; her pleasure the reinforcement he craved.

The atmosphere between them became cozy, bordering on flirtatious. He shouldn't make a move unless he'd thought it through, and he wasn't thinking at all. Her exposed collarbone drew his attention. The knowledge that she had to be naked under that dress kept floating into his mind. That tiny purse of hers was too small to carry underwear, and her wet bathing suit was still in the Target bag. Her pert breasts called to him. Every time she crossed or uncrossed her legs, he thought of her naked body.

Bad, Dean. Bad, bad, Dean.

It's getting late.

I should be leaving.

I'll let you get on with your evening.

There were a million ways to make his exit, but he said none of them.

"I had a good time today." Her voice brought him back to the present moment.

"So did I."

Her eyebrows quirked, as if she didn't quite believe him, though it was the truth.

She stared at her lap, as if she were thinking about saying something specific. Dean had witnessed that action so many times in interrogations— she was getting ready to confess. He said nothing, which was the best and fastest way to get her to say what she wanted to say. "If your friend Jack asks for it, you can give him my number. I gave him the contact info for the top researcher in the field, but he doesn't have the . . . gift. If I can, I'll answer any questions he has about memory removal."

"Are you M&Ming right now?" he teased, trying to keep her from going anywhere bleak. He needed her to laugh again. Or just smile.

She kept her face forward, out toward the lake. "I can't change who I am, and it's been bothering me. People who use what we can do to hurt and manipulate people need to be stopped. Not only for the people whose lives they fuck with, but for all of us who can do the same. There's going to be a tipping point, and we're going to all be registered or monitored or locked up. We can't do anything without consent, but we can take severe advantage once we have a toe in the door."

The depth of her character, her empathy and fortitude, and the sheer emotional strength that she hid behind her snark and her insecurities impressed him. He'd never met anyone so complicated, and that should have been a turn-off, but it wasn't. "I'll tell him you're willing to help."

He should concentrate on the Kolchek case. *Got to go. Check out the time. On that note, I should be going.*

She shifted forward and then stood. The lights from the condo lit her from the front, highlighting her form, washing out the vibrant yellow of her dress but making her blue eyes glow. "I don't want to keep you too late, if you've been trying to figure out how to extricate yourself."

When they were back inside, he was almost in the clear, but for the briefest moment, she turned back to him and he saw her beautiful face and the hint of the smile he couldn't help but want to make bloom.

"Can I kiss you goodnight?" Oh, shit. He'd said that out loud.

She blinked as pink spread over her face.

He winced at embarrassing her and his own baffling eagerness. Maybe she wasn't ready for anything physical. "I'm sorry. I shouldn't have—"

"Okay."

"Okay? Really? Are you sure?" Dean wished that he would stop talking and simply accept her acquiescence.

Kiera puffed out a small laugh. "No, but I think it would make an awkward debate."

Retract and extract. Get the hell out of there and regroup. Instead, he moved into Kiera's personal space.

During the fireworks, she'd pressed into him, the skin of her shoulder still holding onto the warmth of the day, her head solid on his shoulder. The tension between them, that sizzle of attraction that had built all day grew as he edged closer. She was short enough to have to tip her chin to keep eye contact. Her eyes were luminous, her lips parted. Dean's stomach swirled as if he were tumbling down a hill in a barrel. He couldn't shake the idea that it was a mistake and that he was going to do it regardless.

She extended her neck an inch closer to him. Carefully, he rested his fingertips on her face, giving her a chance to change her mind. Her eyes closed. He kissed her, as gently as he could.

Dean hadn't been with anyone since Lyndsey Lynn, which was eight months ago. So maybe that was why his body went haywire, why the barest touch of her lips wrenched him inside out. It was like being dunked in something so cold it burned, a fiery rash along his skin that pooled in his groin.

He kept his body apart from hers, concerned she might take exception to his evident hard-on, particularly if he pressed it into her, which was what he wanted to do. Their kisses deepened, a fire that blazed high and hot. He hoped Kiera had her head about her because Dean was out of his goddamned mind.

CHAPTER TWENTY SEVEN

Kiera

TOO FAR AWAY. DEAN WAS TOO FAR AWAY, BUT every time Kiera inched forward, he countered, keeping the exact same distance between them.

Jesus, how long was her hallway?

Just the pads of three fingers touched her face, the contact so light it was like a ghost. Then those fingers, those small patches of cool against her skin, slid down her jaw, drawing a line of shivers. After her jaw, they moved to her neck, the tingling sensation shattering her control. She moved closer until they were almost touching, snaking her arms around his neck. He kissed her harder, and then she felt it.

Stubble.

Scraping over the delicate skin of her face. Kiera pulled away and mock-frowned. "Just as abrasive as I'd imagined."

He ran his hand over his jaw, never taking his eyes off her. "Got a razor?"

Offering to shave for her comfort sprouted a grapefruit in her throat. She pressed a fist to her mouth, needing a moment to compose her expression. "Can I do it?"

* * *

SHE PERCHED BETWEEN THE SINKS, RESTING HER BACK ON THE MIRROR. They were in the master bath off her bedroom, past the large, comfortable bed she'd named Big Bad John. On the nightstand near the window, her Tiffany lamp glowed, casting the bedroom into a sleepy, sexy glow.

In the bright light of the bathroom, Kiera slathered shaving cream onto his face using far more than he likely used himself. The scent was gender-neutral. The pink razor wasn't. He hadn't commented or seemed to mind the color, which gave him an extra point in Kiera's ledger.

"What shouldn't I do?" he asked at last, the shaving cream making him Santa Claus wannabe-ish. His glasses sat on the other side of the sink.

Ah. She swallowed. "Don't grab me too hard or too suddenly, and never by the back of my hair. No biting." Dean frowned, as if it was a lot to remember, as she ran the razor down his cheek in a tentative stroke. A little glob of shaving cream hung on his earlobe. "Teeth scraping is fine, though." As if that concession would make up for everything else. He tilted his chin to expose his neck, leaving him so vulnerable it enabled her to continue. "Don't call me a bitch or a slut or a whore. Ever, actually. Don't hold me down or restrain me in any way. I don't like to be tickled."

She stroked up his neck, feeling his eyes watching her movements in the mirror. Would he stay? Kiera's body hadn't leveled out at all and a euphoric anticipation bubbled everywhere.

"What else?" He looked at her as if he suspected she was holding back.

She wasn't. Was she? Kiera glanced away. "Well, oral sex isn't going to happen tonight. And . . ." God, it was embarrassing. What if he wanted nothing more than kissing? Kiera hated when men assumed women all felt a certain way about a particular issue, especially sex, so she tried hard not to do the same to men. Not every man fucked whenever they could, irrespective of his partner.

"It's okay. Just tell me." He had a half smile and the half-shaved face made him comical enough to loosen her tongue.

"I enjoy sex, Dean." She had to finish the sentence, get it out, make her intentions clear. "I . . . want you tonight." His body shifted closer. She put a hand on his shoulder, not to stop him but to ground herself. "But I can't get off with another person, and I know it's psychological, but that doesn't matter. Your trying would totally take me out of the moment, and I really, really want to stay in this moment for a while. So please, just take my word for it, okay? If you're interested." Her pitch for him to have sex with her sucked. Who wanted to fuck someone frigid? "Are you? Interested?"

"Yes. Whatever you want; whatever makes you comfortable. I am so turned on right now." His eyes were so lovely and honest they ripped through her soul.

She blinked before tears could form and finished the shave without cutting him once, a good omen. Dean splashed his face with water, then cleared the remains of shaving cream with a hand towel. "Better?" he asked, his grin popping out his dimples.

Kiera reached out and stroked his now-smooth cheeks. "Very nice."

"I knew you were angling to touch my face," he said, shifting to his right, his body nudging her knees apart so he stood between them.

He didn't touch her, except for one hand sitting innocently on her hip. Heat seeped into her skin, and it made her want to explode. Dean stroked her jaw, then slid his hand to the back of her neck, before slowly drawing her into a kiss. If only she could convince him to stop being so damned careful.

CHAPTER TWENTY EIGHT

Dean

DEAN BROKE THEIR KISS AND SAVORED THE WAY she looked at him, the way her body leaned toward his. He didn't have to work tomorrow. There was time to go slow.

With her perched between the sinks and him between her thighs, her dress had ridden to midthigh, but he ignored that for the moment. Slow, he reminded himself as her hard nipples called to him.

"Can I touch you?" he asked, insisting on obtaining permission beforehand. In case she had any doubt what he wanted to touch, he traced the edge of her dress across her chest.

She nodded.

Still, he paused. "I need to hear you say it."

"Yes." The ache in her voice stoked his hunger.

Something wild flashed in her eyes as his fingers dipped beneath the fabric and stroked over the top of her breasts. Her lashes fluttered, and her lips parted. He kissed her as he cupped a breast through her dress. His body demanded more, and he had to pull himself back from burying himself inside her. Slow. Slow. Slow. But his body was trying hard to ignore his mind's orders.

She stroked his now-smooth jaw, her cool fingers tracing over his skin. Kiera was so busy studying him, she must have forgotten to be self-conscious, because she stared at him with open fascination and pleasure. Lyndsey Lynn had never really looked at him except to watch him watching her. Didn't really listen either.

Unless they were talking about her or an extension of her, she wasn't interested. At first, that had been refreshing, not having to talk about the job, but eventually, he had to wonder if she cared at all.

"I freaked you out, didn't I?" Kiera asked, pulling back a little and biting her lip.

She'd caught him thinking about Lyndsey Lynn, which was unacceptable. She deserved his complete attention. Worse, she assumed the hesitation had to do with her. He cupped Kiera's cheek as gently as he could. "No. Sometimes my mind takes a bad turn. I'm here now."

Kiera didn't huff or frown or pout. Not like his other random attempts at dating.

"Well, I wouldn't know anything about bad turns." She laughed at her own joke, grabbed his face with both hands, and pulled him to her. She stopped just short of kissing him, near enough that they were breathing the same air, the electrons on their lip atoms bouncing off one another.

Dean tried to be patient, but she was so damn close, and his body was fluttering and straining. "Kiera," he whispered, her name floating from his lips to hers.

She squirmed on the counter. "Fuck, that's sexy."

When she was that near, her pupils huge, her skin flushed, her lips so near, it made him want to devour her. It made him want to let go and lose it—which he could never do with her. He rubbed his face against hers, his nose trailing over her cheek and temple, into her hair. He wanted to inhale her entire body.

"Say something else." She sounded pained. "Anything."

His body inflated with something light and volatile, like pure oxygen. His nose found her ear, and he ran the tip over the outside before sucking her earlobe into his mouth. She hissed and dug her fingers into his torso, her body sliding forward.

"I want to make love to you," he breathed into her ear with almost no voice at all.

Her thighs clamped against him. "The bed might be more comfortable."

"I would hope so," he said with a chuckle. "You want me to carry you?"

She snorted. "Romantic but undignified. I'll walk." With a flat palm to his chest, she eased him back a few steps before sliding to the floor. Her hip brushed against his gun. "Oh," she gasped. "What do we do with that?"

Dean shrugged. "Drawer?"

She opened a drawer in the bathroom with toothpaste, dental floss, and an assortment of hair ties. Dean removed his firearm, along with the holster and belt. They stared at his weapon for a moment, and Dean feared the mood might have been killed.

Kiera nudged him with her shoulder. "Now you've gone and done it. You're completely at my mercy."

He nudged her back. "So, what are you going to do?"

CHAPTER TWENTY NINE

Kiera

KIERA SLIPPED HER HAND UNDER HIS T-SHIRT, determined to experience his bare skin, which was warm and foreign. She hiked up his shirt, and Dean helped her pull it off his body. They regarded each other for a breath, a paused moment in time. Longing mushroom-clouded up her body, pitching her forward into Dean, her lips desperate.

They tumbled to Big Bad John, their legs bumping as their hands roamed. Kiera crashed onto the bed. Dean followed, perching above her, and they stilled, like the explosion of contact had never happened. The fervor of Dean's gaze captured her.

He untied the fabric at the back of her neck with one hand. Air hit her exposed breasts like a polar plunge.

Dean watched her face and not her breasts, which her foggy brain didn't comprehend. Why would he open her like that if he didn't want to see? But the way he looked at her answered her own question. He was searching for signs of stress or fear or discomfort. It was sweet in a way that made her bones ache. She wanted to smile, so he would understand she was more than okay, but her face wouldn't move—she was too far down into the depths of whatever spell he had cast to respond with her conscious mind.

His gaze went from sharp to unfocused, glowing in the dim light. He tipped his chin down, his entire head following as he lowered his mouth to her breast. Only his lips grazed her nipple, which ached from the barely there contact.

Not enough. Not nearly enough.

The second pass was his tongue, and though her eyes were closed, they still rolled back in her head, making her slightly dizzy. He followed with his fingers, brushing, then lightly pinching. It wasn't hard enough, the sensation dulled by the gentleness. She thought he would work up to harder contact, but he didn't. He sucked and touched and licked, but always with a feather touch.

"More," she whispered. Her body finally moved, arching to his mouth, as if she could force him to touch her harder.

He pulled back again to look at her. His face was flushed, his lips plump and wet. For a moment she was overwhelmed by how deeply she wanted him—it was unnatural and terrifying and inescapable.

There was nothing to be done, so she did nothing. He pinched her nipple harder and watched her reaction. She hated to be studied, and he was clearly studying her, but lust sizzled out everything else. "More." Her voice cracked.

One side of his lips quirked. He pinched harder. He hit a nerve, a cluster of nerves, a network of nerves. Pleasure sparked from her nipples to the rest of her body. Even her toes tingled. Her core clamped and wept with a cramping kind of hunger that should have scared her. Kiera didn't like to be out of control, particularly in matters of sex, where so much could go wrong. But something base inside her, something instinctive, slammed shut all her higher-level functions, all the nattering fears and ghosts of memories.

His eyes darted as he studied one of her eyes and then the other. Did they appear different from each other? He pinched again, and she thought of nothing but the exquisite sting of sensation scorching her.

"More?" Dean asked, his voice rasping.

The sound of his voice made her body quake with longing. "Just like that," she gasped. "Please, Dean."

He blinked several times and licked his lips—and pinched, just like that, twice more. He was panting, his eyes heavy.

She should do something. She'd been lying there, receiving his touch and giving nothing in return. Not that he appeared to mind.

Kiera sat up and raised her arms overhead. Dean shifted, then grabbed the material of the sundress and pulled it over her head. He pressed his body lightly to hers. "So beautiful," he murmured as he kissed her. "So fucking beautiful."

Kiera hated people to talk about her looks—good or bad, but she smiled at his words, the profanity ratcheting up her lust. A flutter skated behind her ribs to the pounding of her heart.

He put a thumb into the waistband of his shorts, pulling them away from his body. "Do you mind?"

Kiera shook her head. Dean arched an eyebrow. She chortled at his insistence of a verbal response. "I don't mind."

That twisting, tumbling cascade of lust spilled through her again as he was stripped down to nothing but his boxer briefs. Dean had a lean body, which might have been called slight if he'd been a few inches shorter, with muscle that came from being active without regular workouts. He came by his physique naturally, and nature had been kind. Everything about him was long—arms, legs, torso, neck, fingers—but he was also elegant, which seemed an uncommon combination. His movements had a careful yet casual quality, as if everything he did was graceful and precise. He crawled over to her and paused.

"There's such a thing as too careful," she said.

"No, there isn't. You may not care if I overstep, but it matters to me."

Kiera looked away. Was this guy real? She caught sight of a jagged scar on his biceps. "Oh my God, were you stabbed?" She grabbed his arm and raised her face to see more closely.

He chuckled. "No, I tripped and fell back into a fence that had a loose chink sticking out."

"Want me to make it better?"

"Baby, just looking at you makes it better."

She scowled. "Don't call me baby."

"I didn't mean anything by it."

Kiera kissed his scar. "There's nothing wrong with calling someone baby." After all, she'd done it herself earlier. Luckily, he either didn't remember or chose not to mention it.

He mock-frowned. "I can't call you baby or bitch or whore or slut. Damn. What am I supposed to call you then? Snooky? Is Snooky okay?"

She bit into the meat of his arm but not hard.

"Hey, you said no biting!"

"No, I said *you* couldn't bite *me*. This is totally different." She was nothing if not a mass of contradictions.

He laughed. "I can't bite you, grab you, or pin you. That doesn't leave many defensive moves."

She nodded wisely. "Better just to submit."

Dean rested his forehead on hers. "Okay, I submit."

Kiera kissed him. "I want you to fuck me, Dean."

"Thank God." He rolled on top of her.

A sensation of falling sent her stomach into her ribs, then down into her core, where Dean was pressing into her, only his underwear between them. She expected him to pull them down, but he didn't. Instead, he kissed her jaw, chin, and throat, working his way down her body. "What are you doing?" she asked, though it was a stupid question.

He laughed, a deep, rumbling noise that reverberated through her body. "Relax," he crooned. As if she could relax while he awakened every nerve in her damn body.

Dean stopped when he got to her belly button and worked his way up again. His hands caressed and traveled toward the apex of her thighs, the part that couldn't stop throbbing and clenching and aching. "That's it," he said as he kissed her ear. "You're almost ready for me."

She whimpered as he touched all around her sex, never making contact with the spots that desperately needed it. Her hips broke loose from her control and rose toward his hand. "I'm ready," she begged. "Dean, please."

His exhale was ragged, and his hands slowed for a moment, trembling. "Don't talk, Kiera. You'll make me come. Don't talk."

Before she could ask him to clarify, he touched her, his fingers slipping over her wetness. She cried out, a high-pitched shriek. He stroked her but didn't penetrate. One of his fingers circled her clit, and her entire body clamped down. The center of her crunched and tightened, with enough pressure to create diamond from coal—it pressed and built and squeezed until Kiera thought she would explode. His touch continued coaxing her higher and higher, and then she detonated. The tightness unfurled and spread through her body in waves, the pleasure riding her, lifting her, making her mind blank and spin and whirl as her skin danced and her core slid and fluttered and bucked. She screamed, a rough, guttural cry as she gripped Dean's shoulders hard enough to bruise.

"Oh fuck," she wheezed. "Oh my fucking fuck." She stilled his hand still working her overstimulated core. Her chest heaved as if she'd spent an hour on the VersaClimber. What he'd done shouldn't have been possible.

Dean groaned and rolled to his side. "That was the hottest fucking thing I've ever seen." He was staring at her, eyes afire and glassy.

The hunger in his face made her body clamp down again, an aftershock of her orgasm. "Am I ready now?"

CHAPTER THIRTY

Dean

DEAN DRAGGED OUT THE UNROLLING OF THE condom, trying to control himself. Making a woman come in a few seconds was a feat of skill. A man coming in a few seconds was a shameful embarrassment. And he was in real danger of popping off at any moment.

Her nails scratched through his hair, and he groaned. Everything she did and said pushed him closer. Her body was more spectacular than he had imagined. She was flexible in ways that made his blood bubble and boil.

He dipped his head to lick her neck, giving himself a moment to lower himself from DEFCON 1 to DEFCON 2, or 3, if he could manage it—which he doubted. Her skin was silk and smooth and smelled of something slightly floral, perhaps the lotion that kept her so damned soft.

For someone so damaged and pained by sexually traumatic memories, she was amazingly open and sensual. It was easy to forget that the experiences weren't hers. She was whole in body. And whoa, what a body.

He leaned over her and stroked her collar bone. Her leg slid up his thigh at his touch. She rubbed her face into the top of his shoulder like a cat scenting. He wanted the scent of her everywhere.

"Give me just a few more seconds," he said. Really, he needed minutes.

Kiera sighed, not with frustration but contentment, and nibbled on the base of his neck. That didn't help him regain control, but he didn't complain or try to stop her.

Dean always cared that the women he slept with got off. But with Kiera, it was more than that. For several moments, he couldn't separate her pleasure from his own. The way his touch sank into her skin, as if she couldn't get enough, had him teetering on the edge. It took all his self-control not to smirk when he remembered her bewildered explosion when she'd come. It hit him with an adrenaline rush greater than if he'd just scaled Mount Everest. On his own. Without a Sherpa. Or a coat.

His cock was hard enough to serve as a blunt force weapon. He'd had to shift his mind, concentrate on something else to prevent himself from coming simply from the way her body tilted toward his—the expression on her face.

Her eyes remained slitted as if she couldn't keep them open and couldn't close them—couldn't stop examining him. She watched his hands quite a bit, as if he were performing magic tricks, as if he were doing something that should have been impossible.

Kiera ran her own hands over his chest, her eyes following her movements as she stroked him in the most pedestrian of places—his rib cage, the crook of his elbow, the tops of his shoulders. Everywhere she touched glowed and shivered. Dean loved that her attention was complete, until it slipped away, like a drowning girl sucked under a dark sea. Then she was in her own body, doing nothing but feeling what he did to her.

And he looked forward to her reaction to what he intended next.

CHAPTER THIRTY ONE

Kiera

DEAN SHIFTED TO HIS BACK. "I FIGURE IF YOU'RE on top, you can control everything."

Kiera never did on top because she lacked the experience to pull it off. She could never get the rhythm right. But after what Dean had done for her, she would have tried almost anything. She threw a leg over his body and positioned herself above him. He watched her with rapt attention, and Kiera felt something like power over him.

She lubricated the tip of him with her wetness until he was slick. Without ceremony, she sank down over his latex-covered cock. He moaned. The advantage to having little sex was tightness. "Holy shit! Stop!" he said once she was fully lowered, grasping her waist. "Wait a sec."

"Okay." He was inside her. So strange to consider—another person was physically joined with her, as if he were a part of her.

"Can you go slow?"

Shifting her weight to her hands, she leveraged her body up and down over his cock. He grabbed her hips, not hard, but loosened his grip immediately, keeping his hands resting against her skin, encouraging her in the rhythm he wanted.

Kiera watched him move in and out of her. The motion puckered her nipples and slicked her core. The sliding became easier with the accommodation and the extra lubrication. She kissed him. His lips were hungry, his tongue insistent, his body tense.

"Is this good?" she asked.

"Fuck, yes." The profanity was a turn-on. Dean swore, but far more sparingly than Kiera. His use of "fuck" as she fucked him, made her hotter.

"More?" She slowed down.

He flinched, almost grabbing her. "Yes. Please, Kiera. I want to come." At his words, she clenched and gripped him from the inside. "Oh fuck," he gasped.

That pleased her because it was exactly what she had said. She spasmed again and wished she could control the clenching. Do it on purpose. She'd have to look up Kegel exercises later.

Dean was close, his breathing hoarse and rapid, and their bodies slick. She pulled her knees to his rib cage and rocked up and down as she imagined squeezing him inside her. He grabbed the covers in his fists and roared, making nonsensical noises, the cords on his neck taut and straining. She whispered in his ear, "I want you to come now, Dean. Come for me."

And he did, his entire body bowing toward her. He flipped her onto her back, their connection never breaking, and he fucked her for a few more seconds, riding out his orgasm as he moved into her at the pace he wanted. Kiera found herself hotter than ever and pressed her thighs into him. He kissed her.

"That just blew my motherfucking mind," he said into her lips.

Kiera felt like the Grinch when he decided to let Christmas into his heart.

CHAPTER THIRTY TWO

Dean

THEY LAY TOGETHER ON HER ORGY BED, COZIER than a nest of feathers in a cloud. Dean tunneled under the most luxurious covers he'd ever touched next to the hardest woman he'd ever touched. Though he'd come to realize that her hardness was a thin veneer that protected someone infinitely soft.

Kiera Brayleigh was layered and complicated and completely enchanting. He interlaced his fingers with hers.

"Is it frightening to be a cop?" Kiera asked.

He faced her, letting his other hand rest on her stomach. "I've never been scared to be an officer, but I've had some hairy moments." Perhaps she expected him to say more because she hummed into his neck and tip-toed her fingers over his chest. "Not so much danger in homicide, believe it or not. The action is all over by the time we arrive on scene. And though we do interviews, it's not usually anything dangerous." Not usually.

"So, when were you the most scared?"

Dean wasn't sure he was ready to share that story. He'd never talked about that day. But maybe she needed something personal from him, some way to believe that he hadn't fucked her without caring. With how open she had been, he figured he owed it to her. He scooted up and pushed a second pillow under his head. "It wasn't a single moment, but a single day."

She crawled up beside him and rested her head on his shoulder, her hand stroking his torso.

He kissed her once. "My mom had fibroids." His mother would be mortified to learn Dean was talking about her fibroids to anyone, but it wasn't as if she'd ever know. "And the doctor recommended a hysterectomy. She wanted me to be there, so I took the day off work." Remembering that day made his heart accelerate.

"Is that sort of surgery dangerous?"

"Not particularly, but you never know."

Kiera stroked down his arm with the tips of her nails, waking his nerves. "Did you have a bad feeling?"

"Yeah." He traced small circles on her hip. Her warm, silken skin reminded him that she was real, and the twist in his gut was a memory. "The surgery went longer than expected, and I got nervous. I had my phone on vibrate, and one of my teammates called." Dean recalled the visceral reaction he'd had when he'd seen Tam's name. She'd known his mother was having surgery. Only something big would make her call. His entire body had gone ice-cold, and he'd had to swipe three times before he successfully answered. "She was calling to tell me that Curt got shot."

Kiera gasped and sat all the way up. "Oh my God. Curt? The guy I met, Curt?"

"Yeah. He was shot in the chest, but he was wearing his vest. It bruised badly, but no penetration." Dean gulped in a hunk of air. "But all I heard was that he was shot. And I hadn't been there."

"He was alone?"

"No, he was with Jason—someone else on the team. Jason's partner had been on furlough, so he and Curt had partnered up. They were at a house to interview someone they thought was a witness, but he opened the door and fired at them with a shotgun. Curt saw the gun at the last second through a side window and jerked Jason away just in time, but Curt took the follow-up hit in the vest." Dean ran the scenario in his mind's eye so often he sometimes forgot he hadn't been there.

She grabbed one hand with both of hers and pulled it to her chest. "Then what happened?"

"Jason shot him." Five times. The assailant had continued to move forward, his gun raised, his body not even flinching, as if every shot had missed or bullets bounced off him. Jason never admitted he'd been terrified but, clearly, he had, with only his firearm standing between the offender and his and Curt's lives. It wasn't a decision any of them ever wanted to make.

"Did he die?"

"Yeah."

She sighed and settled against him again. "Better him than Curt, I guess."

Dean exhaled, glad she hadn't reacted like Lyndsey Lynn, asking if the shooting had been necessary. The guy was an active shooter trying to kill his partner. Of course, return fire had been necessary. Curt suffered two broken ribs and a motherfucker of a bruise. Dean hadn't been there. Nobody blamed him for that except himself, but the reality bit into his soul every so often. If Curt had died, Dean would never have gotten over the loss. For days afterward, he'd pictured himself at the St. Jude parade, the parade to honor those officers killed in the line of duty, carrying a sign with Curt's photo.

Kiera reached out and touched his jaw. She brushed his lips with her thumbs and kissed him. He was glad she didn't say anything, didn't say she was sorry, didn't say how awful that must have been. Her presence grounded him in the present, kept him from slipping too far into the past.

"As I hung up with Tam—the teammate who called—the surgeon came out, and for a second . . . I was sure that Mom had died. Curt being alive meant my mom had to die. My vision went all wonky, like being shitfaced drunk, and I couldn't hear right. It was awful."

"Did she come through all right?"

"Yeah." He couldn't explain the experience right. "But it didn't matter. I lived through her death in that moment, hers and Curt's, back-to-back."

Dean tried to stop talking because he wasn't making sense. "I know it sounds nuts."

"That makes sense to me. The mind does strange things in stressful situations. Just because it sounds irrational, it doesn't mean your experience wasn't real." Kiera sighed theatrically. "And you couldn't even smoke a joint to calm down afterward."

"Smoking weed isn't a healthy coping mechanism," he said, though he couldn't help smiling.

"Ha! You obviously don't have access to medical marijuana. I think there might be an actual strain called Coping Mechanism. Very mellowing."

Dean laughed and wrapped his arm about her waist, glad to hold her close, gladder that they weren't talking about that horrible day any longer. The conversation lulled, and sleep almost claimed him before proper manners made him ask, "You want to tell a story?"

"My mom dosed me with PCP and had me committed."

Something sharp and bright flashed behind his eyes. He was suddenly awake. "What? How?"

"A fucking cheesecake parfait," she replied. "I was always a sucker for those. I thought she was trying to butter me up, but she had a more brutal plan."

"Why would she do that?"

She growled. "I refused a client."

"Your mom drugged you because you wouldn't do a surgery?" That sounded ridiculous, but then he'd seen far more ludicrous reasons for actually killing someone: drinking the last Bud Light, laughing at a girlfriend's fat ass, looking at someone the wrong way, wearing the wrong color on the wrong street.

"The job was worth seven million dollars."

He was stunned into silence. Seven. Million.

Dean would never betray someone like that—but for seven million dollars, he could see the temptation.

She huffed. "If you knew what that woman had gone through, you'd understand why I said no. Her experience makes Brittany's assault seem like a spa day."

Dean didn't try to imagine what would be worse because he could. "So, she drugged your parfait?"

She laughed, the edges hard and dry. "Yeah. I was sitting at the kitchen table, and suddenly the butter started moving, crawling on the table. I was like, 'What the hell.' And I turned to my brother, Ash, and he asked me if I was okay. I didn't hear him say it, but a big, pink bubble came out of his mouth. And I remember thinking he had eaten a trauma, and he wasn't supposed to do that, and I lunged for my mother, because I thought she'd hurt him. The cops showed up in minutes. And Mom said I was under the care of a psychiatrist and where to send me. And the cops didn't even glance at me when I told them she was lying."

Dean realized what the police would think. Mentally ill or on drugs. They would never consider that she'd been dosed, not with the concerned, ordinary family standing there.

"I lost my cool when they tried to cuff me. I had too many bad memories. It was as if someone had unlocked all the boxes where I kept the transfers, and they mixed together, and I couldn't stop screaming. I thought they were going to consume me, take over my body. I wasn't just out of control, but I couldn't tell what was real anymore. And I was terrified it wouldn't end."

"How long were you committed?"

"Two days. That piece of shit shrink was on my parents' payroll. He said I had to either agree to the surgery or stay locked up. Apparently, I was a danger to myself and others."

Dean brushed his hands over the side of her body to comfort her, wishing he could arrest the lot of them. He'd like to ratchet his cuffs tight on the mother. "You took the case?"

She sank into the bed as she nodded. "I'd have done anything to escape that place. But the day I turned eighteen, I left them with three clients on their hands and never went back. Not the fitting retaliation they deserved." She sighed. "The real therapist I found thought it healthier to cut all ties. Trying to fuck them over would do me more harm than good, blah, blah, blah."

"You regret it now?"

"No. She was right. I just have to hope that one day they'll need a kidney." In the following silence, he thought she fell asleep, but she added. "The shrink, however—I got him sent to jail and his license revoked, with a little help from a PI."

"Good." Dean pulled her close, burying his nose into her neck. People might have seen her temper and her fragility and assumed her an easy target. They didn't understand that Kiera was fiercer than any opportunistic predator. It took guts to stand up after a solid hit to the jaw. This woman rose a hundred times in a row and showed no signs of quitting.

Sleep stole over Dean until she whispered, "Sometimes I think I'm just outside the border of crazy."

He felt like that too at times, like the time he spent imagining the minds of killers was slowly tainting him, changing him into a stranger. But he wouldn't share that, not ever. He didn't want her to see him that way. "Everyone has a breaking point, Kiera. You might be the sanest person I've ever met."

She shut off the light, wrapped her arms tightly around his body, and snuggled close, not saying a word. He listened to her breathing deepen as he slipped into sleep, wondering what the hell he'd gotten himself into and how he'd gotten along without it.

CHAPTER THIRTY THREE

Kiera

KIERA WAS THE FIRST TO WAKE, AFTER SIX straight hours of sleep—longer than she'd slept in years. Dean lay on his back next to her, his breathing slow and steady. She watched him and marveled that he'd stayed, that they'd fit together so well— in sex, cuddling, and sleeping. Contentment wasn't something she experienced often.

She tried not to think of the significance of Dean making her come on the first attempt with so little effort. Garrett, the escort she hired occasionally, had never gotten her off, but he'd listened when she told him not to try. She couldn't be angry at Dean. Not when she practically levitated from the bed with her lightened soul.

After drinking in the heat of Dean and listening to the shush of his breath for a few more minutes like a stalker, she crept to her dresser and threw on a silk nightgown and panties, then padded to the kitchen. If she were alone, she would have worked out first, but she didn't want to do that with Dean there. It would smack of showing off or posturing. Plus, that knot in her chest that pushed her was gone. She had no illusions that the pit had vanished forever, but she enjoyed the break.

Wanting to please Dean, she made crêpes, stuffing one with sweetened cream cheese and strawberries, another with bananas and homemade Nutella, and a third with mascarpone cheese and cherries. They were big, so she hoped three would be enough between them.

Dean walked into the kitchen as she was plating them. His hair stuck up on one side, and he wore only his shorts, leaving his chest bare. He also sported the glasses, the ones that made her suddenly want to abandon breakfast, but Dean said, "That smells amazing. I'm starving."

They ate outside in the weak morning sun, the temperature perfect. Kiera owned few sexy nightgowns, because she didn't have overnight guests, so she was glad to have the short, black negligée. It flowed more than clung and had small scrolling flowers along the edges. Dean's eyes kept tracing over the neckline before coming back to her face.

"You're staring," she said once she couldn't bear the scrutiny. Eventually, he'd find a big ole flaw.

"Sorry, but you're so beautiful." He mock-frowned. "Why are you wearing that if you don't want me to look, anyway?"

He meant the comment as a joke, but it hit Kiera the wrong way. "Don't do that."

"Do what?"

"That 'she's asking for it' shit. Wanting to be attractive isn't the same as wanting to be gawked at or raped."

"Whoa." He held up his hands.

She should stop and try to salvage the morning. Comparing his admiration with rape was ridiculous. Her shame at overreacting made her react harder. Kiera compulsively double-downed when she was irrational. "You said 'sorry, but.' That 'but' negates everything. Like I was asking for you to gawk at me. Like when people say a woman should always be able to say no, *but*...why did she drink so much? Why did she walk through that alley? Why did she wear that dress? People always want the victim to share the blame."

He leaned back and crossed his arms. "Now you're a victim? Or do you not know how to be anything else?"

That blow struck deep and hard.

"I apologize." Dean took a breath. "That was uncalled for."

The weight in her gut returned, reminding her that life was pain and to expect anything else was stupid. That he was right made everything worse. She stood and grabbed her dish, her food only half eaten. "You want anything else while I'm up?"

"How about turning back time? Like, ten minutes?"

She almost smiled. "If I could do that, I'd be rich."

"You are rich."

"Makes you wonder, doesn't it?" She returned to the kitchen to mentally kick herself.

Dean followed her with his plate, not leaving her enough time to smack herself upside the head. He set his dish directly in the dishwasher and pulled her gently into his arms, giving her room to pull free. She didn't. He kissed where her neck and shoulder came together.

She held his face for a moment, needing to tell him the truth. "This is what I'm like sometimes." He gazed into her eyes, listening. "I'm not sure if this was a one-time thing or something more, but you need to know that it's not going to get any better. I'm sorry, but this is how it is for me. You should think about if this is worth the trouble."

Dean took a deep breath, probably to keep his irritation in check. "Let me tell you what a relationship with me is like."

Kiera nodded.

"I'll forget your birthday. It won't matter how many times you remind me. You could have your birthday tattooed on my hand, and I'll still forget. I'll also be working. I'll answer my phone every time it rings. Immediately. It won't matter what we're doing or what story you're in the middle of telling. I won't be around. If we don't catch a case, there's follow-up and paperwork and court and witnesses we can only reach at certain times. It's too late to save the victims, but I need to do everything I can to give the families closure and some kind of justice. When I took the homicide gig, I accepted all that. And when I'm not working, I want to sleep. I've also got family, a lawn to mow, and a kitchen remodel. You'll never be first."

As horrible as his story sounded, it made Kiera relax. Otherwise, he was too amazing. "I get all that, you know. I have to answer my phone too, though nobody calls often, but when memory surgeons freak out, we make an event of it."

"Let's see how this goes, okay? Because I do want more than a one-time thing." He reached out and tucked a strand of hair behind an ear, his fingers lingering down her neck. "I'm not asking you to change." He picked her up, slowly, letting her see his intentions, and set her on the counter. "Before I worked homicide, I worked violent crimes, which included sexual assaults."

She was grateful for the support of the counter. He stood between her legs, his hands still on her waist. She barely breathed.

His voice didn't rise, but he thrummed with conviction. "I want you to know that I think everyone—*everyone*—has the right to say no and that consent can be revoked at any moment."

Of course, he thought that. She exhaled. "It's okay."

Kiera mentally slapped her forehead. Not only had she not asked forgiveness, but now she'd somehow accepted his nonexistent apology. Could she be more fucked up? She dropped her face into her hands.

Dean gently pulled her hands away. He studied her. The thrill from last night reappeared and throbbed through her body. How had she not jumped him the moment they'd met? *Please don't let me have messed up everything already.*

Though she had to grip the edge of the countertop, Kiera managed not to beg him to give her a chance. Staying had to be his decision, his choice.

At last, he traced a finger around her ear. "I should do a little work today, but I've got a few hours to spare. Do you mind if I hang out here?"

She shrugged. "Well, I've got a sticking kitchen drawer you could fix." Then the grin she'd suppressed broke free. "Or I still have a bunch of condoms."

CHAPTER THIRTY FOUR

HE RAN THE DVR AGAIN, STARING AT THE television, transfixed by the image. A photo of him—the disguise of him. The cops would have to do better than that to catch him—he'd ditched that skin. The video played. He ignored himself. Brittany. Blond, beautiful Brittany. The footage was black-and-white, but he knew that hair. Hell, he still had a thick patch of it in his freezer. Seeing her alive gave him a thrill. She'd been so fucking easy. Chattering on and on, fluttering her eyelashes, and flipping that hair. Jilly's hair.

At church, Brittany had been the very picture of pure. Always in long skirts and dresses, she'd sat in the pew with her hands folded, and she'd gotten to her knees seconds before called to do so, delicate mouth open for the communion wafer. Outside of church, she was a whore. Flirting with everyone, laughing at them. Like Jilly, she had thought she was untouchable.

He smirked. Hadn't he made it clear that she was not? She was nothing—a single-use, disposable cum bucket. And now she was finally disposed. But he'd been robbed of his high.

Brittany's Facebook page was filled with condolences. The comments made his hands curl into fists. She hadn't been special. In fact, she had been typical, ordinary, and weak. She was a candle flame in the midst of a volcanic explosion. Nobody should have noticed her at all.

Still, he read every comment, licking up the fear, the terror, the horror. The sap was actually pretty funny. Her disappointing end made him return to Brittany's page more often than he should. The never-ending itch compelled him to drill through every post. He was rewarded for his diligence in slogging through the messages when he saw Sarah Kolchek's entry: *She never regained consciousness, but we were blessed to have the famous memory surgeon Kiera Brayleigh attend to her while in a coma. Brittany knew she was loved and loved us in return. It's been a great comfort in all this.*

He'd heard of Kiera Brayleigh. But from where? Google answered that question fast—hardly difficult, but worth his time.

A memory surgeon.

His dick got hard, picturing a memory surgeon beside him, watching his work, experiencing Jilly's death. He rubbed his temples. Brittany's death.

He had an audience. What did she think? Was she in awe? Scared? Overwhelmed? The parents didn't say. Only one stupid comment about passing on Brittany's love. Who gave a shit? Why were people always focused on the wrong things?

Tons of articles and reports about Kiera Brayleigh filled the internet but all from outside sources: doctors, researchers, politicians, victims. The accounts varied, and the photos were all unflattering—her head angled away, a hand in front of her face, a hat pulled down. Some sites claimed she could read your mind with a shake of the hand. Some said she was a fraud. A charlatan. Either way, she would make a proper adversary, a challenge.

"The Psychopath and the Empath," they would call their story. He would be on the book cover, his face filling the space with her limp, dead body in the bottom corner, a rope around her neck, hands and feet hog-tied together.

He was getting harder, images of those bright-blue eyes wide with fear gorging his manhood. She would tremble and whimper and beg, like all of them. He stroked himself fantasizing her body bloated with all those juicy memories, just waiting for him to pop her like the leech she was. His mind floated, riding the rush of power, control. Squeezing her throat, squeezing his penis, squeezing, squeezing, squeezing . . .

CHAPTER THIRTY FIVE

Kiera

T HEY MET AT A QUIET CAFE AT TWO O'CLOCK, when the place would be uncrowded. That was the compromise. Kiera's brother, Ash, wanted to get together at a bustling, exciting restaurant, and Kiera wanted to meet at her house.

Kiera wore a sleeveless wrap dress in power red and came in full makeup with her hair down and styled. She even put that shit in her hair that made it extra shiny. Ash stood when she entered. He was wearing khaki shorts and a Hawaiian shirt in blue and green.

He hugged her close, as if he'd missed her. Her grip on him tightened, the kind of protective reflex that always filled her when around her little brother. She'd missed him too. Ash was the only family she still claimed, and that garnered him a vast chunk of real estate in her heart.

"You're looking great, Kier," he said after their hug broke apart.

She wrinkled her nose. "You're looking . . . tropical."

He laughed. "I knew you would hate the shirt."

"And yet you still wore it."

"I'm a slave to fashion now."

She mock-shaded her eyes. "I don't think Hawaiian shirts can be considered fashion."

Kiera studied the menu in comfortable silence. When she decided what she wanted, Ash signaled the waitress, and they ordered. Ash got a turkey club, and Kiera chose the blue cheeseburger.

"I hope you're not eating too much red meat. It's not good for you." Ash totally should have been a doctor. He had kind blue eyes, a few shades lighter than Kiera's, and the same hair color, though Ash wore his gelled back, curled on the ends just past his neck. Kiera loved that he was handsome, as if he were her son and not her brother, as if his attractiveness and wit and charm were somehow a reflection on her.

"Me love cow," she said in a robot voice. It was a game they had enjoyed as children. Kiera had always played the evil robot, and Ash played the white knight. He had wanted Kiera to be a dragon, but for whatever reason, probably the fun voice, she wanted to be an evil robot—not Terminator evil, more Dr. Evil evil. Not that Dr. Evil was a robot.

"Fair Maiden, I fear I must tell you that your colon does not," he replied in his Prince Valiant voice.

"Colon-schmolon. Me want meat."

"But diverticulitis, that rake, that foe, that bastion of devilry. He awaits thee in the burger."

"Fuck him. And his horse."

"You must take heed. Fucking horses is not the answer." Ash's voice was too loud.

The sideways glances people threw their way put Kiera over the edge. She broke into laughter. "Relax. I'll have a salad for dinner."

Ash bowed his head solemnly, then rocked back in his chair. His grin made her chest cramped and shaky. He was like a ray of sunshine punching through gray clouds. Kiera stared at him, the binding between them wrapping and wrapping tight to her. He was the face of God, and she was the lobster thrown in the pot of cold water, content to sit as the water heated around her, staying and staying even as she screamed.

His smile dimmed. "What's wrong?"

Everything. "Nothing. I think your shirt is giving me a seizure."

"Don't worry, I know what to do. I'll lay you on your side and stick one of those giant breadsticks in your mouth, so you don't bite off your tongue."

"My hero."

He shrugged magnanimously. "What's family for?"

Kiera wanted to have a pleasant lunch, so she didn't respond.

"So." Ash threw an arm over the back of his chair. "How've you been?"

With those few words from Ash, his casual demeanor, the familiarity of him, the way he lived in the moment, the darkness fell away. She smiled, thinking about Dean. "Fine."

Ash stared at her for a few seconds. Nobody looked at her the way her brother did—part love, part frustration, part awe. "What's new, Kier Bear?"

She could have this, a real family connection. "I rode a Jet Ski the other day."

"You did?"

"It was so awesome. You should try it."

He squirmed in his seat like a kid. "I've been. You need to go parasailing next. You always did want to fly."

She had wanted a lot of things before she'd gotten her "gift." Kiera considered telling Ash about Dean, to see his amazed expression, but decided to wait until they had gone out a few times. If the relationship didn't work, she didn't want Ash to ask about it later or, God forbid, tell her fucking parents.

Ash never asked her about relationships because she didn't have them. Kiera never asked Ash about them, because he always volunteered any pertinent information in the sex department.

"Did I tell you Julie and I broke up?" he asked, proving her point.

"No. What happened?"

"She moved to Miami."

"Ouch. And she didn't invite you?"

"No, she did, but she was going anyway. It's not as if she talked to me before telling her job yes. True love doesn't work like that."

Another old argument. "True love doesn't work one way, Ash. Just because she decided to move without talking to you first doesn't mean she doesn't love you. Your standards are impossibly high." He could have been happy with any number of his past girlfriends if he'd let himself.

Ash held out his hands. "I know what's out there."

"So do I." She leaned forward. "But there's a whole world in between what you know and what I know."

He rolled his eyes. "Yeah, yeah, yeah."

Kiera wanted to scream and break things when Ash downplayed her surgeries, as if what he did was the same. The mechanics were the same—they both read memories, and they could both transfer a memory. But the difference made all the difference.

Ash was a memory preserver. He took fun memories, light memories, recollections of love, sex, adventure, and living life to the fullest. Those memories, he didn't store like Kiera did, but passed on to a loved one, giving some family member a literal piece of a loved one back—their actual thoughts and feelings—the most cherished memories. How he believed that those memories were the same as a trauma transfer baffled her. And she had to hold those memories herself, because who the hell would want that sort of legacy? She bore the weight of them every day.

She understood why he thought as he did, of course. Their mother. Their lying, manipulative bitch of a mom, telling Ash that Kiera was overly sensitive, prone to exaggeration, ungrateful for her gift and all the loving support her parents tried to give her.

When Kiera realized she had her fork in a death grip, she set it back on the table. She reminded herself that Ash wasn't the parentals, and they'd harmed him too, instilling in him a too-rosy outlook on life. He expected more than life could offer.

As their food arrived, Ash started in with the parent thing. "They miss you, you know. Mom especially."

Kiera snorted. "I'm sure they do. Heard their business has seen better days." She still had a company keeping an eye on her parents, to be sure they steered clear of her. If they were going to come for her, she wanted to be prepared.

Ash frowned. "They're doing all right. I see a client now and then through them."

Always the devoted son.

"Doesn't quite pay the same as the rougher stuff, though, does it?" People paid for memory preservations—rich people, anyway, but in the five-figure range, not six and above. Her shrink would probably say she shouldn't enjoy these petty victories, but whatever.

"It pays enough, Kier."

"Yeah, and how much of that do you see?"

Ash never discussed the financial arrangement between him and their parents. Since Ash had his own clients as well as his motivational speaking gigs, Kiera suspected her mom and dad kept most, if not all, of the money from those they found for him. "Can't we get past this? Start over again?"

Kiera's gritted her teeth. "Sure. When they have you committed, we can totally have the forgive-and-forget discussion. We'll laugh. We'll cry. We'll learn something about each other and ourselves."

Ash sighed and studied his plate too closely. "They're talking to someone about a book deal." His voice was quiet and careful.

Kiera froze. "You're shitting me."

He shook his head. "I told them the book was a bad idea, and they aren't doing it for sure. They're just considering the option."

Kiera pushed her plate back, her stomach now tight and sick. "Better talk to a fucking lawyer while they're at it, because if they mention anything about me, I'm going to bury them."

"They already did. The lawyers say if it's marketed as creative nonfiction and you aren't specifically identified, they can legally write pretty much anything." The fact that he wouldn't look at her told Kiera all she needed to know. He hadn't said anything to stop them.

"And you're okay with that? Them telling the world your story with their particular spin?"

He tugged his ear. "No, but Mom and Dad say that the world is curious, and they can shed some light and show everyone how hard it is for us."

"Us? Your strolls down happy-memory lane keeping you up at night, Ash? Want to join my therapy group, or can I make a referral for a shrink? I'd hate to think you're suffering alone in silence," she said.

"Please don't put me in the middle, Kiera."

She slammed both hands on the table. "You put yourself in the goddamn middle! Can't we have one fucking lunch without talking about those motherfuckers?"

He rested his hands over hers, and tears welled in his eyes. They ignored anyone who might have been gawking. "I'm sorry. I just thought you should know. If you talked to them, maybe they would—"

"No."

Ash closed his eyes for a moment, probably gathering his emotions. His pain echoed in Kiera—not a flash of his actual mind, but he was her little brother, two years younger, but a lifetime more naive. She had shielded him, taking all the negative cases, so he wouldn't have to be like her.

And her sacrifice had worked. He had a lightness like whipped cream to her cream cheese. He had a quick laugh and a quicker smile. He loved people, all people. Ash was comfortable everywhere. She had paid for that. Though she never regretted her choice—wouldn't have changed it—sometimes she existed on a plane so far out of the world as to leave her alone, as if Ash had taken both his place and hers.

"Ash." Her voice roughened, near tears. "I love you, but you break my heart. Please. *Please*, no more about Mom and Dad."

He nodded. They clasped hands across the table. Kiera tried to release the nasty whirlwind buffeting her, but it spun in tighter and tighter circles.

Ash kissed her hand. "You're right, of course. See? You're not the only messed-up one."

"Don't even think of going for the title, rookie. You can be fucked up, but I get Queen Fuckup for sure."

Using his prince voice, he said, "Long live the queen."

CHAPTER THIRTY SIX

Dean

DEAN SAT DOWN AT THE DESK IN HIS HOME OFFICE, the door closed, so he wouldn't see his demolished kitchen. He needed to concentrate. The FBI was sending a profiler, and Dean was an amateur.

He didn't understand serial killers, but rapists, he'd mastered. Easy enough to begin at that point with the profile. The man seemed like an anger-excitation rapist—well-planned, intending humiliation beyond anything else. He ticked several of that profile's boxes: the need for control, the bondage, the profanity, the trauma—particularly emotional.

Springboarding from that place, Dean combed through his notes and all the information he had compiled on serial killers. He wrote what he supposed. He wrote what might be. On the computer screen, he studied the scanned drawing Kiera had given him of the killer. Dean stared into the man's eyes and tried to imagine looking out of them.

Anger. So much anger, and a need for power and control and retribution. The need made Dean's knuckles throb. His body demanded an outlet, a physical expression of his darkness.

* * *

"I MISS YOUR GLASSES," KIERA SAID THREE DAYS AFTER THEIR NIGHT together. She had invited him over after his shift, though it was almost 2:00 a.m. Dating an insomniac had its advantages.

Dean drank in her presence, every breath a balm for the aches and pains of the day. "I wasn't aware you were a fan of glasses."

She shrugged. "They're sexy."

Sexy. He could work with that. "Should I go home and get them?"

Kiera smiled and tapped a finger against her lips, as if considering. In no hurry, he leaned against her doorjamb. She wore another sundress, this one black, and he considered dropping to his knees and crawling underneath it, but he didn't. He'd read once that women need twenty minutes for their bodies to prepare for orgasm—not that women were a monolith. Still, he liked the idea of building her arousal higher and higher, not just rushing in the moment she was good to go.

"I think you better come inside." Her face turned serious, and her nipples hardened. "Hungry?"

He moved close. "Famished."

Kiera stared at him for three seconds before molding her mouth to his, her body yielding, her chest rising and falling against his own, inviting his heartbeat to merge with hers.

She tugged gently on his hair, then broke away. "Would you rather eat first?"

He grinned. "Only if it's you. I don't give a fuck about food right now."

She moved a step back and bent at the waist. He licked his dry lips as she pulled down her panties, pale yellow and lacy. She kicked them as if they were rags, and they slid across the herringbone wood floor to swish against the baseboard. Dean removed his gun and holster off his belt and set them on the side table, in the fancy silver bowl. He brought his attention back to Kiera, his muscles bunching beneath his skin with repressed longing. But he held still, curious as to what she would do next.

Her face flushed. "Okay, now I'm not sure what to do."

"There's no wrong answer, babe." He'd just stopped himself from saying "baby," remembering she hated that. "Is 'babe' okay?"

"Doesn't trigger anything, so I think you're safe." Her piercing blue eyes glinted in the dim light of the foyer. "Say it again."

The energy tightened between them, the closer proximity making everything denser, like a storm in a bottle. "Can I touch you, babe?"

"Yes."

Another step. "Can I taste you, babe?"

Kiera panted as her hands clenched the sides of her dress. "Yes." Her voice was a dry croak, filled with anticipation.

He moved until they almost touched. "Any memories doing it while standing?" New experiences probably didn't trigger any trauma.

She shook her head. "But I'm not sure how long I can stand." Her voice was small, and she glanced away, staring down the hall at a small window. "My legs are shaking."

"Hmm. You want to perch on the couch, or I can lay you on the counter or the coffee table or outside against the railing or—"

She laughed, a little higher than her usual laugh, but genuine and warm. "Given it some thought, have you?"

"Yes."

"Well, not outside. If someone in one of the taller buildings behind this one was at the right angle, at the right time, they might see us."

Dean didn't care, but he nodded. "Couch?"

She bit her lip. "Okay."

He caressed her jaw, his touch feather light. "Only if you want to, Kiera. I don't need to do that to make you come."

Her dress twitched as if she squeezed her thighs together. God, that was hot. He kissed her. The kiss slammed into Dean like a billy club to the gut. He groaned and pulled her entire body into his. One of her legs slid up his own, bringing their hips into contact. She pressed into his erection, grinding into him. He had only moments to regain control.

"Couch," he whispered, his mouth never far from hers as he backed her to the fur-covered monstrosity. When her back hit the arm, he dropped down to his knees. He would enjoy taking as much time as she needed.

He brushed his fingers over the tops of her bare feet, then circled her ankles. Her lips parted, and he listened to the sound of her ragged breath.

"Keep going," she panted.

He moved his hands up her muscled calves. The combination of hard muscle and velvety skin made his erection throb. Already he scented her excitement, his head only a few inches from the juncture of her thighs. He wouldn't touch her there until she was wild, but he could tease. His fingers crawled past her knees and up past her hips. He kept his hands on her inner thighs as long as possible without stroking her intimately, then shifted to her outer thighs, his touch traveling over her hips to her waist.

"How do you know how to do that?" When he didn't answer, she continued. "I'm serious. I'm pretty sure my glowing body can be seen from space."

Dean rose up high on his knees and pressed his smile into her belly. "It's just chemistry, Kiera." He kissed her through the fabric of her dress.

"Don't your knees hurt?"

He grimaced. "Yes, actually."

She reached back and snagged a magenta pillow and dropped it to the floor. As Dean jammed the pillow under his knees, she pulled her dress over her head. No bra. She was naked in front of him. The flatness of her stomach made the swell of her breasts more pronounced. His hands skimmed down the sides of her body, then back up again.

"Oh, God, babe." He'd almost said "baby" again. "Tell me you're ready. Tell me yes. Please." So much for taking his time.

The insecurity she'd shown earlier was replaced by a carnal smirk. "Yes."

The scent of her arousal triggered something in his body. Lightly, he brushed across her. She was soaked. "Shit," he groaned. "God, that's nice." He slid a finger inside, slow and easy as he ran his tongue around her clitoris.

"Oh, fuck," she cried out in a throaty moan. Her thighs parted a little more, giving him easier access.

He moved slowly, gauging her response, circling his tongue as his finger moved in and out of her. She twitched and made nonsensical noises, all the while coating his finger in her juices. His cock strained against his pants. No doubt she was ready, and he wanted her hot wetness encasing him. He added another finger and crooked them, rubbing her rough, spongy G-spot.

"Oh God, don't stop," Kiera whimpered as her legs shook.

Her pelvis pushed into his face, and she made a high-pitched sound. She whispered, "Please," but he had no idea what she wanted, so he continued. Kiera groaned and jerked, her hips moving in time to his movements. "Yes, yes, yes. Oh, God, what are you doing to me?"

He fought a smile. She clenched down, hungry and desperate. He switched his tongue to an up-and-down movement and reached up and pinched her nipple. Kiera screamed, her orgasm evident in the rhythmic squeezing of his finger and the spasms of her body.

When she'd come down from coming, she smiled, a shy wispy upturn of her lips that made Dean want to wrap her in his arms. "Do you want me to"—she glanced down at the tent of his pants—"reciprocate?"

Oral sex was hard for her, she'd told him. Besides, he wanted to slide into her. He stood, shaking out his cramped legs. She stroked her hand over his erection, and he hissed in pleasure. He sucked in an earlobe, careful not to bite. When she arched into him, he said into her ear, "I'd rather fuck."

Kiera hummed, and her hands gripped his torso for a moment. She always responded like that when he said the word "fuck."

"Such a dirty mouth." She kissed him hard.

The idea of her tasting herself made his dick throb. She fisted her hands in his hair, her mouth kissing down his jaw, nipping now and again, sharp little bites that skated electricity through him. She kissed the hollow of his throat and worked down. He closed his eyes and enjoyed the tickle of her lips on his chest and the slow unveiling of his skin as she unbuttoned his shirt. Desire pulsed through him, growing. He couldn't remember ever wanting anyone like this—a blind, ravaging hunger. What was he doing to her? What was *she* doing to *him*?

"Kiera, please," he moaned as she licked his ribs.

She kissed him again. One hand gripped his neck, the other on his chest. "Do you have a condom on you? Mine are all the way in the bedroom, and I want you now."

He fumbled for his wallet, his hands shaking. Anticipation, he assumed because he wasn't nervous. She worked his pants to the floor. He stepped free as he found the condom tucked into a secret pocket of his wallet, since having a condom right there for anyone to see was unprofessional. *Hi, I'm Detective Dean Matthson, and I practice safe sex.*

Once he extracted the condom, he dropped his wallet to the floor and ripped off the edge of the foil. He kicked his pants and shoes to the side like Kiera had kicked her panties. She surveyed him rolling the condom over himself with rapt attention.

Any chance of taking their time vanished when she leaned against the armrest, grabbed his cock, and guided him into her right where she stood. She was as tight as he remembered, and her interior muscles rippled against him with tiny aftershocks of her previous orgasm.

He kissed her again, slow and languid, like a summer day too hot to allow much movement. The couch was a few inches too short for comfort, and his back protested for a moment until he spread his legs farther apart. Her hips tilted in rhythm to his, and with her delicious wetness, he moved easily through the tightness. He'd never felt anything so good. His cock twitched.

"Faster? Slower? Harder?" he asked between kisses.

She groaned. "Faster. Harder. Fuck me." When she said "fuck," she didn't whisper, she demanded.

He held her steady and pistoned his hips into her, a deep moan vibrating from his lips to hers. He wanted to make the connection last, daze her with his stamina, but she felt too good. If he was going to stop himself, he needed to do it now.

"I'm close," he said, the words popping out in a jumble, begging for permission. The moment stretched as he hovered over the precipice, his skin electric with tingles, and in a moment, he would fall.

"Come for me, Dean," she demanded, gripping the hair on the back of his head.

He exploded, the orgasm coming from everywhere at once, pulling energy from the soles of his feet to the top of his head. The warm, tingling ecstasy making him boneless and in danger of falling over. He kissed her again, less urgent but no less intense. Her lips against his made his entire body thrum.

Dizziness passed through him. Damn. He needed food and sleep—maybe just sleep. But his body continued to spark, wanting to do what they'd done again.

Kiera smiled against his mouth.

"What?" he asked.

"That went so well."

He barked a laugh and gingerly removed the condom. As he walked into the kitchen to deposit it in the garbage, he spotted various containers of food on the counter. "What's this?"

* * *

DEAN LOVED THE ASSURED WAY SHE MOVED IN THE KITCHEN. HE SAT ON a stool like a guest on a cooking show set, wearing only his boxer briefs and his unbuttoned shirt. Kiera wore an oversized T-shirt with a pink-maned unicorn riding a motorcycle.

"Tell me about your family," she said as she stirred rice into a saucepan with a generous amount of butter.

With her actively complicated family, she probably wouldn't understand his passive-aggressively complicated family. "My parents were high school sweethearts who will be celebrating their fortieth anniversary in September. I've got two sisters who are two and five years older than me. My oldest sister, Rose, is married and has a son, my nephew Cal."

"Are you close?"

He looked away, trying to decide how to best describe his family. "Yes and no?"

Kiera poured wine into the pan without measuring. "Are you asking me?"

Dean shook his head, more to clear his thoughts than an indication of no. He toyed with the edges of his shirt. "I love my family, and they're supportive of me. We all get along, and I enjoy their company, but I couldn't say I was close with any of them except Rose."

"Why not?" She ladled heated chicken stock into the rice and stirred.

He'd heard enough of her origin story to surmise she wouldn't hold any sympathy for his familial drama. "You're going to think I'm a douche."

Kiera paused for a moment. "Well, you've got to tell me now."

He sighed. "My parents are traditional, like a fifties couple, with those sorts of values. I don't think they would have had a third child if Peg had been born a boy." And Peg liked to voice that view at almost every family gathering, though rarely when their parents were in earshot.

"They needed a male heir?" Kiera managed not to laugh.

"Something like that. My sisters used to call me the little prince because of the preferential treatment." Did he expect her to sympathize because he was worshiped by his parents? "I know that's a very first-world problem, but it created this kind of expectation that I found—that I still find—hard to live up to. I don't visit as often as I should though they only live in Barrington." He plucked at a thread poking out of one of his buttons. "Every September, we have a family picnic. There's a few birthdays around that time, and it's just before back to school, and I always miss it, even before I had the great excuse of always working." Not that he'd get out of it this year, not with the anniversary celebration tied into it.

"And they made you feel bad about it?"

"Worse. They told me how proud they were of how hard I worked and how I was making the city safer."

"Aren't you?"

Was he? Of course, he was, though some days the slog felt more like trying to run in a dream than anything else. "A little, maybe. Honestly, it's mostly paperwork and legwork. But the issue is that I could have taken time and gone to most of the parties." He slid his elbows back on the counter, which gaped his shirt.

Kiera continued to stir, but her eyes fixated on his chest. He reveled in the attention.

She added another ladle of stock. "So, you don't take time because you don't want to go. Seems like a harmless enough lie to me."

After breaking ties with her family, she couldn't understand. "They don't ask for much, and they're so fucking grateful if I call or when I stop by, but their expectations are crushing. All the worse because they're unvoiced. Mostly."

"Do you think they actually have these expectations, or are you projecting them?"

"Every time I see my mother, she asks me when I'm going to transfer to a nicer department, when I'm going to move out of the city, and if I'm dating anyone, which is just a vehicle for that all-important grandkid and continuing the family name."

His nephew Cal wasn't enough, though he was the cutest toddler ever. And poor Peg had gone and become a doctor, and that still wasn't enough for his parents. His father had even told Peg once that she'd have a hard time finding a husband because men would be intimidated by her profession. No matter how many Thanksgivings and Christmases Dean missed, he remained the golden child. He was the one destined to carry on the Matthson legacy, whatever the hell that meant. And they were sure one day he'd do something worthy of all their hopes and dreams.

Kiera had stopped stirring and gaped at him. It joggled his recall. *Oh. Oh, shit.*

He slapped a hand to his face. "I did not just bring up having kids."

"You did." She concentrated on the risotto. "You've got to know that I'm never having kids, right? E-ver."

Dean sucked in his cheeks to keep from smiling, the late hour making his sense of humor punchy. He slid off his stool and looked her up and down. "Maybe not today, but in five or ten years, you might change your mind." He was playing a dangerous game, but her flushed face spoke of a playful joy aching to break through the discomfort. "I mean, it would be a shame to waste such lovely birthing hips." When he reached over to grab her hip, she slapped his hand away with the wooden risotto spoon. "Ow!"

"You are the worst!"

They both started laughing.

He kissed her shoulder. "I don't care about having kids. I love my nephew, but I've never felt a drive to have any of my own. And even if I did, I've got no time to raise one, so it would only be ego, passing on my genes or some other such bullshit."

She wiped off the spoon on a kitchen towel and then resumed her ladling and stirring. "You would make a good dad," she said in a too-quiet voice.

He plopped back down on the barstool. "And you'd make a great underwear model. Being good at something doesn't require you to do it."

She peered up at him through her lashes. "Underwear model, huh? I don't think my tits are big enough."

"Really? Let me see."

Kiera rested the spoon on the edge of the pan and lifted up her unicorn T-shirt, exposing everything. She arched her eyebrows.

"Size doesn't matter when your breasts are so fucking perfect." His cock swelled, completely forgetting they'd just had sex.

"How can you tell from all the way over there?"

The risotto burned.

CHAPTER THIRTY SEVEN

Kiera

KIERA REORGANIZED HER LIFE TO ACCOMMODATE Dean. It was premature—way premature. But she had too much time, too much money, and her desperation turned her edgy, and the edginess required action. She'd cleared out a drawer in her dresser and the bathroom, made room in the closet.

On her way to group, she obsessed about Dean. So far, she hadn't fucked up—no rages or panic attacks or paranoid rantings. But each day that slipped by without an incident only brought her closer to whatever nightmare she would unleash. Admitting she had something to lose made her lungs itch. She'd wanted to ask the group about sex and relationships for so long, never able to voice her concerns, her needs. But now she didn't have a choice. She needed help to ensure he stayed.

From the back of her hired Caddy, Kiera stared out the window, witnessing life unfolding. Kiera spent an inordinate amount of time watching people, normal people, especially women. She would never be normal. Normal had been razed to the ground, salted, and napalmed. Kiera had to settle for coping.

At least, she had the Center, Ash, Nadira and Beth, her lovely condo, and money. Dean. As fucked up as she was, she had a lot. She should be thankful. As Dr. Patty said, gratitude begets gratitude. Negative self-talk had kept her spirits spelunking. She accepted that truth, but the whole idea of putting Post-it notes all over her home with phrases like "I find joy in life" made her want to slit her wrists. Her brother's Kumbaya, we're-all-one-being, it's-all-about-love philosophy gave her hives. A positive attitude couldn't enforce a restraining order or unrape a woman.

Kiera thought of her mentor, Doreen, and her dark soul. She had worn only black, sworn like a sailor with a rope burn, and said what she thought, always. But though she had tried to twelve-step, she'd died during relapse number three. Kiera missed her.

Doreen had accepted no rules; she had lived like a message in a bottle caught in a whirlpool, destined to drown, break apart, or disappear. Probably there had been a middle ground available, but both Kiera and Doreen liked to live on the edges, not in the middle. The middle was open territory, and who the hell wanted to be exposed like that, even metaphorically?

Doreen had been the one to caution Kiera not to consent to the studies. She had seen the dangers early, the gleam in the scientists' eyes, the perilous paths where someone might want to lead them. Doreen's specialty had been torture. Before her demise, she'd helped political refugees. Kiera had a few tortures mixed into her rapes, forging a continent of common ground.

They'd talked about the stench of blood, shit, and piss. They'd talked about the crack of bone; the way a certain cadence of footfall could make you taste tin in the back of your mouth. Doreen hadn't believed in happy endings, but what if she had? Would she have lived?

Kiera needed to find a space between Ash and Doreen, between toxic positivity and toxic negativity. She needed to strip life down to bare truths. She needed a reality she could bear to live in.

Nadira had agreed to meet her fifteen minutes early. Kiera wanted to see Nadira's face, witness her reaction, when she told her. Nadira had been pushing Kiera to find a "real" lover for ages, but something coiled too tightly in Kiera's belly when she thought about telling her friend. Her opinion mattered. She might not understand how her relationship with Dean had evolved. In person, Nadira would be able to see Kiera's happiness.

"I had sex," Kiera said by way of hello, right in the lobby.

"Unpaid?"

"Yes, unpaid. Otherwise, it's not all that noteworthy; is it?"

Nadira froze and then bounced on the toes of her stilettos before clapping her hands together. "Details, Kiera. I need all the particulars. Who is he? How was it? Are you going to see him again? Is he well endowed?" Nadira arched her eyebrows.

Kiera blushed. She hesitated a moment, recognizing the tough spot, revealing Dean's name. She just had to rush through it. "That detective that came to group—Dean?" She said it like a question.

Nadira slapped a hand over her mouth. "You're kidding! He was kind of attractive." Her eyes danced.

Kiera's belly unknotted, and she almost laughed in relief. Nadira hadn't cared at all. Kiera should have credited her friend more. They could have enjoyed the gossip days ago. "Yes, he is."

"So, how was it?"

Kiera couldn't stop her smile. Nadira giggled and dragged Kiera into the meeting room. They each pulled a folding chair off the stack and set them close together. They sat, their knees almost touching, their heads bent like schoolgirls.

"He was amazing," Kiera mock-whispered, though they were alone. She was tempted to tell Nadira about the orgasm, since it was the kind of detail Nadira shared with her. But opening the conversation invited scrutiny, which might reveal chasms in her relationship. "He's stayed overnight twice."

Nadira's smile faltered, and she curled a lock of hair around her finger. "You let him stay?" When she saw Kiera's confused expression, Nadira continued. "That sounds serious, Kiera. Just be sure you're protecting your heart."

Her friend's attitude switch pricked Kiera. "So, sex is okay, but I shouldn't expect more than that?" Fuck, she'd had the same thought.

"Of course not." Nadira let the hair slip free. "Or maybe? I don't know. None of us has had a successful relationship."

"Maybe all the hooked-up memory surgeons are in another therapy group," Kiera said, trying to shake the tension between them and avoid the dread that clung to her.

Nadira smiled. "Then we should hook up Amy."

Kiera laughed, and it almost lifted the black cloud with sparking lightning overhead. Maybe Kiera had been stupid to embrace Dean so completely, but maybe being stupid was okay sometimes. She hadn't mentioned all the nights he'd stayed over and how she'd installed a gun safe for him.

The awkwardness of her exchange with Nadira made Kiera second-guess everything. She couldn't bring Dean up and couldn't *not* bring him up. Her lungs pumped like bellows. Everyone sat down in their usual spots, their conversations muted and casual. Kiera strained to hear what people were saying, but her ears buzzed, and she couldn't decipher words. She pressed a finger hard into the space between her eyebrows. Her hands shook, but the cold comforted.

Kiera squirmed under their stares. Maybe she'd said something out loud, or she'd done something to attract their attention. Dr. Patty studied her with her lips pursed together. Oh God, Dr. Patty was going to say something soothing, or new age, or trite, and Kiera's head would explode off her body and splatter all over the world's most boring room.

"I met someone." The words tumbled out of her mouth like a drunk falling down stairs.

Nadira smirked, but everyone else looked at her as if her head had, in fact, left her body.

"How do I not ruin it?" Tears pricked her eyes. Oh, hell no. She was not going to cry in group. "I don't have an inkling of how to hold shit together."

"What are you afraid will happen?" Dr. Patty asked.

Not a bad question. "Eventually, I'm going to freak out on him."

"And how do you fear he'll respond?" Dr. Patty asked.

"She's right to be worried," Ramon said with enough force that nobody interjected. He took a deep breath. "You're probably better off telling him ahead of time you're a memory surgeon."

"He already knows," Kiera said. If she wanted this thing with Dean to work, then she had to push her boundaries. She had to try. "It's Dean, that detective who came here."

"He was fine," Beth said and held up her hand for a high-five.

Kiera sputtered a laugh and slapped Beth's hand.

Amy huffed. Kiera supposed Amy thought she'd stolen Dean from her, that if Amy had done the reading, Dean would have courted her. Another day, she might have laughed. Kiera turned her attention back to Ramon.

"What else?" she asked.

"It's easier if they know what's coming. Don't downplay it, either, or he might think you were tricking him. That's happened to me before." Ramon had a nice voice, deep and rich. His eyes were far away.

Kiera's mouth dried. Ramon spoke from experience. While Ramon had been wrestling his demons, some woman had accused him of tricking her into thinking he was more normal than he was. When he'd needed her, that bitch, whoever she was, had abandoned him. Kicked him in the cojones. Scarred him. All of them were vulnerable like that.

"Someone thought that?" Beth said, her voice a scratchy version of Ramon's. "You shoulda said something to us. That's a terrible thing to go through alone."

All of them nodded at Beth's words.

"I was so humiliated." Ramon dropped his head in his hands. But after only a moment, he snapped up to sitting. "But sometimes, reaching out makes it better. The right person can ground you in the here and now. The hard part is finding out if they're the right person."

Dean was the right person; he wouldn't abandon her. He'd seen what she was like after a reading. "Then what? How do you continue?"

Ramon's eyebrows rose, and a smile brought a twinkle to his brown eyes. "You're talking about sex."

Her face flamed. "Uh, that part is actually pretty good so far." But they all knew that wouldn't last. "What happens when something . . . goes wrong?"

Ramon shrugged. "You learn your triggers and stay away from them."

Kiera sighed. "How much of that is he going to put up with? I've already got a huge list of names he can't call me and things he can't do and things I can't do."

Amy made a squeaking sound but didn't say anything, which was a rare treat.

Before Amy could change her mind and talk, Kiera asked, "Anything I can do to make it easier for him? You know, when I start sweating and screaming like a lunatic?"

"If you let him help you, you'll both feel better," Ramon said. "You can call me, if you want."

Kiera wasn't sure if he meant she could call him later or when she lost it. Either offer made her chest burn. "Thanks."

There had to be more, but Dr. Patty opened group, and in moments, Amy was talking about her lactose intolerance.

Though rude, since everyone had given her their attention, she tuned out group. Her car-crash life continued to unfold in her mind—the inevitability of some sort of scene. Maybe she could manage it, as Ramon said, and let Dean into her fucked-up world and hope he wouldn't dash out for a pack of cigs and never return.

Dean would stay or go. The decision was out of her control. The suspense of his ultimate decision, however, might kill her.

CHAPTER THIRTY EIGHT

Dean

DEAN RECOGNIZED THE WOMAN IMMEDIATELY despite her looking little as she had when he'd last seen her, sitting next to him at the crisis hotline. Back then, she'd worn yoga pants and a UIC sweatshirt so large she had to roll the sleeves at the wrist. She always kept an array of snacks surrounding her phone station: Cheetos, Combos, and Charleston Chews she'd frozen and then smashed into bite-size pieces.

Now, she was dressed in a fitted, white, button-down shirt tucked into black slacks and black wingtip shoes with a low heel. Her sloppy, blond ponytail had morphed into a slick version with the elastic hidden by a lock of hair. Her Glock and badge were snapped onto her belt. Grace Page was a Fed. His Fed?

"Hey, stranger." Grace wrapped him in a hug. "I was so happy to see your name in the file."

"You're our profiler?" Dean hoped she attributed his surprise to knowing her and not that she was female. He had assumed the profiler would be a man, and that assumption shamed him.

"Yep. Who would've thought fifteen years ago we'd find ourselves here? Small world, right?"

"Yeah, but in a good way."

Grace mowed through high points of the years since they'd seen each other. She'd gotten a PsyD in forensic psychology, had been with the bureau for over seven years, and lived in Virginia, working out of Quantico. Grace assisted with serial cases: robbers, rapists, killers. She'd been gregarious and sensitive back at UIC, always engaging callers and always knowing the best words to make them feel heard and understood. She was a great fit as a profiler.

Dean's summary of his life took less time because he'd gotten his bachelor's degree in psychology and had done nothing with it, joining the force not even a year out of college. He had a stellar confession rate, but Grace's position as a profiler might have made that a cute accomplishment since she analyzed criminals full-time for a living. His biggest pride was his long-term partnership with Curt, though that was more something that just happened rather than anything he'd done. Still, that was how he focused his share of the conversation.

Dean shifted to business. "You been looking through the files?"

She gestured to the chair to her left. "Yes. Sit, sit. I've been dying to talk to you about the memory surgeon."

His world jolted to a swift stop. "That's what you want to discuss?"

"Hey, I've studied serial killers in depth, but a memory surgeon?" She smacked her lips as if she'd eaten something delicious. "Fascinating. I think they're vastly underutilized tools. So far, anyway."

Tools. Dean swallowed down the acrid taste in his mouth. "Yeah?"

Curt arrived, thankfully killing the moment, and Grace introduced herself to his partner.

"What made you call in a memory surgeon?" Grace asked Curt, resurrecting the conversation Dean would rather remain dead.

Curt shook his head but straightened his shoulders. "I thought it was all bullshit, but having met one . . ." He sighed. "Kiera knew details she couldn't possibly have guessed, and when we followed them up, we found evidence."

"You don't have to convince me," Grace said. "I've seen the studies, and we've got files on most of them."

Dean's gut trembled like an 8.6 earthquake. "Files?" Did the Feds know about him and Kiera? "There's surveillance on them?"

Grace waved her hand. "Homeland Security doesn't have the budget for that, but they dug into their financials, tax returns, some of their internet usage, things like that. Nothing intrusive."

Sounded intrusive to Dean, and Kiera certainly wouldn't find such attention unintrusive. Not that he could tell her about it. He wasn't going to feed her paranoia, with the damage already done and nothing to gain with the knowledge. Still, part of him raged on her behalf.

And yet, he apprehended why the government surveilled them, the threat they saw in Kiera, considering what she could glean about terrorists in custody, politicians, and world leaders. In theory, nobody could keep a secret from a memory surgeon.

"Learn anything interesting?" Dean asked. The inquiry into sensitive information wasn't a betrayal of Kiera. Anything he discovered could help him protect her. His curiosity was exclusively for her benefit.

Grace waggled her eyebrows. "She pays for sex."

Dean had too many thoughts at once: Kiera hadn't mentioned paying for sex; they hadn't discussed their past lovers; and just because Grace used the present tense, that didn't mean anything. The file was static, not an ongoing investigation.

"Huh," Curt said, his jaw moving back and forth as if he were chewing, which was just his I'm-considering-this-new-information tell. "I can see that. She's got money, and I don't see her setting up a Tinder profile."

"A girl's gotta do what a girl's gotta do," Grace added.

Dean should have contributed to the conversation, but his instincts and loyalties were too disparate for him to form words. Cop humor pushed him to join the banter, but he cared too much about Kiera to mock her. "Have you had a chance to review the case files?"

"I've looked them over." She grinned. "But I've got your memory surgeon coming by in a few hours, and I want to start there before I dig in."

Dean thought he might have to spend the next twenty minutes in the bathroom to either shit or vomit or both. Kiera occupied a separate part of his life now and the thought of her there, of acting . . . he didn't know what he feared most, her temper and scathing wit or that she might want to curl into him for comfort.

He couldn't comfort her and keep Grace's respect and probably his team's. Other officers would notice, and the rumor mill would crank to life. If his relationship ended up in the Second City Cop blog, then the *Sun-Times* might pick it up, then Channel Seven and then his mom would call him and ask questions about her, wanting him to bring her to the family picnic, asking him how serious they were and if she was "the one." Meanwhile, his career would tank, with officers smirking at him, Dennison giving him shit at every opportunity, and poor Curt getting sucked into the mud with him because Curt would stick by him and support his decisions, even if he disagreed and thought Dean was a fucking idiot.

The problem wasn't really Kiera but their ignorant society and people's habits of judging others no matter how little evidence available. The world didn't know or accept Kiera, not really, though they had no trouble using her. Just like Grace. Just like him. He would find a way to support her and still hold onto his status in the department.

But then Garrissey arrived. The lead detective on the second victim's case was the most egotistical detective Dean had ever met—and that was saying something. He would make a smooth interview impossible, and he would insert himself everywhere, positioning himself to take lead, if the cases were consolidated. Dean wanted that role, and his past with Grace gave him an edge he needed since he wasn't "connected" to the bosses like Garrissey. Kiera, however, could ruin everything.

CHAPTER THIRTY NINE

Kiera

THE NEIGHBORHOOD SURROUNDING THE CENTRAL Area Detective Building was derelict and depressed. Kiera wouldn't want to work there. Litter clung to the sides of the road—Styrofoam cups, Mello Yello cans, crumpled McDonald's bags. Youths ambled down the sidewalks in tank tops and jeans at half ass.

Inside the squat brick building obviously built in the seventies and never updated, officers in their starched uniforms and visible guns answered phones, walked with purpose down halls, laughed in loud voices. It was another world. A fake world.

Kiera gave her name to the front desk clerk, a high-cheek-boned black woman. The officer displayed a brief flash of teeth before going back to her bored bureaucrat routine. The officer went to a side desk to call upstairs.

Walking to the benches in the waiting area, Kiera tried to calm her breathing. She didn't want to talk to a profiler. Her aversion was almost as strong as the idea of having another memory surgeon in her head. She hoped Dean wouldn't be upset with her. Though she should have told him she'd been called down, she couldn't shake the possibility that someone might notice if he wasn't surprised.

Dean in his natural habitat. It might make up for her dislike of new places. For a few minutes, she stared at the asphalt parking lot and entertained a few fantasies of them talking in coded messages, his fingers "accidentally" brushing over the back of her neck.

"Ms. Brayleigh?"

A tall and trim stranger in a dove-gray suit stood on the public side of the wooden partition between civilians and law enforcement. His tanned hand extended as he walked toward her. "I'm Detective Aaron Garrissey, homicide." With his buffed nails and whitened teeth, he seemed more like a Hollywood detective than a real one.

"Nice to meet you," she said, accepting his handshake.

He grinned at her as if she were an old friend and warmly squeezed her hand twice. "Let me show you upstairs."

Garrissey deftly placed a hand on her elbow, as if he had been cast in the role of Gentleman. Kiera scolded herself to keep an open mind but shifted her purse over her shoulder to break contact with him. Dean hadn't mentioned a Garrissey, so he wasn't one of his teammates. Who the hell was this guy?

"We sure appreciate you coming down to speak with us today." Garrissey had a deep voice, soothing but with an affected quality, as if he'd practiced it, honed it. "I understand you've gone over a few things with Detectives Matthson and Haze, but we think there might be more details that can help."

"Who is 'we'?"

Garrissey laughed as if she'd made a joke.

The detective division was on the second floor. If they'd taken the stairs, they would have been there by now. But, no, Kiera had to be stuck on the world's slowest elevator next to a used-car salesman with a badge.

It only got worse.

The elevator opened to a hallway on the second floor, where Kiera heard the tumble of conversations in the distance. They walked past an empty reception desk, then into a large room jammed with people. Most of the spots among the rows of tables were filled with armed people in front of computers. Phones rang. People talked simultaneously. Detectives jostled one another and clogged the aisles. The air was heavy and didn't move. Where was the air conditioning? The room smelled of sweat and coffee and something else . . . something metallic. Guns?

On one side was a wall of cops, Dean and Curt among them. Everyone was so tall. Was there some sort of height requirement to work homicides? Someone brushed past her, his arm touching hers. It was hard to breathe.

"Ms. Brayleigh," a blond woman said. Her cute ponytail did nothing to diminish the authority she projected. She extended her hand, revealing short and neat nails. "I'm Special Agent Grace Page. Thanks for coming down."

Page's hand was warm, but Kiera's had gone cold. She hadn't sweated much yet, so at least, her handshake wasn't clammy.

"You've met Detectives Matthson and Haze," Page said, gesturing to Dean and Curt along the wall.

The guys both shook her hand as if they hadn't met. First, Curt, which was fine. But Dean? He didn't even squeeze her hand. Kiera had anticipated support, and without it, she wobbled, unmoored and fragile in the face of ominous clouds and an ill wind.

"The rest of Brittany Kolchek's team," Dean said, taking over the introductions, his voice alien. "Detectives Jason Roegarden and Kristin Sanchez." He gestured to a huge white dude next to a sleek Hispanic woman.

Kiera pulled up the bits of information Dean had given her back when he had acknowledged her presence. Kristin and Jason, the ones who liked to work out. Jason also had the wife who had been raped. She detected no sign of the pain of that. Likewise, she got no read on Kristin, who had large brown eyes but wore the same bland expression as her partner. Kiera had heard enough about Dean's team that she'd anticipated the comfort of the familiar, but they were strangers. Everyone a stranger.

Dean brushed her elbow, the barest touch. She hated how much she yearned for that brief touch again.

She focused intently on his words, distracting herself with the details and keeping names and faces straight in her mind. Anything to not acknowledge her vulnerability.

"And this is Detective Liu Sung and Detective Tamara Brandon."

Liu and Tamara. Tam, true to Dean's description as the friendliest of the group, smiled. She was a slim black woman with short hair and bright-red lipstick.

"It's so nice to put a face with the notes," Tam said.

Liu's hands were cool but dry. He said nothing as they shook hands, but his lips softened. His deep crow's feet only made him more attractive—he looked like a man used to smiling.

Any grounding she might have gained was ruined when Page stepped too close and put a hand on her arm. Why were all these cops touching her? She wanted to rub her arms and take three steps backward. Too many new people in a chaotic environment. This was why she only went to her usual places.

"Detective Garrissey is from the Area North Division and is the lead detective on another case involving the same perpetrator," Page said with a game show gesture. "There's one more lead detective from the first case, but she can't make it today."

Kiera breathed a sigh of relief that at least one cop in the city wasn't there.

Garrissey showed off his glow-in-the-dark white teeth. "Kiera and I have already introduced ourselves." As if they were friends.

She was relieved not to have to touch him again.

"I've arranged for a conference room for us," Page said, and the wall of cops moved.

"Hold on," Kiera said, her voice sharper than she'd intended. She addressed Page since she had been the one to call Kiera. "You said you just had a couple of questions."

Page walked back to her. "Too many people?"

Garrissey appeared on her other side, as if to box her in. She startled. "Do I need a lawyer?" she asked Page, though she wanted to ask Dean.

"Not if you've nothing to hide," Garrissey said in a friendly tone.

A shiver slid down her spine.

"You don't need a lawyer," Page said.

She remembered Dean talking about interrogations and how there were rules, but the interviewees rarely knew them. He could lie, to a point—not about rights, but about procedures, probable outcomes, things like that. He controlled his interviews. And now she perceived their hunting behavior, the way they circled like orcas around a baby harp seal.

"You know what? I'm not feeling this." She swirled her hand to encompass the entire group.

"He's killed three women," Garrissey said, not raising his voice, not losing his smile. He moved closer. "Don't you have an obligation to those victims to help in any way you can?"

Obligation? "Fuck you, Garrissey. Take your guilt trip and shove it up your ass."

The room fell quiet. Only the clicking of fingers on keyboards, the distant ringing of a phone and a few conversations continued, but the knot of cops working Brittany's case froze. The tension wasn't only the lack of talking but that hollow reverberation of shock. Even Dean and Curt looked taken aback. Kiera's skin flushed hot. Before she flinched or attempted to mollify anyone, she fished her cell out of her purse.

Nobody tried to stop her, which was fortunate, because she had no idea what to do if they did. Cortney McIntyre was number seven on her speed dial—not because Kiera called her all that often, but because she thought it hilarious to have a lawyer on speed dial. Not so funny today. All she had to do was press down one digit. Her hands trembled. Goddamn it.

"Can we start again from the beginning?" Curt asked. Curt. Not Dean. "Maybe order a little food? I'll pick it up."

His small smile won her over. That and the odd memory of how he hated walnuts.

"No. I want you to stay." She gave Garrissey a hostile glare. "Let Mr. Zero Percent Financing fetch the food."

His own glower was cold and calculating, a glimpse of his true face.

Ugly. "I'm a homicide detective, not an errand boy. This involves my case, and I'm staying."

"You stay, and I go." She stared at Page, whose face showed nothing. "Your call, Special Agent Page."

"I'll be in touch with you later this afternoon, Detective Garrissey," Page said without hesitation.

Garrisey's tan face blossomed red like a bruised tomato. Kiera suppressed a shudder. He glanced about, as if needing something to kick or knock to the ground before storming out like a child.

That was somewhat satisfying.

"Ms. Brayleigh?" Dean's voice was quiet, but it carried. He looked at her—the Dean she recognized and the Dean who recognized *her*. "Would it be all right if I sat in on the interview too?"

Kiera wanted to say no because she'd been scared and trapped, and he'd just stood there and watched. She hadn't expected him to introduce her as his special lady friend. But he'd always been friendly toward her when he worked, a quiet, solid presence during the maelstrom of emotions that swirled when she read a memory.

Dean had won her trust and then made her question it.

What was she doing? No, she wasn't going to yank away that earned trust because she—shocker—felt vulnerable. She mentally rolled her eyes at herself.

Dean lowered his head and looked up at her, an apology in his eyes. After making so many mistakes herself, she couldn't judge Dean.

Maybe she'd give adulting a try. "All right, Detective Matthson. As long as you're on your best behavior."

* * *

THE CONFERENCE ROOM HAD INDUSTRIAL CARPETING, GRAY WITH BLACK checks, and a beat-up wooden table with several scuffs and a huge gouge on one side. Kiera sat away from the gouge, though it put her back to the door. But that wasn't where the danger lay.

Page sat across from her, letting her interlaced fingers rest across the groove. Kiera thought human nature should make her avoid the crack, like avoiding cement breaks on the sidewalk. What did you break if you rested your hands on a crack?

Dean and Curt positioned themselves to Page's right and left, both tilting their shoulders so they weren't all staring her down.

Page launched right into her questions and rarely paused, starting with ones Kiera had already answered about the similarities of the victims and their attacks.

Sometimes Kiera could answer the inquiries, but some baffled her. How could she tell how sexually active someone was from a handful of selective memories? Page and Dean volleyed questions at her like an Olympic tennis doubles team with Curt overhead smashing a question every so often.

After victim similarities, the next hour was Kiera going through the Westchester assault step-by-step. They broke for lunch. The chicken and waffles were delicious, particularly the side of greens. They moved on to Brittany's attack.

"What comes to your mind first?" Page asked.

"Piercings. Two rings in the center of his bottom lip."

"No earrings? Or a stretched earlobe or plug?"

She thought back. "No. No other piercings." It hit her. "They're fake, aren't they?"

Page shrugged. "You tell me."

Kiera pressed her hands over her face, the heels of her hands digging into her eyes. "Uh, wow. Probably. He licked the piercing a lot, now that I think about it." Her leg jiggled under the table. "His whole hipster presentation was an act. The entire thing. He dressed like that for her."

"Does Brittany have a history of dating men with piercings?" Page asked Dean.

"I'll have to talk to the parents," Dean said, a small line between his brows indicating either deep consideration or displeasure.

"Regardless, she did find him attractive," Kiera said. "He was cool to her."

"We should find out what kind of men the other two dated," Dean said to Curt.

Curt grimaced. "Let's have Tam call Garrissey."

"No need. I'll talk to Aaron," Page said, distracted.

Aaron? Dean and Curt exchanged a look. It made Kiera smile to witness the moment between them. Curt was Dean's best friend, not just his partner. Dean had been Curt's best man. Kiera had Nadira and Beth, and though they weren't as functional as the cops, she understood how deep a person could be connected to another.

"You think he's playing a part for each victim?" Dean asked Page.

His words focused Kiera's attention to the killer, sharpening her mind. *Playing a part.* Everyone played a part. She grabbed the ends of her hair and tugged. "Jesus Christ, I'm starting to feel like I get this sick fuck. That can't be good."

"What do you mean, Kiera?" Page asked as Dean stared at her, almost alarmed.

She blew out a breath, letting her thoughts unfold, concentrating on Page. "Back in the day, he was a stalker. He knew too many details about the victim: her room, where she hung out, the people she was friends with." She swallowed, even though her mouth was dry. It hurt. "Possibly he interacted with her. He drugged her, had her unconscious and could have done anything, but he wanted her awake, needed her to witness her own defilement. Now he's the same but different."

"Different?"

She concentrated, but that was a question that didn't have an answer. Not yet. "I can't tell how. Just an impression. He stalked Brittany. I'd bet my life on it. He asked her for tea, not coffee. How did he know she drank tea unless he'd seen her copper kettle and a shelfful of teas?"

"Anything else?" Dean asked, his voice gentle.

"I hate that motherfucker."

Dean bit his lip, but a smile hit his eyes. "Anything pertinent?"

"He had better eye contact when he was pretending than when he was himself," Kiera said. "Like the confidence is all an act."

Page tapped a pen against her lips. "Could be the high he gets from fooling his victims provides him an extra burst of confidence."

Dean nodded, then said, "It might also be that inhabiting the persona drains him to such an extent that he can't hold onto the confidence during the assault."

Page smiled at Dean. "True. We don't know enough about him yet, but we'll get there."

Something passed between Dean and Page. Maybe it was professional kinship, but their intuitive bond stabbed through Kiera's heart. Dean's eyes were so focused and alive, as if his mind were fully engaged.

This was what she'd wanted, to see him in his element and witness him at work. And he'd been just as engaged with Curt. But watching Dean and Page interact made Kiera realize how much better someone like Page would be for Dean. She probably already knew how to anticipate his emotional needs.

Kiera shoved the ache into the fists on her lap and continued to recount the attack. "He said, 'That's right. I'm the one that kills you.' Those were the last words she ever heard."

And suddenly, Kiera needed to go home, to a safe space filled with familiar objects and soothing scents and medical marijuana. She understood her place in the world while in her condo; she understood Dean there too.

* * *

"I'll walk you out," Dean said in a quiet voice.

"I can find my way." Kiera didn't want to act unaffected and didn't want to watch Dean feign disinterest for another second. She was too unbalanced to manage the tightrope.

He smiled. "Civilians have to be escorted."

Figured. "God forbid someone walks off with one of those corded phones from 2003."

"It's more having someone pop into the gun locker." He didn't touch her, not even her shoulder or elbow, but his eyes went soft for a second. Her stomach unclenched. "Come on."

She was glad an overweight woman with an armful of manila folders shared the elevator with them. Dean stood a respectable distance, but the back of his hand brushed hers once. An electrical pulse shot through her.

How did he do that?

"I'll call you later," he murmured as he walked her through the wooden half door that kept the public separated from the police.

"Sure."

She forced herself to look away and sent her driver, Tony, a summons text.

Dean paused as they reached the glass door that would finally free her. "You did really well."

"Did that surprise you?" As if she hadn't gone through fifty million times worse all on her own.

"No." He lowered his voice. "I think you're the strongest person I've ever met."

She snorted, though the compliment gave her a gust of energy. "If that's true, the human race is screwed."

CHAPTER FORTY

Dean

KIERA STRODE TO THE WAITING CAR WITH HER head high. Dean watched until the car pulled away, suppressing the urge to bang his head on the glass. The interview had gone well, Grace hitting the perfect notes to open Kiera, and Kiera diving deep to unearth details and theories he hadn't discovered with her.

Dean, however, had almost ruined everything. Professionally, he'd salvaged his misstep, but he still needed to repair his relationship.

He'd been so concerned about appearing involved that he overcompensated in the other direction, even as he witnessed Kiera struggling to find her footing. That prick Garrissey threatened her, and Dean clamped down his jaw instead of standing beside her, walking her through what they intended, easing her, comforting her—all of which he could have done in a businesslike manner.

Not that she'd needed him. Kiera might snap like a stray dog kicked too often, especially when scared or challenged, but he'd forgotten the core of strength inside her. When pushed, she found a way to work through her fears or limitations. But he'd hurt her with his aloofness.

Dean shook out his hands as he jogged up the stairs to debrief with

Curt and Grace. He would fix the damage he'd done later, in person. She deserved nothing less.

Grace sat alone at the conference table, Curt gone. Dean approached, loosening his stride, sloughing off his self-recrimination to concentrate on the job. "She was really helpful, wasn't she?"

"They're plenty useful, but so damn selfish." Grace spun her pen in her fingers.

"Selfish?" That wasn't a word he would have applied to Kiera. He sat across from Grace, in the seat Kiera had taken. Hyperconscious of his body, he cupped his hands on the table, thumbs up to display openness.

Grace dropped her pen and steepled her fingers, a sign of authority and confidence. "Think of what they could do." She opened her hands before steepling them together again. "We've been studying serial killers since the seventies, and everything we learn is self-reported. You think the ones that agree to talk to us tell us the truth? We have to figure out what's real from the spin and the manipulation and the delusion. A memory surgeon could tell us *exactly* what went on in their minds. They could tell us *exactly* how they choose their victims. We could have an accurate, objective profile of a serial killer."

Dean hadn't considered that, though it wouldn't be as objective as Grace intimated. Still, it would revolutionize profiling. They would need numerous subjects if they wanted a thorough view.

Grace opened her arms. "What wouldn't you sacrifice to be able to find these killers faster? To stop them after one or two victims?"

The word "sacrifice" prickled, and Dean barely stopped himself from pulling his hands back, signaling a retreat. "I doubt it's that simple."

Images of Kiera crouched over the wastebasket in Brittany's hospital room flicked through his mind.

"Certainly. But if even one of those memory surgeons would help us, think how many advances we could make. What might we learn from the inner workings of a rapist, a pedophile, a killer? Think of what we might understand about sociopaths and psychopaths by getting into their minds. What would happen if their pathological memories were erased? Would they be cured? Or is it something too deeply ingrained? Aren't you curious? The Dean I remember wanted to know all those answers."

She hadn't known him well enough to say that. Still, he did want the answers. Grace had spun her web, and Dean had gotten himself stuck. If he could read a killer's mind himself, he would. He'd destroy himself for the chance to find out the answers, to save future victims, to prevent future killers.

However, admitting that to Grace might provide the foothold she needed to persuade him to coerce Kiera. "I still want answers, but I wouldn't sacrifice someone else to do it." Certainly not his girlfriend.

She held out her hands. "Nobody's asking you to throw a body onto the pyre."

He smiled, though he had to work at it, because that was exactly what she was asking.

"But Kiera does trust you. She likes you." Grace tilted her face. "Like-likes you. I'll bet you could talk her into it."

Dean coughed to hide his astonishment and only half faked it, because his mouth had gone so dry. "I don't think she likes me *that* much." That was the truth. Nobody was worth putting herself into that sort of situation.

But could he manipulate her into it? Yes. She'd gifted him with enough glimpses of her vulnerable spots that he could exploit her in any number of ways. He had power over her. And if he let his mind drift that way, to all the implications, he could understand how that might become addictive to some. Like Brittany's killer.

Of course, Kiera also had power over him. He wanted her happiness enough to do almost anything. The difference was she didn't know it.

"You underestimate your charm," Grace said with an easy punch to his arm. Dean thought about the emotional cost of him mentally inhabiting rapists and killers, and then he considered how awful it would be to live the reality instead of imagining.

Grace stood, her ponytail swinging behind her jauntily. "Something to think about once this case is solved." She didn't understand what she was suggesting. She didn't grasp the true cost.

"Don't you want to debrief the interview?" he asked.

Grace shook her head. "I work better if I marinate on it myself for a bit. Want to meet up after work and talk through it? It would also give us a chance to catch up more."

He needed to make restitution with Kiera, but contemplating that conversation made his body weight triple. Anyway, he wanted to dive into the profile, witness how Grace parsed information, and he was genuinely interested to hear the full story of how she became a federal agent. "We aren't on the uplist." She might not know what that meant. "Our squad isn't scheduled to take the next homicide, so unless there's extenuating circumstances, I shouldn't need to work OT, but my shift doesn't end until one. Is that too late?"

She shrugged. "I never sleep well on assignment, and I've always been a night owl, so that's fine."

They worked out the details and Grace left to isolate herself so she could process the case files and Kiera's insights. Curt showed up with an assortment of deliciousness from Insomnia Cookies.

He handed Dean a chocolate peanut butter cup and a double chocolate mint, then held the box out to Tam and Kristin and the rest of the team. Best partner ever. It was a nice respite from homicides and serial killers, if only for a few minutes.

* * *

AT THE END OF HIS SHIFT, DEAN PIT-STOPPED AT THE LOCKER ROOM to take out his contacts, his eyes burning with the extended wear. Grace followed him to Murphy's, a corner bar in the Bridgeport area, not too far from Area Central. The dim lighting, tucked-in seating, and cloistered atmosphere was perfect for letting go and relaxing. Scents of leather, beer, and a lingering whiff of cigarette smoke from decades past added to the neighborhood-bar charm.

Grace slid into a booth tucked behind the door.

Dean remained standing. "I'm going to hop to the bar. What can I get you?"

"Do they have any local brews? That's my thing when I'm out of town, trying out local small-batch beers."

"They have a few. What kind do you like?"

"Pale ale if they've got it. Weiss beers are good too, but I'm not all that picky." Grace settled back into her seat and glanced at the crowd. Dean suspected she peered deeper than she appeared, like how most officers habitually assessed crowds and egresses. Perhaps she profiled everywhere she went as a mental exercise.

Dean ordered a red zinfandel and an Alpha King pale ale for Grace. The murmurs of conversation distracted Dean as he waited for the drinks. When he returned to their table, Grace thanked him and clinked her glass on his. "I had dinner with Bob Cranston last night."

"You call Dr. Cranston 'Bob'?" For Dean, calling his mentor "Bob" would have been like calling his parents by their first names. Some people could pull that off but not him.

"I'm trying." She chuckled. "It is weird, though."

Dean hated that his suspicious nature assumed she'd pivoted her position to align with him and establish a connection that she could later leverage. "How is he? I talked to him recently, but it was a brief conversation."

After five minutes of Cranston updates, including a new granddaughter, talk shifted to the job. Grace propped an arm on the back of the booth, the arm closest to Dean, which shifted her body to open toward him. Dean didn't mirror her position exactly but set his elbow on the table, which tilted his body similarly.

"What do you think about our guy?" she asked.

The question galvanized Dean. "Obviously, he's organized and intelligent. He's shown a pretty thorough knowledge of Chicago, so he's probably traveled around the city quite a bit, either with his job or growing up here."

Grace nodded but didn't say anything.

Dean continued. "He's got a lot of anger but control, so I've categorized him as a power-assertion rapist. I've researched the kinds of serial killers, and I think he's power seeking. He spent considerably more time raping and controlling Kolchek than killing her."

"I agree." Grace took a deep pull from her beer. "Nice choice." Then she talked about the killer's shifting identities and his compulsion to concoct a persona catered to each victim. The contact lenses particularly fascinated her, that level of detail. "His experimentation might also have an internal component."

"You think he wants to be someone else?"

"It's certainly possible. Identity, I believe, is key for him. I keep coming back to that." Grace put her elbows on the table. "I've seen your work."

Dean hadn't expected that. "What do you mean?"

"I've watched some of your interrogation videos. Your technique is impressive. This conversation solidifies what I suspected. You would make a great profiler." Was she recruiting him? "Have you ever considered making a change? You could actually use your psych degree."

But wouldn't the stakes be higher? The pressure more intense? "I'm happy with CPD."

"But it's hard, isn't it? Getting inside the mind of a killer, knowing what makes them tick, so you can convince them to confess?" She spoke as if they were talking about the difficulty of a proper dovetail joint. Somehow, she'd gleaned how he got his confession rate and the price he paid for it.

"There's a cost." He kept his voice neutral, his expression closed, trying to block her profiling of him, though she'd likely already finished.

"If you're going to pay the price, why not make the most of it?"

Dean didn't respond, his mind unable to focus. What about Curt? Kiera?

Perhaps sensing his unease, Grace shifted tacks, regaling him with stories from her FBI testing. A subtle temptation. *Look how fun it is to become an FBI agent.*

It worked, to a degree. Dean enjoyed Grace's company and her insights and enthusiasm for profiling. Yet as they approached closing time, his legs wouldn't settle, his whole body restless. Grace confused him with a world of opportunities she expected him to want.

But what he wanted was Kiera. For all her rules and peculiarities, she provided Dean with solid ground. She dealt in straight lines and hard truths.

He'd make things right between them. If she'd let him.

CHAPTER FORTY ONE

Kiera

KIERA DUG INTO HER HOMEMADE CHICKEN POT pie, the comfort food she'd prepared for herself to counter the exhausting interview. Dean's behavior ran through her memory again, no doubt leaving a track she'd be able to follow ten years from now.

He and Page seemed so in tune with each other, as if they'd been pals for years and not people who only met today. Page was attractive in a Fed Barbie kind of way, taller, blonder, and with bigger tits than Kiera and far better suited to Dean.

This was the anxiety talking, the spiral that accompanied copious stress. When she performed memory surgeries too close together, her thoughts latched onto the first paranoid idea with promise and pumped it full of steroids and adrenaline.

Kiera should have made Page, Dean, and Curt come to her.

Dean hadn't given Page any secret glances or "accidental" touches or any other indication that they were more than colleagues. Yet even with that epiphany, she couldn't stop the panic because Dean's discomfort with her presence had been evident before her rational mind took a sabbatical.

She shoved the remains of the pot pie into the fridge. She hadn't eaten much.

Kiera could imagine a future with Dean for herself. He was patient and intelligent and witty and beautiful and someone she'd always want by her side. Dean made her life infinitely better. But one person could be perfect for another but not the reverse.

Dean needed someone who could walk beside him. A profiler like Page could talk about catching perps, laying down cover, and innovations in law enforcement procedures. They could have kids: Frank, Bart, and Isabelle and would joke about their FBI family. And Page would never puke during sex.

Kiera dug her fists into her temples trying to wrangle her thoughts into a line and not a Rorschach test.

Listen to me, loopy brain. Dean and I have been great together; I accommodate his schedule, and he accommodates my crazy. We talk and laugh, and, good God, the sex is transformational. Somehow, we're right.

Eventually, he'll want a date to the Lyric or a Blackhawk's game or a departmental holiday party or a family birthday celebration. Eventually, you'll have to agree to go. And eventually, you'll show him exactly why you won't work long-term by vomiting on his boss or telling his mom to fuck off or causing a scene during his nephew's choral concert.

No. Dean cared about her. His eyes as he walked her out of the station had been warm and regretful. But what if he'd had an epiphany of his own? Maybe Dean had sat in that conference room and realized how easy his life would be with the profiler beside him as his lover instead of the snot-crying mess across from him. Maybe that regret was because he'd decided to end things with her.

Her phone buzzed.

You still up?

Her legs shook. *Yes.*

Can I come over?

* * *

He wore the goddamned glasses.

"Hey." Dean stopped at the threshold looking like a dog who'd knocked over the garbage.

Kiera bit her lip to keep stop them from visibly trembling. "Hi."

"Babe." Dean covered the few feet between them and caught her face in his hands. "I'm sorry. I . . . I was unprepared for you to show up at work, and I panicked." He pressed his forehead to hers. "There's nothing *official* that says I can't date you, but you are tied to the case, and eventually, if the cases remain unsolved, they're going to consolidate, and when they do, there will be only one lead detective. And I want it to be me."

The energy from her near panic attack stopped gaining gale-force winds but had nowhere to go. Her body shook but now in relief.

"So, we're okay," she said, to show she comprehended his dilemma. Thank fuck. "You just needed to look as professional as possible. I get that. God forbid that ass-punch Garrissey be in charge." Garrissey would make everything about himself and not about the victims.

"Yeah, we all hate that guy." He pulled her forward until her chest hit his. When she embraced him, he wrapped his arms around her in a tight hug. Dean hugged better than anyone she'd ever met. "But I should have done better, Kiera."

The crisis had been averted, but the issue remained. "You and Special Agent Page have a nice rapport." She spoke into his chest so she wouldn't have to read his reaction.

"Yeah, we knew each other at UIC when she and I both worked the crisis hotline for Dr. Cranston."

"Oh." How could she have guessed that? She scrambled for a pivot. "Did you know that Ted Bundy and Ann Rule both worked a crisis hotline together?"

"Are you comparing me to Bundy?" Dean's mouth twitched.

"No, I'm comparing Page to Bundy."

He sank his fingers in her hair and studied her blotchy face with tenderness rather than repulsion. "Were you jealous of Grace?"

"I'm jealous of everyone that's better than me." She squinted. "Did you just call her Grace to annoy me?"

He stroked his thumbs over her cheeks. "No, that was my 3:00 a.m. brain not working properly." Slowly, as if afraid she might object, he bent down to kiss her.

His lips were soft as ever, their kisses as flammable as ever, only more so, because she'd almost lost him—if only in her mind.

After a minute, he broke the kiss. "People aren't *better* than one another, babe," he said. "But if there were some kind of grading system, I don't think anyone would rate higher than you."

Nobody had ever talked to her like that before. And he clearly meant what he said. He pulled her into a hug, squeezing hard, and the discomfort that usually came from being held too tightly never came.

Knives stabbed the back of her eyes, and wet heat built there. "I'm not that easy to be around."

"Why? Because you're a bit prickly? Because you have some anxiety?" He kissed the top of her head. "So what? You're intelligent and funny and brave and selfless." He lowered his voice and said "beautiful" as fast as he could.

She laughed because he respected her mixed emotions about comments on her appearance and because he wanted her to laugh.

"And you allow me to be myself. You don't ever ask me to feel or act in any particular way, and you have no idea how rare that is. It isn't hard to be with you, Kiera. I don't want anyone else, and I don't want you with anyone else."

"Okay." She should have replied with a list of all the things she liked about him, but her eyes still stung, and her tongue felt thick. All she wanted was to bask in the moment and hold onto it, hold onto Dean.

"Come with me." He interlaced his fingers with hers.

They walked directly to the bedroom. He put his gun in the safe, then held her hands. He stared at her for a moment before tracing a finger from her ear to her jaw and chin and back to the other ear. His attention remained fixed on her. He guided her to the bed and straddled her, easing his body on top of hers, moving slowly and carefully. He set his glasses on his nightstand.

Dean held her hands loosely by the wrists and stretched them over her head. Her chest constricted, but she didn't say anything, wanting to be cool.

"Don't be afraid, Kiera," he said, his voice as gentle as his hands. He was studying her, his expression open and vulnerable. "I would never hurt you."

The tears that had built spilled over, the tributaries pooling at her temples and in her hair. Dean kissed the corners of her eyes, drinking in all the emotion flowing out of her. Neither of them spoke. Kiera couldn't have spoken, not coherently, if she'd wanted, but they were beyond words. He'd been in a hard position earlier in the day, and he'd locked up in fear and caution. Another man might have defended his cold professionalism, might have called her out on her insecurity. Dean had tended to her emotional wounds, and she loved the way he saw her. She wanted to see herself like he did. She wanted to give him everything she had and everything she would ever have.

I love you.

The thought sprang to life like a jack-in-the-box and just as startling. She kept her hands over her head, even when he released them, his hands stroking down the inside of her left arm, and though he raised goose bumps, the caress didn't tickle. His hand continued down the side of her body to her hip. His eyes followed his fingers and then came back to hers. He really saw her in that moment with all his attention on her—and the panic never came. She was alive in his gaze. He kissed her again.

I love you.

The thought repeated until she was afraid the refrain would burst out of her mouth. It was too soon to say that, too soon to think it, yet the conviction grew stronger in her mind.

"You okay?" he asked, whispering centimeters from her lips.

I love you.

The words wanted to come out. "Yes. Kiss me, Dean. Please." *Kiss me before I make a complete ass out of myself.*

He did.

CHAPTER FORTY TWO

Dean

DEAN'S BODY MOVED ON AUTOPILOT AS HIS BRAIN tried to find a way to sleep standing up with his eyes open. He'd sleepwalked his way through the courthouse at Twenty-Sixth and California to the second floor, thinking about the scent of Kiera's hair and how gorgeous it looked fanned over her pillow.

"You look a little sleepy," Curt said as he sidled next to him at the check-in room entrance. "I didn't sleep enough either, but I had a very satisfying night." Curt brushed his thumb over his mustache, trying to nudge down a smile. "How about you? How'd Kiera take you and Agent Page having a drink? She doesn't strike me as the jealous type, but you never know."

Everything in Dean's body locked up at once. Luckily, it was his turn to have his time-due slip stamped, and the administrator snatched the paperwork from his frozen outstretched hand. Now he was officially on the clock. "What do you mean?"

"Seriously, dude? I'm a detective and your partner. Give me a little credit." Curt picked imaginary lint off his brown suit coat as his own sheet was time-stamped.

"Shit. Does everyone know?" Dean wiped his face trying to rattle his mind online. They found the printout for room 702 from the stacks of sign-in sheets set up on the long table.

"No, just me. Otherwise, they would have talked differently after yesterday." Curt signed next to his name and pushed the paper to Dean, who fidgeted, distracted by the image of the team discussing Kiera. Curt knocked into his shoulder. "Mr. Zero Percent Financing? I think Jason might have proposed to her if he wasn't already married. Man, I barely held it together myself."

How could he have forgotten about that? Dean laughed. "I hope that gets around."

Curt broke out a grin, his amusement contagious as they headed to the back offices of room 702 to await their turns to testify. "Oh, it did. Someone posted the comment on the Second City Cop blog."

Garrissey would lose his shit if he found out about it, and cops gossip, so he would.

Dean smiled, his fatigue lifting. "Yeah, my girl done good."

* * *

THEY WERE RELEASED FROM COURT EARLY BECAUSE OF A PLEA DEAL. Dean considered stopping by Kiera's to hang with her, but duty cock-blocked him. Yesterday's interview and postmortem combined with a few hours of sleep had given him an idea.

"I want to go back to Holy Trinity," Dean said as they reached their unmarked.

"Why? We already passed out the sketch, and nobody recognized him," Curt took the passenger seat, which meant he wasn't opposed to a detour.

"This guy," Dean said, the resonance with the profile vibrating within him, "his disguise isn't for the masses but tailored to his victim. I don't think he's walking about in public with that persona but honing it in private from what he observes."

Curt nodded. "Okay, I see what you're saying. You think he was at the church but disguised or watching from behind a building or in the trees or something."

"I think it's possible."

Curt called Father Thomas, and he agreed to meet them within the hour. Dean and Curt shared that low-level excitement they got when a case moved forward, both optimistic that the offender had likely cased Brittany for some time. Something might've been missed.

The white stone facade boasted a wide, round stained-glass window that impressed even from the outside. The church had a Gothic appeal with its flying buttresses and angels anchoring the roof where gargoyles might roost. Father Thomas had gray hair and a craggy face but a smile full of genuine warmth that likely enraptured his congregation. He met them in the front yard. "Detectives, you mentioned you have more questions for me. How can I help you?"

Curt took lead on the interview. "Thank you for taking the time, Father. We were wondering if you can remember anything unusual in the month or so before Brittany's attack. A utility truck, landscapers, something like that?"

Father Thomas pursed his lips and glanced across the street. Dean and Curt waited, letting him access his memory. "No, I don't think so."

"How about something amiss in the church?" Dean asked. "Items out of place, someone unexpectedly sick, anything?"

Father Thomas's chin jerked back. "Now that you mention it, we did have a broken lock about two months ago. Something was jammed into the lock, and we had to have it replaced. Mr. Fine, the caretaker, would know more about the incident."

Curt and Dean exchanged a glance, then followed Father Thomas to the rectory in back to find Murray Fine, the caretaker. Murray was an older man with a round body, white hair, and a jolly disposition. He was probably an excellent Santa around Christmastime.

He rubbed his snow-white beard. "We thought it a fluke because nothing was missing. Why would someone break in and not take anything?"

"Is it all right if we take a look?" Dean asked, keeping his face calm but still shooting Curt a look.

The rectory was against the church, the outside built out of small, buff-colored bricks, which Dean noted needed some tuck-pointing, the mortar gouged and chipping. Holy Trinity must have spent all its money on upkeep for the building's public face and let the back fall into disrepair.

Past the back door was a kitchen, and to the left, a spiral staircase. Dean and Curt moved toward the stairs in unison. Up at the top was a storage area filled with boxes, sections of pews, wooden crosses, and trunks, all coated with dust. Murray stayed on the second-to-the-last step, perhaps curious. Father Thomas had already left.

At the back right corner of the room, they found a two-foot-square section cleared of clutter. A thin break between the wood-panel slats shone like a spotlight. If Dean put his eye to the crack, he hypothesized he would see straight into the sanctuary where "Dillon" had observed Brittany. He and Curt searched, precise about where they set their feet, but found no wrappers or other signs someone had been there beyond the cleared space.

Dean studied the small section, careful not to disturb anything. The corners of the cleared space were sharp and symmetrical. Precise. All the details of Brittany's attack filtered through his mind. The killer had come here to study her but couldn't simply stand in the shadows and watch. His space, the place he stood, had to be clean. The break in the slats—was it natural wear, or had the offender made it? Dean peered at the edges, keeping to the side to preserve the scene. Chisel, he thought, noting the rough edges. A blade would have made a cleaner line. The offender drove a van. Maybe he was in a trade, some profession where a chisel and hammer, rags, and solvents were all at hand.

"He didn't just clear the space. This is clean," Dean said to Curt.

Curt nodded. "What's that smell?"

"Mineral spirits," Dean said, his nose catching the scent that luckily hadn't dissipated.

"You think it's from our guy?"

"Absolutely. No reason to have mineral spirits up here." Dean bent down. "Yep. It's stronger down here."

"What does this mean?" Curt's eyes glinted, as if he sensed Dean's brain churning.

"Could be a woodworker. It's a profession that requires attention to detail, planning, and perfect execution. If he makes furniture and delivers it, it's possible that's how he knows the neighborhoods."

Curt frowned. "No way people are having custom-made furniture delivered to those shitty neighborhoods where he's dumping."

Dean sighed. "True."

"Maybe he makes armoires by day and delivers pizzas by night." Curt grinned. Another cop in violent crimes always suspected pizza deliverymen.

Dean laughed. "Collins would lose his shit."

Curt put on gloves and examined the studs, then along the horizontal support board, and found old chewing gum. "Hello, evidence," he said in his slow jazz voice.

Dean pulled out a paper evidence bag and Curt dropped the gum into it. Dean filled out the information and sealed the envelope closed. He liked the odds that the gum belonged to his offender. Saliva didn't hold DNA, but if there were some cheek cells there, they *might* be able to extract some DNA. Two-month-old gum wasn't the best evidence, but he'd bet big money there were prints there too.

He peered again through the spy hole, sinking down into the murk. The killer had stared at vibrant Brittany, sitting between her parents, thinking about what he wanted to do to her. He struggled, watching her walk away, out of his view. His prey.

Dean considered the gum again. The offender enjoyed the delayed gratification of the wait. Gum implied leisure and relaxation and leaving it at the scene of his stalking said he didn't fear discovery—so sure of his safety that he had no qualms about the potential DNA evidence. Arrogant. Dean loved arrogant offenders; they made mistakes.

"Let's bring someone out to look for prints," Curt said.

"Yeah. If we can find a match between prints here and Brittany's apartment, that would be telling."

Curt nodded at Dean as he pulled out his phone. After weeks of stalled progress, they were moving forward. This was why he loved his job.

As they emerged outside to wait for the tech, Dean and Curt searched for cameras to find video footage of the man breaking into the rectory. They spotted one camera, but it was in the front, and the footage was recorded over every week. Damn. Well, two steps forward, one step back beat no momentum at all.

CHAPTER FORTY THREE

SOMEONE AS FAMOUS AS KIERA BRAYLEIGH SHOULD have been easy to find. She was everywhere online and nowhere physically. No properties, no utilities, no FedEx or UPS accounts. Nothing. If he had access to the IRS, he could find her, but he didn't have skills on that level. And he couldn't risk discovery. So far, he'd managed to keep himself separate from his toys.

He found the parents and the brother easily enough, but neither of those yielded his quarry. Wasted time. The brother, especially, was never in one place for long, always on his way to the next thing—health clubs, restaurants, concerts, lakefront runs, wine tastings, movies, gallery openings. The man went everywhere but where he needed him to go.

Of course, if Jilly were still alive, he certainly wouldn't be visiting her. So, he shouldn't have been surprised the brother didn't know where Kiera lived. If he did, he'd kill her himself. Killing the sister who got all the press, all the accolades, all the attention, all his mother's love. Cunt.

No. No, no, no. Kiera wasn't for the brother to kill. She was his.

He could kill her. Slowly. He could kill her slowly enough that she relived her own death as he murdered her. In those minutes it would take, she would remain trapped in that gift that made her think she was so fucking special.

No. No. He needed her.

He didn't need her. He wanted her, wanted her gift, wanted to chase that high when Jilly died, as she stared into his eyes. Jilly, when she died as she was meant to die, not in that stupid car accident.

No. He kills her. He kills her and kills her and kills her.

And when he has the memory whore, he can kill her every day.

CHAPTER FORTY FOUR

Kiera

KIERA HADN'T SEEN DEAN IN OVER A WEEK. DEAN had ruined her with a steady diet of touch, and now she'd turned into a lust beast, preparing to pounce on him and shred his clothing the moment he stepped through the door. Or maybe in the hallway. Then she'd wrap herself in his pelt all night long.

Was that normal?

Who was she trying to kid? Every time she saw him, she fell so hard, she cracked every bone in her body. Dean made her better than normal. Oh God, she was happy. Surely, that was a sign of an impending apocalypse.

She didn't watch the lobby camera footage, but she was in the library, the room closest to the door. Her legs were shaved and moisturized; her underwear was lacy and uncomfortable. She never wore uncomfortable anything. But she wanted to please him, to make up for all the ways she sucked.

Kiera paced and studied the spines of her books without seeing them.

Her phone rang with the ringtone reserved for the lobby desk—the theme from *Star Wars*. She gripped it hard enough to hurt. "Hello?"

"He's on his way up," Manny said.

Kiera's stomach flipped, and she was lightheaded for a moment. "Thanks, Manny."

Her hands clasped together, dropped to her side, to the back of her neck, then balled into fists. She shook them twice, trying to tame her wild energy as she perched in the open doorway to spot Dean the moment he left the elevator.

At last, the elevator dinged, and Dean strode through the doors before they had fully opened. Kiera met him in the hallway, and he kissed her. For a moment, she thought they might have sex right there. She kind of wanted them to. He pressed his body into her, and she wallowed in his greedy need. She wasn't the least bit claustrophobic.

He broke the kiss. "Hey."

"It's been too long, Matthson."

Once inside with the alarm armed, he picked her up and carried her to the bedroom. She wrapped her arms around his neck and stared into his blue-green eyes. He didn't fling her on the bed but set her down, the backs of her legs against the mattress.

His gun went in the drawer, the safe too far away. He kissed her, gentle at first, his fingers slipping under her tank top. When he found her breasts, he kissed her harder, his hands cupping her, stroking her, making her smolder. "I'm trying hard to go slow, but . . ." He kissed her again.

"You don't need to go slow. I'm ready," she said during the brief pause between one kiss and the next. Her comfort and confidence were unprecedented. Maybe Dean was that flying unicorn that would take her to the Land of Normal.

"Thank God." He unbuckled his belt. He usually took his shirt off first.

She found his urgency exciting, and she followed suit, naked in moments. He caressed up her leg to the center of her body, between her legs, not stopping.

He moaned, and they lay crosswise on the bed, and Kiera liked that, the different orientation. Dean kissed her and entered her at the same moment, and she contracted around him, and he moaned again. He moved faster, overtaken by passion. Kiera watched his face and followed his body, enjoying his excitement in a way that was sexual and tender at once.

216

"Oh, Jesus," he panted. "Can't slow down."

Kiera lifted her hips harder into his, encouraging him. She loved how possessed he acted. He arched his back, raising above her like the sexiest version of cobra pose.

"I should . . ." He pumped and pumped. Kiera's core tightened, though she couldn't orgasm from that position. Or could she? Dean's hips punished in the best way.

"I'm sorry," he said. "Oh, God, I'm so sorry . . ."

It hit her. The "sorry" with the "oh God."

All at once, she couldn't breathe. She couldn't see. Her skin flushed in an itching heat that made her want to scream. The memory erupted, and she couldn't feel Dean any longer. The weight of her father—heavy and sweaty and so, so, so fucking sorry—pinning his bulk on top of her.

Not hers. Not her memory. But she couldn't shove away the reek of his sweat, the flab of his stomach sliding over her. Kiera slid a foot toward her butt, leveraging her lower body and shoved Dean with all the strength in her arms and her hips, flipping him clean off her.

He cried out and said something, but Kiera couldn't hear anything beyond the ringing in her ears. She stumbled and fell but reached the bathroom in time to throw up.

Her body broke out in hives, a red patchiness that spread from her arms to her neck to her chest. She threw up again, and again, and again, until her stomach dry heaved. Anything to purge the sickness of Anna's father's touch. She pressed her forehead into the cool porcelain, rocking her head from side to side to cover as much area as possible.

* * *

DISTANTLY, SHE HEARD DEAN'S VOICE.

"Kiera? Kiera!" He had been shouting her name for a while.

She rotated her neck to stare up at him. He was naked from the waist down and no longer hard. His face was pale and drawn. "I'm so sorry, Kiera. I'm so—"

"Stop!" Her voice sounded foreign to her ears. "Don't apologize. That's the trigger. Don't say you're sorry again. Don't say anything. Give me a minute."

He stepped back, saying nothing, and Kiera's chest almost cracked over yelling at him. It wasn't his fault. How could he have known? She wouldn't have thought to add that on the list. *Hey, no matter what you do, don't apologize during sex.* God, she was fucked up.

Suddenly, she was cold to her bones, but her stomach was too tenuous for her to move. Time. She would come out the other side of this episode. But the thought of Dean seeing her like this—vomiting, shaking, shrieking—made everything worse. She struggled to cobble herself together knowing full well that it had to run its course. There was no fast-forwarding through the process.

It was probably better this way. She no longer had to worry that she'd reveal just how broken she was. Ta-da.

Dean reappeared at the door holding her cashmere robe. "Thought you might be cold." He held it up. "May I?"

When she nodded, he wrapped the robe over her.

"Anything else I can do?" he asked in a subdued voice.

She shook her head.

"Are you sure? I've got a terrible singing voice," he said.

She snorted. "I'm trying *not* to throw up, thank you."

"You want a distraction?"

"Does it involve your dick?"

"Believe it or not, I have powers beyond my formidable dick."

"Who'd have thought?" She peeked at him, remembering Ramon's advice to let Dean help. "Will you just talk for a bit? About anything other than what just happened?"

He slid down to sit on the floor with her, his back against the sink cabinet, still wearing only his dress shirt, the top two buttons undone. "Oh yeah. To be an effective detective, you have to be able to talk to people, make people want to talk to you."

Kiera nodded. His voice was soft but textured. She listened to the rhythm of his speech, the cadence of his words, more soothing than a Valium but twice as addictive.

"Sometimes, I find people need something for their minds to focus on while the important stuff runs in the background, especially when I'm working a confession. People can't always come to terms with something hitting them flat in the face, so I run a story while they reconcile themselves to being held accountable for their actions."

"Is it hard to do?" Her chin was tilted to him, her cheek resting on the rim of the toilet. Classy.

He brushed hair away from her face, his fingers light. "Sometimes. There are moments when my mind blanks, usually when I'm completely sickened by whoever I'm talking to, and I'm working hard not to show it. That takes a lot of energy." He continued to stroke her hair, the act so comforting Kiera thought she might start crying, so she clamped her eyes closed. "Other times, though, stuff pours out of my mouth, and I can talk for days." He kissed her temple.

"Would you do that for me?"

"I'd do anything for you, babe."

Now she really was going to cry.

"You want to hear about the run of naked arrests Curt and I had back when we were on the streets?"

She opened her eyes, the absurdity a mental life preserver. "Definitely."

He smiled at her. He had his knees up, his arms balanced on top, his hands clasped loosely together. He appeared relaxed and content, as if they weren't sitting on the floor of her bathroom during one of Kiera's panic attacks. She couldn't see his lower half from her vantage point, but she pictured his rod and tackle resting on the cold marble.

"There's a stretch of time when the afternoon guys are getting off, which they want to do as soon as possible, and the midnight guys start, and they're trying to procrastinate, where there aren't as many cars out. It was during those strange hours when we had the naked run."

"Is that what you call it?"

"It is." He straightened the robe over her shoulders. "First one was a disturbance call. We arrive, and in the middle of the road is this naked guy in his sixties. We weren't well versed in how to deal with mental cases back then, and this was clearly a mental case. The guy was yelling at us that his wife was poisoning his clothes. Curt wanted the guy in pants—I mean *really* wanted it—so he pushed too hard and too fast, and the guy went from grumbling to throwing himself at Curt."

Kiera sat up. "Curt got attacked by a crazy naked guy?"

"Yeah, and Curt made the most hilarious sound I've ever heard, this high-pitched girlie noise. I wish we had body cameras back then." Dean grinned. "He knocked Curt over, and I was scared he was going to go for his gun, but he didn't. He just grabbed him by the vest and yelled that Curt was one of them, and I came up behind him and pulled him off Curt and cuffed him right there in the street. Once he was secured, all the fight went out of him, and he went limp body on us. Fucking Curt had to put on his gloves before helping me get him to standing. The guy's legs kept buckling, and we had to hold him up between us while the neighborhood residents laughed at us until the ambulance got there, which was probably pretty fast, but it felt like forever."

"Did you arrest him?"

"No, he was a mental case, so Curt didn't sign a complaint. The guy was hospitalized instead." Dean smiled as if he were in the moment again.

"Mental? That's not PC."

He shrugged. "That's what we call them."

She grunted but didn't press the issue further. "And that was the beginning of a run on naked guys?"

"Not only guys." He cocked his head. "You okay enough to move this to a more comfortable place? Couch? Library? I could start a fire."

He was always like that—sensitive and considerate. Her stomach only twinged with nausea, her shaking had stopped, and though her heart skittered, she no longer thought she might pass out. "Help me stand?"

CHAPTER FORTY FIVE

Dean

DEAN SAT ON THE COUCH IN A T-SHIRT AND boxers, his eyes on fire from lack of sleep and mental exhaustion. Kiera walked to him, her steps tentative. She looked like a fluffy cat who had been soaked to the bone, small and delicate in her super-soft robe.

He held up an arm, and she curled up and tucked herself into his body, fitting perfectly. He pulled her favorite alpaca blanket over her.

As she settled against him, Dean's mind took a sharp left. He flashed on her pain—the angry red splotches over her pale skin, the sheen of sweat on her upper lip and brow, the bend of her body over the toilet, the splashing sound as she threw up in the bowl, the raw fear in her eyes. Those images plunged into his gut and twisted, but even as he held her close, part of him observed, cold and detached. He'd long ago learned to turn his dark moments into profiling practice.

For some men, what Dean had just witnessed was porn. Some men would be hard to the point of pain witnessing the broken agony of Kiera. And though he didn't want to, though the very idea made him want to puke himself, he didn't stop trying on that personality. He relished the overblown sense of power, superiority, and lust at what he'd wrought, the destruction he'd unleashed on her.

Flipping the switch to evil took so little effort, and Dean feared that sort of switch might one day never switch back. God, he was tired. That was all. He was himself. He didn't savor others' pain. And certainly not Kiera's.

Holding her close flipped that switch back into the off position. She was good for him and so damned strong. He just wished he could help her see that about herself.

She smiled and put her hand across his stomach. Dean closed his eyes and almost fell asleep. Kiera nudged him awake. "You're supposed to tell me the rest of the naked run."

Dean understood the desire to act normal, to seek distraction until the adrenaline drained. He wrapped his other arm around her and told her about the other naked arrests he and Curt had had his first summer as a police officer.

The next incident was the drunk woman in the bushes who peed in the squad car. Thankfully, fleet had to clean that up and not him and Curt. Kiera laughed outright, her mood changing like the full moon emerging from the clouds. She stroked his chest.

Dean ignored his semiaroused state and adjusted his position so Kiera wouldn't notice. Not every erection needed a parade or a key to the city.

He told her about the third naked incident, not even a week after the first, which was a couple in Hyde Park having sex on the swings at a playground. That couple, at least, had clothes on hand, so they didn't have to arrest them naked, but it still counted in the streak. The last had been a homeless man in an alley. They had called for an ambulance, though they thought he was dead, but when Dean reached over to check for a pulse, the man rolled over, hand on his johnson, and almost sprayed him. The narrow escape of the ejaculate shot made Dean arrest him. Otherwise, they might have insisted he dress and leave it at that.

"Four in how short a time period?"

"Two weeks," he said. "We were on high alert for the next few months after that. Any calls that came in that sounded like they possibly involved someone naked, we were not so quick to respond."

Kiera snuggled tighter to him. "So, tonight."

Was she ready to talk about what just happened? A promising sign. "Yeah?"

She spoke into his chest. "We hadn't been together in what felt like forever, so I was like a horny teenager."

"Me too. Perhaps we were too exuberant?"

"No. I loved how carefree and out of control we were. And I want to feel like that again. It was next level until . . ." She leaned back and gave him a theatrical grimace. ". . . the puking."

Dean chuckled. One of the things he appreciated most about Kiera was her humor amid chaos. No matter how dire the situation, she managed to crack a grim joke. It reminded him of cop banter, of how he and Curt easily barbed each other at the most gruesome crime scenes. Civilians didn't always get that sort of inappropriate levity.

"Well, it certainly wasn't boring," he replied with a quick kiss to her shoulder, hoping she wanted to play that way.

She groaned. "Ha. I think I'm going to remove that memory when you're asleep."

"Can you do that?"

Kiera rolled her eyes. "No, I need consent."

Dean stretched his arms and yawned for dramatic effect. "Too bad for you then, because I'm keeping it."

"Why would you want that memory?"

Outside, a gale of wind whistled, a reminder of the unpredictable nature of the world. He brushed his fingers over her cheekbones. "I want all our memories."

She rested her head on his chest. "I'm sorry."

He kissed the top of her head. "Don't say you're sorry, or I might throw up."

CHAPTER FORTY SIX

Kiera

THEY FELL INTO A ROUTINE OF LATE-NIGHT/EARLY-morning dinners together around 2:00 a.m. When he took his day or days off, it was like a holiday or vacation, and they often stayed in bed, talking for over an hour before starting the day.

Kiera never lazed, not as a teenager and definitely not now—she woke up and got up. Dean preferred to relax before he rose—which made no sense to Kiera. But she remained in bed to be closer to Dean and then found she liked it. She enjoyed the playful and childlike lounging on Big Bad John, like playing desert island. They started leaving snacks in the side tables.

One morning, Dean flipped so his head was near the footboard. She wore nothing at all, and he wore only his boxer briefs and the glasses she loved. In his maneuverings, he'd cocked up the comforter, so it lay mostly on the floor. Before she could fix the mess, he grabbed her foot and pressed his thumbs into the arch.

She groaned in pleasure.

"Okay, choose a superpower," he demanded, a quizzing game he often suggested they play.

She and Ash had debated superpowers several times, so she had a ready answer. "Flying. What about you?"

Dean, though he had proposed the discussion, didn't have a quick response. "I don't know. Super strength or lie detection."

"Lie detection?" Kiera sat up to mock him properly. "God, you're such a cop. Knowing when someone lies would be a curse, not a superpower."

He raised his eyebrows at her. "Oh yeah?"

"Yeah. Can you imagine finding out that everyone hates your tie and that you're not aging well and that your cooking sucks and that you're not as large as you think you are—"

"Wait a minute." He tugged her foot hard, and she flopped back on the bed. His strong hands gripped their way up her calves. She squealed. Dean kept rising up her body, closing in on her. "Are you challenging my manhood?"

She couldn't catch her breath with her laughing, a giddy sort of fear warring with sexual heat. He scared her with his predatory movements, though she knew, *knew*, he was playing.

It was Dean. She trusted him. And she realized she was safe.

That didn't stop a shriek from exploding out of her mouth.

Dean stopped moving, his hands on her left thigh. He kissed her hip bone and arranged the sheet over them until only his head poked out. "You okay?"

"Uh, yeah. I can take you."

He shot up until they were facing each other. "Before you take me, I need to ask you something."

"All right." God, he suddenly looked so serious. Had she said or done something—

"What if I'm larger than I think I am?"

She laughed—really laughed—then tackled him, rolling them over until she was on top again. "You'd be the first man ever."

His phone rang. They stared at each other, then Dean leaned over and snatched his phone from his side table. He checked out the display, groaned, and pushed it under a pillow.

"Work?" Kiera asked.

"Worse, my mom."

His mom was worse than work?

Kiera tried to comprehend his aversion to a mother that loved him too deeply, which had been his only complaint about his parents. Something more was going on, but she didn't want to pry. Pains and fears should only be shared willingly.

"You want me to give you some privacy?"

"No." He sighed and retrieved his phone from under the pillow. He put on shorts and a T-shirt before he called his mother back. "Don't look at me like that. Talking to my mom when I'm only in my underwear is creepy."

That made Kiera laugh. "You want me to get dressed too?"

He looked her up and down. "The answer to that is always no." Then he sat on the edge of Big Bad John and took two deep breaths before calling his mother.

"Hey, Mom." Dean's voice was soft yet brittle. She draped herself over his back like a dentist's iron cape. He stroked her forearms.

Kiera couldn't hear the exact words, but Dean's mother had a deeper voice than she'd expected. She imagined his mom having a breathy, higher-pitched voice, probably because Dean portrayed her as submissive and stereotypically feminine. Kiera hated to discover she bore the same prejudices as most people. A high-pitched, breathy voice didn't mean anything, and it was a disservice to women to assume anything based on voice alone.

"Yeah, sorry, work's been insane," Dean said before sighing. "I told you, Mom. I took a personal day, so I won't have to work . . ." His body stiffened. Kiera slid off him, recognizing he might need to move, to pace out his stress. He laughed. "I promise."

His mother talked and talked with Dean only contributing "I'm listening" noises. He collapsed onto his back on the bed, eyes shut. Kiera imagined unzipping his shorts and putting his dick in her mouth. The fantasy excited her, but she couldn't risk some sort of panic attack while within earshot of his mother.

But maybe one day.

She contented herself with stroking his hair with her fingernails. Dean opened his eyes to slits like a pleased cat, then closed them again.

He sat up abruptly. "Actually, one of the cases is mine." He scooted off the bed and began pacing. "That's just the movies, Mom. Serial killers don't typically stalk the detectives investigating them . . . Mom. Mom! Trust me: I'm not in danger . . . I know . . . I know . . . Yes, I appreciate that . . . Mom, did you call—"

Kiera covered her mouth to hold in her laugh. Dean narrowed his eyes at her and shook his head, which only made her laugh more.

Dean ran a hand over the back of his head. "I'll be there. You don't have to ask me every week." He rubbed his eyes. "No, I'm not upset, just tired. Sorry, I didn't mean to snap." He laughed. "That would be great . . . Yes . . . Okay . . . Love you too. Bye."

He tossed his phone behind him with a groan and turned to Kiera. "She calls me every week about that stupid barbecue."

"The one you back out of every year?"

"Yes." He reached out and took her hand. "I don't know why I find it so stressful. She brags about me a lot to whoever shows up, which is embarrassing, but . . . I don't know."

Kiera leaned over and kissed his forehead. She had a wild impulse so strong that the words came out of her before she could stop them. "Do you want me to go with you?"

"What? Really?"

She shrugged, though it wasn't a shrug-worthy issue, and she'd surprised herself. "I'm not the kind of woman parents love, but you'd have my support."

"You don't have to do that."

The weakness of his response told her that he wanted her to go. Kiera had never been the hero before, and she loved the idea of shielding him from parental affection and expectation. "I don't like to go out, but I'm not agoraphobic or anything. I can handle an afternoon with people." She sounded like she meant it too.

CHAPTER FORTY SEVEN

Dean

DEAN LAUGHED AT JASON, WHO SAT NEAR HIS partner, Kristin, eyeing her lunch like a dog begging for scraps. His teammates had a partnership almost as good as his and Curt's.

"She didn't bring enough to share," he grumbled at Dean's attention.

Curt had taken a personal day to celebrate his anniversary, which left Dean working alone. Ordinarily, he would have been bummed, but he'd been wanting to talk to Jason for weeks.

Even though things with Kiera had been going well, he wanted some tips for when things turned pear-shaped. He would never find a better opportunity. "Want to hit Pizza Capri?"

Jason brightened. "Works for me." He knocked Kristin's chair. "I'm not bringing you back squat."

"I weep," Kristin said with a mouthful of chicken breast.

* * *

JASON DID HIS THING WHERE HE REARRANGED THE OBJECTS ON THE table. He liked the salt and pepper on his right and all flip menus, condiments, and napkins to be on the far left. If Jason discovered anything offending on the table, it wasn't enough to have the spot wiped or cleaned; Jason would need a new table. When his food came out, he would rearrange his plate too, most likely. Curt hated eating with Jason, but Dean didn't mind. He found the show entertaining.

"So, they started tearing down the wall between the kitchen and dining room." Jason pulled the Velcro loose from his vest. Like Curt, Jason always removed his vest to eat. Dean always left his on. Jason slung his vest over the back of an adjacent chair. "And there's fucking plaster behind the drywall."

Dean shook his head. "I warned you about those old houses."

"Amelia thinks there's horsehair or something in it. She's making that up, right?"

"Nope. They used to use horsehair or goat hair back in the day." Hearing Jason talk about Amelia in such a normal way, like before, gave Dean hope for promising news.

Jason pounded a meaty fist, the sound too loud. "Damn. I owe her twenty bucks now."

"Why do you keep betting her? Have you ever won?" Dean didn't bother to hide his laugh.

Jason ignored Dean and picked up his menu, though they'd all eaten there enough not to need one.

* * *

WHEN THEIR FOOD CAME, DEAN DECIDED TO FINALLY ASK JASON'S ADVICE. Before he could, Jason gave him a shit-eating grin. "So, you gonna to tell me about your girlfriend, or are you still keeping her a secret?"

"She's not a secret," Dean replied with a mock slam down. "She's just none of your business."

Jason raised his brows, suddenly serious. "Even if it's starting to affect your work?" That took Dean off track for a moment, which Jason intended because he full-on cackled. "I'm fucking with you. Kind of. We've all noticed you're in a better mood the last month."

Dean tossed his napkin at Jason's face, but he caught it and tossed it back. This was the opening he'd needed. "Yeah, I'm dating someone I really like. But, listen, I wanted your advice."

"Now *you're* fucking with *me*," Jason said with a laugh.

Dean sighed. "No, I'm not. She's got a few issues."

Jason frowned. "What kind of issues?"

"I can't go into specifics, but I thought maybe your experience with Amelia might help me with her." Dean used a soft voice as if that would cushion the pain bringing up his wife's attack would cause.

Amelia's sexual assault had been bad enough to require hospitalization. Jason never talked about how the ordeal affected him.

Jason shook his head. "Don't do it, man."

"Do what?"

"Get out now. You don't want to take that on. I'm serious. Get out before it's too late." Jason's voice was urgent and hard, without a pause or peek of doubt.

Dean tried to corral his thoughts. The conversation wasn't going the way he had anticipated—any of the ways he had anticipated. "Why?"

"You don't get it," Jason said, pushing his plate aside, plonking his elbows on the table, his hands fisted together. "Think of the worst possible thing she could say, and I guarantee it will come out of her mouth multiple times. You weren't there. You don't care. You don't understand. All you care about is the bastard who did this. You're selfish. You're the job. You're a fucking monster."

Dean flinched. He was the job—sometimes—too often. And he'd had to think like a monster to catch a monster, and though it was different, it wasn't *that* different.

"And God forbid we catch a big case when she's having one of her bad days. You'll be rolling the body, standing at the end of the morgue table documenting the injuries of some gunshot vic, and your phone won't stop buzzing because your fucking wife is feeling unsafe and alone, and you can't go to her no matter how much she cries. So you're trying to find her some support *and* do your job, but whatever you do won't be the same as you being there, and she's not going to appreciate all you do to watch out for her because you carry a gun and she thinks you're never scared and you're so irritated and conflicted and you're *not* thinking loving thoughts, you're *not* wishing you could be with her, and our lives are so full of violence, and when you get home, you'll find that so is hers because that's all she plays on repeat."

Dean listened in some kind of paralytic stupor as Jason shredded his napkin into long, thin strips, his voice somewhere between a mumble and regular speech. When he finished one napkin, he moved to another, the strips like paper fresh from a shredder.

He couldn't stop. "You can't do a damn thing with what's bugging her, and she sure as shit doesn't want to hear about your bad day, and you're in the bathroom at 4:00 a.m. scrubbing blood out of your shirt from some witness grabbing you, and your wife is going to walk in and freak out, and when you go to hold her, she's going to scream and hold up her hands as if she's scared of you, like you were the one that hurt her. And even when she apologizes in the morning, you'll know she equates you with that piece of shit. She'll see everything about you that reminds her of the man who destroyed her. And after a while, you'll get so fed up with it that maybe she's not wrong."

Jason sat back, took a long pull from his water glass, then wiped both eyes with his hands. He wasn't crying, but his eyes had gone shiny and pinched. Mostly, he looked tired to the depth of his soul. "Sorry, dude—didn't mean to unload on you. Amelia and I had a rough couple of days this week."

The paralysis broke. "I didn't intend to bring all that up," Dean said as his own soul seemed to inhale all the poison Jason had just exhaled.

Would Kiera come to equate him with all the males who had hurt all her clients? Would she see the violence that tainted him by association and come to associate him with it? When he dove deep into the feelings and perspective of killers, would she see the abyss that clung to him afterward? He wouldn't let it come to that.

CHAPTER FORTY EIGHT

Kiera

"**C**OME HERE." DEAN GESTURED WITH HIS entire arm from his sprawled position on Goliath.

"I'm making lunch."

"Who cares about food? You're too far away." His limb flopped to the floor in mock despair. "Kiiiiiera."

She laughed and tip-toed to the side of the couch to watch Dean wallow. His eyes were closed, but he popped one eye open when she'd gotten close. He lolled his head to stare up at her. "Hey, beautiful."

Nobody looked at her the way Dean did. Every other man fell into one of three categories. They didn't see her at all, they saw only the packaging, or they burrowed their gaze too deep inside. Dean saw her without flaying her first, without looking for anything more than who she was. "Hey, handsome."

"Snuggle with me." He held his arms open like a toddler, and Kiera rolled over the back of the couch to splat onto him. He caught her and tucked her into a spooning position, letting her take the outside where she wouldn't feel trapped.

"This is nice." She backed into him, allowing his body to support her own.

His fingers made meandering trails along her skin like a drunk trying to find her way home. She thought of Doreen, who'd never had anything like this and now never could. Kiera gripped Dean's arm tighter, wanting to go back in time to when Doreen was alive and bring this oasis of peace with her. For all that the memory surgeons did, all the people they connected to more closely than their own families, they were—Kiera had been—lacking real connection. Lying next to Dean with his breath on her neck, his body framing hers, his hands touching in a way that soothed, she thought she might die from happiness.

"Dean?"

"Hm?"

"Thank you."

His sleepy voice rumbled. "For what?"

She almost laughed, thinking of how to encompass everything, the ever-present pain of loss and betrayal that he assuaged with the rhythmic stroking of her skin and his solid presence. "This," she said as a weak start. "You're so patient with me."

His face dipped to her neck, and he pulled her tighter for a moment. "You might be a little bit more sensitive than most—"

She snort-laughed at that.

"—but you handle everything remarkably well, Kiera. You're amazing. So, if I have to be a little more mindful with what I do and say, it's not a big deal. Probably everyone would be better off if they took more care."

Kiera scoot-rolled to face him. His hazel eyes were mostly open, but the usual sharpness dimmed with indolence. It made looking into his eyes easier, and she slipped into a warm-bath kind of relaxation herself. "I should take more care with you."

She ignored the snap of truth to her words. Dr. Trent was always telling her to claim any good moments that came her way and let go of guilt. Every bit of pleasure and wholeness needed to be savored and experienced in the now. Kiera had never perceived the importance of living in the moment more.

Dean kept his arms loosely around her. "You okay, babe?"

With her right arm pinned between them, she could only hug him with her left, but she pulled him close. "I'm good. I wish we could stay like this forever."

He rested his cheek on the top of her head. "I'll hold you whenever you want. Just ask."

Kiera tilted her chin. "When you're here."

His body stiffened but then relaxed. "I'm sorry I can't give you more."

She kissed him, but some of the magic sloughed off at her careless words, uttered less than a minute after she'd admitted she should be more careful. "You have nothing to be sorry for. What you give me is more than enough to make up for the erratic schedule and long hours. Please. Forget I said that."

"Said what?"

But they couldn't go back, couldn't shift into the lazy, hazy intimacy. Why was it the best moments of life were impossible to recapture but pain, self-doubt, and misery were 24-7 accessible? Returning to any number of shitty mental places was as easy as blinking.

Not today. How could she demonstrate her care? "This will all pay off when I distract your parents at the family picnic."

"Do I want to know how you're going to do that?"

"I can juggle." Which was true, though that sort of spectacle was a last resort.

It worked, though; Dean laughed.

CHAPTER FORTY NINE

Dean

DEAN HAD HIS OWN KEY CARD FOR THE ELEVATOR now, and he liked that. It made him feel he had special privileges and he'd earned Kiera's trust and forgiveness after the way they'd met. He still asked Manny at the front desk to let Kiera know he was on his way so the opening of the door wouldn't startle her. And he loved walking out of the elevator and finding her waiting. When he got to her floor, however, her door was closed. He knocked, though he knew the code.

She flung open the door. "Are these boots stupid?" she asked.

It took Dean more than a few seconds to compute what she was asking. His brain had stuttered. Kiera had always been beautiful, but tonight she was stunning. She wore a black-and-gold corset in some sort of upholstery material that pulled in her waist and boosted up her breasts. Her pants were simple black dress pants, but they clung to her body. The outfit alone would have made him mute, but on top of that, she had done her hair and makeup.

Her hair was thick and glossy and fell in wisps over her face. The dark color of her clothes highlighted her bright-blue eyes, the makeup turning her eyes anime big, and her lips were red and wet.

"What?" She slipped a thumbnail in her mouth. "I should change, right? I look ridiculous." She turned away, muttering, "So stupid."

"No," he said louder than he should. "No, no, no, don't change. Nobody's going to notice the boots, but they're fine." They were black and blocky, but they only made her look like she could kick ass.

Hot.

"I'm going to grab a purse," she said, glaring. "When I get back, I expect you to not be so weird."

Just before she turned away from him, he saw the corner of her smile. And dear Lord, the view as she walked away. The back of her was as exquisite as the front, the corset coming halfway up her back, exposing her bare skin. The pants hugged her curves. Kiera was sensitive, and if he didn't stop acting all googly-eyed, she was going to freak out on him. But goddamn.

* * *

DEAN HAD NEVER BEEN TO GEJA'S BEFORE, BUT CURT INSISTED IT WAS the place to go. He was right. It was dimly lit and intimate. Their side booth was composed of thick mahogany, and heavy red drapes pulled back gave the illusion of privacy. Kiera relaxed when she was tucked away. The waiter was young and solicitous, and though he didn't stare at Kiera, his attention wandered to her often, though Dean, presumably, would be paying his tip.

The cheese fondue came out fast, and Dean had real hope they wouldn't be there for hours. Kiera speared a chunk of French bread.

"This is so fun." She plunged the bread into the cheese, then let go of the stick to watch it sink.

"So, when's the last time you were on a date?"

"Are you trying to make me self-conscious?" She tugged on her lip and sighed. "I haven't traditionally dated in years. I'm not out enough to meet people, and you know how I am." She brushed her fingers together, smearing the lipstick that had stuck there.

"So, you . . . untraditionally dated?" He really wanted her to tell him about the paid sex. He'd tried to let it go, but then he worried that the guy fulfilled something that Dean wasn't giving her. Sometimes it was easier to ask for what you wanted when you were paying for it.

"I had an escort I hired when I . . . you know . . . really needed to be touched." She scowled. "Don't judge me."

He'd kept his forward lean, both hands on the table, palms tilted up, all to portray openness and acceptance. He wanted to assure her—and himself. "I'm not, but I'm curious."

"Garrett was a professional, so it wasn't as awkward as you're imagining. And before you switch into cop mode, what we did isn't illegal. I paid him for his time, and only some of it was spent dancing in the sheets."

He tried to laugh, but her words tripped something primal. Garrett. Probably wasn't his real name. "What else did you do, then?"

She shrugged and played with her water glass. "He held me a lot, which I know sounds pathetic. He was great at making me feel like he was a friend."

"I'm glad you had that."

"Are you?" Kiera pressed the heel of her hand into her eyebrow and growled. "I'm not going to apologize for needing human contact and not feeling safe any other way, Dean."

"I don't care that you hired someone." That much was true. Still, the image of an underwear-model-type guy holding his girlfriend made his skin feel a size smaller than his body. "Sorry." He took a breath and ignored the security gate that wanted to crash between them. "I hate to admit this, because it's completely irrational, but I'm a little jealous—not about the sex, not really."

She finally looked at him. "Then what about?"

"I want to be the one who satisfies that need. The idea of you being in pain and it's somebody else comforting you . . ."

"We hadn't even met."

"I did say it was irrational." He sipped his beer. "I get you hiring an escort; it makes perfect sense. This is just me fighting with my inner caveman."

She gripped the back of her neck then stroked down, processing what he'd said. "You're jealous of someone I had to pay to be with me?"

"Sad, right?" he said. "I'm trying to want you all to myself in a way that's healthy and not stalkerish, but I'm not doing as well as I'd hoped."

Kiera raised her eyes to his. "You're doing better than you think." She slid out of the booth and slipped in next to him. "Now you've gone and permanently ruined escorts for me. Why would I want the lie of an escort when I can have something real?" She fisted his shirt and kissed him.

* * *

KIERA RETURNED TO HER SIDE OF THE TABLE IN TIME FOR A SERVER TO bring out the meats, a fondue pot filled with oil, and different sauces on the side. It wasn't the tastiest meal Dean had ever had, but the atmosphere was drowsy and sexy; Kiera was seductive and playful. He fed her from his fork and studied her as she took a bite. Her lips weren't as red, but they were still full, and Dean recalled exactly how soft they were.

Suddenly, Kiera stiffened and cowered back in the booth.

"What's wrong?" Dean peered into the restaurant. A young man in too-tight gray pants was toting a young, tattooed brunette toward them. "You know those guys?"

"No." Her voice was like a guitar string ready to snap.

"Kiera Brayleigh, right?" The young man sounded both excited and angry. "See? I told you it was her."

Kiera's face was a mask, which told Dean she was uncomfortable.

The guy either didn't notice or didn't care about her discomfort. "You could tell if someone was cheating, yeah? If Krystal here said she'd been faithful, you'd know if she was lying, right?"

"I'm not a lie detector," Kiera replied, voice cold.

"Bullshit. You could pull up the cheating memory in a second if you wanted. They talked about it in my psych class last semester. I'm not some uninformed idiot." His voice was as hot as hers was cold.

Dean stood, and the man backed up a few steps. Lyndsey Lynn had once commented that he had a "cop face" that he used on occasion, and Dean had no doubt he was wearing it right then. "We're trying to have a private dinner."

The guy glared at Dean's chin, a sure sign he was intimidated. "Fuck you, man." Then he turned to the woman, Krystal, and muttered, "What a bitch." He stalked back across the room, tugging Krystal with him.

"You tell him to get lost, and I'm the bitch," Kiera mumbled. "Asshole."

He noticed her face pale. "Should I apologize?"

"For what? Running off a creep? I . . . I just need a few minutes to calm down, and I'll be appropriately grateful." She tried to smile, but it came out more as a grimace.

"You don't need to be appropriately grateful."

"Maybe you should find out what that entails before you wave it off like that." Her tight voice belied her stress.

Dean stretched his hand across the table, palm up. She took his hand. Talking it through might dissipate the tension faster than pretending it wasn't there. "Does that happen a lot?"

"No, but I cringe every time anyone recognizes me. I mean, you wouldn't insist a famous chef whip you up a baked Alaska when you run into them on the street, right?" She wanted to deflect.

He could deflect. "Or a musician play a concerto."

"Or a lawyer review your rental agreement." Her shoulders rocked, indicating a swinging foot or leg under the table, a sign her mood was lifting.

He kept going. "Or insist a dermatologist remove a hairy mole."

The banter continued that way for several more minutes until they were both laughing too hard to continue. They were nothing like Jason and Amelia.

CHAPTER FIFTY

Kiera

IERA WAS DANGEROUSLY CLOSE TO BLOWING THE date. Dean had her giggling until her stomach hurt, but as soon as they stopped laughing, her mind returned to its usual post-accosted loop.

The asshole's sneer ran on repeat, the expression. His tone had said it all, like her ability made her a public servant, and he'd come calling for what he was due.

Hopefully, the woman *was* cheating on that prick. Anyone else was guaranteed to be an improvement. It would serve him right if she left him tonight for a kinder, more respectful lover.

When Kiera refused one of those public requests, which she always did, she was a selfish bitch. It surprised her how often they said the words aloud. Her mother had never called her a bitch to her face, but selfish was a familiar refrain.

You're so selfish.

Her mother's voice grated in her memory. Pious, philanthropic Mom who'd never taken a case pro bono.

God granted you this ability. These people are in pain, Kiera.

As though the price of having a gift she'd never asked for was that she had to live in service to everyone else.

The waiter came with the chocolate fondue and fruit, pound cake, and marshmallows. Kiera loved pound cake, and though using food as a pharmaceutical wasn't encouraged, it wasn't verboten. She speared a chunk as her phone sang "I Will Survive." It was Nadira's ringtone.

Damn it.

Nadira was a texter—a phone call indicated something serious. "It might be important."

"Go ahead." Dean submerged a marshmallow and pulled out his own cell to give her a little privacy.

"Hello?" Kiera said. She heard crying. "Dir? You okay?" More sobbing. Kiera's stomach dropped down to her knees. "Are you hurt?"

"No." The voice whispered. For a moment, Kiera had the daft thought that it wasn't really Nadira.

"Are you safe?"

"Just . . . bad day." Nadira's voice.

Kiera looked down at Dean. When had she stood?

"Everything okay?" he asked in a quiet voice.

She shook her head. "What can I do?" she asked Nadira, hating herself because she hadn't wanted to offer.

"Can I come over?"

Kiera's shoulders sagged, but she'd never let down Nadira. "Of course."

"Would you mind if I stayed the night? I . . . I don't want to be alone right now."

Kiera swallowed the lump in her throat. Nadira's pain affected her like nobody else, and her friend had to be in a bleak place to need a face-to-face. "We'll have a pajama party." She tried to sound cheerful.

Nadira's weak laugh was a hopeful sign. "No flannel."

Kiera snorted. "Fuck you, I have plenty of decent sleepwear."

Dean's eyebrows shot up, and he smirked. At least, he didn't seem angry.

"Can I bring champagne?" Nadira asked.

"You better," she said. "See you in about an hour?"

After the call ended, Kiera had to face Dean, and pray he would understand. "I'm sorry. We've always been there for each other."

Dean stuck his credit card into the bill. "Called off for an emergency?" He huffed out a dramatic breath. "I certainly can't relate to *that*." Then the guy winked at her. *Winked*. And made it work.

* * *

DEAN PULLED UP TO THE DOOR AND STARED AT HER FOR SEVERAL SECONDS as if he wanted to consume her. Kiera leaned over and kissed him. His response was brief, as if he expected a peck. She wasn't having that. Kiera drew his face closer and kept her lips pressed to his. He responded and gripped her upper back as their tongues met.

Knowing they couldn't do anything made it exciting, or perhaps the rush was the culmination of the entire evening. Kiera squirmed in her seat, her body like a lit match dropped into a box of fireworks.

After a few minutes, Dean pulled away and gripped the steering wheel. "I'm not taking my hands off this until you get out of the car." He took a deep breath. "Damn, Kiera."

* * *

KIERA WORE ROYAL-PURPLE SILK PAJAMA BOTTOMS WITH A MATCHING camisole. She thawed some chocolate-covered cherries, which were Nadira's favorite. Kiera was stuffed, but she had room for at least one.

Nadira showed up an hour after their conversation. When Manny called to announce her, Kiera disarmed the alarm and waited for Nadira's soft knock, trying not to remember Dean's flushed face. Nadira's eyes were bloodshot, but her makeup was perfect. She had a bottle of champagne, a Louis Vuitton travel bag, and a matching garment bag.

Kiera laughed when Nadira revealed her pajamas, navy silk with tiny white dots, hanging in the garment bag. The shirt was short-sleeved like a business shirt, with buttons in the front. The pants were just pants. "I didn't want them to wrinkle," Nadira said, as if she were making sense.

"Yeah, I'd have to kick you out if you showed up in wrinkled pajamas." Nadira arched a brow and shrugged one shoulder. Kiera rolled her eyes. "Go change already."

As Nadira entered the living room, Kiera held out a glass of champagne. They settled on opposite ends of Goliath, Kiera curling up on one end and Nadira sitting properly on the other.

"What happened?" Kiera asked.

Nadira set down her flute and dropped her face into her hands. "One of my former clients is . . ." She broke into sobs.

Kiera handed her a tissue and waited, sipping the sparkling apple juice in her champagne flute. Probably, she should hug her. Then she did, reaching across the couch and squeezing Nadira. "Once you get it out, you'll breathe easier."

"She's trying to get her father out of prison."

Kiera pulled back. "Oh shit."

That was one of Kiera's worst fears—that the client would believe the trauma had never happened. False memories were a real thing. A memory could turn funky in the retelling, like a game of telephone—sometimes affected maliciously by a third party and sometimes naturally. And more often with children, whose brains were still forming. The mind was a funny, funny thing. With the absence of the root, a false memory was more possible. That was one reason why none of them transferred until the court case was closed. Not even Kiera, with all her paranoia, had considered an appeal.

"Are you going to testify?" Kiera asked.

"I can't! Our testimony is inadmissible." Nadira hid her face in her hands again.

"This is bullshit!"

"I know." Nadira reached out and took Kiera's hand. "Oh, Kiera, the things he did to that little girl."

Kiera squeezed her hand. "Aren't there medical records for that shit?" One of the "advantages" to physical abuse as opposed to emotional abuse were the obvious effects.

Nadira released her hand and stood, pacing in front of the fireplace. "Same old song." She used her fingers to list off the excuses. "She was clumsy, she bruised easily, she was bullied at school, and my favorite: she sleepwalks."

Kiera took a deep breath. "Have you considered giving her a memory back? Just one?" She didn't say anything else, but this very situation was one of the reasons Kiera didn't do a full wipe. Her clients always knew something bad had happened. Of course, she couldn't judge, because she didn't do children, and she wasn't privy to the particulars of the case.

"No way." Nadira smoothed imaginary wrinkles from her thighs. "I don't know if I could, even if I tried."

"How old was she?"

"Six." Nadira sighed, maybe remembering the girl. "That was five years ago. She's still only eleven."

"What about the mother?"

"Alcoholic." Nadira swirled her champagne glass, making the bubbles scurry. "She's not the ideal parent, but she never abused her. He was one of the worst, Kiki. The verbal abuse was dreadful."

"He hit the wife, too?"

"They were never married, but yeah. I took the memories of the mother's abuse too, though."

Kiera nodded. She'd have also taken those memories. Nobody comprehended better than a memory surgeon about secondary trauma. "Shit."

"Exactly."

"You could write a letter to the court, I guess. It wouldn't have legal weight, but I can't imagine your input would be completely ignored. Her past has to count for something." It was a weak plan of attack, but nothing better came to mind.

"I suppose I could try."

* * *

IN THE MORNING, NADIRA BOUNCED INTO THE KITCHEN. "I TALKED TO the state's attorney. He said that they can't just reopen a case and that child abuse and domestic abuse victims often recant, so the court isn't likely to do anything. Maybe I got worried over nothing."

"Are you kidding? The idea is horrifying."

At least, that little girl was safe for now. Kiera shuffled in the kitchen, finishing up Nadira's favorite, eggs Benedict.

"Sometimes I'm glad we can't testify. I think about being cross-examined, and I don't know if I could maintain my poise. It would be like I was on trial." Nadira tucked her hair behind her ear. "But it would feel better to do more, you know?"

Kiera nodded. "That's kind of how I felt about the coma victim. You and I worked together on that sketch, remember? They even used it on TV."

"That was strange sharing that blip of a memory." Nadira rested her elbows on the counter. "Too bad we couldn't download all the DMV photos in the state into Beth's brain. She'd find him instantly."

Kiera giggled. "We'd make the most dysfunctional crime-fighting team ever."

"Possibly rendering your boyfriend irrelevant."

"Believe me: he's got plenty of relevance outside his work." Kiera conjured the memory of Dean standing up to the douche nozzle at dinner, then his joking her out of her foul mood, and then that last kiss.

"Oh yeah? He's that talented?"

Kiera whisked the hollandaise sauce with a sway in her hips. "Last time he spent the night, I thought I saw God." They both laughed. But she didn't want Nadira to think that sex was all she had with Dean. "I slept eight hours, Dir, with his arm around me. Eight. Hours. Like a normal person."

"Wow." Nadira picked up her fork and wiggled it between her thumb and index finger. "It's going so well. Doesn't that worry you?"

It did. "Too good to be true, right? I keep waiting for him to realize that

I'm not worth all the hassle. But it's motivating me to grow. I even agreed to go to a family picnic. With, like his mom and dad there."

Nadira gaped at her. "Go you. Social gatherings are not your strong suit."

Kiera forced a smile. "Doesn't mean I can't pull it off."

* * *

KIERA SUFFERED NO ANXIETY THE WEEK BEFORE THE PICNIC. NADIRA'S client couldn't reopen the case, and Dean seemed happy and lively. Every time he came over since she'd boasted about her talent, he begged her to juggle for him, promising her sexual treats. She'd refused, intending to practice first.

But with the barbecue tomorrow, tendrils of nerves wormed their way into her. She kept dropping the balls of socks. Not that she'd ever juggle in front of strangers, but she was working on a strip juggling routine for Dean to make him laugh. For his family, she would make chocolate chip cookies. Everybody loved those, and she couldn't arrive empty-handed, regardless of Dean's assurances.

Ash phoned as she mixed up the cookie batter. "Can you meet me for dinner?"

Kiera snorted and shook a generous portion of milk chocolate chips into the mixing bowl. "You just assume I don't have plans?"

Ash mimicked her snort. "Because you never have plans."

Kiera decided to tell Ash about Dean. "As a matter of fact, I can't go out because I must prepare for my boyfriend's family picnic tomorrow. So, ha!"

"You what?"

"Your shock is quite unflattering, little brother." And somewhat satisfying.

"Oops." Ash hummed. "Can we meet just for a bit?"

A trickle of dread slid from the inside of her left eye. Her brother should have been whooping and probing like a puppy on uppers. "Why?"

After too long of a pause, Ash said, "I need to talk to you."

The dread reached her gut where it expanded until it corseted her, making it hard to breathe. She turned off the heating oven. "We're talking now. Just say it Ash because you're freaking me out. Are you . . ." She swallowed down something thick and metallic. ". . . sick?"

"No." He spoke too loud, but Kiera didn't mind, as the air running freely through her lungs gave her a dizzy kind of high. "No, Kiera, nothing like that. It's—Mom and Dad gave an interview on NPR that's airing tomorrow morning, and I didn't want you to be surprised by it."

All that air caught in her chest. "Interview?"

"About their book." Ash's tentative phrasing indicated more bad news coming, something worse.

"They've already written it?"

"No, they're in the process, but they wanted to start the media campaign early." Media campaign. "Anyway, they . . . mentioned your breakdown."

Kiera's face flamed as her stomach froze, and her knees gave out. She collapsed to a sitting position on the kitchen floor. "What?"

Her mother wouldn't. Kiera's supposed breakdown was the family's darkest secret, both because the commitment had been orchestrated by her mother and, in a sense, unreal, and because potential clients would have been scared off by dealing with someone so unstable. But Kiera wasn't seeing clients through her parents any longer. Her distancing herself from them had given them the space they needed to attack her without it affecting them. She should have seen that coming. She should have prepared, especially when Ash had warned her about that book.

"Please. Please, don't cry, Kiera. It's not as bad as you think."

* * *

CORTNEY, HER LAWYER, GAVE HER LITTLE HOPE. STOPPING THE interview from airing wasn't possible in so short a time. Worse, Cortney's research affirmed that if her mom and dad wrote the novel as creative nonfiction, they likely couldn't stop publication.

Kiera's hands shook as she held the phone, shoving all the papers off her desk looking for her Airpods so she could talk hands-free. "But I have proof that shrink took bribes and—"

"Kiera, unless you have proof that he did that in your case—"

"I was seventeen years old! How the fuck could I have gotten hold of my parent's financial—"

"That's not what I'm—"

"There has to be—"

"Let's meet next week and hash out a strategy."

Kiera threw a glass paperweight that looked like the galaxy into the wall, expecting the globe to shatter, but it punched a hole in the drywall instead. She couldn't even get destruction right. "No."

"No? You want to meet—"

"No, forget it." She couldn't win. Putting her energy into a losing fight would cause more damage than it could possibly repair. She'd underestimated her parents, and this was the cost. "I cut them out of my life a long time ago. If I pursue this, it will move them into the center, and I can't do that."

"You don't need any direct contact. I can—"

"Cortney, I appreciate your willingness to take them on." As Kiera spoke, her convictions solidified. "Likely, they've anticipated my reaction and have an entire media blitz waiting for this opportunity, for some huge, public feud. I'm not going to give them that."

Kiera took her monthly allotment of Valium and one toke of Mary Jane. It didn't remove the pain or anxiety, but built a nice buffer, where she could study the shape of the clusterfuck about to hit her life. She thought of all her mental anguish, and how her mother would portray her in their "novel."

Her parents could humiliate her with the truth, but they wouldn't stop there. Under the guise of creative license, they would enlarge her temper tantrums and dive deep into her withdrawal and self-pity. Worst of all, they'd cast themselves as heroes. Kiera could hear her mother's voice, the one she wore for other people, cloaked in a mother's love, telling everyone how she begged Kiera not to push herself too hard, how it broke her motherfucking heart.

CHAPTER FIFTY ONE

Dean

DEAN FORCED HIS EYES WIDE TO FURTHER WAKE himself. The team had caught a case last night that they hadn't finished until five in the morning. Even with his going straight home, Dean hadn't slept more than three hours, and he'd find no time for a nap before the picnic.

Despite the otherworldliness of his exhaustion haze, part of him looked forward to the family event. He anticipated introducing Kiera, solidifying her presence in his life, and he wanted Kiera to meet everyone, learn her take on their family dynamics, laugh about it later.

The radio cut out, signaling an incoming phone call. Kiera canceling? His stomach dropped out the back of his car and tumbled onto the pavement. But it was a CPD number.

"This is Matthson."

"Hey, Dean, it's Belinda Lighthouse at the crime lab."

His stomach leapt back into his body. "Hi, Belinda. What's up?"

"Don't get too excited, because there's no match, but we pulled enough DNA from that gum to have a profile when you find a suspect. Thought you'd want to know right away."

"Yes!" Dean slapped his hand on the steering wheel. "Thank you for letting me know, Belinda. Great work!" The fingerprint linkage between Kolchek's and the church was tenuous, only a few partials that were a likely match. A few edges weren't as solid as a full print. But if the DNA and partial prints matched to the same suspect, it would solidify his case considerably. Now all he needed was a suspect. But today wasn't the day to worry about that.

Dean kept pushing his speed to reach Kiera sooner. He couldn't wait to share the good news.

*　*　*

KIERA'S CONDO WAS DARK, SETTING DEAN'S SENSES ON ALERT. BY TEN IN the morning, Kiera should have opened all her drapes and blinds. "Kiera?"

No response.

Dean toed off his shoes and headed for the bedroom. When he nudged open the door, enough light hit the room that the lump of Kiera in bed became visible. Was she sick? "Kiera?"

She groaned and pulled the covers over her head. "No."

He made himself smile, to force his body into lightness as he approached the bed. "You feeling all right, babe?"

"No, I'm hung over."

Dean's head throbbed, and something sharp scoured in his chest. Kiera never drank alcohol alone and never to excess. "What's happened?"

"It's unimportant."

He sat on the edge of the bed. "Nadira okay?"

"Yeah, she's fine." Nothing else.

Kiera wouldn't come. No matter her commitment, no matter his good news about the case or that he craved her support. He was jumping to conclusions, but his throat tightened. "Can I get you something? Water? Tea? Toast?"

"Ibuprofen and some water. Thanks."

Like a puppet, he fetched her water and painkillers and leashed the bitter disappointment that turned his mouth sour. He hadn't expected this degree of grief.

Over a picnic.

But it had been about a lot more than a picnic to him.

He'd told his family about Kiera, how much he liked her, even admitting it was serious. His mother made macarons just for her, wanting to impress this woman who wouldn't even get out of bed. And now he'd have to tell them she wasn't coming and couldn't explain why. This was worse than if she'd never offered to come.

Breathe. Okay, it wasn't as if Kiera timed this breakdown on purpose. Maybe he'd spent too long thinking about Kiera's issues to avoid looking at his own. What grown-ass man dreaded his family because they cared too much? Lots of people had families that didn't really know them. He shouldn't need his girlfriend to feel grounded.

He handed everything to her and stood at the side of her bed breathing deep to keep his voice calm. "So, no picnic then?"

She snorted. "Obviously." Then she slapped a hand over her forehead. "I'm sorry, Dean. I intended to go, even made Nadira help me pick an outfit, but I can't face your family today."

"I'll tell them you aren't feeling well, and we'll schedule another time for them to meet you."

"Better not get their hopes up."

A hot itch crept up the back of his neck. "What do you mean?"

"I'm not the kind of woman every parent wants for their son. You should prepare them for what a mess I am."

He grabbed her ankle through the covers and shook it once. "You're not as messy as you think." Then he considered her red eyes. "Usually."

She didn't laugh but sighed as if it hurt to breathe. "Every time I think I'm getting better the universe likes to remind me that I'm not."

He kept his voice as calm as he could. "What happened, babe?"

"Not now."

His pulse boomed in his ears, and his hands shook. He should assure her or comfort her or distract her but couldn't. "I brought you a chocolate peanut butter cup cookie from Insomnia. I'm going to go put it in the kitchen."

"Sure."

He didn't know what she was going through because she wouldn't share it. She had every right to wait until she was ready. Fuck him, right? So what if he'd never asked her for anything except this one day. So what if he needed her, and she refused to even attempt to wrangle herself together. Asking her to try would make him the bad guy, and she would lash out. And it wouldn't change a goddamned thing.

Whatever.

The internal pressure grew, removed, like an alien presence. Killers, he supposed, felt this all the time, the desperate need to relieve the tension. Dean even experienced intense fantasies. He imagined yelling, unloading every unkind, betrayed thought. Before he could stop himself, Dean embodied his serial killer, how he would assuage his frustration and anger.

His knife. His victim—not the woman he despised but a placeholder, a specter of a human being, a doll. His delight when the blade slid deep into her uterus, the organ that made a female a woman, the biggest fuck-you in the universe, to her and the rest of the cunts in the world. Watch the life leave their eyes. The power of it consuming him, eating away everything that ached and pinched. The blessed high. The blessed relief.

Dean crushed the cookie in his hand and dropped it to the counter, crumbs everywhere.

He hadn't pictured Kiera when he thought it, hadn't even felt like himself, but that didn't matter. It was one thing to fall into that pattern of thinking on the job or entertaining a stray thought under duress, but he had connected too closely to that evil. Maybe it was the perfect storm of too little sleep, the news about the case, and his anger at Kiera, but this wasn't who he wanted to be. Maybe Kiera didn't ground him. Maybe he couldn't be grounded.

CHAPTER FIFTY TWO

Kiera

THE BACK OF KIERA'S NECK PRICKED AS IF SHE'D been jabbed with a handful of needles. Dean's footsteps echoed in the quiet, their rhythm a rebuke. She should have told him about the NPR interview. But how could she justify her freak out when she hadn't listened to it to determine how invasive it was? The chances that anyone had caught the NPR story were slim, but the idea of his family hearing about her committal made her stomach churn. She couldn't meet those people important to him when her psyche was barely held together with pushpins and year-old envelope glue.

"I've got to go," Dean said from the doorway, his backlit face obscured in shadow. "Kiera, listen—"

She said nothing, but he stopped as if she'd interrupted him.

He gripped the door frame with both hands, and his voice sounded empty. "I hope you feel better. Call me later if you want to talk about it."

Silence slammed through the room, and time paused for a moment. A panicked animal scrambled up her throat. He'd never acted so emotionally withdrawn from her before. "I can try—"

"No. It's just a family picnic, and I'll be fine on my own."

Fine on his own. Damned if that didn't sound fucking prophetic. Her head throbbed, and her belly roiled. She was never, ever doing Valium and weed together again.

Kiera struggled from under the covers and went to him. Cold air assaulted her as she walked to Dean, toward the light. She put her arms around his neck and hugged him. Dean's familiar body radiated warmth and strength. She inhaled the subtle scent of his aftershave, slightly spicy and slightly minty. Before she could think beyond the tiny details, before her mind unspooled her heart, she pulled away.

She darted back to the gloom, hunkered. "Have a good time."

Kiera Brayleigh was the worst girlfriend ever.

CHAPTER FIFTY THREE

Dean

D EAN SPENT MOST OF THE BARBECUE THINKING about how it would have gone if Kiera had been there. Peg brought Lyndsey Lynn. Sure, she and Peg were friends, but inviting an ex-girlfriend to a family picnic was a dick move, particularly when Kiera should've been there. Lyndsey Lynn hadn't changed—tall, blond, feminine, well-groomed. She smiled at Dean with a confidence that made him nauseous. That wasn't the smile he wanted.

He gave Peg a look he'd never given her before, filled with disapproval and fury. She flinched, reddened, and pretended keen interest in the potato salad. His mother loved Lyndsey Lynn and kept cooing and fussing over her.

Lyndsey Lynn was the daughter-in-law of her dreams. Kiera was the daughter-in-law of her nightmares. There would be no mother-daughter shopping trips or visits to the beauty salon. They wouldn't sit side by side and watch sappy Hallmark Christmas movies where the characters learn that God's love can cure any ill. They could forget about Midnight Mass.

Would his love for Kiera have been enough? His mother wouldn't say anything outright. Dean would have had to prepare for a barrage of passive-aggressive comments and disapproving looks. Kiera would sense them, see them, internalize them, and they would hurt. For all her fuck-yous, Kiera had vulnerabilities all the more precarious because people assumed she didn't have any.

Dean had planned to stay by Kiera's side the whole time. They would have needed to take frequent breaks, walking the park by themselves, so she could settle or recharge. His family wouldn't have understood, but they would have accepted it. They could have been outcasts together. He could have felt real and not some glamour-shot clone of his true self.

His mother told everyone that Dean was the lead on the serial-killer case, and crowed about what an honor that was, despite him repeatedly telling her that leads were assigned on rotation not on merit. Coincidental selection was not a talent. But nobody heard him when he explained. The only one who would have hadn't come. She'd abandoned him.

Lyndsey Lynn circled him, as if he were prey. Her too-sweet perfume overpowered the smells of grass and grilling meat. She went out of her way to touch his arm several times. With a heft of self-control, he halted the impulse to shrug off her hand. He didn't want her.

"How've you been? You look tired." She sounded concerned.

"Been working a lot. More than usual." He hoped the subtle reminder of her main complaint when they were together might curb her onslaught.

"I never appreciated how hard that was for you. I'm sorry about that."

Dean kept his eyebrows from rising. "Thanks."

Peg sidled up after that. "She wanted to come and apologize. What was I supposed to say? I didn't know your girlfriend was going to be sick."

"And what if she'd been here? How do you think that would have made her feel?"

His sister frowned and lowered her voice so as not to be overheard. "What do you mean? You chose her. You said you'd never been with anyone so loyal and supportive before and that she made Lyndsey Lynn look like a plastic doll caught in a fire."

Kiera had been supportive. Nobody was more Team Fuck Family than her, and she enabled him to laugh about it, about the absurdity of always surpassing his parents' expectations even when he hadn't. Still, she wasn't there.

Not because she didn't want to be—he'd seen the look on her face when she'd volunteered to try. But they'd both known she couldn't accompany him without sacrificing herself, and he wouldn't do that to her. Not today.

But a part of him wanted to push, to fix her like he'd fixed her washer. If being with him didn't make her better, didn't improve her life, then what the hell was he doing? He couldn't bear another emotional failure.

God, he was overthinking. His lack of sleep had turned him melodramatic and maudlin. But he couldn't turn it off.

His father tried to speak to him, and his sister Rose tried too, but Dean continuously talked to Kiera in his head and couldn't enjoy his family at all, not even his nephew. They were all so bright and cheerful, believing that the world was a safe place and that most people were generally good. They were clueless.

For as horrible as the day would have gone if Kiera had been there—a blowup, a panic attack, her dazing his proper mother with her improper vocabulary—that was the afternoon he wanted, what he craved. Not the sanitized version he got where people talked about their jobs and people who weren't there, and Dean nodded and smiled while nothing moved inside him except regret and longing.

CHAPTER FIFTY FOUR

Kiera

P ACING FOR HOURS DID NOTHING BUT MAKE HER feet sore.

She desperately wanted her mentor, Doreen.

Not available. Dead.

She could call her shrink, who'd tell her to stop sweating the stuff she couldn't control.

Pointless.

She could call Nadira, who'd tell her life sucked and would only get worse.

True, but not what I need.

What she needed was some rainbow glitter or bare feet on a sandy beach or finding unicorns in the shapes of clouds. Only one person she knew could give her that.

* * *

ASH TOOK A DEEP DRAG ON THE PIPE, THE SMOKE CURLING INTO HIS mouth and up his nose as if he'd missed his calling as an indie film actor.

They sat cross-legged on Goliath, their knees touching.

"This is some sweet shit," he said while holding the smoke in his lungs. He passed the rainbow glass pipe to Kiera.

She nodded. "Not a bad one yet." She thought about the young man at the medical marijuana place. Shit. What were those places called, again? He had curly orange hair, freckles, and a thin mouth. As an expert in all the strains, he got excited about each one, like a pothead sommelier.

"And this about a dude? It isn't about . . . anything else?"

Kiera let the pipe clatter onto the coffee table and glared, working up the energy to dispense a wicked friction burn on his arm.

He held up his hands. "I didn't say anything! I'm totally abiding by your stupid rules."

She sighed and fought back giggles. It wasn't funny. "Did you listen to the interview?"

"What interview?"

She smacked him with a pillow twice.

"Okay! Okay! They made it clear the novel was fiction, but they also said it was based on their lived experience." Ash winced in anticipation of Kiera's reaction to "lived experience."

Kiera screamed into the pillow and came away with a few fuzzies in her mouth, which took an eternity to pick off her tongue. "Did they mention my committal?"

Ash covered his face for a moment. "They said they wanted to share the story to fight the stigma of mental health issues." He rubbed his palms over his jeans. "I know. It sounds terrible, but it wasn't that bad."

Kiera opened her eyes as far as possible and leaned her face close to Ash. His mouth twitched, and they broke into laughter.

Her parents were baiting or testing her, but she didn't care. Let them tell whatever story they wanted. Their words couldn't change the truth, and that was what mattered. "Fuck them."

Ash snorted and collapsed into her shoulder. She tried to shake him off, but he pressed his head tighter into her. "First-love relationships are tough."

"Dean isn't my first love, asshole."

He hummed. "Then you're this upset because your boyfriends are few and far between?"

"Not. Helping." If she weren't high, she'd clench her teeth. Dean. "He understands me in a way that nobody else ever has."

"You know, you could always show me."

"I'm not in the mood for interpretive dance." Why had she thought calling Ash was a bright idea?

Ash held out his hands to her, palms up, his face serious, steady, and calm. Realization prickled along her scalp. "I want to understand you too, sis. Come on. It'll be fun."

"It's too dangerous, Ash. I would never risk you like that." Only a memory preserver would think trading memories was some sort of party game.

He sighed. "I'm a professional, and I'm not an idiot. I'm not going to grab some traumatic memory by mistake. You think, because my clients are rich and have something precious to pass on, they don't have tragic memories too? Heartbreaks, disappointments, terrors? Of course, they do. Like your clients probably had a fun day every so often."

Kiera thought of her client Emma and her boyfriend's loving gaze, but she still scowled at Ash. As always, he underestimated the risk. "I'm starting to think that all those good memories are only going to make it worse when it ends." She drummed her fingers on her thighs, the weed making her skin sensitive. "Or maybe they weren't as great as I remember. I might just be fooling myself because I want so desperately to feel like other people do."

"Want to find out? You know the root memories don't lie." He trailed off for a moment, his eyes glassy. "Let me see something special that happened to you. Something epic, and then you'll know it was real."

"But what if it isn't real?" For someone who claimed not to be an idiot, Ash sounded like a complete dumbass.

"Then you'll know, and you can stop this internal debate." Ash must have seen her deliberation because he grinned. "Come on. Show me something cool."

She did want someone to understand. "What if it hurts as much to remember the good as the bad?"

"This is what I do." Ash wiggled his fingers. "Trust me."

* * *

ASH AND KIERA SAT CROSS-LEGGED ON GOLIATH, FACING EACH OTHER with knees and palms touching, Kiera's on top. When she was the surgeon, she always kept her hands on the bottom. Did all surgeons do that or if it was a Brayleigh predisposition?

Kiera closed her eyes and fought the urge to slam everything shut and death grip her memories. She saw spools in a rainbow of colors—Ash's mind—his memories. The filaments swirled, and in the middle, little by little, a space appeared. A space Ash made for her. He was far more receptive than Nadira had been when Kiera had given her the snapshot of the killer.

She opened herself, needing the connection to another person. But before she had time to select a memory, something tugged within her mind. Suddenly, she remembered the night after she'd gone to the police station to meet with the profiler, when she'd worried Dean would break up with her. Why the hell would Ash want to see that? And then she recalled how the night had ended. Dean had taken her to her bedroom, pinned her wrists over her head, and—

Kiera tried to jerk her memory back, but it was too late.

Moments later, Ash yanked his hands away. "I did not think this through." He shook his head and jumped to his feet, pacing the living room, twitching.

Her face flamed. "Yeah, well, if you waited for me to pick a memory and hold it out to you, that wouldn't have happened."

Ash intertwined his fingers around the back of his neck. "Why didn't you shut the whole thing down before it got to . . . you know."

"You think I didn't try? You should know once you grab the memory, it runs to the end."

He wiped at his eyes. "Oh God, it's like incest."

"It's nothing like incest. It wasn't his memory."

"I just lived my sister having sex. Do you have any idea how creepy that is?"

"Uh, yeah." She stood so he couldn't look down on her. She poked a finger in his direction. "This was your plan and your fault, so quit looking at me like that, fucknut."

Ash gaped at her, his lips puckered as if he'd eaten an unripe lemon. "I've never experienced sex from a woman's body before. That was weird."

Kiera held out her hands. "Please don't share anymore."

He stared at her, as if her face had been rearranged. She said nothing, wanting the conversation to end. The awkwardness hit a tipping point, and they burst out laughing.

Ash collapsed to the ground, his back on the wood floor, knees bent, holding his stomach. When they stopped giggling, he sat up. "That was intense, Kier bear. I get it now."

She got it too, the refresher of the memory as Ash lived it. Her laughter faded, though she kept a smile on her face for Ash. Kiera's love for Dean was more real and deep and terrifying than she'd thought. The realness didn't make it better; it made it worse.

* * *

KIERA WAITED UNTIL AFTER GROUP WHEN SHE, NADIRA, AND BETH HAD their traditional debrief at Intelligentsia. The coffee shop was sparsely populated, but the primo location made the space long and thin, so the place could feel cramped, though it was largely empty. Or maybe Kiera's mood affected her perception.

Their threesome sat at their favorite metal table for two.

"She broke up with the drummer," Beth said, dipping her finger into her espresso to test the heat. "I seen a picture of him a while back." Of course, with Beth, her photographic memory meant she recalled every detail of the ongoing saga, even if she wasn't updated for months. "I think she made a mistake."

That was Kiera's opening. She leaned forward, licked her lips, and let the words careen loose. "Dean and I aren't going to make it."

Nadira had her cup to her mouth but didn't drink. She set the cup on the table hard enough for coffee to splash over the sides. Beth wiped it up as Nadira stared at Kiera, her eyes filling with tears.

"Did something happen?" Nadira asked.

"It's my fault."

Nadira dabbed at her eyes with a napkin. "It's always my fault too."

"How? Aren't you the one who does the leaving?" Kiera asked as gently as she could.

"Only when I sense them pulling back. You can feel it, right, when they're ready to bolt? And I cannot bear even the idea of sitting there through that conversation, so I end it before they can hurt me." Nadira managed a smile, though she blinked convulsively to keep back more tears. "I know it doesn't make sense."

"Makes sense to me," Beth said, and Kiera nodded her agreement.

"Maybe you're right," Kiera said, reaching out to hold Nadira's hand. "I pulled away from Dean several times, but only because I was scared, not because I didn't want to be with him. But how many times is he going to put up with that? And why should he have to? I missed his family picnic, the only thing he'd asked of me."

"He break it off?" Beth asked.

At the too-small table, they leaned in, a private huddle. Kiera cradled her cold hands on her warm cup of tea. "No, but he hasn't called, and it's only a matter of time." She'd already shared the NPR interview debacle to group, so they comprehended the situation. "I should've told him what was going on. Knowing Dean, he would've sympathized and pulled me out of this funk. I should've tried to go to the barbecue, but instead, I made it all about *me*, thinking of how *I'd* feel if people found out and how uncomfortable it would be. I didn't take *his* feelings into consideration at all."

Her own tears pricked, but she dug her nails into her palms to quash the impulse. She didn't want commiseration, she wanted atonement. "He never said it explicitly, but it was obvious how much my going meant to him. He needed support, and I let him down."

Damn if Dr. Trent wasn't right; confessing the ugliest parts of herself had lightened the burden, and neither Nadira nor Beth appeared horrified.

"Shit," Nadira said.

As always, Nadira using profanity made Kiera smile. "Indeed."

"You tell him all that?" Beth asked.

Kiera snorted. "Of course not. My apology isn't going to roll back time and undo what I've done." Then she considered it. "I'm scared to talk to him. If I do, I'll have to tell him that it won't work. I can't burden him with me if I truly love him."

"Then you're doing exactly what I do," Nadira said. "You're pushing away before he can do it to you."

"Or I'm saving him."

"Doing nothing ain't no different than pulling away," Beth said. "Tell him you was afraid and see what happens. You already got the worst in your heart, so why not try?"

"You should try." Nadira reached out and held Kiera's left hand. "But I would certainly understand if you didn't."

Beth took hold of Kiera's right. "I wouldn't understand. He might be the po-po, but he is fine."

They laughed and sat like that for a few minutes, looking as if they were either saying grace or conjuring the spirit of Great-Grandma Pearl. For years, her friends and a little paid companionship had been enough. But Dean had awakened something in her. Not a new need, but an ache so deep she wasn't sure she could live without it.

CHAPTER FIFTY FIVE

Dean

W ORK WAS BETTER—IT HELD DEAN'S FOCUS
more than anything else, but he still had a hard
time concentrating and a harder time caring about anything. The team
must have sensed something, because nobody asked him to knock on doors
or chase down videos. Dean might have fared better if they'd given him
all the legwork, but he didn't say anything. He put in his hours and all the
extra hours required by rote.

Dean called Grace to go over what they had so far. Profiling inspired
his mind to a more productive path. Besides, if—no, when—they caught
a solid lead, he could call Kiera and tell her. Because if neither of them
reached out to the other soon, they might never. Already, it felt more weird
to call than not call.

Grace predicted the offender would strike again in the next month.
Dean didn't need the extra sense of urgency, but it helped with his lethargy.
Together, they reviewed the timeline. Two stressors, Grace had determined,
and Dean agreed. The first led to the rapes, then something occurred to
cause him to escalate to murder.

"What if it's a sister he keeps killing by proxy?" Dean asked, studying the victim photos. "Don't you think he'd target older women if he was fixated on the mother?"

"Why do you think it's family?"

Ever since the barbecue weekend, Dean had a strong sense of family. His hypothesis felt right, but he needed to back up his intuition with something more factual. "Because the victims are so diverse. If he was killing a girlfriend, wouldn't all the victims be more alike, more like some idealized version of her? These women ..." Something caught in his mind. "He's taking parts of them, building his true target with the parts, like Brittany Kolchek's hair and the second victim's nose. He wants a perfect representation, and it's more firmly set in his memory because he's known her for so long. He feels more familiarity than he'd have for a girlfriend, don't you think?"

Grace didn't hesitate. "I like it." He could hear the smile in her voice. "You do have a gift for this, Dean."

He smiled for the first time in what felt like days. "Thanks."

"Seriously, you should apply to the FBI and leverage that talent. I'll send you a link, and if you submit an application, tell me, and I'll talk to my friend in HR. I can't guarantee anything, and you'll have to start out as a regular special agent, but I'll vouch for you."

Suddenly, her offer didn't seem impossible. He'd hate to leave Curt and his family. And Kiera—if he even still had her. But if he self-destructed, if he went full dark, he'd like to do it in service of something bigger than closing a few domestic disputes or drug-related homicides.

For the first time, Dean could imagine making a radical change. Maybe he'd throw himself on that pyre instead of Kiera.

CHAPTER FIFTY SIX

WAS IT PROVIDENCE OR A PUNISHMENT? HE found his prize. Well, he found her business, anyway. The Center. A stupid name, snotty, as if she didn't need to say more. He only had to camp out two days before she showed up in her black Caddy with the bulky driver. Probably a bodyguard. She went from the car to the back door. At four, the dude returned.

He was ready with a vehicle of his own. The bodyguard took a direct route, nothing indicating they caught on that anyone followed. Now he knew where she lived.

She presented an interesting challenge. Her routine was predictable, which should have made taking her easy. But she was never alone. After her meetings on Tuesdays, she went for coffee, but always in the company of two other women. Her therapist's office on Fridays had tight security.

Kiera didn't run errands. Only meetings, coffee, and therapy.

Once, he'd gotten past the desk clerk where she lived and to the elevator, but the elevator wouldn't go to the ninth floor. The stairs were locked, but the locks could be picked. Still, nine floors were a long way to have to drag her. Cameras in the lobby. Lake Shore Drive had little foot traffic but heavy car traffic. If he found a way to render her unconscious, if he drove his van to the back alley, there would still be exposure. The risk was too high.

His break occurred when Intelligentsia Coffee needed help. He'd studied the customers and staff long enough to figure out who they wanted, and he gave it to them. He carefully altered his appearance with long hair, green eyes, and glasses, so nobody would recognize him from the sketch on TV. Two interviews back-to-back, and he was hired.

If he'd ever doubted she was meant to be his, he'd gotten a bigger break at her building. After planning every detail, watching her, monitoring her, he was ready to have it all.

CHAPTER FIFTY SEVEN

Kiera

THE LAST PERSON KIERA EXPECTED TO CALL phoned her four and a half minutes into her planking. Vanessa. Maybe she wanted to check and see if her attacker had been caught. Kiera's abs hurt almost as much as her heart, and she was relieved to break the posture.

"I took your advice and talked to someone," Vanessa said, breathless.

"That's great." Kiera wiped sweat from her face with a towel. She hoped Vanessa hadn't called just for that. "Where are you?"

"Estepona, Spain. Look, the woman I spoke with was an old friend, my best friend in high school."

The name and image of a short, brunette girl with a crooked nose formed in Kiera's mind. She'd been Vanessa's best friend at the time of the rape. "Gabby?"

Vanessa hissed in a breath. "Yes." She laughed in a way that held little humor. "I forget that you already know . . . what you know. Yes, Gabby." Vanessa swallowed hard enough Kiera heard it. "I told her what happened—well, what I remember, anyway. I don't know why, but I was sitting on the beach, and I didn't want to hold it inside any longer."

Kiera smiled, glad Vanessa couldn't see her because that I'm-glad-you-finally-understand smile was irritating as fuck. Maybe Kiera couldn't fix her sucky life, but at least, she mostly made other people's lives better.

"Anyway, Gabby remembered the party before what happened happened, and she sort of remembers me . . . going off with some rando guy." Kiera could hear Gabby's voice in her head from Vanessa's memory.

Kiera breathed as deep as possible to keep present. "She knows him?"

"No. She'd never seen him before, and that's all she recalls. She doesn't think he was at the party alone, though, but she can't recall who he came with. It was a lifetime ago, so I can understand, but I thought maybe . . . could you do your thing? Help her remember?"

If Gabby identified Vanessa's attacker, it would basically solve Dean's case.

* * *

KIERA HAD NO IDEA HOW TO BRIDGE THE TWO-WEEK-PLUS GAP OF silence between them, so when she called, she got right to the point. "My client from Westchester had a change of heart."

"Fantastic. Can you give me her number or have her call me to set up a time to meet?" Dean sounded just like she remembered, which was a stupid thought. Did she expect him to sound like a stranger?

"Um, it's more complicated than that but potentially better. She's out of the country right now, but she finally talked to someone from her past, an old friend, and that friend recalls the party the weekend before Vanessa's rape."

"Your client's name is Vanessa?"

"Yes, but that's not important. I guess some girl they both hated fell in a pool at the party when Vanessa was roofied or whatever—drugged. Anyway, it was ten years ago, so she only has a vague memory, but she's willing to let me refresh it, so to speak. I can go in and pull it up and see if she might recognize the guy or any buddies he might have showed up with." Damn. She needed to stop talking and breathe.

"Whoa."

"If you're interested." She didn't care if she sounded smug.

"Are you kidding? That's amazing. When?" He said something to someone else, likely Curt, but she couldn't make out his words with that low buzz taking over her hearing.

"I scheduled her for tomorrow at two, figuring you and Curt will still have time to get to work by four. She's agreed to come to the Center. I'll text you the address."

CHAPTER FIFTY EIGHT

Dean

D EAN FIGURED SEEING KIERA AGAIN WOULD BE hard and awkward, but he didn't expect it to be like this.

She didn't smile when he and Curt walked into her office. She looked good, no makeup except rose-tinted lip balm. Burt's Bees. Dean also recognized the black cashmere dress, sleeveless with delicate silver buttons as the only ornamentation. It was one of Kiera's favorites because it was soft and thin enough for summer, and professional. He'd forgotten the intensity of blue in her eyes.

He wanted to hug her, run his hand down the velvety material, then underneath to her silken skin. But they had an audience, and the connection between them had frayed. Her eyes returned to him often but wouldn't stay.

She asked Curt about new restaurants. The conversation soon meandered into a debate about bubble tea as they walked through the space. Her entryway was all white and silver, the space open and bright. She led them to her office, the walls and credenza white, the floor-to-ceiling windows allowing lots of light and a view of the grass-covered embankment next to the parking lot in the back. The furnishings were black and all the decorative items bright colors. It was as tranquil as her home. Simple. Elegant. Kiera.

As she ushered them inside, Dean and Kiera's gazes locked, and for a moment, Dean thought he might reach out and touch her, something innocent and human, and that maybe they were all right. But she wrapped one arm over herself and turned to face a woman sitting on a black leather sofa. "Gabrielle Marquis, this is Detective Matthson and Detective Haze."

Gabrielle Marquis was a short, curvy platinum-dyed blond with a hooked nose and pinched lips. Her handshake was limp, as if she'd rather not shake at all. She gazed hard at Dean then flicked a glance at Kiera. "You guys are going to supervise, right?"

"If you'd like," Dean said, wondering what the hell the woman thought Kiera would do if unsupervised. If what Kiera and his friend Jack said was true, they wouldn't even know she was doing anything untoward.

Kiera pushed a button on a remote, and the windows suddenly frosted, providing absolute privacy. Staffers brought two simple desk chairs, and Kiera had the furniture set up so that Dean and Curt had a view of Gabrielle's face and Kiera's back.

Dean couldn't stop staring at the tendrils of hair on the back of Kiera's neck that had escaped her twisted hairdo. If he stroked her neck, goose bumps would erupt. He wanted to kiss the exposed, delicate skin. God, he missed her.

She focused on Gabrielle, walking the woman through a relaxation exercise. "Okay, Gabby," Kiera said, her voice low and hypnotic. Gabrielle's eyelids fluttered. "I want you to think about the night of the party when Molly fell into the pool. The more details you can recall the better. Did it smell like beer or sweat? Packed with people? Was it hot inside?"

"Yes," Gabrielle opened her eyes. "I had these embarrassing sweat stains."

"Close your eyes," Kiera said, holding Gabrielle's hands, unperturbed, now that she was in her element. "Focus on the feel of your clothes sticking to your body." Her chin dipped. "Yes."

CHAPTER FIFTY NINE

Kiera

"**O**h my God, you are so drunk!" Gabby couldn't stop laughing, bending over to catch her breath, only semi-aware that her tank top was low enough that her breasts could spill out at any moment. She'd sweat enough to cause an embarrassing ring, but everything made her laugh harder.

Vanessa swayed on her feet, her face red and sweat trickling down her temples, plastering her hair to her face. "Groove is in the heart," Vanessa slurred, swishing the skirt on her designer dress back and forth.

Gabby ignored the spike of covetousness that pierced her chest. Vanessa's home was a safe place for Gabby, and she appreciated that, but she would have loved designer clothes, a mansion, and a room all her own.

She jumped into the crowd dancing, expecting Vanessa to follow. When she turned to Vanessa to point out that she could see Patricia Cornel's thong sticking out of her jean skirt, Vanessa wasn't there. Gabby looked around and saw Vanessa weaving up the stairs with a brown-haired boy, his arm clamped to her waist. She didn't recognize him from school, but she'd seen him in the kitchen talking to Ben Tuk and Jake Harris, so maybe he went to their school. He looked yummy with those sharp cheekbones and athletic body. Gabby liked her men even brawnier, like Scott Cho. Was he at the party?

* * *

Kiera broke the connection. She opened her eyes and dropped Gabby's hands. The memory hadn't been traumatic. If anything, it had been fun, with all the freedom and infinite possibilities of youth. Fun, if you didn't know how it ended, if you didn't know that you were watching your best friend walk away with a rapist serial killer.

"That's it? Did it not work?" Gabby scowled at Kiera as if pranked.

"No, it worked. I—"

"I didn't remember anything more than I had before. What a crock." Gabby rose and clenched her purse close to her body as if Kiera might make a grab for it. "Did you guys see that?"

Dean and Curt also stood. Dean frowned. "What exactly are you accusing Ms. Brayleigh of?"

"She's a hoax, and she took hundreds of thousands of dollars from my friend, Vanessa Sanrow. You should arrest her!"

Kiera didn't have to be kind to Gabby, as she wasn't a client or a victim, but she'd connected to her through the memory. Misguided and ignorant, Gabby still stood up for Vanessa. So, Kiera overlooked the accusation. "She didn't recognize your guy."

"Ha!" Gabby said. "See!"

Kiera continued, "But she did see him talking to a Ben Tuk and Jake Harris who went to the high school in Willowbrook."

"What?" Gabby took a step back and stared at Kiera as if she'd pulled off her face. "I do remember those guys. Kind of. H-how did you—"

Curt shuffled Gabby out of the room in a courtly manner, leaving Kiera alone with Dean. She yearned to scratch her bared arms to kill the itch that built with the tension. Concentrate on business. She had to tell Dean everything Gabby knew—had known.

"Tuk is spelled T-u-k. I think they were a year older than Gabby and Vanessa, so your guy must be somewhere close in age, maybe thirty." She scrambled to her desk. "Here, I wrote a general timeline before you guys got here. Gabby hadn't seen him before so—"

"Kiera."

The way he said her name made her shiver, her shoulder jerking back. Professional. Professional. She was a goddamned professional. He rested a hand on her upper arm, his skin as warm as ever. It felt so comforting that her eyes watered.

"Are you all right? Do you need to sit or anything? I know that you get a bit disoriented after a reading." He didn't stroke her, but he also didn't remove his hand.

"I'm fine. That wasn't traumatic, so I don't need any kind of recovery." She needed him to see that she wasn't always broken, even if it was too late. "I could use some water, though." Kiera moved away from his touch and pulled her insulated water bottle out of a drawer and took a long pull.

He studied her with a pinched expression. Oh shit, this was it. "We should probably talk about what's going on with us."

The pain was a thunderclap, like being rolled in tacks and nails and ground glass, like sinking into black water, weighted down, knowing there was no chance to breach the surface again.

"I'll be fine." She sounded normal, and that was enough.

"Kiera—"

She just wanted this part over. "Look, we both know this isn't going to work between us. You deserve someone better."

He stared at the ceiling, his head cocked all the way back, exposing his throat. The throat she'd loved to kiss and run her tongue over the stubble, which invariably grew by the end of his shift. She was doing the right thing, but goddamn it, it hurt.

"Better? Because I'm so perfect?"

"Yeah, you are, and I'm not even *good* for you. And I never will be." She closed her eyes and spoke the hard truth. "I realized it when I ditched out of going to your family's party. Maybe you're willing to put yourself through that over and over." She opened her eyes, aware she was crying but too deep now to stop. Maybe she should have told him about the NPR interview, but what did it matter? If it hadn't been her parents, it would have been something else. "But I care about you too much to do that to you. You should be with someone who's as supportive and strong and wonderful as you are. This is my choice, Dean. It's over."

"Okay," he finally said. When he exhaled and lowered his head, his eyes locking onto hers, he looked resolved and cold. "If that's what you want." At the door to her office, he turned back, his professional mask in place. "Thanks for your help today on the case. I think this is what we need to catch this guy."

And then he left.

Kiera's heart splattered against the back of her rib cage before starting a slow, steady slide down, down, down to her stomach, where it throbbed and beat and grew ever heavier.

CHAPTER SIXTY

Dean

DEAN DROVE WITH HIS EYES FIXED ON THE ROAD while Curt made phone calls. His mind whipped like a tilt-a-whirl with a blown fuse. He'd been so sure she understood the pressure on him to live up to other's expectations. She was supposed to love him despite his flaws, not miss them altogether and idolize some fantasy version of him.

If she'd bitched about him coming over at 2:00 a.m. for sex and food and expecting her to do his laundry—which wasn't true because she was the one who had insisted on washing the clothes he left at her place, joking about her owing him for fixing her washer—or complaining he didn't make enough time for her, or that he had to stop trying to fix her, or that he hadn't been honest about the demons—

If she'd named *actual* problems, if she'd looked at the real him and found fault, he would have fought, argued, used every persuasive technique he'd ever learned to keep her. Because she was the one who deserved better. But if she didn't see his weaknesses now, she'd see them one day and resent the fuck out of him for not telling her sooner.

What could he do?

Hey, don't break up with me because I'm actually not that great a guy deep down inside and possibly part monster. Don't you want to be with me?

What if he did?

He could lay it all out there for her and let her decide instead of deciding for her. Maybe if she saw the darkness within him and recoiled it would make it easier for her. Or maybe she'd love and accept him as broken as he was—every bit as broken as she. But he couldn't bear the thought of her disgust or, worse, fear. He just wasn't strong enough. The temptation of Grace's offer: a new life, a shift in his bleak perspective, grew.

He filled out the application, just in case. It wasn't running if he found a higher purpose, right?

* * *

Curt tracked down the two men and a source for yearbooks from Willowbrook high school. Tam agreed to find yearbooks so Dean and Curt could focus on the rest. Since it was technically their day off, they could drive out to Willowbrook if Tuk and Harris turned out to still live there.

"Kiera looked good," Curt said between calls.

Dean kept his attention on driving, but the memory of Kiera's words hadn't loosened its hold. "Yeah?"

"That memory reading was a bit boring, but this is the best day off I've had in a long time," Curt said.

Dean laughed at the old joke between them, how leads always seemed to land on their days off. The mirth almost felt genuine.

Curt elbowed his arm. "I think Miss Gabrielle only wanted us there to catch Kiera pumping a hallucinogenic gas in the room or some other kind of bullshit."

Dean shook his head. "She really wanted to find the wizard behind the curtain."

"I thought Kiera handled her pretty well." Curt tapped his cell phone on the dashboard. "You going to thank her properly?"

"That's all over," Dean said as he changed lanes. Saying it out loud suddenly made it true.

* * *

It took an hour to find Jake Harris through the high school's alumni records, but he'd moved to Dallas and wouldn't return Curt's calls. Finding Ben Tuk took a day, but Verizon had him in their database. He lived in the Edgewater neighborhood of Chicago. Dean found his LinkedIn profile, and he worked at a computer repair service near his apartment. He and Curt decided to stop by his work on Monday rather than risk his refusal to speak with them.

Dean functioned on autopilot, glad the tasks weren't cerebral as he'd likely fuck up. He missed Kiera—her laugh, the honey-citrus smell of her skin, the small noises she made when they kissed. At least he no longer had to worry he'd fall short of her expectations, which lifted a weight. But that only felt wrong, like ditching his duty belt while doubling up on his Kevlar.

* * *

Ben Tuk had the physique of a football player past his prime, wide shoulders and generous portions of both fat and muscle. He had thick brown hair, glasses too small for his face, and fine lines around his eyes from excessive smiling. "Can I help you guys?" he asked when they entered the Computer Clinic.

He sobered at the appearance of their credentials.

"Got a few minutes?" Dean asked.

Ben looked over his shoulder, though there was nothing and no one behind him other than some metal shelving stuffed with various computer parts. "Uh, I suppose. Am I in trouble?"

"No," Curt said. "We're trying to track down someone you might have known about ten years ago."

"Me?" Ben looked between Dean and Curt. "Who?"

"We don't know his name. We're hoping you can help us with that. Is there a place we can sit?"

If Molly, who had sponsored the party, hadn't fallen into the pool, Dean suspected they wouldn't have been able to jog anyone's memory to a night so long ago. Ben had laughed at the prompting and shook his head. "Oh shit, I do remember that!"

"Do you recall talking to a boy in the kitchen? About six feet tall, brown hair, thin?"

"Sorry, no."

They were too close. Dean tried another angle. "He was seen walking upstairs with Vanessa—" Dean pulled out his notebook, but he didn't need it.

"Vanessa Sanrow?" Ben frowned. "Yeah, I do remember that. Dalton . . ." Ben pushed his fingers into his forehead. "Jackson? Jameson? Shit, I don't remember his last name. He was in my shop class when I was a sophomore, and he was a senior."

Dean and Curt exchanged a look. Dalton wasn't exactly Dillon, the name the offender had given Brittany, but it was close. Dean finally had that the-case-is-about-to-be-solved feeling. After he closed this case, a world of possibilities would open, and he just might impress the FBI recruiters.

* * *

THEY FOUND A DALTON JANSSEN IN THE GRADUATING CLASS TWO YEARS prior to Ben. Dalton looked enough like their sketch that Dean couldn't eliminate him. Progress. Secretary of State records gave them a Humboldt Park neighborhood address for him and a registered vehicle: a white utility van, and his driver's license picture was a close enough match that Dean's gut fizzed all the way to the top of his chest.

No social media presence. Spotty work history and no known employer at the moment, which only meant he was paid under the table or the system hadn't updated his information yet. His sister had died eleven years ago and his mother last year. Stressors. Maybe he couldn't do relationships, but *this*, this he could do well.

* * *

DALTON JANSSEN LIVED ON THE GROUND FLOOR OF A SIX-FLAT. THE windows were small, and several had A/C units sticking out so they weren't equipped with central air. No parking lot out back and the cars in the area were old and rusted. Glass and garbage littered the sidewalks and easements. The Humboldt Park neighborhood was closer to Garfield Park than Logan Square, and gentrification hadn't spread there yet.

Since Kiera's testimony wasn't admissible and Vanessa's sexual assault had never been reported, they didn't have enough evidence for a search warrant. However, with the owner's permission, they could access all the public spaces.

They watched his apartment for several days, but Dalton never appeared. Dean decided to risk it. He buzzed Dalton's apartment an hour before the evidence tech was set to arrive and received no response. He either wasn't home, or he'd holed himself in tight. Dean wanted to know where the man was, but he didn't want to wait.

Kristin and Jason watched on both ends of the block on the lookout for the white van or Janssen on foot. The evidence tech arrived before the management-company representative and Dean hated the exposure as they waited. Janssen never showed, which pleased and worried him. Janssen missing from his home might indicate he had found his next intended victim and was stalking her. Dean couldn't make a mistake, but he also couldn't afford to delay too long.

When they finally accessed the building, the evidence tech pulled prints from a few lucky spots in the public areas: Janssen's mailbox, his front doorknob, and, best of all, the gray Trek bike chained outside his storage locker in the basement, a match to the one seen with Brittany Kolchek's killer.

Ident called Dean a few hours later with the fingerprint analysis and linkage results. "It's the same guy," Parker, the analyst, said. "We found a couple of partials that match the ones from the apartment and the church exactly. The guy's not as smart as he thinks."

"What do you mean?"

Parker laughed. "My guess is he's using an acid or some chemical to erase the prints, but he didn't get the whole surface, so it leaves an edge. He's made the print distinctive and far more identifying than if he'd left his fingerprints alone." He clicked his tongue. "Though, to be honest, if we'd only seen it at the two locations, we might not have caught it."

Huh. Dean considered the strange twitch of the offender's fingers, the way he rubbed his thumb and index finger together. Was he distracted by overly smooth skin there? Not that it mattered.

Thank God for stupid criminals. But before he could call Kiera to update her—a sorry excuse to hear her voice—the team got called to a fresh homicide.

* * *

DEAN SAT IN HIS CAR IN THE AREA CENTRAL PARKING LOT, HIS HANDS at ten and two on the wheel. They weren't shaking, but they didn't feel like his hands, but a stranger's hands. Finally, he made the call.

"Hello?" Her voice disemboweled Dean with how much he needed to hear it.

His managed only one word. "Kiera."

Shuffling in the background. "Dean? Are you okay?"

He couldn't talk. If he did, he might fall to pieces in the middle of the parking lot. That was unacceptable. He made a sound but no words.

Her voice slicked over his skin, cocooning him with his name. "Dean."

His name on her lips softened him in the most dangerous way. He knew better than to open himself to her and this feeling, but he was lonely, and he was desperate, and she was the only thing that brought him peace.

"It's okay if you can't talk," she said. "We can stay just like this as long as you need. I'm going to keep on talking for a while, or say the word, and we can sit quietly together. You're also welcome here if you want."

"Kiera," he said, hating how sun-beaten and shriveled he sounded.

"You want me to come to you?"

Dean sucked in a breath. She'd never offered to meet him anywhere before. She'd never even been to his house in the months that they'd dated since she was only comfortable in her own space.

He thought of the softness of her hair and the blue of her eyes. He thought of her peaceful condo with the herringbone wood floors and photos of serene places in nature. "I'll come there."

CHAPTER SIXTY ONE

Kiera

DEAN EXITED THE ELEVATOR, HIS HEAD DOWN, AS if he were afraid his feet couldn't be trusted. He was at the door when he noticed her standing there. "Oh, hey." His eyes were bloodshot, and his jaw grizzled—not the trendy, purposeful stubble he used to wear, but I've-worked-all-night natural stubble.

Kiera opened the door and stepped back, so he could enter. He looked her up and down, not checking her out, she didn't think, but reminding himself who she was. She had never seen him so lost, so out of sorts. She rearmed the alarm.

"Come on." She grasped his hand gently and tugged him toward her relaxation room. "Let me show you where the magic happens."

He stopped, and she was jerked back an inch. "Kiera, I'm sorry . . . I can't—it's been—"

She rolled her eyes. "No need to tighten your chastity belt; your virtue is safe."

Dean blinked as if he didn't speak English. She squeezed his hand. "We're going to the relaxation room."

She opened the door to the small, cozy room. In preparation for him, she'd filled the reservoir on the wall fountain with distilled water and started it going and jacked up the air conditioning to sixty-eight degrees.

The lights were on whisper, which was a low, soothing setting. Inside, the room was hushed and quiet.

Dean made a small noise.

"Take off your shoes and tie, and your gun, and sit in the recliner, okay?"

"Gin," he replied, as if she'd asked him what he'd like to drink.

Kiera wanted to try this her way first. "I've got something else prepared, but if you still want gin later, I'll get it for you."

Dean stripped off all the requested items and handed them to Kiera before collapsing onto the massage recliner. He stared at the wall fountain, which was partially obscured in the dim light. The acrylic panel was painted in deep hues of purple and blue with a little gold mixed into the swirls. It reminded Kiera a little of van Gogh's *Starry Night*. Water streamed down, making a trickling sound, the background shimmering through the streams.

Kiera juggled Dean's belongings and grabbed the chair's remote to run a ten-minute customized massage program. Even worn out and weary, he was handsome. She wanted to see the tiny divots of his dimples, poke a finger into one, see him smile.

"Whoa," Dean yelped as the zero-gravity massage chair tilted him backward, the calf sections gripping his lower legs in place. Rollers would massage up and down his neck and back.

"Relax and let the chair do all the work." She flipped the switch for the fountain lights. Purple light suffused the space, faded to blue, then green took its place. Kiera switched off the overhead lights and left the fountain to provide the illumination. She started her favorite music and slipped out the door with the vestiges of his work.

She stowed his shoes and tie at the front door and his gun in the silver bowl in the entryway in case he wanted to leave in a hurry. The drinking chocolate was ready. She had made it with whole milk and semisweet chocolate and a pinch of cayenne and salt. She added a pour of Bailey's to the pan so he would taste the alcohol enough to satisfy his craving.

When she returned, the chair was upright again, the program completed. Dean stared at the fountain. She handed him the mug of chocolate.

"Ah, damn, I forgot the blanket," Kiera said, spying it on the chaise. She shifted to pick it up.

"It was a kid."

Fuck. She let the blanket pool over his legs and up to his neck. She placed a hand on his shoulder to comfort him. He drank deep and sighed. "This is really good."

Kiera moved to the chaise and waited. And waited. Willing to wait forever, just being there for him.

Dean drank his hot chocolate, then set his cup on the beautiful blue topaz side table next to the recliner. He rose, clutching the blanket to him and looked at her with a mutt of raw emotions, too many strains and strands to name it any one thing or any single color. When he sank beside her on the chaise, she pulled him close, leaning them both back. His head nestled on the top of her chest as his body relaxed into her. She held him, stroking his hair, pretending she didn't notice he was crying, pretending she wasn't crying herself, whisking away each tear before one could fall on him.

His voice was a hoarse whisper. "She left her child bleeding on the floor, possibly still alive, and cleaned up the room. She cared more about appearances than her own daughter's life. What if that little girl died watching her mother make her bed?"

Kiera kissed the top of his head. "You can't control that."

Dean clutched her as if she were an overgrown teddy bear. After a few minutes, he resituated his head on her chest, and a thrill went through her body. She slammed down the arousal in case Dean might sense it. Maybe he could, because he kissed her collarbone, and he was painfully close to her nipple. Kiera grabbed his face to stop him. She didn't want him like that, not when he wasn't thinking clearly.

He pulled away. "I'm sorry."

She disentangled and patted his arm. "Want to try to sleep now?"

Dean nodded, deflated. He brushed his teeth with her toothbrush and collapsed onto Big Bad John instead of the guest room. "Will you stay until I fall asleep?"

CHAPTER SIXTY TWO

Dean

THEY HAD BARELY SETTLED IN THE DARK COMFORT of her bed, their bodies close but not touching, when Dean blurted out, "We never talked about what happened. I never reached out to you." He needed to explain but had no idea how.

"I noticed." Amusement tinged her voice.

"I wanted to, but I . . ." He couldn't finish. How did he put into words something so impenetrable? How he thought of her every hour, how, in his head, he still told her about his day and accumulated funny anecdotes to share with her later.

"Hey, I get it. You needed to find the right greeting card. It happens."

Dean laughed and groaned. He'd missed her wit. "Damn it, now I'm going to have to find some inappropriate stationery. Like Hello Kitty or Pokémon."

"Don't send Hello Kitty. I'll spend three days trying to figure out if there's a hidden pussy joke in there somewhere."

He chuckled again but it didn't catch. Something had its claws too deep for him to break free. "I shouldn't have let you think that the breakup was your fault."

She huffed out a breath. "We aren't going to have an it's-not-you-it's-me conversation because I am not down with that. We both know—"

"No, you don't know. That's the problem, Kiera."

She sat up, the covers shifting over Dean with the movement. "What don't I know?"

"There's a monster inside me."

"What do you mean?"

He took a breath deep enough she could probably hear it. "Do you know how I get criminals to confess?"

"I assumed you hit people with phone books and stuff."

He flopped his hands on top of the covers. "Stop making jokes."

"Start making sense."

She had a point, but he needed to say it right. "I sort of go into their minds," he said. "Kind of how you do it, only not literally. It's like trying on clothes, but they don't come all the way off when I'm finished."

Kiera reached out and stroked his arm once. "I can relate to that. When I do a memory read, I'm certainly affected by the other's experience and emotions. But, Dean, empathizing with someone doesn't make you become them."

"But my thoughts can go so dark."

She snorted and lay back down. "I imagine lighting Amy's hair on fire every week. I've shoved my mother down elevator shafts, metal stairs, and slammed a stiletto into her eye. Fantasies don't mean anything if you never act them out."

He found her hand. It didn't matter if they weren't together and couldn't be together. Even if nobody else ever did, he wanted her to know the whole truth about him. "What if I become so jaded that I stop feeling anything at all for the victims? What if I start to think just like the criminals I arrest? What if hitting a six-year-old with a book becomes the only way to get her to shut up?" The picture of tonight's child victim wouldn't fade.

She waited, not saying anything.

He rubbed at an itch on his cheek only to discover hot tears trailing down his face. "I try too hard, then not hard enough, and I can't always reconcile what I do with who I want to be, and sometimes the ends don't justify the means, and sometimes they do—and sometimes that makes it worse. And although I call myself a good guy, my . . . shit, I don't know, my soul . . . isn't pure."

Kiera turned on her side to face him, never releasing his hand. "Nobody is pure, love."

He wanted to say that she was, but they both knew she wasn't. And he didn't want pure. He wanted this tangled mess of a woman, and so far, she hadn't shrunk away from him. His soul ripped into tiny pieces, wanting to be worthy of her faith in him.

She sighed. "I had a mentor once, and she told me to never let anyone else tell you what you should be doing or set your limitations. People always overestimate or underestimate others, depending on whatever fucked-up shit is going on in their own lives." Kiera smoothed over his chest in a small circle. "You decide who you are, and fuck anyone who says otherwise."

His family loved him, and his workmates appreciated him, but he'd never believed he'd been or done enough before. He placed his hand over hers. "God, I missed you."

"I missed you too." She rested her cheek on his shoulder. "Thank you."

He snorted and laughed at the same time. This woman. "Why would you thank me?"

Her breath ghosted mint toothpaste over his face. "Because you let me see you at your worst." His heart cracked. "And there's no bigger sign of trust than that. I am so . . . honored that you would share that with me."

When she said the word "honored," his cracked heart exploded, taking his chest and throat with it.

Sobs bubbled out of him, and for once, he didn't try to stop them or shield her from the chaos. She pulled him close and stuffed tissues in his hands and lay with him, stroking his hair until he fell asleep.

CHAPTER SIXTY THREE

THE TIME IS NOW.

CHAPTER SIXTY FOUR

Dean

A KNOCK AT THE DOOR WOKE DEAN FROM A DEAD sleep. For a moment, he forgot Kiera had said goodbye and left. He rolled out of bed, pulled on his pants, and put his arms through his business shirt as he padded to the door. The rap came again, louder and more urgent. Dean looked out the peephole and saw Manny. He opened the door, and the alarm chirped a warning. Dean held up a finger, closed the door, then disarmed it before opening the door again. What time was it?

Dean scratched his chest and tried to fully wake. "Kiera's not here. Can I help you with something?"

Manny shifted his weight between his feet, and his fingers tugged at the hem of his navy sports coat. "Are you sure?"

Dean gripped the handle on the door. "What?"

"Kiera's not here? Because she never came down, and her driver's waiting for her."

Dean shook his head once to jolt his brain into functioning. He'd been so tired. When he pressed his memory, he couldn't remember hearing the alarm beep or the door close. He swiped a hand over his face and called out, "Kiera?"

Had she said she was getting ready or going? Manny hung back, unwilling to step across the threshold. Dean doubted Kiera would mind Manny inside, but the place wasn't his to invite him in. "Kiera!"

The condo had an echoing emptiness that grated on Dean's nerves. He hadn't been abandoned; she'd gone to group therapy. Only she hadn't. Where would she go without her driver? She wasn't in the dining room or library or workout room or relaxation room or guest room or laundry room or kitchen or bedroom or bathroom or balcony or anywhere else.

"Not here," Dean said, jogging back to Manny. "You're sure she didn't walk out and you missed her?"

"I haven't left the desk since before you arrived this morning." He scratched the back of his neck. "Tony's waiting for her. What do I tell him?"

Dean's muscles ached as if he'd sprinted a 10K yesterday and hadn't stretched afterward. His eyes stung, and his stomach shot filaments of lightning through his body. Something was wrong.

"I'll go down and talk to Tony," Dean said. "Just give me a second."

He buttoned his shirt on his way to the bedroom to fully dress. Maybe Kiera hadn't accepted his confession as open-mindedly as he'd thought. No, the way they'd connected had been real.

Dean slid on his belt, ran his hands through his hair, and thought, absurdly, of superpowers. He wanted to change his answer to the ability to find anyone anywhere.

CHAPTER SIXTY FIVE

Kiera

Earlier . . .

AFTER KISSING A GROGGY DEAN GOODBYE ON THE cheek, Kiera left for group. She stepped in the elevator just as Tony called to say he had arrived. Perfect timing. It was a sign.

She savored the image of Dean sleeping in her bed, the gentle rise and fall of his chest. They hadn't resolved everything or, really, anything. No future plans, no relationship discussion. But the invisible wall that always lay between them, constructed by them both, had disappeared. If Kiera decided to share in group, she was going to call that barrier a sneeze guard. Everyone would laugh because (a) it was funny and (b) they would sense the lightness in her and (c)—

The elevator stopped on the third floor. When the doors opened, a tall, slim blond woman beamed at her. Goose bumps broke over Kiera's skin, and her throat burned a kiln. Her back hit the wall.

Kiera had spent most of her life on edge: paranoid and expecting the worst. All the same, she didn't even open her mouth to scream when the prongs of the stun gun struck.

Her pec muscles locked and squeezed. She couldn't move, her entire body stiffening. And, fuck, it hurt. She grunted and swore in a prolonged litany.

That smirk. Brittany's killer.

He held the trigger forever. She hadn't fallen over, but she hadn't been able to control her torso, and almost dropped to her knees. Once she became unstuck, he had a glimmer in his eyes, as if he expected her to fight, as if he wanted her to attempt to defy him, so he could zap her again. She stared up at him, from under her lashes, her hand gripping the interior rail, wondering when the pain would dissipate.

"You're holding up the elevator. Get out."

His voice. It wasn't the Batman voice he'd used with Vanessa ten years ago. And it wasn't the voice he'd given to Brittany. Was this his real voice, or a voice made just for her?

Kiera had to think, but she couldn't stop staring at the wires connecting her chest to the killer's stun gun. She and the killer were attached to each other.

He frowned and extended the stun gun. "If I have to say it again—"

She stumbled out, her upper torso aching, the tightness giving way to a jellylike warbling. Would she notice if she had a heart attack now?

"Come on." He spoke in a singing voice, as if she were a child or a dog. "A little bit further."

Farther, ignorant asshole, not further.

But she said nothing. His dress covered too much to be acceptable for the Indian summer weather, with its three-quarter sleeves and full-length skirt. The muted-orange cotton color brought out the green of his eyes. Green eyes today.

If she turned and ran, would the wires pop out of her? Could she pull them out before he could electrocute her again? Or did they have to be surgically removed? She wanted them off, off, off.

He stopped outside 3F and opened the door.

What the actual fuck.

He lives in my building?

Of course, he did. He couldn't trick her, he couldn't snatch her off the street, he didn't have the access to reach her—without living where she lived. And his study of her—oh God, she couldn't think about the details of that—he'd apprehended her schedule. He'd known when she'd be in the elevator.

Dean.

Six floors above her, Dean slept. Or maybe he woke with a sort of premonition of her danger. Maybe his supercop instincts would bring him to the door, to her rescue.

Yeah, right.

The killer beckoned her. "Right this way, Kiera. Try anything and I'll fry you again."

* * *

KIERA HAD NEVER BEEN INTO ANY OF THE OTHER APARTMENTS IN THE building, so she didn't know what to expect. Even if she had, nothing could have prepared her for the psycho decoration of the space.

Foam was nailed or stapled into every surface. They were from different sources, several colors and textures layered over each other, from thin yellow squares to a gray-green thick foam that had peaks and valleys like an egg carton. Pieces were attached at strange angles with no gaps, as if he'd completed the project in some sort of manic episode.

He led her through the empty entryway and down a long hall. The walls were likewise covered. Where had he gotten all that foam? How had he brought it into the building without raising eyebrows? He opened the first door. Kiera followed, wires still protruding from her chest. She couldn't feel the prongs, but her muscles still ached and trembled from the zap. Surely, it should have stopped hurting by now.

This room was also covered in foam—soundproofing. She could scream and scream, and the only person to hear her would be the attacker. Trickles of cold fell in thin lines from the top of her head to her lower back.

This might be the last room she ever entered. She wouldn't give him the satisfaction of crying or begging. At least, she hoped she wouldn't.

Would Dean work the crime scene when they found her? The image of him seeing her like that, literally broken, made her eyes prickle. *Bad train of thought*. She had to focus on what she could control, which shouldn't be too hard since there was so little.

"What's your name?" she asked.

His eyes bore into her as he pulled off his long, blond wig. "You can call me Dillon."

"But that's not your real name?" She'd meant to sound confident, but it was difficult to speak authoritatively with wires sticking out of her chest and stomach.

"I suppose I could tell you my real name," he said. "But you need to earn it."

She hadn't earned any of this, but she only nodded.

Dillon, who wasn't Dillon, moved aside, and Kiera saw a metal bar secured about three feet from the ground with iron manacles attached. Oh, shit.

"Have a seat," Non-Dillon said with a nasty smirk.

She couldn't run. Even if she managed to yank out the probes, he'd catch her long before she reached the door. But if she allowed him to shackle her, she'd never sprint free. Apparently, she'd taken too long debating, because he hit her again with a shock from the stun gun.

Everything locked, her chest tightening, and the agony . . . the agony continued forever. This time she crashed to the floor, and pain exploded in her knee. The crackling stopped, and the fist gripping her entire chest loosened, but she didn't have time to do anything before Non-Dillon kicked her in the thigh, expressionless. The lack of emotion on his face scared her more than anything else. He wasn't human. Not in the ways that mattered.

CHAPTER SIXTY SIX

Dean

DEAN STUDIED THE LOBBY. ONE CAMERA THAT would catch everyone entering and exiting. "Does the camera stream, or is it recorded somewhere, Manny? If I can, I'd like to look at the last twenty-four hours." Ordinarily, he'd ask if Manny had the authority to grant him permission; that was the correct procedure. But he wasn't taking chances. No cameras at the back, so her abductor had likely taken her out that way.

The elevator was Kiera's last known location, so he started there. A metal interior would have possibly told him more, if there'd been a struggle, showing smears and fingerprints to the naked eye. This elevator with its wood paneling gave away nothing. Or maybe there was nothing to give away. Dean began at the ceiling and worked his way down, checking every inch in a grid pattern so he couldn't miss anything. When he finally reached the floor, he found a tiny pink circle tucked into the edge of the carpeting and the wall.

Dean picked out the circle and studied it on his index finger. Plain. Pink. Slightly shiny. His breath hitched. He flipped over the circle and saw the miniscule black script too small to read. It was an AFID, antifelony identification. They dispersed whenever a stun gun was discharged. Someone had been stun gunned here. Dean's stomach plummeted as if the cable had been cut from the elevator. An icy hand clamped to the back of his neck, and for a moment, Dean thought he might puke. He stepped back so if he did vomit, he wouldn't contaminate the crime scene. Crime scene. His gorge didn't settle, but he didn't spew out last night's hot chocolate.

He strode back to Manny's desk. A stun gun had been deployed. That was all that was certain. It could have happened months ago. His surety that Kiera had been stun gunned in the elevator could be his concern overwriting his objectivity. He'd had gut feelings fall off the mark plenty of times.

"Manny," He concentrated on speaking slow and even. "Have you had any incidences of a stun gun being used in the elevator?"

"No."

"Are you sure? Maybe when you weren't on shift?"

"No, Detective. I'm head of security, so I would have heard about something like that." Manny frowned. "Why would you think that?"

Dean showed him the AFID.

"Confetti? I thought I'd gotten all those. Here, give it to me, and I'll throw it away."

Manny reached his hand out to take the AFID, but Dean grabbed his wrist. "There were more of these? When did you find them?"

"This morning on my way up to check on Miss Kiera." Manny scratched his cheek. "What are they?"

"ID tags that deploy whenever a stun gun is activated. It enables authorities to trace back the stun gun that was used. Who arrived here after me?" Dean's hands shook.

"Nobody's gone up." Manny puffed out his cheeks and slowly blew out. He clenched his hands together. Dean managed not to throttle him. "Maybe five people came down."

Dean gently rested the AFID on the desk as he fished out his phone. He needed assistance. "Can you give me a list of those who came down after I got here?"

"Sure." Manny eyed the tiny circle. "You want all of them?" Manny gestured under his desk. "I have the rest right here in the garbage."

"Yes."

"Okay. And I got the video system recordings ready in the security office. You want to watch those now?"

"Hold on," he said to Manny as he started dialing. "Is there a way to shut off the elevator? It's officially a crime scene."

CHAPTER SIXTY SEVEN

Kiera

"**D**O YOU KNOW WHY YOU'RE HERE?" Non-Dillon asked as he sat down in front of her, cross-legged, wearing jeans and a Jack Daniels T-shirt, his dress discarded. His green eyes glowed, from the contacts or his own special brand of derangement.

"I wouldn't want to presume." She kept her voice even. The stun gun rested on the dust-covered hardwood floor, not far from her left foot. He hadn't taken out the stun gun's probes, though she was now shackled to the wall. The wires cascaded from where they lodged in her chest and stomach to her lap to the floor, like a waterfall. Maybe he wanted to scare her, or maybe he would jolt her again just for kicks. Her ribcage trembled with tightness or aftershocks, her heartbeat barely perceptible though her heart had to be racing. The stun gun was a hefty deterrent to resistance.

"You've been spying on me." His voice sang but remained flat, like someone pretending to be human. "How much did you see?"

"What are you talking about?"

"You told that cunt's parents that she knew she was loved, which she hadn't mentioned to me. I assumed you were the real deal, but maybe you aren't." He reached for the stun gun.

Kiera's thoughts crashed into each other in a mad scramble: *fucking-Kolcheks-not-the-stun-gun-again-please.* "I'm the real deal." She'd never referred to herself like that before, but she was willing to call herself whatever he wanted to avoid another shock.

He smirked, and she fantasized kicking him in the face.

"So, how much did you see?"

She hesitated only a moment. "All of it."

"Can you show me?"

Show him? Wasn't he there? "You want me to prove it? You want me to tell you what happened?"

He glared at her and kicked her thigh in the same spot as before. Hard. And, oh, fuck, that hurt.

Overly enunciating, he repeated his words, "Show. Me."

And then she realized what he meant. He wanted to use her like a video player, forwarding and reversing, so he could revisit his favorite moments. But memory reads didn't work like he wanted, and when he found out, he was going to be so pissed. She had to stall. "I'm not sure. I've only shared memories with other memory surgeons."

"Your brother shows memories all the time, doesn't he? Isn't that his specialty?"

Shit. She scrambled for a response.

Non-Dillon continued. "Not that it was easy to find much about him. No, all the articles were about you. Kiera, Kiera, Kiera, taking all the glory for yourself." He rocked a little, and pink crept into his cheeks.

Glory? Oh, yeah, she lived such a glamorous life.

He didn't stop. "Living in a penthouse, refusing interviews while your brother gets almost no coverage. Your parents are always going on about how proud they are of you."

"You don't know what the hell you're talking about."

Non-Dillon froze, and his predatory stillness snapped Kiera's rage. What the fuck was she doing, antagonizing a serial killer?

She backtracked as fast as possible. "They're not proud of me. They only pretend for the media. It's my brother they're proud of. He's the one they love. I was just a cash cow to them and nothing more. We haven't spoken in ten years."

Non-Dillon frowned. "They only love him?"

He wanted her to confirm that, something eager in his eyes. "Yeah. Why do you think he gets all the good memories, and I'm stuck with all the awful ones?"

Shit. She shouldn't have called the memories of him awful. But it didn't matter because Non-Dillon seemed pleased by her answer. "I knew we were alike."

"Of course." Agreeing with the serial killer who has you chained and is holding a stun gun with prongs attached to your body is common sense. Dean's words about interrogation came back to her. Understanding built trust, and trust could be manipulated. Could she find a way to weaponize it? An idea budded but wouldn't form, and she didn't have time to cajole the answers.

"I want to see Brittany's end." His face split open in a wide grin.

She didn't have a plan yet. Holy fuck, she needed a way to delay his demand. "I would, but I can't."

"Yes, you can. It's your whole purpose!"

"No, this is different. I don't have Brittany's memory. I did a read only, no surgery for her."

He frowned. "What does that mean?"

Knowing what he wanted helped her find the right way to explain. "It's like I watched a show on TV live and not on DVR. There's no way to go back and see it again."

"Then give me *your* memory."

As if she'd give that asshole any part of herself. Her fucked-up memories were her own, and they'd stay that way. "It doesn't work like that."

His face flushed pink and his eyes bugged out like a frog's. "Don't. You. Lie. To. Me. Memory whore."

Oh shit. She was trapped—mentally and physically. "I'm not ly—"

"Your brother does it."

Okay, okay. She could manage him. "No, he takes the memory and then gives it to a loved one. It isn't his memory of the memory," she explained as gently as she could.

Non-Dillon stared at her in a way that made every hair on her body stand on end. If she hadn't been attached to the wall, she would have run, despite knowing she couldn't escape. Nothing could have stopped her from scrambling away like a wild animal.

But then he just left.

*   *   *

KIERA STRAINED TO HEAR WHAT NON-DILLON MIGHT BE DOING, BUT the soundproofing worked too well. Though futile, she struggled to pull her hands out of the restraints. Her wrists were small, but the manacles were too tight. The room stank like off-gassing plastic. Her cells were probably mutating to cancer as she sat there.

The door burst open, flying into the padded wall and bouncing back. Amy stumbled and landed hard on her knees in front of Kiera. Lines of mascara streaked her face. Kiera's world stopped for a moment as their eyes met.

"I heard you talking about her, so I thought you might appreciate this little gift," Non-Dillon said.

Amy was dressed in a violet tank top, white bra straps showing, and a denim skirt, all fitted to her curvy body. Not enough clothes on her, leaving her vulnerable.

"Kiera," Amy whispered, then sobbed. Kiera had witnessed Amy crying more times than she had digits, but never like this. "Help me."

CHAPTER SIXTY EIGHT

Dean

IT TOOK DEAN LESS THAN FIVE MINUTES TO MAKE all his preliminary calls. He called 9-1-1 first, giving his name and star number and all the particulars dispatch would need to get a squad there fast. Dean phoned Sergeant Mike next. Kiera's abduction was most likely related to his case, which meant his team could investigate, but because of his personal relationship with the victim, he'd have to step out, according to department policy. That didn't mean he couldn't assist. A lot. They would need to interview him anyway, and he knew more about the suspect than anyone.

Mike responded with only a pause when Dean explained his involvement with Kiera before agreeing their team should handle the investigation. Dean offered to call Curt and Grace while Mike called in the rest of the team and updated the bosses.

"Sounds good," Mike said. "I'm going to put Haze in charge of this one until I get there."

Putting Curt in charge was Sergeant Mike's unspoken blessing for Dean to guide the investigation. "Thanks."

His call to Curt was short, needing only a few words. He saved the call to Grace for last, hoping her insights would push the case forward.

Before he pulled up her number, however, the mail carrier wheeled his cart inside and raised an arm in greeting to Manny. Delivery people didn't sign in at places and often went unnoticed.

"Manny," Dean said leaning on the counter. "Any strange deliveries in the last week or two? Or different drivers? Anything unusual?"

Manny set down the telephone handset. "Yes! There was a replacement UPS driver last week, Tuesday, I think. I remember because he came two hours early and then Miss Ellie had something outgoing, and it took me twenty minutes to convince the UPS people to send the driver back."

"Do you keep a list?"

He shook his head. "But they all come through the front, so they should all be on the video. You want me to pull up footage going back more than three days?"

"Can you give me two weeks?"

"Yeah, sure."

"Thanks."

Dean walked to the corner of the lobby to make his call, barely noticing the pastel pink trim accenting the white wainscoting, the old-world charm. He ignored everyone as he focused on Grace's words. She grounded him but didn't offer much consolation. They agreed that a public abduction and the use of the stun gun were not part of his usual MO, but that Kiera posed unique challenges since she wasn't approachable and far too jaded to fall for a confidence ruse.

"Could it be a coincidence? Someone else? I mean, how would he even know about her? Her involvement wasn't public knowledge." Not that a separate kidnapper made the situation better. "Maybe someone looking for ransom?" She had quite a bit of money, so kidnapping made sense.

"If someone wanted money from her, wouldn't they kidnap the brother? He's probably stronger than her, but he's far more easily accessed. No, I think it's our killer."

So did Dean. Part of him had known the moment Manny had knocked on the door.

Dean almost asked why, but the answer popped out instead. "He's going to try and use her to run his greatest hits, isn't he?"

Grace audibly exhaled. "The idea has to be tempting. Killers tend to find their high from their kills aren't as high and fade faster the more they kill, which results in escalation and eventually to mistakes being made. Maybe he wants to use Kiera to lengthen his refractory period."

Worse than imagining him raping and killing her, Dean envisioned that bastard keeping her for years like a pet.

No. No fucking way.

CHAPTER SIXTY NINE

Kiera

MY STARED AT KIERA AS IF SHE BELIEVED KIERA could save her.

Help her? How exactly was she supposed to do that chained to the wall with stun gun wires sticking out of her body? Kiera couldn't help herself, so Amy had no reason to think she could help her.

Non-Dillon grabbed Amy's hair and yanked her head back. Amy yelped. Her face looked sunburned. Tears gushed from her eyes. Strips of memories from transfers spun around Kiera. Screams. Cigarette burns on her forearm. Body odor stench. Floating. Disappearing. Escape where there was no escape. It wasn't real. It wasn't real. It couldn't be real.

Twine came from nowhere, tan and thin. Kiera remembered the bite of the rope on Brittany's skin—itching and cutting. Non-Dillon trussed Amy like a cowboy roping a calf. A little sacrificial calf with blond hair. He twisted and threaded the bindings, attaching each arm to the same-side leg, using his knee to spread her legs apart.

Kiera's mind detached, observing everything without seeing. She'd understood it was possible, of course, since several of her clients had dissociated. It wouldn't stop anything, wouldn't make the torment any less awful, but it would delay the impact.

"Please don't," Amy said to Non-Dillon, but she kept her attention on Kiera. Begging wouldn't work. Brittany had begged, and so had Vanessa.

Sure enough, Non-Dillon slapped the back of her head. "Shut up."

Amy whimpered. If Kiera let herself numb emotionally, she'd have an easier time, but she'd never be able to help Amy. Or herself. Being in the moment wouldn't unshackle her, but it would leave her mind free to plan an escape. She blinked and blinked until her focus sharpened.

Non-Dillon yanked Amy's underwear hard enough that her entire body rocked as the fabric ripped. He tossed them aside. They were white. Amy screamed but didn't thrash, didn't fight it. Later, Amy would hate herself for not fighting, even ineffectually. Almost all victims did. And if she did fight, she'd hate herself for making things worse. This was a game in which there was no way to win.

No time. Think. Think. Think. Please, think.

Amy gently rested her chin on the floor and looked up at Kiera. This time when their gazes locked, it grounded Kiera. Something passed between them, and Kiera caught a spark of anger in Amy's eyes, defiance even.

Yeah. Fuck this guy.

Non-Dillon shoved Amy's skirt up to her waist and unzipped his jeans. He cackled, enjoying Kiera's presence, her attention on him, on what he was about to do. He pushed his jeans down his hips. Oh, God, Kiera spied his erection.

"Wait!" Kiera's voice had purpose; she just had to figure out what it was. Control. She had to take control of her mind. And his. He needed her for his fantasy. "Let's make sure this will work first." Too croaky, she sounded too weak, and she still didn't have a fucking plan, but she pressed forward. "It would be a shame to waste her death. We should perfect the process first." Forced teaming. Using the word "we" was meant to make Non-Dillon feel as if they were in this together, on the same side. Rapists used the tactic sometimes, but that didn't mean it couldn't be implemented by victims. Thank you, Gavin de Becker for writing *The Gift of Fear*.

Non-Dillon frowned. "How?"

Good question. How? Part of a plan sprouted. "Let's try this with an older transfer first, since we can't start over if it doesn't work."

He jutted out his chin. "I don't want one of your other stupid memories. I want mine."

"Actually, I have one of yours. Vanessa Sanrow."

CHAPTER SEVENTY

Dean

DEAN CALLED LIU, WHO WAS THE ONLY ONE ON the team with access to the license plate reader (LPR) system. Sergeant Mike had already explained Kiera's disappearance, so at least, he didn't need to go through that again. "Can you run Dalton Janssen's plate through the LPR and see if anything hits?"

The system compiled everything the Automated License Plate Readers captured from squads patrolling as well as all the stationary cameras. If Janssen's van was caught anytime in the last few weeks, it might give them a search area. The offender planned so he'd have to prepare a space to take her, something like that would take time to create. If his plate turned up repeatedly in a neighborhood, they could catch a break.

"I'll be at the office in ten minutes, and I'll run it. Call me if you need anything else, anything at all, okay?"

"Great. When you're done, check out any camera pods in his neighborhood and this one, see if we can get movement on the van, figure out time frames and location, match them to the crimes. Thanks, Liu."

Curt showed up at the same time as the squad with coffee and a hug long enough to show support but short enough that Dean wouldn't lose his shit.

Dean leaned his arm against Curt. "Can you call Tam and get her to submit the search warrant for Janssen's place to the judge? When she gets it, I want them to look for paperwork first, and once they're inside, search any desks or bookcases looking for anything that pertains to Kiera."

"You mean Kolchek," Curt said with a hard glare.

Dean winced. He needed to sharpen his mind, not just to avoid missteps in paperwork and policy but for Kiera. "Exactly, for Brittany, but they might let us know if they accidentally find anything else."

"On it," Curt said. "I'm going to have Jason and Kristin print up a few copies of Janssen's driver's license and canvass the building. Probably most people are at work, but some might still be home, and we'll catch people returning as the day wears on. Maybe one of them has seen Janssen."

"Yeah, good."

Curt squeezed his arm as the officers approached to take Dean's statement and start securing the crime scene.

CHAPTER SEVENTY ONE

Kiera

Non-Dillon blinked twice, his face blank. "How do you know about Vanessa?"

"She was one of my clients," Kiera replied. "Westchester, about ten years ago, right?"

Non-Dillon didn't move from his position over Amy, but he'd lost his erection. Amy remained still, but her focus made Kiera feel less alone.

"That wasn't your memory to take. I want her to remember," Non-Dillon said.

Well, fuck. "She remembers parts of the night, and she suffers from insomnia and panic attacks, even now." Kiera couldn't believe she was trying to comfort that asshole.

He frowned and rose to his feet, towering over her, his right thumb running over his index finger. Adrenaline shot through her. His tell. She knew things about him, from Brittany and Vanessa and from Page and Dean. There had to be a way to use what she'd learned.

Kiera dug her heels into the hardwood floor, willing herself to stay focused. "This is going to be great."

His twitching fingers stopped. "What do you mean?"

What does he *want*? To reinhabit his exploits. For his living victims to bear his memory forever. "You can relive Vanessa's experiences. This will be a fantastic test run."

"Test run?"

"We can iron out anything you don't like." She had no idea what there might be to iron out, but every minute she delayed was another moment for someone to find them. "You can let me know what you like. That way, when we get to Amy, we can perfect the experience before we move on to the next victim."

"A perfect experience." He stared at her with no sign of recognition or humanity. "I like it."

Amy pursed her lips and glared at Kiera. "You won't ever be able to go back." Amy's voice came out hoarse and papery. Her words sounded familiar, but she couldn't place them at first. Then they slotted into place—Kiera had said that to Amy after she'd volunteered to read Brittany's memories.

Non-Dillon pulled a knife out of his pocket. "Shut up, bitch."

Before Kiera could breathe enough to cry out, he'd cut Amy's bindings. He jerked her to standing and shoved her out the door. Kiera wanted one last moment between them, but she was gone too quickly. He must have just dumped Amy in the other room because he returned in seconds. "Let's go. How do we do it?"

This was it. She couldn't delay any longer.

Kiera looked at him, really looked. His sharp cheekbones and full lips were attractive, his eyes creepy and dead, his sneer ugly. Kiera had always known she'd die violently. Her life could end no other way. Once he experienced a read . . .

He'd never be able to go back.

Holy shit, Amy was onto something. The trauma. The idea sprang whole, like warrior Athena from Zeus's head.

It wouldn't work. *Not with that shitty attitude.* It could work. Or she would be ripped in half and die in a puddle of her own blood. *Shut up.*

She would fight. Kiera had done enough transfers to realize that fighting didn't always change the outcome, but, of course, women who triumphed didn't need her.

What she needed from Non-Dillon for her plan to work was trust. How the hell was she supposed to build trust? Flattery? "You were very clever with the contacts."

He grinned and spread his arms wide. "I have every color."

Maybe it was working. He didn't look as if he wanted to carve her to pieces. "Your ability to change your appearance is pretty remarkable. I didn't even recognize you."

He rocked back on his heels. "I worked hard on each character. It takes weeks to get it just right."

"It shows." Okay, keep going, build that rapport. "These women that you killed, they're, like, stand-ins for someone else, right?"

He took a step closer as if she'd perked his interest, but in a good or bad way, Kiera couldn't tell. She kept going. "They just seem . . . not quite—"

"Nothing. Those bitches are nothing. They're pieces, little pieces." Non-Dillon paced near Kiera, muttering and clenching and unclenching his fists. "I can't find her. She's gone, and all I can get is pieces. Cut the pieces. Kill the pieces. She's dead. Dead. Dead."

Excellent plan, Kiera, agitate the psycho.

He stilled. "You want to know who I keep killing?"

She nodded because she couldn't do anything else. Her mouth was too dry for speech and she was chained to the fucking wall.

"My sister." The words sounded like a prayer.

She'd been expecting a girlfriend because of the whole rape thing, even though rape was about power and not sex. Huh. Being wrong wasn't a sign she was mistaken about everything else. It wasn't.

Was it?

He stared at Kiera as if he were deciding her fate.

Non-Dillon sat down in front of her, closer than before, breathing his stale breath in her face. He had faint freckles spattered across his nose.

"She was always the favorite. My mother gave her everything. She used to beat me and say horrible things, but never to Jilly. No, Jilly was perfect, but she was the real villain. She told on me whenever I did anything and sometimes made things up. When I was beaten, she laughed."

"How awful. It's terrible to be overlooked." She tried to mean the words. He was vulnerable, and she was vulnerable. She could use their shared insecurity, somehow. A trickle of sweat slid down her side.

He stared at Kiera's neck. "The night she died, she was on her way home to tell my mother something bad about me. I'll never forget her laugh." His eyes rose to hers. "Except she never made it back home. She died in a car accident, and I'd never been so happy."

If he was so thrilled, why was he killing women? She didn't ask—better to pretend she grasped why. And then she didn't have to fake it. His words echoed in her mind. *I'm the one that kills you.*

This was her chance. "It should have been you that killed her."

His hands shot out and grabbed her head. Before she could process anything, he mashed his lips onto hers. He kissed her. His tongue invaded her mouth, and she tried not to taste him, bite him, pull away, or throw up. She kissed him back—not well, but he didn't seem to notice. His thick tongue tasted of old cigarettes. She whimpered but hoped he'd think it was a moan. He kissed her harder.

No escape from this shit show, and she was losing her nerve. Time to see what fate had ready. She eased out of the kiss and attempted a smile. "Do you want to see Jilly pay?"

CHAPTER SEVENTY TWO

Dean

DEAN SUGGESTED HE ASSIST JASON AND KRISTIN with the canvassing, but Curt refused. "I want to keep an eye on you."

Sergeant Mike arrived and another squad car. A few residents stopped in the lobby, asking Manny questions about the police presence. Everywhere people moved and talked, the sound reverberating in the space and filling it. Dean struggled to filter out all the extraneous sensory input and concentrate on his next steps.

Updating Mike physically hurt because he asked too many probing questions, trying to unearth every detail. Dean didn't want to talk—he wanted to act.

Kristin and Jason jogged through the door with a stack of papers, Dalton Janssen's blown-up driver's license photo visible. Kristin pushed Dean's shoulder. "You okay?"

Dean nodded because he wanted to stay. The chaos of the active crime scene seeped into Dean's body, wanting to turn and tear and trip him into making a mistake. It demanded a mental discipline Dean couldn't find. He needed air and a moment to calm himself and collect his scattering thoughts.

"Let's get started, yeah?" Jason asked Mike.

"Detective Matthson!"

Dean turned and saw an officer blocking Nadira Shula and Beth Hamilton near the door. Beth waved a hand at him and bounced on her toes. Nadira stood still, her arms tight to her sides, lips compressed, and tears sliding down her cheeks.

"Let them through!" Dean called to the officer and gestured them forward.

Nadira and Beth both picked their way through the crowd as if wanting to touch others as little as possible. They held hands and moved together, Nadira leading the way. "Kiera didn't show up to group, and she never misses. She won't answer her phone." Nadira wiped tears off her cheeks. "Is she dead?"

The question punctured his heart, and Dean thought he might bleed out on the lobby floor. Before he could recover, Curt said, "There's no reason to think that at this time, but she is missing. Do you have any information that might help?"

"That the guy?" Beth asked, pointing a finger at Janssen's photo. She leaned to peer closer, and Kristin lifted the top copy to give Beth a better view.

"He's a person of interest," Curt replied.

"'Cause I seen him before."

The world slowed, as if something heavy were dragging on time and it couldn't flow right. "When?" Dean asked as Curt asked, "Where?"

Beth turned to Nadira. "You remember? Intelligentsia two weeks ago. I mean, he had blond hair in one of them buns and a beard and wore those little granny glasses, but that was definitely him." Nadira stared at Beth with the same wide-eyed stare Dean was sure he wore. Beth frowned. "Remember? New guy who cleaned the tables real slow and had real long nails?"

"That guy?" Nadira asked and studied the picture.

"You don't think so?" Dean asked as Curt asked, "Which Intelligentsia?"

Dean and Curt shared a glance filled with hope at a lead and frustration that they had talked over each other.

"The one on Broadway, near group. And I don't recognize him, but Beth remembers everything, people especially. If she said she saw him, then she did. That means he was stalking her, right? That he has her?" Nadira's voice started calm but worked up to frantic.

"You want to sit down?" Curt asked Nadira, hovering a hand next to her shoulder in case she required some physical support. The crowd pressed into their group.

Dean should have been the one to comfort Kiera's best friend, but he couldn't take his eyes off Beth. Her skills at spotting disguises was exactly what he needed. "Ms. Hamilton, would you be willing to look through video footage to see if you can spot this man? He'll likely appear different from how he looks in his license photo and at Intelligentsia."

Beth tilted up her chin. "You bet your sweet ass I will. This prick got my friend? If he's hiding on that video, I'm gone ferret him out."

CHAPTER SEVENTY THREE

Kiera

NON-DILLON SAID NOTHING, ONLY STARED AT her as if she glowed. Kiera's mouth was as dry as her palms were wet. Her vision tunneled.

She couldn't stall any longer.

"I need your hands," Kiera said in a shaky voice.

What she really needed were her own hands, but her opening move didn't free her. He reached up and took her hands, still secured over her head. Their lips were inches apart. She tried to time her inhales to not taste his exhales.

Kiera grimaced. "I don't know if it will work. This is really uncomfortable, but I'll try. Close your eyes."

Could she even do a memory read if she had to, with him not sharing the gift and her Zen left back in the elevator? She searched for his bundle of memory. Even with the discomfort, she found the snarl of his mind, muted but accessible. But he didn't know that.

After a few seconds, she slumped. "I'm sorry. Can you unlock my hands?"

Non-Dillon sighed, but he unlocked her left, the weaker hand. "If you can't make this work, I'll have to find another way to motivate you."

Where was the trust? She needed both hands, damn it.

He sat a few inches farther away, like kids readying for a game of patty-cake, holding her left hand in his right.

His brain snapped into focus and pulsed, like the belly of a snake that has eaten a mouse. The colors were garish—lots of pink in the core, but that wasn't the predominant color. Great skeins the color of dried blood flickered like a bulb about to die. Interwoven were an assortment of oranges and metallic browns. The colors glowed so bright she wanted to look away; they hurt her eyes.

"I can see you. You're beautiful," she whispered, figuring it would be harder to detect the lie in hushed tones. "You need to open to me in order for me to share the memory."

The filaments of color slithered, and Kiera's stomach convulsed. Never had she wanted to drop a connection so badly. *One chance.* He opened wider than she expected, the coils like the yawn of a mouth with sharp teeth and a brain that only desired consumption.

If what she was planning to do didn't work, the repercussions were going to be bad. Not paper-cut bad, but arms-ripped-out-of-the-sockets bad. If she did nothing, she'd be raped or killed, or raped *and* killed. Amy too. Kiera would have to play his game better than he did. She couldn't do this half-assed. From the storage boxes in her mind, she pulled out Vanessa's root memory.

CHAPTER SEVENTY FOUR

Dean

"TAKE YOUR TIME," DEAN SAID TRYING NOT TO loom over Beth and Nadira as they sat side by side at the security office's metal desk. Manny kept the lobby tidy with nothing marring any surface. In the back, however, it was a hoarder's paradise with piles of paper advertisements, plastic silverware settings, and several mugs partially filled with coffee, according to the acrid scent permeating the room.

The office was about the size of a walk-in closet, and Kiera would have hated the tight quarters. With Manny, Dean, Beth, and Nadira all crowded together, the air heated in a breath. Sweat trickled down Dean's back.

Beth controlled the speed, and she did not take her time. Dean squelched the urge to tell her to slow down or to pay closer attention to the deliveries. But he had no idea how Beth's brain worked, and he needed to trust her.

After only a few minutes, Beth stopped the video. "There."

"Miss Janet?" Manny asked, frowning. He peered forward, his face inches from the computer screen, his bulk pressing between the two women who both edged away. "No way."

"That's him." Beth pointed at the image while pushing her hair off her round face. "I ain't lying, and I ain't guessing."

"She's right," Nadira said. "That's him."

"Miss Janet? She's subletting 3F." Manny bit his thumbnail. "She moved in earlier this month. You telling me she's transgendered?"

"No, he's not transgendered but wearing a disguise. He creates a persona specifically for each of his victims. A man could never get close to Kiera and gain her trust," Dean said, his mind finally grasping something solid.

Even a woman, as a stranger, would have a hard time getting past Kiera's bullshit detector. Thus, the elevator. 3F.

Janssen lived in the building.

"Kiera's still here," Dean said, his stomach disappearing. Knowing she was so close didn't provide the kind of relief he wanted. What the hell was that bastard doing to her at that moment, two floors up? "We need to see all the paperwork on Miss Janet."

Manny scrambled to the file cabinets as everyone else stared at the small security monitor to watch the footage of a tall blond woman walk through the door in an orange dress, wave at Manny, and then head toward the elevator at eight last night. Dean bent down and hit the keys to play the video back and forth. Dalton made a convincing woman.

"He got on a wig and dress, but see how he walks, right? It's the same guy," Beth said to Nadira in a hushed voice.

"The set of the shoulders too," Nadira whispered back.

"Ain't you gonna go get her?" Beth asked when Dean hadn't moved.

"We need a warrant first," Dean said, his gut twisted like a pretzel in a blender. He pictured himself slipping up the stairs.

"And SWAT. Busting in there without a plan could get her killed," Curt said, poking his head into the room, as if he'd had a premonition about the revelation. "TAC team hit Janssen's place. No Kiera or Janssen, of course, but they did find body parts. No doubt our guy. Tam got the judge to give us a full search warrant, so he'll sign off on a warrant for this location quick. I'll put it together and email it to Tam in five minutes, and then we'll get SWAT out here."

SWAT wasn't just around the corner, and everything took so much damned time. Dean hoped they wouldn't be too late.

CHAPTER SEVENTY FIVE

Kiera

K IERA HELD OUT VANESSA'S MEMORY FILAMENT near the cluster of memories that were Non-Dillon's. She remembered how greedy Ash had been for a good memory, how he'd snatched it from her like an ill-mannered dog with a treat. And how she'd given a snapshot of memory to Nadira, and how delicately Nadira had taken the fragment.

Dalton wanted to relive the misery he'd wrought, and Kiera wanted him to choke on it. The coil closed over it, and he took hold. She released it—the root memory, the full, potent experience—with a shove. The events wouldn't just play but transfer to Non-Dillon. He likely didn't have a storage box to store it, a built-in mechanism to cope with another's trauma.

Kiera counted on him trying to drop the memory, which would slam the entirety of it into his consciousness instead of letting the memory unfurl in its own time. It should overwhelm him.

But what if his apathy, his complete disregard for others made him immune to a transfer? What if his fucked-up brain loved it? What if it worked just as he'd hoped, but rather than a paralyzing punch of sympathetic and parasympathetic nervous systems firing simultaneously, he received a whopping jolt of endorphins? What if his body delivered enough adrenaline for him to crush her into oblivion with his bare hands?

She opened her eyes wanting to see her destiny and face whatever happened next. Non-Dillon clamped down on her hand, and his eyes gaped wild and unseeing.

He moaned and thrashed but didn't close the access to his mind. If anything, the trauma made his brain softer, looser, as the coils spun away from one another. And she could see the spools of color with her eyes open, which had never happened before. Somehow, she'd connected deeply with that creep.

She didn't have to relive Vanessa's assault again by giving it to him, but—flashes of colors, the growl of grunts, the taste of tears—they rippled over her. So much pain.

Karma is a bitch, Non-Dillon. Taste a drop of the poison you spilled into the world.

A sob. Non-Dillon of the present. His coils loosened even more, the open space beckoning, and vengeance unfurled from her like a cobra lily plant, which tricks insects into thinking they're heading to freedom when they are only burrowing deeper, into their doom.

Follow the trauma, motherfucker.

She opened the box to the worst root memory she'd ever taken and rammed it into the middle of his threads. Seven million dollars' worth of rape and torture coming right up. Non-Dillon shrieked, but Kiera gripped his hand harder. The tight contact made dropping into him every strand surrounding that surgery, all the echoes, easier.

Despite the fear that she would lose control, Kiera madly crammed every transfer she had, every root memory, every echo. Sweat poured down her face. As the transfers flowed—blurs of pinks and screams and shivers and whispers and tears and temper—she grew stronger and stronger, he weaker and weaker. Non-Dillon cried, curling around her hand, his forehead on her thigh.

The swirling mass of his memories roiled like spiders from a burning building, bringing all the pink memories to the top. He held more than she'd expected, and they all started to glow. She should have retreated, let go, but she couldn't turn away from the blaze of pink. A shell pink memory vibrated, and then the edges frayed as the recollection pulled apart.

* * *

Darkness.

No, Mommy. It was too dark, and he had to pee, but if he did, if he made a mess . . . He couldn't stop the tears. Snot ran down his nose and into his mouth. Quiet. He had to be quiet, but he needed to breathe, and when he took a breath, the sob escaped.

* * *

SHE JERKED FROM HIS CONSCIOUSNESS, BUT A VOICE FOLLOWED LIKE A wolf howl in a breeze, resounding through Kiera's mind. A woman's voice. Mother. She screeched a name. *Dalton.*

So fucking weak . . . So pathetic . . .

Dalton slammed his face onto her leg, then onto the floor. "Stop it! Stop it right now! I'm going to kill you!"

Kiera had emptied all the trauma not her own. And she wouldn't share any of herself—not even to save her own life.

Nothing left. No weapons. She was light. Insubstantial. Half specter. Out of options. Dean. Dean! What would he do? What would—

She uncrossed her legs, nudging away the stun gun, but Dalton was too close for her to kick him solidly. She needed just a little more room. But he would be coming back, his mind coiling back together, his rational thoughts surging up from the bottom of all those memories.

"Dalton!" she shrieked, trying to mimic his mother's shrill, harsh cadence. He froze, mouth gaping, eyes swimming. "You're so fucking pathetic!"

He scrabbled backward in blind panic, but she kept tight hold of his hand. All those brutal workouts to keep her mind calm had bolstered her body, and she possessed a strong grip. Once she had enough space to clear her foot, she kicked him hard in the face. His chin snapped back. She kicked him again. And again. Their grip was slick, and Kiera couldn't hold him if he got enough sense to yank his hand away. If she couldn't kill him, he would recover before anyone found her. If she was lucky, he would kill her quickly in a fit of rage. She'd never been lucky.

CHAPTER SEVENTY SIX

Dean

T HE SWAT TEAM SPREAD THE FLOOR PLAN FOR 3F across the security desk. Simple setup: open living room and kitchen, two bedrooms, and a bathroom. Only the hallway was a fatal funnel.

Each floor was separated by concrete, so SWAT didn't need to worry about gunfire affecting other floors. They were going in with a team of nine, so they could breach both bedrooms simultaneously if they didn't find them in the living room/kitchen area.

They found an open unit with the same floor plan, so they did a dry run of the op, running through it in minutes. Smoothing out the strategy was supposedly worth the short time it took, but the minutes branded into Dean.

If he could have taken a pill to render him unconscious for ten minutes, he would have swallowed it without water. The closer they got to go time, the sicker he became.

Hold on, babe. Please.

He couldn't breathe.

Come back to me. Come back to me. Come back to me.

CHAPTER SEVENTY SEVEN

Kiera

KIERA RAISED HER LEG HIGH AND HAMMERED HER heel into the side of his head, which had flopped to the floor. The contact was solid, but with some give. She expected a cracking sound but heard nothing except her own breathing and her foot thumping.

Random snippets of images and memories bombarded her—cracks on a plastic chair, the ache of a rotten tooth—raw meat on the verge of going off, red and brown, brown and red, juicy, stop the smell—stop stop—

She thought of the movie *Halloween* when the girl cries in a corner while Michael Myers sits up behind her. She imagined Dalton sitting up, his face bloody, pulling out the knife he'd used to scalp Brittany. He was going to kill her. *No. No. No.* She struck again and again and again, a frenzy overtaking her. He had to be dead. He had to be dead. He had to be dead.

* * *

KIERA CAME TO, THOUGH SHE DIDN'T THINK SHE'D BEEN UNCONSCIOUS. In a breath, she was back in the moment, with no recollection of where she'd gone. Would her root memory, if extracted, show everything that happened under a veil of red or black or psychedelic magenta?

Dalton lay only an arm's length away from her, his face mercifully turned away from her, but his head had collapsed. Blood pooled, but the ooze slowed. Still, she edged away. Blood coated the entire sole of her shoe. She'd have to throw the shoes away. Her foot ached and throbbed, especially her heel.

Kiera jerked the probes out of her chest and stomach, not caring if it was verboten. Holy shit, she'd killed a man. She had taken a life. Her heartbeat was everywhere—her chest, her arms, her legs, her ears, her eyeballs.

Puffy clouds. Puffy clouds. She cackled at her own insanity. Then she screamed, screamed like a mortally wounded animal until her vocal cords fractured.

She closed her eyes, and that was better. She had to break free, had to find Amy, who was locked in her own hell. Had to get away from the dead body.

"Okay, okay, this is going to be nasty. You know it's going to be nasty. Whatever. No big deal. Just a little dead flesh." Her voice rasped, as if she'd been screaming, which she had.

"You can talk to yourself. Who cares? Nobody will ever know; you're in a soundproof room." Kiera opened her eyes and stared at the ceiling. Even that had padding. "I'm a killer! Don't fuck with me!" Her cauterized throat wailed.

She had to find a way to escape. No way had she killed someone only to starve to death in this macabre wannabe sound booth while maggots poured out of the corpse and wriggled toward her. Looking at death, her own death, had cleared the cobwebs and the side quests. Kiera had reasons to live and unfinished business.

When she saw Dean again, she would tell him how desperately she wanted him. She might be seriously flawed, and this little episode probably didn't do her mental health any favors, but—blood pooled under Dalton—she'd be seeing that in her dreams—but she'd survived. And if she put her heart on the line and Dean didn't want her, she'd survive that too. And if he did, then she'd leverage the fight inside her to hold onto him.

"Enough fucking around." She grabbed Dalton's collar with her left hand and hauled him up between her legs, using her lower body to shift him closer. His blood was everywhere, her jeans soaked. She was going to need a full panel workup after this.

Don't think.

The body was heavy yet pliant. When did rigor mortis set in?

Shut. Up.

When she reached his pocket, tears poured down her face. She needed to conserve water, so crying was stupid, but she didn't try that hard to stop herself.

No key. How was that possible? Then she saw it, sitting on the floor a foot from Dalton's body, completely out of reach.

CHAPTER SEVENTY EIGHT

Dean

Dean's legs cut out from under him as he waited to discover if Kiera was alive or dead. Better to stay on the ground because Curt and Jason looked concerned. If she were gone, he would never again hear her laugh, or watch her eyelashes flutter when she slept, or smell the silk of her hair, or hold her until she melted into him.

Please.

"We've got two victims up here," the radio squawked. "Both with minor injuries. Suspect appears dead. Okay to send in the medics."

She was alive. Kiera was alive. Dean grabbed the handle of the car door and hauled himself to his feet. Curt slapped his back, and Jason and Kristin fist bumped. But until he saw Kiera with his own eyes, his chest wouldn't unclench. He'd taken one step to the building when Curt clamped a hand on his shoulder.

"Later," Dean snarled, shaking off Curt's grip.

Jason shifted in front of Dean and held up his hands. "Hold up a sec, brother. No way you don't blow everything if you go off like that." He kept his voice firm but kind. Jason didn't do kind often. "You can't lose it now."

Dean squeezed his fists and dug them into his forehead. Jason made sense, but . . . "I can't." Now that the pressure of finding her had vanished, nothing held him together. "What do I do?"

"Try dropping into the zone," Curt said. "Just like any other victim. You read people better than anyone I know. Figure out what she needs."

Jason put an arm around Dean. "Exactly. She's going to need you. Those first moments set the tone, and they can't be undone." He shook Dean's shoulder. "You need to be in control so that she doesn't have to worry about you on top of everything else."

"You don't understand," Dean said, fighting to manage his pelting emotions. "I never got the chance to tell her—"

"You have that opportunity now." Curt slapped the back of his head. "So, don't fuck it up."

That advice was far too vague to be helpful.

But it was too late for clarification, as the radio barked again. They were coming out.

CHAPTER SEVENTY NINE

Kiera

AMY HAD EXITED FIRST WITH AN ESCORT OF armed men. They hadn't spoken, but Amy turned before leaving the apartment, her face streaked with tears, and clapped a hand over her heart. Kiera mimicked the gesture, her gut tightening though the rest of her remained numb. Something inside her had broken. Maybe everything.

Then a pair of men in army green guided Kiera out of the building. She was already outside when she realized she'd walked past Manny. Air hit her face, not cool, but refreshing. Her hair rose off her neck. Lights flashed to her left—an ambulance. People, strangers, littered the sidewalk, where uniformed officers kept them back. Probably, they were watching her, but she couldn't care.

And then Dean stood a foot away. He wore the same shirt as the night before, though it was considerably more wrinkled. She stopped, but her escort continued, dispersing into the spinning lights and throngs of people. Kiera wanted to throw her arms around him, but she was covered in blood.

The large paramedic from upstairs tossed a blanket across her shoulders. "Just a quick examination to be sure you're fine," he insisted.

She shook her head, already having refused medical attention, though she did clutch the blanket to her. Hopefully, it would calm her shaking, and she liked the barrier between her bloody clothes and Dean.

"Shock can hide—"

"Give us a second," Dean said, waving him back. "Just one second."

The paramedic scowled but took two steps back, eyeing Kiera as if she might drop dead at any moment, and he was not taking the blame for it.

Dean slipped a hand under the blanket and brushed up and down her arm. Every inch he touched bloomed with warmth. When the blanket threatened to fall off, Dean held it in place. "You're safe now, Kiera."

She spluttered a crazy kind of laugh that wanted to turn into a sob. He captured her gaze and her hand, and as she stared at him, her quaking slowed.

He visibly swallowed, his eyes wet. "Are you okay?"

"I'm tired," she whispered.

Dean squeezed her hand. "You can rest soon. Let me tell you what's going to happen, all right?"

She nodded.

"They'll clean you up in the ambulance," Dean said. "Address your injuries, take you to the hospital if—"

"No." She didn't care that it came out too loud. "I'm fine. I don't need a hospital." What she needed was safety, and some hospital wouldn't give her that. Besides, she barely felt any pain. She refused to think of what could have been done to her.

"Okay. Nobody's going to force you to go anywhere or do anything. They just want to take a look to make sure there's no injury that adrenaline is hiding. Is that all right?"

She nodded.

He nodded with her, encouraging her, syncing with her. She'd never needed anyone so much in her entire life, and though it should have scared her—and it did—she trusted Dean would see her through it all.

"Good. Evidence techs will take away your soiled clothes and photograph any injuries, so I'm going to run upstairs and get you fresh clothing while you're being treated." His hands never stopped soothing her, as if he didn't mind the blood. "Once you're medically cleared, they're going to want your statement. Everyone will understand if you're not up to it today, and we can do it—

"No, I want to do it now. I want to do it and be done. Please, I just want this to be over."

"Okay, okay." He pulled her close enough to touch, the blanket the only thing keeping Dean from Dalton's blood. The thought of Dean being tainted by it made her belly lurch, but she couldn't resist the comfort of him. Dean continued in the hypnotic voice he used when she freaked out. "We'll get it out of the way today. I'll be with you the whole time, if you want, except for the actual interview."

She made a small noise at the thought of being separated from him again.

"I can't be in the room because I'm too close to you. But I'll be right outside, and you can ask for me if you need *anything*. You can stop whenever you want, take as many breaks as you want, and I'll be right there. You can refuse to answer any question you don't like or, even better, just tell them you don't remember." He sounded so calm and matter-of-fact that her muscles loosened one by one.

"Do I need a lawyer?" she croaked.

"No, babe."

"But I killed him."

Dean's eyebrows shot up. "Good for you," he said, a small smile quirking his lips. He squeezed her shoulder. Like the blood truly didn't scare him. "There isn't a state's attorney in the world who would press charges against you. But if it eases your mind, I'll be listening, and if I think, for any reason, you need a lawyer, I'll interrupt the interview."

"Can you do that?"

Dean shrugged. "It's not illegal, and if the bosses don't like it, I really don't give a fuck." He brushed his fingers across her cheek.

That small touch opened up a chasm of emotion that she couldn't voice—not until they were alone.

* * *

KIERA FELT TOO MANY EMOTIONS, AND HER THOUGHTS WOULDN'T settle, as if her mind had put on those magical red shoes that wouldn't allow the dancer to stop dancing. But she felt no guilt over killing Non-Dillon—Dalton. Possibly that would come later, but the universe was a better place without him.

She was free of all the surgeries. The ordeal had sucked hairy balls, but her slate was now clean. Kiera might never do another surgery again. Though she still had all her memories of the transfers, her head was so light it floated, like pollen in the spring. If not for the sickness in her gut and the aches in her body, she might have enjoyed the sensation.

The interview lasted just over an hour, and Dean somehow arranged for Tam to conduct it. Kiera wished they were talking under different circumstances so she could ask Tam about Dean, what he was like on the job, and ask her what it was like to be a black, female homicide detective, and how she liked working with Liu, and if they had the same kind of relationship as Dean and Curt, and a dozen other questions that weren't about what had happened in that awful room.

Kiera told the truth, only omitting the memory dump, claiming instead that she'd only pretended to give him Vanessa's memory. Her official story was that she'd tricked him into closing his eyes, and then sprung her attack. Tam never questioned it, never asked her about memory surgery or readings at all. Had her deception really been that easy?

Dean captured her in a tight hug the moment she left the interview room, a hug that lasted until she pulled away.

"I can take you home," he said. "Or I can take you to my place if you don't want to go back there tonight. You can stay as long as you'd like."

Kiera almost melted at not having to brave the elevator or haul herself up nine flights of stairs with her bone-bruised foot. Whether his offer was simple kindness or protectiveness didn't matter. Dean made her relax—had always had that effect. She wanted every moment possible with him. "I'd rather stay with you for a bit."

* * *

THE FADED RED T-SHIRT HAD A STICK-FIGURE PERSON RUNNING FROM A stick-figure cop. The caption above the characters read *Running*. The caption below said *Sometimes all we need is a little motivation*. It almost made Kiera laugh as she pulled it over her freshly scrubbed body.

The T-shirt came to the tops of her thighs and didn't hide her motherfucker of a bruise, but it was soft as flannel, as if it had been washed a thousand times. Though the shower had melted off a layer of skin, Kiera still shivered. She took the black cotton robe off the hook on the back of the door and clomped downstairs, following the sounds of Dean (it was Dean, right?) rummaging about in his dystopian kitchen.

Although she hadn't made any noise, he turned the moment her feet hit the bottom of the stairs. He wore his glasses, and though it was probably because he'd had his contacts in far too long, he might have worn them for her. He'd also changed into a T-shirt and cotton pajama pants.

His smile was genuine as he held out a cup of tea. "Chamomile," he said, like an apology.

She took the mug, liking the heat on her hands, appreciating the gesture, but finding herself unmoored from reality and the moment. Where did they go from here?

CHAPTER EIGHTY

Dean

"WHAT CAN I DO FOR YOU?" IN HIS HEAD, Dean begged a God he didn't believe in for her to come up with something, so he could be of use. What he wanted was to solidify their relationship, but he wasn't selfish enough to push for that now.

"Will you hold me?" She wouldn't look at him, her eyes darting, her lips trembling. "I don't want him to be the last person who touched me."

Fuck. Me.

His chest squeezed as if a giant were using his heart as a stress ball. He took her mug of tea and set it down on the nearest flat surface, then pulled her into his arms. Her wet hair now smelled like his shampoo. "You want to continue this somewhere more comfortable?"

"Is a bed an option?"

He ran a hand up and down her arm. She was adorable in his oversized bathrobe. "Anything I can give you, it's yours. Upstairs, then?"

She nodded, and he led her up the tight stairs. He should have made his bed and shoved all his dirty clothes into his closet when he'd changed, but it was too late now. Small hillocks of shirts and socks created an embarrassing landscape in his too-small room. The bed was queen-size, and though the black-and-white-checked comforter was crumpled to the end, at least, the sheets were clean.

She dropped his robe onto the ground and crawled into the bed. He dropped his glasses on the nightstand and followed her, scooting close, laying so that they faced each other.

He brushed her damp hair away from her face. She looked as she always did, though a little pale. Dean would have pulled out his own throat for the right words to make her situation even a tiny bit better, but he was off-kilter. "Uh, where should I touch you?"

She rolled onto her stomach and shoved the covers to the side to poke out a foot, keeping her head turned to him. "If you don't mind."

In her official statement, she claimed she'd kicked him several times, and the redness on her heel, threaded with blue indicated just how hard she'd nailed him. She flinched when he touched the spot, so he switched from his fingers to skating his lips over the deep bruise. He stroked her calves and the back of her knee.

Her eyes closed as she sighed. The realization that she was safe and alive and there with him drenched him like a monsoon. His hands shook and tears backed into his throat and leaked out his eyes. He'd almost lost her. He fought the desire to drive down to the morgue and shoot that fucker in the face, just as Kiera had asked him to do months ago. She'd been the one crying then.

"Dean?" Her eyes were open and glassy. "I have to tell you something."

Oh God, Janssen had raped her. Dean shoved down the howl of grief worming its way from his gut. "Okay." He stayed lying beside her, his face near her stomach, so she could look down on him. This wasn't about him. Not now. "No matter what you tell me, I promise I won't hurt you. I won't leave you."

She nodded. "I didn't tell the whole truth when Tam interviewed me."

When no more came, he said, "Okay."

She swallowed and covered the hand resting on her hip. Her fingers were so cold that they almost burned when she placed her hand over his.

"I did manipulate him into uncuffing one wrist, but after that, I didn't just . . ." She smiled that self-deprecating tweak of her lips when she joked about something not funny. "I didn't just break out my killer moves."

He waited.

"I gave him Vanessa's memories."

He squinted, trying to ascertain the worry beneath that revelation. "I'm not sure that particular detail matters. I mean, so what if you did?"

She inhaled. "It had the effect I'd hoped. He was definitely stunned, and—I don't know—I guess I kind of got angry about the situation?" Kiera's fingers jerked over his hand. "Okay, I just—I was upset, about myself and all the others and every client I ever had, and I thought . . ."

"Keep going."

"I unloaded the worst memory I ever took. And it felt good. And then I kept going." She looked at him, her eyes desperate. "I put every bad memory I've ever taken into him."

"And you feel guilty about that?" Because that strategy was brilliant.

"No, the opposite. I don't feel guilty at all, and I'd do it again." She brushed her face into the pillow, breaking eye contact for only a moment before looking at him again. "I broke him. Using my gift, I obliterated his mind so badly I experienced it falling apart—not inside him, but from the outside, like watching through a window. The traumatic memories I made him relive shattered his own horrible memories, and I caught little snippets and sensations, and I shouldn't have been able to do that. I've always needed permission to access someone's memories, but I could have done anything. I think I could have wiped him like a hard drive."

He shimmied up to face her to ensure she saw his conviction. "You were fighting for your life. Of course, you used everything at your disposal."

Her icy hand fluttered to the sleeve of his T-shirt and played with the edge, as if she wanted to touch him. "But I'm a killer now. And even worse, I'm like those charlatans your friend Jack is suing. I'm capable of doing terrible things with people's minds."

Dean laughed, more at himself and the situation rather than her words.

"Oh, babe." He plucked her frozen hand and tucked it underneath his T-shirt, between his ribcage and arm, barely managing not to hiss at the icy contact. "Weren't you just telling me last night that what we're capable of doesn't matter, only what we do with it?"

Her fingers spread and gripped his side. "But if people found out what memory surgeons could do, how badly we could hurt people—"

"Even if they did, how does that make you any different from, say, a Navy SEAL?"

She huffed a laugh. "Or a ninja?"

Dean smiled. "Exactly. Consider yourself a brain ninja."

She tilted her face closer, studying him, searching for truth. "It doesn't bother you? What I can do?"

"No."

Her eyes filled with tears, though none spilled over. "You might think differently about me when you see him."

She'd never been more wrong. "I already know what I'm going to think." He kissed her forehead.

"You don't know . . . when you see what I—"

"Babe, I don't care if he looks as if he just fell asleep, or he's so disfigured he isn't recognizable as human." He cupped her face and drilled his gaze into her, pouring his conviction into his eyes and his voice. "I'm going to look at those photos and feel nothing but *pride*. You are a badass."

She blinked, snorted, and rolled her eyes. "I am *not* a badass."

"Kiera, you bested an armed serial killer one-handed. Nobody is more badass than you."

Her body relaxed. "So, how come I don't feel like I won?"

"Because although you did win, you also lost something." Something she could never get back. But that didn't mean she wouldn't emerge stronger than ever. She was a phoenix.

She twisted a lock of her hair. "Did I lose you?"

His body shuddered. "No." Too much to say—but only one thing mattered. "No, Kiera. You'll always have me."

343

If she believed him, her expression didn't show anything. That was okay. He believed it—and she saw he believed it. The rest was up to her.

Dean stroked her hair. "I'm sorry I let my insecurities keep us apart. I'm sorry I didn't come to you sooner, but every time you warned me about how messed up you were, it reminded me of how messed up I was. I was terrified that you didn't seem to notice, and when you eventually did—I couldn't endure that moment, Kiera, when you realized that this person you admired wasn't who you thought. That I was more monster than man, more cold than—"

"Stop." She covered his mouth with her finally warm hand. "Listen to me. Everyone has a shadow side or a dark side. I got up close and personal with mine today, and it saved my life. There's a reason we're in touch with the shady side of ourselves, and it isn't because we're monsters. But. . ." She lowered her hand from his mouth. "I understand better than anyone what it's like when the part of you that hurts the most is the part that everyone else values."

Before he could breathe again, she kissed his chin. He'd never been able to put his fears into words, but she'd slapped down truth like an unbeatable hand of poker. "Let's be done playing the I'm-the-most-fucked-up game." Her smile lifted only one corner of her mouth. "For one, I just got a *real* unfair advantage today."

Dean snort-laughed, which ticked up the other side of her smile.

She reached out and cupped his cheek. "I love you, Dean."

He wrapped his arms around her back and guided her flush against him. "Damn it, Brayleigh, I wanted to say it first. I even had this grand gesture planned."

"Oh yeah? Does it involve a mariachi band or sky writing? Because I'm not into spectacles."

Dean laughed and nuzzled her neck. "No, I just took a six-week sabbatical from work, and I thought we could—"

She stiffened and pulled back, studying his face. "You did what?"

Had that been a mistake? "I . . . uh . . . in case you needed me."

"That is so much better than a Jumbotron proposal." They laughed and she rested her head on his chest. "So, now you think *I* need *you*?"

"Well . . ."

"Because I do. You're the only thing in my entire life that's ever made any sense." Kiera broke into a smile, this one reaching her eyes, and she squeezed him hard enough to hamper his breathing.

He laughed with relief. And love. And the certainty that with every fiber of his being, he needed her too.

CHAPTER EIGHTY ONE

Kiera

"ANYWHERE ELSE I SHOULD TOUCH YOU?" Dean asked, his hand brushing lazily down her neck.

"Everywhere?" Until she felt the drag of his skin over her entire body, she wouldn't believe they were together again, that she'd survived the worst and come out of it with the best man she'd ever known. "Can I touch you too?"

"You can always touch me," he said and kissed her again, his lips and tongue familiar and exciting and banishing the assault on her mouth from earlier.

She stroked her hands down his chest, then dipped her fingers underneath his T-shirt. He watched her, and she'd longed for him so much that it didn't bother her—almost dying put her fears in perspective. She dragged her hands up, which tugged up his shirt. He sat up enough for her to pull it over his head.

"I missed you," she said, spreading her fingers over his chest, sucking in his warmth, and feeling the beat of his heart under her palm. He'd taken six weeks off work just to be there for her. Because he loved her. He. Loved. Her.

"Kiera." He said her name as if it carried power. And it did.

She breathed in the totality of his presence. More. She needed more.

"I need to make love to you," she said.

Their mouths moved together, their kisses deep but slow and purposeful and full of everything they'd said and everything they couldn't say. Dean slid down her panties as she lowered his pants and boxer briefs.

Once naked, his erection pressed into her belly, but neither maneuvered for penetration just yet. His lips were better than Valium or pot or alcohol or any other drug in the world. Drunk on his lips and his body, Kiera surrendered to the moment.

They touched like two beings freshly born, with no knowledge of what felt good, where the erogenous zones lay, or what the other might want— they stroked everywhere with feathered caresses, scratching nails, and gripping fingers. And they kissed, their mouths finding each other every few minutes. He drowned her in his warmth and constant touch.

She rolled, pulling him with her body until he lay on top of her. He interlaced their fingers—both hands on either side of her head. He wasn't holding her down, and he wasn't holding her together. He connected them and held that connection.

"You're sure, right?" he asked.

"Yes."

He gazed at her, relishing the anticipation—and then he slid inside, hard and hot, and they both groaned with the intensity. She squeezed her hands against his and tilted her hips so he could reach deeper. She stared into his hazel eyes and drank in the sight and feel of him.

"More," she said again, loud and insistent, a request and a demand.

He pumped faster, timing his thrusts to her heartbeat. He said her name again, and she came hard, the tension flipping her insides. Dean followed close, his face buried in her neck, his cries tickling her skin.

"I love you so much," he said. "Shadows and all."

"Shadows and all," she echoed.

Four Months Later

CHAPTER EIGHTY TWO

Kiera

A FTER A TENTATIVE KNOCK AT THE DOOR, IT opened a few inches, and her brother, Ash, stuck his face in the gap. "Hey," he whispered.

Kiera gestured him inside. "It's an office, not a library."

Ash eyed the three manila folders on her glass desk, laid out like giant tarot cards. Kiera put her hand on each, knowing her future lay among the contents. Her assistant had pared down all surgery referrals to these three. It would be her first since the Purge.

"You thinking of resuming the memory transfers?" Ash reached out and nudged the corner of the closest folder, as if it might spring to life at his touch.

Kiera stuck a pen in her mouth and chewed on the clicker. "I don't believe in the whole everything-happens-for-a-reason bullshit, so don't ever say that."

He smirked and slouched in his chair, throwing one arm over the back. Ash was such a walking *GQ* ad that Kiera almost waited for him to check his watch. "But?"

She clasped her hands together on top of her desk. "I used to be so scared that I'd lose myself with the gift, but the worst happened, and I held onto who I was through the whole thing. Now I know I can help people and keep my sanity. It's empowering to have a purpose—my own purpose."

Kiera glanced at her buzzing phone though she wanted to ignore it. Sure enough, another GIF from Amy, this one featuring a cat riding a Roomba. And damn if it didn't make her smile.

Amy had grown on Kiera like a puppy fungus, equal parts annoying and adorable. By saving Amy, she'd created a bond Kiera couldn't have foreseen, and somehow, it didn't bother her. Nadira and Beth, however, had threatened a revolt if Kiera ever invited Amy to Stan's Donuts, their new hangout place after group. Their fears were unfounded. Kiera hadn't completely lost her mind.

Ash cleared his throat. "I promise this is the last time I bring this up, but I talked to Mom and Dad, and—"

Kiera pitched her pen at Ash and hit him square in the chest. They both watched as the pen fell from his chest to his lap to the floor. Ash raised an eyebrow. "Feel better?"

"No."

"I told them, if they went ahead with the book deal, then I would never take another client or speak to them again. So, no more book. I didn't want you worrying about it. Okay?" He wiped his hands against each other to demonstrate the matter concluded.

Kiera tried to scowl but couldn't.

Ash put one loafered foot on her desk, then crossed it with the other. The weather was too cold for loafers, but since she wasn't qualified to dole out fashion advice, she kept her feedback to a raised eyebrow.

"So, whatcha got in those folders?" Ash asked.

CHAPTER EIGHTY THREE

Dean

"THIS IS GOING TO SUCK," DEAN SAID AS HE SAT on the stone step facing the twenty-foot-wide swath of concrete trail that followed Lake Michigan.

Kiera laughed and pinched her knees together, rollerblading backward. "Hey, you're the one who insisted we do something outside."

He had. But Dean hadn't skated since he was eight, and he hadn't been six feet tall then. It was far to fall.

Though warm for February, they could still see their breath in the air. They both layered to regulate their temperatures. For the top layer, Kiera wore a fuchsia sweatshirt with a surfboarding penguin, easily spotted in a crowd. Not that swarms of people made use of the lake at zero dark hundred. At least, the streetlights kept the lakefront well illuminated. Dean's sweatshirt was plain gray, but his flailing arms would make him easy enough to find should the masses converge and Kiera decide to venture ahead.

Kiera donned wrist guards, yoga pants, and knee pads. Dean insisted on a helmet, gloves, wrist guards, elbow pads, jeans, knee pads, and a sullen expression. He latched his inline skates and glared at Kiera. "It's too early for this."

Of course, that was part of the compromise. Kiera had agreed to go outside, but only to the lake and only at the ungodly hour of 6:00 a.m., the safest time. Dean didn't argue. He was also armed and under strict instructions to shoot anyone who might want to harm her.

She skated close and hovered. Dean stood, his arms stretched out to help him balance. Kiera giggled and taunted him.

He was fine as long as he didn't venture out of reach of the stone riser. "How is it you skate so well when you're practically a recluse?"

"I wasn't always a recluse." She glided toward the water, which made Dean's heart lodge into his neck and expand there like a frog. "My 'gift' didn't manifest until I was seventeen. Before then, I skated all the time. I could even do a few tricks like jumping and grinds."

"Grinding? I'd like to see that."

Kiera rolled her eyes. "Grinds, pervo; it's riding on the edges of things like railings or stairs."

"Great. Now skate back over here. You're too close to the water."

She bent her knees and spun in a perfect circle, right near the edge. "Does this make you nervous?"

"Yes. Now come here."

Kiera raised her hands in the air and skated backward, then forward, her movements sinuous and graceful, but less than a foot from the lake. "Would you jump in to rescue me if I fell in?"

"No. I'd fall and crack my head open on the pavement and bleed out as you drowned, so knock it off."

A pair of joggers huffed by, two men who rubbernecked to observe Kiera. She skated over to Dean after that, but she continued to tease him with the easy way she moved. "Come on, Detective, take my hand."

For a few seconds, she flowed backward, pulling him forward. "Bend your knees. You'll have better balance."

Like a little kid, he gripped her hand. She twisted and maneuvered, so she was next to him, holding only his left hand. They progressed slower than he could walk, but Dean still wanted to slow down.

After he mastered stopping, he relaxed a little. It took Dean half an hour more to leave the safety of the stone steps. One day, after Dean had practiced enough, he was going to make Curt and his husband, Mark, join them. Curtis Haze on inline skates was something Dean needed. He would video the whole thing with his phone and hold that over Curt for the rest of their careers in their new section, special victims. Dean had moved divisions for Kiera, and Curt had moved for Dean.

Dean had decided he needed a change, and Kiera's kidnapping put life in perspective. Less glory, less stress; more life, more Kiera.

Several bikes passed by and a few more joggers. The sun broke over the water, spearing the high rises with a golden-pink light. Kiera's hair absorbed the rays and glowed. She grinned at him, letting go of his hand to glide ahead, only to return a minute later. Eventually, he held her hand for pleasure and not for safety. Her grip was easy but solid, her smile infectious. Everything about Kiera was addictive, even her colorful temperament.

Dean released her hand. "Okay, skate all the way to that point down there before you come back. I know you want to open the throttle."

She tugged up the sleeves on her sweatshirt. "You sure?"

He smiled. "Yeah."

"Will you keep an eye on me?"

"Always."

IF YOU'RE HURTING AND NEED HELP:

RAINN (Rape Abuse & Incest National Network)
1-800-656-4673

National Suicide Prevention Lifeline
1-800-273-8255

ACKNOWLEDGEMENTS

WRITING IS A SOLITARY PROCESS THAT, FOR ME, IS IMPOSSIBLE WITHOUT the help of so many people.

Thanks to my editor, Steph Morgan. You helped me tighten everything like a fitness trainer. The novel wouldn't have been nearly as good without your input. I also need to thank my critique group: Susan, Carolyn, Dani, Meg, and Rae. You guys are not only awesome with the feedback but always there when I had a question or needed support. And speaking of support, shout out to my accountability/brainstorming people: Susan (again!), Tracy, Sheri, and Lyssa. Without our weekly check-ins, I probably would still be working on the novel. Thanks to June Diehl for taking a quick look even when you didn't have to and reassuring me.

Big thanks to my copyeditor Ginny Glass. I also want to thank Olivier Darbonville for the interior design and formatting.

I had a lot of experts who helped me out: Sergeant Randy Nichols, Sergeant John McCarthy, and Louis Boone III from CPD, Dr. Cynthia Clark for looking over my early serial killer profile, Geoff Simon for crime scene procedures, and Lee Lofland and all the instructors at The Writer's Police Academy—I learned a lot of cool shit there, including how to do a PIT maneuver, which I am totally putting in a book someday. There is no doubt I made some mistakes, and I can assure you, they are all mine.

Shout out to my cover designer Sarah Hansen at Okay Creations.

I need to thank Sisters in Crime, particularly the Chicago branch and the Guppies. The classes and camaraderie have been so important. And

OCWW (Off-Campus Writers' Workshop) for the great speakers and social interaction. I miss meeting all of you in person!

Thanks to the Soon to Be Famous Illinois Manuscript Contest people for their support and humor: Mitchell, Kate, Jeffery, Nikki, Emily, Anna, Eva, and Lucy. You guys gave me my first real validation, and I'll never forget it!

There were too many beta readers to list them all, but thanks for everyone who read an early draft and gave me feedback.

I need to thank my family: mom, dad, and the stepparents for all your support over the years. Thanks to my son, Quinlan, for mostly understanding when I'm always writing and for telling me that I'm a great writer, even when you haven't read anything of mine. I love you, Bear. And, most of all, I need to thank my husband, Randy, who has supported me through everything and always believed in me, even if I sometimes doubted myself. He is my alpha reader, my cheerleader, my sugar daddy, and my love. We both know who got the better end of this deal.

And thanks to my readers. As I'm writing this, you are merely a dream of mine that I can't wait to make a reality. I hope you have enjoyed the story and will follow me to the next one. Without you, I'm a tree in the woods falling down in silence.

If you're interested in a deleted scene and writing updates from me, please go to **www.holliesmurthwaite.com** and sign up for my newsletter.